Simply Learning, Simply Best!

Simply Learning, Simply Best!

倍斯特出版事業有限公司
Best Publishing Ltd.

用英語來學節慶

English Learning at the Festivals

East & West

倍斯特編輯部◎著

經由對東西方文化節慶的介紹，
幫助你的英語學習，學得好，學得深入。

提升英語閱讀與寫作功力

閱讀寫作要加強，就要品味好文章。本書文章分為簡單和完整版，介紹節慶來由、典故和背景知識，再輔以閱讀測驗，幫助你熟悉內文再強化閱讀，吸收語法，加強寫作能力。

節慶版會話 讓您做好國民外交

幫助讀者在關於節慶對談的英語會話中，提出多元有趣的話題和外國友人交談，增進彼此的友誼和對東西方文化的認識，溝通無障礙。

單字、句型有一套，學到賺到 英雄絕對有用武之地

精選重要而關鍵的單字和句型，討論節慶主題時，一定馬上用到，生活又實用，讓您的英語表達力更加靈活和充分。

互動遊戲，強化學習動機

每章節都有「互動時刻真有趣」的單元，藉由生字遊戲與謎語、英詩賞析與美味佳餚特製等等活動內容，增加學習樂趣。

從習俗活動的生動描述中，
引領你的思想，用英語進一步來了解多元的文化。

特約編輯序之一

I have always enjoyed holidays! As a child I looked forward to each one with joyful anticipation! There were some traditions that were the same every year. My favorites were Christmas and Thanksgiving because we shared them with lots of family and friends. Now that my husband and I have our own children, we have tried to come up with our own traditions. Hopefully, our kids will look back on these holidays with wonderful memories.

In writing this book, I loved learning about the Asian holidays and the traditions associated with them. A few years ago my family was in Taiwan during Chinese New Year. It was a great experience to see how a different country celebrates a part of their culture.

May you enjoy learning to speak English better as you learn about some western holidays in this book. Talk about them with your family and friends! Speaking English is the best way to learn it.

我總是很喜歡假期的！當我還是孩子的時候，我期待著每個愉快的活動參與！有些節日的傳統是每年都有的。我最喜歡的節日是耶誕節與感恩節，因為我們可以和許多的家庭和朋友們一起分享。現在，我的先生和我有我們自己的小孩了，我們也已經試著發想出屬於我們自己的傳統。希望我們的孩子在回想這些節日時會有著美好的回憶。

寫這本書的同時，我喜愛學習有關亞洲的節日和與它們有關的傳統。幾年前，我們全家在台灣過中國新年。這是一個很棒的經驗來看一個不同的國家慶祝其文化中的一部分。

當你在本書中學習到一些西方節日時，希望你能高興地學習將英語由此說得更好。可以和您的家人和朋友聊一聊！最好的英語學習方式就是勇敢地說出英語來！

Melanie Venekamp

特約編輯序之二

　　在雪梨唸書時，養成了一個習慣，每年在拿到學校新的行事曆後，總是會認真的加填上台灣的重要節日。對於在外求學的遊子而言，這些節日總是會引起滿滿的鄉愁，所以在這些節日中組織聚會，彼此互相加油打氣，是大家行事曆中的重點事項。回台工作之後，因為工作性質的關係，我的行事曆上又加入了美國的重要節日，而也時常遇到外籍朋友詢問我一些有關我們的傳統節日由來。每當這個時候，我就會發現自己好像不夠了解這些節日，有只知其一，不知其二的茫然感。相對於外籍朋友在談起他們的節日時的侃侃而談，像是準備了演講稿似的，我的心虛感就不斷的上升。但在這些討論的過程中，讓我發現到有些被我們視為理所當然的節日習俗，往往是節日的精髓所在，也讓我見識到更多東西方節日的不同面貌。我將我和朋友們所討論及我所認識的節日面貌寫進這本書，希望能對大家在和朋友或是孩子們在介紹及討論這些節日能有所助益。

陳欣慧

編者序

　　「節慶英語」是否帶給您濃濃的節慶的氣氛呢？不論是東方或西方，節慶本身總是帶給人愉悅或悵惘的感受，隨著節慶的不同，感受也不一樣。大體來說，人們總會為節慶預備些什麼或有些活動，使人心快活，也紀念節慶的來由。不知您是否有一些喜歡的，或非過不可的節日呢？有時藉機呼朋引伴，出去走走，這也是不錯的忙裡偷閒的時機喔！本書以精鍊的中英文文章介紹了節慶文化與由來，讓讀者一邊品味好英文，一邊進入英語節慶文化的領域，開拓英語聽說讀寫的知與能，一覽節慶英語的有趣和特別之處，使讀者分外有收穫。佳節一到，放下手邊的工作，用心的採買與為即將到來的活動預備，著實增添了生活的樂趣。特別是中西文化的不同處，從這裡就可以看得到，也增添了本書內容的活潑生動之處。

目　次

東方節慶篇

西方節慶篇

Eastern Festival

東方節慶

Chinese New Year
中國新年

節慶源由──簡易版

Lunar New Year is also called Chinese New Year. It is a holiday in a lot of countries. It is the first day of the Chinese Lunar calendar. Some countries celebrate for two weeks. Stores and banks close. Schools close, too. People will clean their houses because they want to sweep away the bad luck and to get ready for good luck to come. They might put red paper on their door. Red means happy.

農曆新年又稱做中國新年。這在很多國家是個節日。它是中國農曆的第一天。有些國家慶祝兩個星期。商店和銀行會休息。學校也會休息。人們會清掃他們的房子，因為他們想把壞運清掃掉，並準備迎接好運來臨。他們會在門上貼上紅紙。紅色表示開心快樂。

On New Year's Eve, the family will have a big meal. They might cook all day for this meal. They may cook chicken, duck, seafood, rice and sweets. After the meal, many people set off fireworks. It can be a loud night! Moreover, on New Year's Eve, each child is given cash in red envelopes. On Lunar New Year, you should forget the bad things and wish each person peaceful and joyful.

在除夕夜那晚，一家人會吃大餐。他們會為這頓大餐煮一整天。他們會煮雞、鴨、海鮮、米飯和甜點。在大餐過後，很多人會放煙火。這是個熱鬧的夜晚！除此之外，在除夕當晚，每個小孩都會收到一個紅包。農曆過年時，你應該忘記不好的事，並希望每個人都平安、快樂。

單字大集合

1. **lunar** *adj.* 農曆的

   The word "lunar" has to do with the moon.
   「農曆」這個字跟月亮有關。

2. **bank** *n.* [C] 銀行

   I got some money from the bank.
   我從銀行提了一些錢。

3. **clean** *adj.* 乾淨的

   After washing my hands, they are clean.
   在洗完我的手後，它們很乾淨。

4. **chicken** *n.* [U] 雞肉

   Kelly had a chicken sandwich for lunch.
   Kelly 中午吃一個雞肉三明治當午餐。

5. **fireworks** *n.* 煙火

   I saw the bright fireworks in the sky.
   我看見天空有明亮的煙火。

6. **cash** *n.* [U] 現金

   I had cash in my pocket.
   我有現金在我的口袋。

節慶源由──精彩完整版

　　The Chinese calendar follows the farming seasons and the cycles of the moon. Lunar New Year, often called Chinese New Year, is the first day of the Chinese Lunar calendar. It is usually celebrated sometime between late January and mid February. It is the most important yearly festival for the Chinese people. Lunar New Year is celebrated in many countries. Some countries celebrate the holiday for two weeks. Stores, banks, businesses and schools close. Many people return home to their families for a reunion celebration.

　　中國農曆伴隨著農耕的季節與月亮的陰晴圓缺。農曆新年，常叫做中國新年，是中國農曆的第一個日子。通常是介於一月底到二月中來慶祝的。它對中國人而言，是最重要的年節慶典。農曆新年在許多國家被慶祝。有些國家用兩週的時間來慶祝這個節期。店家，銀行，企業和學校都關起來。許多人返家和家人團聚慶祝。

　　In preparation for the holiday, families clean their houses. They sweep away the bad luck from the past year. They get ready for good luck to come this year. Rice bins are filled, debts should be paid and any quarrels should be ended. Families then decorate with colorful decorations or with red paint. Red is a symbol for happiness. The tradition of Lunar New Year is that you should forget all the bad things from the past year. You should sincerely wish each person peace and happiness.

　　為了這個假期做準備，家家戶戶清潔他們的房子。掃除從前一年而來的霉運。他們準備好迎接今年要來的好運。米倉滿滿的，債務還清應該沒問題，爭執應該得以終止。家家戶戶用彩色的裝飾或紅色印字來佈置。紅色是喜氣的象徵。農曆新年的傳統是你應該忘記去年所有不好的事。你應該真心的期盼每個人平安和幸福。

　　On New Year's Eve, the family will have a reunion feast. The family might spend all day cooking for this feast. They may cook chicken, duck, seafood, rice and sweets. Tradition says that after the meal, no one should sweep the floor. All brooms should be put away, so that your luck does not get swept away. That night, many people set off fireworks. Some people believe these fireworks will scare away evil spirits. It can be a very noisy night!

在除夕夜，每一個家庭都有團聚的團圓飯。大家可以花上一天為煮好團圓飯。他們可以烘煮雞，鴨，海鮮，飯和甜點。依據傳統，在吃完飯後，沒有人可以打掃地板。所有的掃把都應放著，所以你的好運才不會被掃掉。這天晚上，許多人會放煙火。有些人相信煙火可以嚇走惡靈。 這也可說是個很吵的一晚。

On New Year's Day, each child is given money in a red envelope. The money is supposed to bring good luck. Many people also bring gifts to their friends and family during the New Year celebration. These gifts are often in red envelopes, red bags or red boxes. Nothing unpleasant should happen on New Year's Day. This is to make sure that good fortune will be with you for the rest of the year.

在大年初一，每個孩子都會拿到用紅色信封裝的壓歲錢。這個壓歲錢可以帶來好運。許多人也在這新年慶典中，帶著禮物給他們的朋友和家人。這些禮物常放在紅色信封，紅色袋子與紅色盒子裡。沒有任何不愉快的事物應在大年初一發生。為了確保好運在接下來一年會跟著你。

In China, this holiday is also called Spring Festival. This is because the spring season begins with the first day of the lunar year. Spring Festival begins on New Year's Day and ends fifteen days later with the Lantern festival. Chinese New Year has been celebrated for centuries in countries with large Chinese populations. It is also celebrated in Chinatowns in other countries, such as the United States.

在中國，這樣的節日也叫做春節。這是因為春節伴隨著農曆新年的第一天而來。春節從大年初一開始，到十五天過後隨著元宵節而結束。中國新年已經在有著廣大人口的許多國家，慶祝了好幾個世紀了。它也在有像唐人街般的其他國家被慶祝，美國就是如此。

單字大集合

1. Calendar *n.* 月曆

The first month on my calendar is January.
我日曆上的第一個月份是一月。

2. Festival *n.* 節日；慶典

There was a festival in the park.
在公園有一個慶典。

3. Reunion *n.* 團聚

I am excited for the reunion with my family.
我對於和家人的團聚感到很興奮。

4. Quarrel *n.* 爭吵；爭執

I had a quarrel with my brother.
我和我哥哥有點爭吵。

5. Colorful *adj.* 彩色的

Her clothes were very colorful.
她的衣服是富有色彩的。

6. Unpleasant *adj.* 不愉快的

There was an unpleasant smell in the room.
有個難聞的味道在房間裡。

7. Population *n.* 人口

The population of Taipei is very large.
台北的人口很多。

8. Sincerely *adv.* 真心誠意的

I love my mother sincerely.
我心的愛著我的母親。

閱讀測驗

1. The color red is a symbol for: 紅色是＿＿＿＿＿＿的象徵
   (a) Health 健康
   (b) Wealth 財富
   (c) Happiness 幸福

2. Where is Lunar New Year celebrated? 農曆新年在那慶祝？
   (a) Only in China 只在中國
   (b) Only in countries that speak Chinese 只在有說中文的國家
   (c) In many countries 在許多國家
   (d) All around Asia 全亞洲

3. Why should you not use a broom after the reunion meal?
   為什麼你應該在團圓飯後，避免使用掃把呢？
   (a) So you do not get too tired 所以你就不會太累了
   (b) So you don't sweep away your luck 所以你就不會將你的幸運掃掉了
   (c) You have to hurry to light fireworks 你需要趕快去放煙火

4. How many years has Chinese New Year been celebrated?
   中國新年已慶祝了幾年了呢？
   (a) Since the year you were born 從你出生的那一年開始
   (b) Since my grandmother was a child 自從我的祖母孩提時
   (c) Since the world began 當世界剛開始時
   (d) For many centuries 已經好幾世紀了

活動慶典和習俗

　　農曆新年（Lunar New Year，但一般稱為 Chinese New Year）是全球華人最重視的傳統節日，也稱做春節（Spring Festival）。慶祝的時間一般是從農曆（Agricultural/ Lunisolar Calendar）正月初一到十五日的元宵節（Lantern Festival），有些地區的慶祝活動則會持續至正月結束。

　　在台灣，從冬至（winter solstice）祭祖之後，便開始有了年節氣氛，接著還有農曆 12 月 24 日的祭祀送神（一般稱為過小年），及 26 日的尾牙活動。到除夕前的這段期間中，我們還會做歲末大掃除（Year-end cleanup），更換春聯（spring couplet），也會添購新衣，理髮等一些含有「辭舊迎新」（bid farewell to the old and usher in the new）寓意的活動。這些活動不僅僅是有好的寓意，也是為了過年時的一些禁忌作準備。在過年期間特別是在初一到初五之間，為了求取好兆頭而衍生初一些特殊的禁忌，例如不可掃地、倒垃圾，以免將家中的財富掃出去；也不能動刀剪，才不會引來兇殺或是口舌之災。除此之外還要避免孩童哭鬧，不能打罵孩童，忌打破碗盤。如果不小心犯了這些忌諱的話，則可以吉祥話語來及時化解，如打破碗盤時，我們說「碎碎平安」，取其諧音為「歲歲平安」來化解未知的災厄。

　　在農曆新年的這段期間，除了行為上的規範之外，在吃的方面也有所講究。團圓飯（reunion dinner）一般又稱年夜飯、團年飯或是圍爐，在除夕這一天，全家人齊聚一堂吃飯，如有在外無法回家的遊子，家人也會為他擺上一副碗筷，表示團聚。團圓飯的食材和菜式多半含有吉祥寓意，例如長年菜象徵長命百歲，餃子象徵元寶，髮菜則取其諧音象徵發財等。而在年夜飯桌上擺放的魚，則不得取用，以象徵年年有「餘」。招待上門拜年的客人，必先奉上以甜味為主的糖果蜜餞類的茶點，意欲讓客人有甜頭可嘗。而這些茶點中也大多會包含一些有吉祥象徵的食材，如核桃（和氣），棗子、花生、桂圓、栗子（早生貴子），橘子（吉利）等。

實用生活會話

Q1: Hi, Jenny, where are you going?

嗨，珍妮，要去哪裡？

A1: I'm going to have a grocery shopping for the Chinese New year.

我正要為了農曆新年去採購一些東西。

Q2: Is it the most important holiday for Chinese?

過年對中國人而言是最重要的節日嗎？

A2: Yes, it is.

對啊。

Q3: How do you celebrate it?

你們通常都怎麼慶祝呢？

A3: On Chinese New Year's Eve, all family members will gather for the annual reunion dinner. Children will dress up with their new clothes and get red envelopes from parents and relatives. Many People stay up late and set off firecrackers for the coming year.

在除夕夜時，全家人會聚在一起吃團圓飯。小孩會穿上新衣，還會收到父母及親戚給的紅包。很多人還會守歲及點燃鞭炮來迎接新年的到來。

Q4: Wow, that sounds interesting.

哇，這樣聽起來好有趣喔！

A4: Yes, it is indeed.

沒錯，的確很有趣。

實用單句這樣說

- Gong xi fa cai. / Wishing you a prosperous new year.
  恭喜發財。

- During the Chinese New Year, every family decorates their gateposts with the spring couplets that express happy and hopeful thoughts for the coming year.
  在春節期間，家家戶戶都會在門口貼上含有對未來一年樂觀及展望寓意的春聯。

- It is traditional for every family to cleanse the house before the Chinese New Year, in order to sweep away the bad luck, and make a way for the incoming good fortune.
  照傳統每個家庭會在過農曆新年前做大掃除，為的是掃去壞運，迎來好運。

- It is customary to eat rice cake during the Spring Festival.
  習俗上，在春節期間會吃年糕。

- The firecrackers are spluttering and crackling.
  鞭炮劈裡啪啦的響。

- "Nian" was afraid of the color red, and loud noises.
  年獸害怕紅色及吵雜的噪音。

- Youngsters stay up all night after the reunion dinner to wish longevity for their parents.
  年輕人會在年夜飯後開始守歲，以祈求父母能長命百歲。

- Married women visit their birth parents' home on the second day of the Chinese New Year.
  已婚婦女會在農曆新年的第二日（正月初二）時回娘家。

互動時刻真有趣

A 十二生肖 Chinese Zodiac

鼠 rat	牛 ox	虎 tiger	兔 rabbit	龍 dragon	蛇 snake
馬 horse	羊 goat	猴 monkey	雞 rooster	狗 dog	豬 pig

B 找出十二生肖的英文單字

H	O	R	S	E	D	O	G
D	R	A	G	O	N	O	X
R	O	O	S	T	E	R	W
R	A	T	T	I	G	E	R
B	C	R	A	B	B	I	T
G	O	A	T	Y	P	I	G
S	N	A	K	E	F	H	J
M	O	N	K	E	Y	L	Q

Answer:

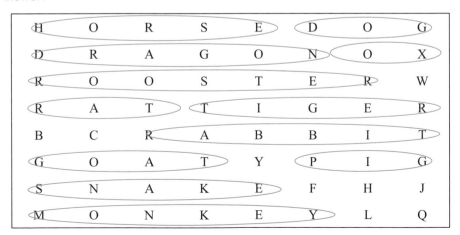

Lantern Festival
元宵節

節慶源由──簡易版

　　Lantern Festival comes two weeks after Chinese New Year. It is the end of the New Year holiday. This is the first full moon in the new lunar year. While the moon shines, lanterns hang outside. They are made of many colors. People carry lanterns shaped like dragons, fish, birds or red balls. Sometimes, children dance a lantern dance. They solve riddles written on the lanterns. The riddles are about good luck, the good harvest, or love.

　　元宵節在農曆新年後的兩個星期到來。它是新年假期的尾聲。是農曆新年的第一個滿月。當明月照耀，燈籠掛在外頭。它們被製作成許多顏色。人們提著龍、魚、鳥或是紅球狀的燈籠。有時候，孩子們跳起元宵舞蹈。他們解決寫在燈籠上的謎語。謎語都是有關好運、豐收或是愛。

　　Later, people let go of their lanterns. They fly up in the sky. This is to bring good luck and blessings. It is also to let go of yourself and get a new self. Some people write a wish on their lantern. They pray for the wish to come true.   Long ago, lanterns were very simple. Only the rich had fancy lanterns. Today, any lantern can have a fancy design.

　　之後，人們將他們的燈籠放走。它們飛上天空。這是為了帶來好運及祝福。也放掉自己得到一個新的自我。有些人將他們的願望寫在燈籠上。他們祈禱願望可以實現。很久以前，燈籠是非常簡略的。只有富人才擁有花俏的燈籠。在今天，任何一個燈籠都有花俏的設計。

單字大集合

1. **Lantern** *n.* [C] 燈籠

   The lanterns were very colorful.
   燈籠非常的鮮艷。

2. **Dragon** *n.* [C] 龍

   The book is about dragons.
   這本書是有關龍的。

3. **Riddle** *n.* [C] 謎語

   The kids solved many riddles.
   孩子們解決許多謎語。

4. **Blessing** *n.* [C] 祝福

   We hope for blessings in the new year.
   我們希望在新的一年得到祝福。

5. **Yourself** *pron.* 你自己

   Tell yourself you can do it!
   告訴自己你可以做到！

6. **Design** *n.* [C,U] 設計；構思

   I love the design on my lantern.
   我喜歡我的燈籠的設計。

節慶源由──精彩完整版

Lantern Festival comes 2 weeks after Chinese New Year. It is the fifteenth lunar day. It marks the end of the New Year celebration. This is the first night that there is a full moon in the new lunar year. Ancient Chinese believed that celestial spirits could be seen in the first full moon of the lunar year. People lit lanterns to see the spirits.

元宵節在農曆新年後的兩個星期到來。在農曆十五日。它標誌著新年慶祝活動的結束。是新的農曆年第一個滿月的夜晚。古代中國人相信，神仙在每年的農曆的第一個月圓可以被看見。人們點亮燈籠以看見神仙。

Today, while the moon is shining, there are thousands of colorful lanterns hung outside. People carry paper lanterns shaped like dragons, fish, birds or red globes. Sometimes, children perform lantern dances. Often they solve riddles that are written on the lanterns. These may be messages of good fortune, abundant harvest and love. At the end of the evening, the lanterns are released. This is to bring good luck and blessings. It can also symbolize letting go of yourself and getting a new self. Some people write their wishes on the lantern and pray for their wishes to come true.

在今天，當月亮在發光時，便有數千個色彩繽紛的燈籠掛在外頭。人們提著龍、魚、鳥或是紅球狀的紙燈籠。有時候，孩子們表演起元宵舞蹈。他們常常解決寫在燈籠上的謎語。這些可能是好運，豐收和愛的訊息。在夜晚的尾聲，燈籠們會被釋放。這是為了帶來好運及祝福。也象徵著放掉自己得到一個新的自我。有些人將願望寫在燈籠上並祈禱他們的願望實現。

There are many legends about the origin of Lantern Festival. One tells about a beautiful crane that flew down to earth from heaven. On earth it was killed by some villagers. This angered the Jade emperor in heaven because the crane was his favorite one. He planned a storm of fire to destroy the village on the fifteenth lunar day. A wise man suggested that every family should hang red lanterns around their houses. They should set up bonfires on the streets, and explode firecrackers. They should do this on the fourteenth, fifteenth, and sixteenth lunar days. This would give the village the appearance of being on fire. On the fifteenth lunar day, troops were sent down from heaven to destroy the village. They saw that the village was already ablaze.

They returned to heaven to report this to the Jade Emperor. Satisfied, the Jade Emperor decided not to burn down the village. From that day on, people celebrate the anniversary on the fifteenth lunar day every year by carrying lanterns on the streets and exploding firecrackers and fireworks.

這裡有許多關於元宵節由來的傳說。其一講述一隻美麗的鶴從天庭降臨到地球。在地球上被一些村民打死。這激怒了在天庭的玉皇大帝，因為這隻鶴是祂最喜歡的一隻。祂計畫在農曆十五以暴風雨般的火摧毀村莊。一位智者建議每戶人家應該在家裡四周掛紅燈籠。他們應該在街道上設置篝火及燃放鞭炮。他們應該在農曆十四、十五和十六做這些事。這將帶給村莊被火燒的外觀。在農曆十五，天兵天將從天庭被派遣下來摧毀村莊。祂們看到村莊已經起火。祂們返回天庭將此向玉皇大帝報告。令人滿意的是，玉皇大帝決定不燒毀村莊。從那天起，人們藉由在大街上提燈籠及燃放煙火及鞭炮來慶祝每年農曆十五的週年。

Long ago, lanterns were very simple. Only the emperor and other noblemen had ornate lanterns. Today, any lantern may have a very complicated design. In Taiwan, the government builds a giant zodiac animal lantern every year. Around the giant lantern, many lanterns from grade schools, organizations, and foreign countries are displayed for competition.

很久以前，燈籠是非常簡略的。只有皇帝和其他貴族擁有華麗的燈籠。在今天，每個燈籠都有非常複雜的設計。在台灣，政府每年都建造一個巨型生肖花燈。在巨型花燈四周，許多來自學校、機構及外國的燈籠為了比賽被展示。

單字大集合

1. Ancient *adj.* 古代的
I was not alive in ancient times.
我不是活在古時候的。

2. Celestial *adj.* 神聖的
An angel is a celestial being.
天使是個神聖的存在。

3. Giant *n.* [C] 巨人
The giant could not fit through the door.
巨人可能不適合進門。

4. Abundant *adj.* 豐富的
There was abundant rainfall this spring.
今年春天的雨量充沛。

5. Appearance *n.* [C] 出現；露面；演出
My appearance at school surprised my teacher.
我在學校的演出讓我的老師吃驚。

6. Firecracker *n.* [C] 爆竹；鞭炮
Firecrackers are too loud for me.
鞭炮對我來說太大聲。

7. Complicated *adj.* 複雜的
My homework was very complicated.
我的作業非常複雜。

8. Foreign *adj.* 外國的
We had visitors from a foreign country.
我們有來自外國的訪客。

閱讀測驗

1. In ancient times, why did people light their lanterns?
   古時候，人們為什麼點亮他們的燈籠？
   (a) To see where they were going. 為了看見他們要去哪裡。
   (b) To see the celestial spirits in the moon. 為了看見月亮上的神仙。
   (c) To let their neighbors know they were home.
   　　為了讓他們的鄰居知道他們在家。

2. Why was the Jade emperor angry when his crane was killed?
   為什麼當祂的鶴被殺的時候，玉皇大帝會生氣？
   (a) It was his favorite one. 因為那是祂最喜歡的一隻。
   (b) He wanted to see it again. 祂想要再看到牠一次。
   (c) He could hear it crying. 祂可以聽到牠在哭。

3. When the village lit bonfires and firecrackers, what did it look like?
   當村莊點燃篝火和鞭炮，看起來像什麼？
   (a) Like they were having a party. 像他們正在開派對。
   (b) Like the village was on fire. 像村莊起火了。
   (c) Like everyone had moved away. 像每個人都已經搬走了。

4. Who had ornate lanterns long ago? 很久以前誰擁有華麗的燈籠？
   (a) Anyone who wanted one. 任何想要的人。
   (b) All the children. 所有小孩。
   (c) Only the emperor and noblemen. 只有皇帝和貴族。

活動慶典和習俗

　　元宵節又可稱燈節，所以在英文中一般稱為 Lantern Festival，而也有直接音譯成 Yuanxiao Festival。在中文中則有上元節、小正月、元夕、小年的稱呼。在這一天會舉辦燈會及猜燈謎的活動，孩童也大多會提著紙燈籠上街，家中會吃元宵（Yuanxiao）以示慶祝。

　　根據記載，早在漢朝時期，元宵節就已經是一個重要的節日，因漢文帝是在農曆一月十五日登基，所以每年到了這日晚上，他便要出宮與民同樂，因為一月又稱「元」月，而夜有可稱「宵」，所以漢文帝將這一日訂為元宵節。而這一天是傳統新春定義的最後一天也是農曆新年的第一個月圓之夜，除了宣告假期的結束之外，也象徵著嶄新一年的開始。。

　　在東漢時期，明帝為宣揚佛法，便訂在元宵節這天燃燈表佛。到了唐太宗時期，因私塾多在十五日後開學，所以在元宵節當天，孩童會帶一個精巧的花燈到私塾中請博學的先生替他點燈，這個入學儀式稱做「開燈」，象徵著前途光明。因此逐漸演變成燈會（lantern show），及孩童提燈籠上街的習俗。到了宋朝，則加入了猜燈謎（riddle guessing）這一項受人歡迎的益智活動。

　　在台灣，元宵節當天除了燈會之外，在各地皆有極具特色的慶祝活動。其中最著名的有新北市平溪區的放天燈（sky/Kongming lantern flying）；台南市鹽水區的鹽水蜂炮（Yensui fireworks display）；台東縣的炸寒單（blasting Handan）及澎湖縣的乞龜祈福儀式。這四個地區性的活動並稱為「北天燈、南蜂炮、東寒單、西乞龜」為台灣的元宵節增添許多色彩。

實用生活會話

Q1: How do you call those colorful dumplings in Chinese?
那些彩色的團子中文叫什麼？

A1: We call that Yuanxiao.
我們叫它做元宵。

Q2: Is it a special food for the Lantern Festival?
那是元宵節的應景食物嗎？

A2: Yes, it is. It is made with glutinous rice flour.
對，沒錯。它是用糯米粉做的。

Q3: Is it delicious?
那好吃嗎？

A3: Sure it is. Sweet dumpling filled with sesame paste is my favorite.
當然好吃。我最喜歡的是包芝麻餡的元宵。

Q4: Have you made a lantern before?
你之前有做過燈籠嗎？

A4: Yes, my favorite one is in the shape of the horse.
是的，我最喜歡的一個是馬的形狀。

Q5: How about some riddles guesting?
想要猜個燈謎嗎?

A5: OK, Let's start.
好的，讓我們開始吧。

實用單句這樣說

- They wrote riddles on the Chinese lanterns.
  他們將謎語寫在燈籠上。

- On the night of the Lantern Festival, you can see people on the streets with variety of lanterns.
  在元宵節的晚上，你可以看到街上的人們提著各式各樣不同的燈籠。

- On the Lantern Festival, people watch lantern show, solve riddles, and also eat yuanxiao for good luck.
  在元宵節這一天，人們賞燈猜謎，而且也吃元宵以求得好運。

- Penny is making Yuanxiao for us. She places the red bean paste stuffing into a bamboo sieve with rice flour and sprinkle water continuously, and rolls those fillings to form balls.
  佩妮正在為我們製作元宵。她將紅豆餡料放進竹篩中，加上糯米粉，及持續不斷的灑水，將那些餡料滾成球狀。

- We cook savoury filled tangyuan in boiling water, and then served with clear soup broth.
  我們將包有鹹餡料的湯圓放入滾水煮熟後，再放入清湯裡一起吃。

互動時刻真有趣

● 謎語 Riddle

1. 千里隨身不戀家，不貪茶飯不貪花，水火刀槍都不怕，日落西山不見他。

   Each morning I appear to lie at your feet. All day I will follow, no matter how fast you run. Yet I nearly perish in the midday sun. 每天早上我就會出現在你的腳邊。整天我都會跟隨，不管你跑得有多快。但每當中午太陽出現時，我就快要不見。

2. 按住我的心，屋裡有響應，主人真殷勤，出來看究竟。

   What is something never asks any question, but demands a great many answers? 什麼東西從來不問問題，但卻要求得到許多回應？

3. 肚裡有熱湯，解渴又聞香，脫掉帽子看，好像小水缸。

   What begins with T, ends with T, and has "T" in it? 什麼字開頭是 T，結尾是 T，還有 T "Tea 茶" 在裡面？

4. 兩個兄弟數數字，數來數去不停止，一個只算二十四，一個能算到六十。

   What has a face and two hands but no arms or legs? 什麼東西有臉有手，但沒有胳膊或腿？

5. 紅河細長不起浪，只有高矮無瘦胖，夏日中午騰雲起，寒冬夜裡直下降。

   The higher I climb, the hotter I engage. I can not escape my crystal cage. 我爬的越高，我就越熱。我沒辦法從我的水晶牢籠中掙脫。

6. 稀奇稀奇真稀奇，鼻子當馬騎，猜一物。

   Without a bridle, or a saddle, across a thing I ride a-straddle. And those I ride, by help of me, though almost blind, are made to see. What am I? 沒有籠頭，沒有鞍，橫過某物我跨騎。被我騎者，得我助，雖近乎盲者，也能看的清。

Answer:

1. 影子 Shadow　2. 門鈴 Door bell　3. 茶壺 Teapot　4. 鐘 Clock
5. 溫度計 Thermometer　6. 眼鏡 Spectacles or Glasses

Girl's Day
女兒節（日本）

節慶源由──簡易版

Girls' Day, or the Doll Festival, is March 3rd. On this day, families in Japan make a wish for their daughter. They wish for good health. They wish for her to be happy. The girls dress up in nice clothes. They honor dolls that are set up on a red cloth. They eat sushi, clam soup, and sweet rice cakes.

女兒節，或稱作娃娃節，在 3 月 3 日。在這天，日本的家庭會為他們的女兒許願。他們希望身體健康。他們希望她能快樂。女孩們會用漂亮的衣服打扮。他們尊重擺放在紅布上的娃娃。他們吃壽司、蛤蜊湯和甜年糕。

When a girl is born, she is given a set of fancy dolls. Long ago, people thought these dolls could hold bad spirits. Some of the dolls were sent away on a river. These dolls took the bad luck away with them. Girls all over Japan set up these dolls today. They wish for good luck in their life.

當一個女孩出生時，她會被給予一套別緻的娃娃。很久以前，人們認為這些娃娃可以容納妖魔鬼怪。有些娃娃被送到河裡。厄運也隨著娃娃被送走。今日，所有的日本女孩擺放著這些娃娃。她們希望在生活中帶來好運。

Families set up the dolls a few weeks before the festival. They take them down right spirits. after it. If the dolls are up past March 4, bad luck will come.

各家會在節日前的幾個禮拜擺放娃娃。他們帶來好的靈魂。之後，若娃娃在 3 月 4 日後擺放，壞運就會來了。

單字大集合

1. **Wish** *vi. vt.* 希望

   I wish for a good grade in school.
   我希望在學校能有好成績。

2. **Clothes** 服裝

   I got new clothes for school.
   我得到學校的新衣服。

3. **Soup** *n.* [C,U] 湯

   My mother gave me soup when I was sick.
   當我生病時我媽媽會給我湯。

4. **Fancy** *adj.* 別緻的；花俏的

   She wore her fancy dress for her birthday.
   她為了她的生日穿了她花俏的連身裙。

5. **River** *n.* [C] 河

   There was a boat on the river.
   那裡有艘船在河上。

6. **Week** *n.* [C] 週

   There are four weeks in one month.
   一個月有四周。

節慶源由——精彩完整版

The Japanese Doll Festival, or Girls' Day, is held on March 3rd. It is also known as the Peach Blossom Festival. On this day, young girls decorate their homes with fresh peach blossoms. The peach is a symbol of long life. The Japanese believe it also has the traits of peacefulness and gentleness. The young women dress up in special clothing. They eat colorful sushi, clam soup, and sweet rice cakes. They honor elaborate dolls that have been set up on a special platform covered in red cloth.

日本娃娃節，或是女兒節，在 3 月 3 日舉行。它也被稱為桃花節。在那天，年輕女孩們用新鮮的桃花裝飾她們的家。桃子也是長壽的象徵。日本人相信它也有寧靜和溫柔的特質。年輕女性用特別的服裝打扮。她們吃五顏六色的壽司、蛤蜊湯和甜年糕。他們尊重精心製作的娃娃，將她們擺放在鋪有紅布的平台上。

An ancient Japanese custom on this day is called doll floating. Long ago, people believed the traditional Hina dolls had the power to contain bad spirits. Straw Hina dolls were floated on a boat to the sea. They took troubles and bad spirits away with them. Today, several towns in Japan sell special paper dolls which are made to float. As in the past, the dolls are taken to a river and released into the water. They take away all the evil, sickness, and bad luck from the young women who release them.

這天在日本有個古老的習俗被稱為漂浮娃娃。很久以前，人們相信傳統的雛娃娃有能力可以容納妖魔鬼怪。雛娃娃被放到船上送出海。麻煩和惡靈隨著她們被帶走。今天，許多日本的鄉鎮販賣被作來漂浮的特別紙娃娃。跟以前一樣，娃娃被帶到河邊並放到水中。她們帶走了流放她們的年輕女性身上所有邪惡、疾病和壞運。

When a girl is born, her parents or grandparents buy a set of gorgeous Hina dolls. During this festival, girls all over Japan set up their displays. They hope to find good luck in their marriages. Families wish for good health and happiness for their daughters.

當一個女孩出生時，她的父母或祖父母會買一套華麗的雛娃娃。在節日期間，所有日本女孩們會將她們陳列出來。女孩們希望能為她們的婚姻找到好運。家人們希望他們的女兒們能有健康和幸福。

Five platforms covered with a red carpet are used to display the set of ornamental dolls. There is the Emperor, the Empress, their court and musicians. They are all dressed in the traditional Japanese kimono. On the first platform（at the top）are the Emperor and Empress. The second platform holds three court ladies. The third platform has five male musicians. The fourth platform holds two guardians. The fifth platform holds three servants. There can also be two more platforms holding furniture, tools or carriages from the royal palace.

鋪著紅布的五層平台通常被用來陳列一套的裝飾娃娃。有天皇、皇后、他們的大臣和樂隊。他們都穿著傳統日本和服。第一層平台（最上方）是天皇和皇后。第二層有三名宮女。第三層有五名男性樂師。第四層則有兩名隨從。第五層是三名僕人。也可以另外多兩層用來擺放貴族宮殿的家具、工具或馬車。

Families generally start to display the dolls in February and take them down immediately after the festival. Superstition says that leaving the dolls past March 4th will result in a late marriage for the daughter.

家人通常在二月開始陳列娃娃，並且在節日結束後立即撤下她們。迷信說，在 3 月 4 日後還留下的娃娃將會導致女兒晚婚。

This beautiful festival is an example of how the Japanese combine ancient customs with style and creativity in their modern lifestyle.

這個美麗的節日是個例子，展現日本如何結合傳統習俗與現代生活方式的風格與創意。

單字大集合

1. Blossom *n.* [C,U] 花；開花期

The cherry tree has beautiful blossoms.
這櫻桃樹有很多漂亮的花。

2. Decorate *vi. vt.* 裝飾

We will decorate our house for Chinese New Year.
我們將為農曆新年佈置我們的房子。

3. Trait *n.* [C] 特質

Patience and kindness are good traits to have.
耐心和善良是值得擁有的好特質。

4. Float *vi. vt.* 漂浮；使浮起

The leaves were floating in the water.
葉子們漂浮在水上。

5. Trouble *n.* [C,U] 煩惱；憂鬱

She had many troubles in her life.
她的生活中有許多麻煩。

6. Release *vt.* 釋放

They will release the fish into the river.
他們將把魚放到河裡。

7. Gorgeous *adj.* 華麗的

I bought a gorgeous dress for my wedding.
我為了我的婚禮買了件華麗的連身裙。

8. Ornamental *adj.* 裝飾的

The old door has ornamental wood around it.
這老舊的門有裝飾的木頭包圍。

閱讀測驗

1. Why is Girls' Day also called the Peach Blossom Festival?
   為什麼女兒節又被稱作桃花節？

   (a) It is the time of year when peaches are blossoming.
   是桃花一年之中盛開的時候。

   (b) Girls decorate with peach blossoms. 女孩們用桃花裝飾。

   (c) They all eat peaches that day. 她們在那天都吃桃子。

2. What color cloth must the dolls be displayed on?
   娃娃必須被陳列在什麼顏色的布上？

   (a) Any color the girl likes. 任何女孩喜歡的顏色。

   (b) The color the girl's mother chooses. 女孩的母親選的顏色。

   (c) It is always a red cloth. 始終是紅布。

3. What do the floating dolls take with them? 漂浮娃娃將什麼隨著她們帶走了？

   (a) Food for their journey. 她們旅程的食物。

   (b) Trouble and evil spirits. 麻煩及惡靈。

   (c) Food for the fish in the river. 河裡的魚的食物。

4. How are the dolls dressed? 娃娃們是怎麼打扮的？

   (a) In fancy clothes the girls puts on them. 穿著女孩為她們穿上的華麗衣服。

   (b) In any clothes that can be found in the house.
   穿著任何家裡可以找到的衣服。

   (c) In the traditional Japanese kimono. 穿著傳統日本和服。

活動慶典和習俗

在日本，女兒節/雛祭（Girl's Day/Hinamatsuri）是專屬於未出嫁的女孩的節日，又可稱做人偶節（Doll's Day），桃節（Peach Festival）或是上巳節（Double Third Festival）。其原本是在農曆的三月三日，而在明治維新之後改在西曆的 3 月 3 日慶祝。

由於日本在奈良及平安時代大量的引進唐朝的章典制度及文化，一般據信這個本是中國傳統古老的上巳節及其慶祝習俗便是在那時傳到日本的。在中國，上巳節是親近水的日子，在古老的風俗中除了文人的曲水流觴（在迴環彎曲的水渠中放進酒杯，流到誰的面前，便可取杯喝酒）之外，還有在貴族婦女間流行的臨川浮卵（將煮熟的雞蛋放入河川，漂到誰的跟前便歸屬於她）及農村婦女的洗腳大會和拴娃娃等的活動。文人的活動以即興詩賦交流，且認為可以藉以除去厄運，而婦女間的活動則多半為了求子。到了唐代，更有在上巳節時，婦女結伴出遊的風氣，在杜甫的麗人行中寫道：「三月三日天氣新，長安水邊多麗人」，所以古時候的中國也有人稱這天是女兒節。而與日本女兒節不同的是在中國的習俗活動中也包含了已婚婦女，而在日本則是針對年輕的未婚女子。

在日本，女兒節並不是國定假日（national holiday），而有女兒的家庭一般在女兒節前一、二個星期便會開始著手雛人偶（Hina dolls）的擺放，一般是有 15 個做工精巧的人形娃娃及七階的檯子，再加上一些小家具。但因其造價昂貴，所以也可選購一、三、五階的檯子。而整套的雛人偶擺飾通常會在女子出嫁時做為嫁妝，以供世代傳承。應節的食物則有菱餅（麻糬），雛霰（彩色米果），散壽司，白酒及因兩片殼緊緊密合而象徵愛情專一的蛤蜊（clam）。女孩兒們在這一天會盛裝打扮，而第一次正式為女兒過女兒節的家庭，會邀請親朋好友參加，而賓客則會準備玩具，或與桃花相關的禮物，或是以禮金（gift money）替代，而主人家的回禮則是喜慶用的紅白方塊糖。

實用生活會話

Q1: Chika, what is it?

知佳，這些是什麼呢？

A1: This is the seasonal food for the Girl's Day. We call it "Hishimochi" means diamond-shaped sticky rice cake. They are usually colored red, white and green.

這是女兒節的應節食物，稱做菱餅，是一種切成菱形狀的麻糬。它們通常會被染上紅白綠三種顏色。

Q2: It looks pretty. Is there anything special about the color?

它看起來好漂亮。顏色有特殊涵意嗎？

A2: The red is symbolic of Peach blossoms for chasing evil spirits away. The white represents snow and purity. The green means spring and restorative.

紅色象徵著可驅除厄運的桃花。白色則代表白雪，有純淨的意思。綠色則代表春天及恢復健康。

Q3: What kind of activity you like the most on Girl's Day?

你喜歡女兒節的那一個活動呢？

A3: I like to make the delicate "Hina dolls".

我喜歡製作精巧的雛人偶。

Q4: Have you bought a gift related to a peach blossom?

你已經買了與桃花一樣的禮物嗎？

A4: Not yet, I'm ready to use gift money as a substitute.

還沒，我正準備用禮金代替。

實用單句這樣說

- In Japan, families and communities celebrate Hinamatsuri on March 3rd every year to wish good health and happiness for girls.

  在日本，家庭及社會團體都會在每年的三月三日時慶祝女兒節，以祈求女孩兒們能幸福健康平安的長大。

- In the past, the Doll's Festival was also a day to appreciate women busy working for the family.

  在以前，女兒節也是個感謝女子為家庭忙碌付出的日子。

- Traditionally, parents or grandparents of a newborn girl will buy a set of gorgeous hina dolls, unless there's a set handed down from generation to generation.

  除了家中已有可供傳承的雛人偶組之外，傳統上，父母或是祖父母會為新生的女嬰添購一套漂亮的雛人偶。

- In an ancient Japanese custom, paper dolls are set afloat on a small round straw boat and send down a river on the Girl's day, supposedly taking troubles or misfortunes with them.

  在古老的日本習俗中，在女兒節時把紙人偶放入用草編織的小圓船中並隨著河川的水流走，將可以一併帶走麻煩及厄運。

- Families generally display dolls from the end of February to March 3rd. Superstition says that leaving the dolls past March 4th will cause the late marriage for the daughter.

  一般來說，在 2 月底到 3 月 3 日之間會在家中擺放雛人偶。按照迷信的說法，如果將其放到 4 日才收，女兒將會晚婚。

互動時刻真有趣

● 雛人偶擺放介紹

　　家中擺放的雛人偶檯一般為三到七階，在最頂端的金色屏風前放置兩樽衣著豪華的雛人偶分別是衣冠束帶的天皇及穿著十二件宮廷單衣和服的皇后，中間放上花瓶。我們以七階為例，面對人偶由左至右的方式來介紹其擺設方法。

第一階　內裏雛 天皇（The Emperor）皇后（The Empress）

第二階　宮女（Court Ladies）宮女三人，手拿飲酒用的酒器，分別為酒壺、酒杯及酒勺，執酒杯的宮女為坐姿狀。

第三階　樂師（Musicians）樂師五名，分別拿著太鼓，小鼓，大鼓，笛子及手中拿扇的歌手。

第四階　大臣（Ministers）隨臣二人，分別為右大臣及左大臣，左大臣的人偶通常留有長長的白鬍子。兩位大臣中間通常會放女兒節的應節食品：菱餅，雛霰及甜白酒。

第五階　僕人（Servants）僕人三名，方別手執華蓋（古時遮陽用的器具），脫鞋用的台子，及雨傘。也有的家庭是擺放三名不同表情的武士（Samurai），分為泣、怒、笑。

第六、七階　嫁妝（Dowry）在第六階放梳妝台，櫃子等家具，最下層則為轎子，放食物用的漆盒及牛車。

　　在明治維新前，因受到中國文化的影響，在左者為大，所以會將天皇擺放在皇后的左手邊，而西化後則將其改放在皇后的右手邊。傳統上在女兒節當日傍晚，便會收起雛人偶。據說如果沒能及時收起，而放到隔天的話，女兒則會晚婚。

Children's Day
兒童節

節慶源由──簡易版

　　All children must have time to play.　Parents should play with their kids, too. Children's Day is a good time to do this.　Children's Day is a holiday in many countries.　In China and Taiwan, it is on April 4th.　This is the day before Tomb Sweeping Day.　Some years, they are on the same day.

　　所有的小孩都必須要有玩樂的時間。父母也需要陪他們玩。兒童節便是做這件事情的好時機。兒童節在許多國家都是節日。在中國及台灣，訂在 4 月 4 日。在清明節前一天的日子。某些年他們會在同一天。

　　On Children's Day, schools offer special activities.　They often honor good students.　Amusement parks let children in for free.　Many groups offer crafts and games.　Children play with their moms and dads. The kids should feel like King for the day. Parents should enjoy being with their children.　One Chinese saying says "There is a little child in everyone's mind."　A parent cannot be a child again. But every parent can enjoy time with their child.

　　兒童節當天，學校會提供許多特別的活動。他們常常表揚好學生們。遊樂園也讓兒童免費進入。許多團體提供手工藝品和遊戲。小孩們和他們的爸爸及媽媽一起玩樂。孩子們在那天會覺得自己像個國王。父母應享受和他們的小孩在一起。有一句中國諺語說：「每個人的心裡都有個小小孩。」，父母不能再重新當一遍小孩，但每位父母可以享受和他們的孩子在一起的時光。

單字大集合

1. Play *vi. vt.* 玩耍；玩（遊戲等）

I love to play games.
我喜歡玩遊戲。

2. Activity *n.* [C,U] 活動；活動力

There were lots of activities to do in the park.
公園裡有很多活動可以做。

3. Honor *vt.* 使增光

I honor my mom when I do what she asks.
當我做到媽媽的要求時，我使她增光。

4. Enjoy *vt.* 享受

I enjoy watching movies.
我享受看電影。

5. Everyone 每人

The room was too small for everyone.
這房間對所有人來說都太小了。

6. Parent *n.* [C] 父親；母親

My mom and dad are my parents.
我的爸爸和媽媽是我的父母。

節慶源由──精彩完整版

Children's Day is celebrated in many countries. In 1954, the United Nations recommended that all countries around the world should set aside a day to celebrate children. They wanted Children's Day to be a symbol of worldwide understanding. They also wanted to promote the well-being of children.

兒童節在許多國家被慶祝。西元 1954 年，聯合國推薦世界上所有國家應該制定一天來慶祝孩子。他們想要兒童節變成遍及全球的一個象徵。他們也想要推動小孩的福利。

This holiday has been celebrated in China since 1931. Unfortunately, the holiday was cancelled in 1998. In 2011, it once again became a national holiday there. China has now designated April 4th as Children's Day. Children's Day must be a lot of fun. Some parents demanded to accompany their children in the celebration. Because of this, Taiwan celebrated Women's Day together with Children's Day on April 4, 1991. Since then, April 4th has been known as "The Combined Holidays of Women's Day and Children's Day". It has been a public holiday in Taiwan since 2011. Every leap year, Children's Day falls on the same day as Tomb Sweeping Day. Those years, there are not so many activities for children. Most of them are celebrating Tomb Sweeping Day, instead.

這個節日自西元 1931 年開始就在中國被慶祝。不幸地，這個節日在西元 1998 年被取消了。西元 2011 它再一次成為國定節日。中國現在已經將 4 月 4 日定為兒童節。兒童節必定是很有樂趣的。有些父母要求在慶祝活動中陪伴小孩。因為如此，台灣在西元 1991 年 4 月 4 日將婦女節和兒童節一起慶祝。從那時候起，4 月 4 日被稱為是「結合婦女節和兒童節的節日」。從西元 2011 年起在台灣變成眾所皆知的節日。每次閏年時，兒童節和清明節會適逢在同一天。那些年便沒有這麼多給孩子的活動。大部分他們會以慶祝清明節作為取代。

It has been said that the most important thing for children to do is to play hard and to play happily. It is especially important for kids to play together with their parents on Children's Day. Children's Day is a day to bring joy to children. It is a day to strengthen bonds between parents and children. Schools offer special activities. They often honor model students. Some amusement parks offer free entrance for children on this day. Local groups offer activities for children and their parents. The kids should feel like King for a day. Parents should feel excited about being with their children. There is a Chinese saying that says "There's a little child in everyone's mind." Although parents cannot be children again, they can still be excited about the holiday together. After all, it is important for moms and dads to remember that their child is worth making time for.

　　有人說，對兒童最重要要做的事情便是盡興且愉快的玩。在兒童節當天對孩子們來說，和父母一起同樂是件特別重要的事情。兒童節是個帶給小孩歡樂的日子。是個加強父母和孩子間聯結的日子。學校提供許多特別的活動。他們常常表揚模範學生。有些遊樂園也提供孩子在這天免費入場。本地團體提供活動們給小孩與他們的父母。孩子們在那天會覺得自己像個國王。父母也會因為陪伴著他們的小孩感到雀躍不已。有一句中國諺語說：「每個人的心裡都有個小小孩。」雖然父母無法再當一遍小孩了，他們仍然可以為這個節日一起感到興奮。畢竟，最重要的是爸爸和媽媽們記得，這是個值得他們的孩子們度過的時刻。

Here are some questions for you to discuss:
這裡有些供你討論的問題：

1. What kind of activity is the most popular for kids to play?
   那種活動是最受孩童歡迎去遊玩的呢？

2. Do you agree with the saying that "There's a little child in everyone's mind"?
   你同意這個諺語，「每個人心裡都有一個小小孩嗎」？

單字大集合

1. Recommend *vi. vt.* 推薦

The doctor recommended I take vitamins.
醫生建議我服用維生素。

2. Understanding *n.* [U] 理解

Understanding means being able to see the other point of view.
理解意味著能夠看到其他的觀點。

3. Designate *vt.* 指定；稱呼

We have designated today as no homework day.
我們已經指定今天是無功課日。

4. Accompany *vi. vt.* 伴奏；陪同

I will accompany my grandmother to the store.
我將會陪著我奶奶去商店。

5. Especially *adv.* 特別是

I like all ice cream, but especially chocolate ice cream.
我喜歡所有的冰淇淋，但特別是巧克力冰淇淋。

6. Amusement *n.* [C,U] 消遣；樂趣

The amusement park has lots of good rides.
遊樂園有許多良好的遊樂設施。

7. Combine *vi. vt.* 結合；使結合

We combined the third and fourth grade classes.
我們結合了三和四年級的課程。

8. Strengthen *vi. vt.* 變強大；加強

I have to strengthen my muscles.
我必須強化我的肌肉。

閱讀測驗

1. Why have Women's Day and Children's Day been combined?
   為什麼婦女節和兒童節已經結合？

   (a) Because there was not time for both holidays
       因為兩個節日都沒有時間。

   (b) Because parents wanted to celebrate with their children.
       因為父母想要和他們的孩子一起慶祝。

   (c) So that children do not have to be left alone. 這樣小孩才不會被單獨留下。

2. What is the most important thing for children to do?
   對孩子們來說，最重要要做的事是什麼？

   (a) Play hard and play happily. 盡興且愉悅的玩。

   (b) Get lots of sleep. 獲得大量的睡眠。

   (c) Take their vitamins. 攝取維生素。

3. What does it mean "there's a little child in everyone's mind"？
   「每個人的心裡都有個小小孩」意指什麼？

   (a) Parents can become children again. 父母可以再次成為小孩。

   (b) Parents can enjoy doing children's activities. 父母可以享受孩子們的活動。

   (c) Everyone has a child they are always thinking about.
       每個人都有個時常惦記的孩子。

4. In which year the holiday has been celebrated in China?
   這個節日自幾年開始就在中國被慶祝了呢？

   (a) In 1954

   (b) In 1931

   (c) In 1991

活動慶典和習俗

　　在 1925 年 8 月，由來自世界 54 個不同國家的代表參與了在瑞士日內瓦召開以保護兒童相關福利為訴求的國際會議，在會議上國際兒童幸福促進會首次提出（first proclaim）了「兒童節」（Children's Day）。而我國則在 1931 年時，由中華慈愛協濟會提議，訂 4 月 4 為兒童節。在政府於 1949 年遷台後，仍沿用之前的規定，國小（含）以下學童於兒童節時放假一天。在 1991 年及 1997 年時則與婦女節合併放假一天。在 1988 年週休二日（two-day weeken(d)實施後，則取消放假，在 2011 年時又重新修法，恢復兒童節為國定假日，並規定，如與民族掃墓節同一日時，於前一日放假，但逢星期四時，於後一日放假。如遇週休，有時會有 4 日的連續假期，也頗為符合國人於初春時出遊的習慣。

　　除了我國 4 月 4 日的兒童節之外，在其他國家則依照其文化而訂在不同的日期。而其中以 6 月 1 日或是 11 月 20 日為多數國家的兒童節。6 月 1 日又稱國際兒童保護日（International Day for Protection of Children），或是國際兒童節。這是在 1949 年時，國際民主婦女聯合會在莫斯科舉行會議時，由義大利代表提出為了要確保該各國兒童生活、衛生和教育全力的任務，需訂立國際兒童節。而為了紀念在 1942 年 6 月 10 日被納粹德國屠殺的捷克利迪策村的 88 名兒童，提議將國際兒童節訂在 6 月 1 日。而接著在 1954 年的 12 月 14 日，聯合國（United Nations）教育科學文化組織訂定 11 月 20 日為國際兒童日（The Universal Children's Day）。

　　在台灣，兒童節的時候，各縣市政府多會為了慶祝兒童節而舉辦一些免費的活動。例如台北市各國小會發放兒童節活動折頁，而兒童能憑折頁享有相關展覽會場門票免費的優待，如台北市立動物園（Taipei City Zoo）、兒童育樂中心（Children's Recreation Center）、國立故宮博物院（National Palace Museum）、自來水園區（Water Park）等。縣市政府也會舉辦免費的親子活動，相關的藝文節目。許多的遊樂場則會推出優惠門票，推出一些活動如卡通人物遊行（parade of cartoon characters）等來吸引兒童的目光。

實用生活會話

Q1: What day is Children's day in Japan?

日本的兒童節在什麼時候？

A1: May 5, and it is a national holiday, but we usually celebrate children's day thrice a year; March 3 for girls, May 5 for boys, and November 15 especially for girls who are aged three or seven, and boys who are aged three or five.

5 月 5 日，是個國定假日。但我們通常一年中有三個不同的慶祝日子，3 月 3 日是針對女孩，5 月 5 日是男孩的節日及 11 月 15 日別針對 3 或 7 歲的女孩，及 3 或 5 歲的男孩。

Q2: Wow! What are the differences of the celebrations?

哇！那在慶祝儀式上有什麼不同呢？

A2: On Girl's Day, we display a set of ornamental dolls at home to pray good health for girls.

在女兒節時，我們會在家中展示雛人偶為女孩祈求健康。

A3: Children's day in Japan also known as Boy's Day, we fly carp streamers outside, and display Samurai dolls and Japanese military helmets at home.

日本的兒童節也叫做男孩節，我們會懸掛鯉魚旗，及在家中擺設武士人偶及日本盔甲。

A4: The last one is "Shichi-Go-San", means 7-5-3. It's a unique traditional festival day in Japan held annually on November 15 to celebrate the growth and well-being of young children. 3-7-5 children will get their "Chitose Ame", literally "thousand year candy", which symbolize longevity and health.

最後一個是七五三節，是一個獨特且傳統的日本節日，每年會在 11 月 15 日時舉行來祈求年幼孩童能健康平安地長大。歲數在 3、5、7 的孩子會收到象徵長命百歲及健康的千歲飴。

實用單句這樣說

- In response to a letter written by a 6-year-old boy inquiring if Mr. President would make a Children's Day for him, President Bill Clinton proclaimed Children's Day to be held on October 11.
  一名 6 歲大的男孩寫信請求總統先生是否能為他設立一個兒童節，因此柯林頓總統宣布將 10 月 8 日訂立為兒童節。

- Children's Day is recognized on various days in many places around the world.
  兒童節在世界各地被訂立於不同的日期。

- Children's most wanted Children's Day present is cell phone in South Korea.
  在南韓，行動電話是兒童最想要的兒童節禮物。

- Korean children wanted to spent the Children's Day with the girl band "Girl's Generation" the most, with one third of respondents saying so.
  有約三分之一受訪的韓國兒童表示，最想要和女子團體"少女時代"一起過兒童節。

- Children's Day is the most expectant day for all the kids; during the day, teachers and parents are less than punishing the kids as usual.
  兒童節是所有孩子們最期待的日子，當天老師和爸媽比較不會處罰人。

- The symbolic meaning which contains behind the Children's Day is far beyond how people could imagine complicatedly and deeply.
  兒童節背後蘊含的象徵意義，遠超過人們所能想像的複雜與深刻。

互動時刻真有趣

● 有趣問答

1. 一年當中，最早過兒童節的是那個國家？

2. 在兒童節時，兒童會 cosplay 的是那個國家？

3. 那個國家的兒童節最重視健康？

4. 那個地區有最長的兒童節？

Answer:

1. 烏拉圭（Uruguay），1 月 6 日。在烏拉圭除了官方版本的 1 月 6 日兒童節之外，還有一個是在 8 月的第二個星期天。在這兩天，兒童都會收到父母或是親戚送的禮物，有趣的是，在 1 月 6 日時，成人偶而也會收到禮物。

2. 瑞典（Sweden），在瑞典，也將兒童節分為男孩節及女孩節。男孩節是在 8 月 7 日，又稱龍蝦節，在當天男孩們會裝扮成龍蝦，表演節目。有鼓勵男孩要學習龍蝦勇敢精神的含意。12 月 13 日則是女孩節，又稱露西亞女神節，女孩們要打扮成女神，並為其他孩子做善事。

3. 巴西（Brazil），8 月 15 日這一天也是巴西的全國防疫日，在這一天全國的醫生會為孩童做身體檢查，及 5 歲以下的兒童注射小兒麻痺疫苗。另外在 10 月 12 日的聖母顯靈日，也常被視為是兒童節，會有慶祝活動。

4. 非洲西部（West Afric(a)，在非洲西部一些國家有長達一個月的兒童狂歡節，儘管生活條件並沒有那麼的好，但孩童們都會在節慶上盡情歡樂，有時還會戴上動物面具跳舞，非常熱鬧。

Tomb Sweeping Festival
清明節

節慶源由──簡易版

Tomb Sweeping Festival is also called Clear and Bright Festival. It takes place in April. It is a time for families to think about their dead relatives. People visit the tombs of their relatives. They sweep them clean. They pull weeds. They put flowers on the grave. They paint the grave with new, shiny paint. They place chicken, eggs and tea on the grave. This is a gift to the spirit who lives there. This should be done in the morning. The spirits walk around during the day. They come home to sleep at night. Families want to remember their relatives while the spirits are still home in the grave.

掃墓節又被稱為清明節。在 4 月舉行。這是家人想到他們已過世的親人的時刻。人們造訪他們的親人的墳墓。他們將它們掃乾淨。他們拔草。他們將花朵擺在墳上。他們用新的、有光澤的塗料粉刷墳墓。他們擺放雞、蛋和茶在墳前。這是給住在那的靈魂的禮物。這必須在白天進行。靈魂在那天四處走動。他們在晚上回家睡覺。家人們想要在靈魂仍住在墳墓裡時記得他們的親人。

This sounds like a solemn day, but it is not. The tombs are often in the country. So the visit is a fun family outing. The family will have a picnic. They might play games and even fly kites.

這聽起來是個莊嚴的節日，其實不然。墳墓通常在郊外。因此掃墓拜訪是一個有趣的家族郊遊。家族將有一次野餐。他們可能會玩遊戲，甚至放風箏。

單字大集合

1. **Bright**　*adj.*　明亮的

   The sun is very bright today.
   太陽今天非常的明亮。

2. **Relative**　*n.* [C]　親戚；親屬

   My relatives came over for dinner.
   我的親戚過來吃晚餐。

3. **Shiny**　*adj.*　發光的；閃耀的

   I got a shiny new bike today.
   我今天得到一台閃耀的腳踏車。

4. **Picnic**　*n.* [C]　野餐

   We took a picnic to the park.
   我們到公園野餐。

5. **Spirit**　*n.* [C,U]　靈魂；心靈

   A spirit is like a ghost.
   靈魂就像鬼一樣。

6. **Solemn**　*adj.*　嚴肅的；莊嚴的

   My father was solemn when I told the lie.
   當我說謊時我爸很嚴肅。

節慶源由——精彩完整版

Tomb Sweeping Festival is sometimes called Clear and Bright Festival. This name comes from its Chinese name, Ching Ming. Ching means clean and Ming means brightness. Most years, it takes place on April 5th. It is 104 days after the winter solstice. Winter solstice is the day the sun is at the farthest point south of the equator. Because it must be 104 days after the solstice, during leap year the holiday falls on April 4th, the same day as Children's Day.

掃墓節有時被稱作清明節。這個名字來自於它的中文名稱「清明」。「清」指的是乾淨,而「明」指的是明亮。在大多數的年份,它會在 4 月 5 日舉行。冬至後的 104 天。冬至是太陽在赤道以南的最遠點的那天。因為清明節必定在冬至後的 104 天,在閏年時,節日便會落在 4 月 4 日,和兒童節同一天。

Tomb Sweeping Day is a time for families to remember their dead ancestors. People visit the tombs of their ancestors to sweep them clean. They pull weeds from around the grave and place flowers on it. They repaint the family names in gold paint. Often whole cooked chicken, hard boiled eggs and tea are placed on the grave. Three sets of chopsticks and three cups of wine are placed on the headstone. These are all given as an offering to the spirits. This must all be done early in the morning. The spirits wander the earth during the day and return to their graves each night to sleep. So families want to pay their ancestors their respects while the spirits are still home in the grave.

掃墓節是家人回憶他們去世祖先們的時刻。人們造訪祖先的墳墓,將它們打掃乾淨。他們拔下墳墓四周的雜草並且擺放花朵。他們在祖先的名字上重新漆上金漆。通常完全煮熟的雞肉、水煮蛋和茶葉被放置在墓地上。三組的筷子和三杯酒放在墓碑上。這些都是給靈魂的祭品。必須全部在清晨完成。靈魂在白天時四處遊蕩,每晚返回他們的墳墓睡眠。因此家人們想要在靈魂仍然居住在墳墓裡時,表達對他們祖先的尊敬。

Tomb Sweeping Day was first declared a national holiday in 732 AD, during the Tang Dynasty. This day has long been a public holiday in Taiwan, Hong Kong and Macau. It was re-named a holiday in China in 2008. Legends say that unhappy spirits wander the earth on Tomb Sweeping Day. It is considered bad luck to do important business or have an operation on that day.

掃墓節第一次被宣布為國定假日是在西元 732 年，唐朝期間。這天在台灣、香港和澳門已經成為國定假日很久了。在西元 2008 年，中國將它重新命名一個節日。傳說中不開心的靈魂在掃墓節這天會在地球各處四處遊蕩。這天也被認為是作生意或是動手術會不幸運的一天。

This is not a totally solemn day, however. Because the tombs are often in the country, the visit is a fun family outing. Usually the family will have a picnic. They might burn incense for their ancestors and even fly kites.

然而，這天不是完全莊嚴的日子。因為墳墓通常都在郊外，因此掃墓拜訪是一個有趣的家族郊遊。通常家族將會野餐。他們可能會為他們的祖先燒香，甚至放風箏。

Here are some questions for you to discuss:
這裡有些供你討論的問題：

1. Does your family have a habit to visit the bombs of your ancestors?
   你的家人有去掃墓的習慣嗎？

2. What do you usually do to plan for the Tomb Sweeping Festival?
   你通常都如何計劃清明節的？

單字大集合

1. Solstice *n.* [C] 至

The winter solstice is the shortest day of the year.
冬至是一年當中最短的一天。

2. Remember *vi. vt.* 記得

I remember doing that when I was a kid.
我記得當我還是個孩子的時候。

3. Ancestor *n.* [C] 祖宗；祖先

My ancestors lived in China.
我的祖先住在中國。

4. Headstone *n.* [C] 墓碑

The headstones on the graves are falling down.
墳墓上的墓碑倒下了。

5. Offering *n.* [C,U] 祭品；貢獻

We will make an offering to the gods.
我們將準備祭品給神。

6. Business *n.* [C] 公司

Our business is always closed on holidays.
我們的公司總是在假日關閉。

7. Operation *n.* [C,U] 手術；運轉

I need an operation to fix my broken leg.
我需要一個手術來修復我受傷的腳。

8. Incense *n.* [U] 香

I like the smell of incense burning.
我喜歡燒香的氣味。

閱讀測驗

1. Why is Tomb Sweeping Day also called Clear and Bright Festival?
   為什麼掃墓節又稱作清明節？
   (a) Because you sweep the graves clean.
   因為你將墳墓清掃乾淨。
   (b) The meaning of the Chinese name is Clear and Bright.
   中文名稱的意義是清淨及明亮。
   (c) It is a clear and bright day.
   這是個乾淨又明亮的一天。

2. Why is food placed on the grave? 為什麼食物被擺在墳上？
   (a) Because everyone is hungry.
   因為每個人都很餓。
   (b) For the animals to eat.
   給動物吃的。
   (c) As a gift for the spirits.
   作為禮物送給靈魂。

3. Why should the tomb sweeping be done in the morning?
   為什麼掃墓必須在早上完成？
   (a) Because the afternoon is too hot.
   因為下午太熱了。
   (b) So you can all take naps in the afternoon.
   這樣你才可以在下午打瞌睡。
   (c) So the spirits are still home in the grave.
   因為靈魂仍然在墳墓裡。

4. What makes the day fun? 是什麼讓這天變得有趣？
   (a) Sweeping is always fun. 掃除總是快樂的。
   (b) Family picnics and games. 家族野餐及遊戲。
   (c) There is nothing fun during this holiday.
   在這個節日期間沒有有趣的事情。

活動慶典和習俗

　　清明節是我國的傳統節日之一，也是最重要的祭祀節日，在這一天我們除了祭拜祖先（Ancestors worshipping）之外，其主要的紀念儀式則是掃墓（Tomb/ Grave sweeping），是後人慎終追遠及孝道的表現。清明節在英文中稱 Ching Ming/ Qingming Festival, 也可稱 Tomb Sweeping day 或是 All Souls' Day.

　　清明是農曆二十四節氣（24 solar terms）之一，每年會固定落在國曆 4 月 4、5、6 日其中一天，是少數與國曆大致吻合的傳統節日，也是兩岸三地中唯一一個根據節氣而訂立的假日。

　　在古代，清明只是節氣之一，人們重視的是在清明前一日的寒食節（Hanshi/ Cold Food Festival）。寒食節的主要習俗則為當日不生火煮食，只吃準備好的熟食及冷食，還有掃墓。因與清明日子相近，而逐漸演變成將寒食節的習俗移至清明，而清明也因此從一個單純的節氣躍升成為我國傳統的大節日之一。我們在清明節常吃的潤餅/春捲（Lumpia/ Spring Roll），則是源於寒食節不生火的習俗中所衍生而出的食物。

　　掃墓時，因各地習俗不同，而準備的東西也有所差異。在台灣，因約有七成以上為閩南後裔，所以在掃墓時大多只準備線香（incense/ joss stick）、蠟燭（candle）、紙錢（joss paper）及酒（wine）。先以雙手祭拜，告知守墳的土地公及先人要開始掃墓，以鐮刀清除四週雜草，並做簡單的修繕工作。然後進行祭拜，祭拜完成後，再以小石頭壓住墓紙以代表掃墓完成。

　　在清明節的時候，除了掃墓為最主要的習俗活動之外，因正值萬物生長之時，所以郊外踏青（spring hike）也成為受歡迎的活動之一，除此之外在不同地區還分別有盪鞦韆（play on the swing）、放風箏（fly a kite）、帶柳枝（carry willow branches）、甚至還有畫蛋、鬥雞（cockfight）等慶祝活動。

實用生活會話

Q1: Daddy, what is Ching Ming Festival?
爹地，什麼是清明節？

A1: Ching Ming Festival, we also call it Tomb Sweeping Day.
清明節，我們也稱做是掃墓節。

Q2: What should we do on the Ching Ming Festival?
那我們在清明節時該做些什麼？

A2: We normally visit our ancestors' graves on this day, and remove weeds, touch up gravestone inscriptions and then make offering of wine and fruit.
我們通常會在清明節時到祖先的墳上，清除四周雜草，修繕墓碑，之後再獻上酒和水果。

Q3: Why should we do that?
那我們為什麼要這樣做呢？

A3: It's a way for us to commemorate our ancestors and pay respects to them.
這是我們緬懷先人及對祖先表達敬意的一種方式。

Q4: What is the important meaning of Ching Ming Festival?
什麼是清明節的重要意義呢？

A4: It combines with the worship of people towards ancestors and the nature,and presents the moral goodness to uphold filial piery.
清明節結合了人們對祖先與自然的崇拜，顯示國人崇尚孝道的美德。

實用單句這樣說

- Tomb Sweeping Day is a national holiday in Taiwan.
  在台灣，清明節是國定假日。

- I heard that there were many fire disasters by burning joss paper on Ching Ming Festival last year.
  我聽說去年清明節，因為焚燒紙錢而引發多場火災。

- Many fire disasters were caused by careless, so we should be paying more attentions when burning joss paper.
  火災大多是因為人為疏失而造成的，所以我們在燒紙錢時必須特別的小心。

- On the Ching Ming Festival, all cemeteries are crowded with people who came for the tomb sweeping, and caused serious traffic jams in those areas.
  在清明節的時候，墓園總是會湧入大批掃墓的人，而造成週邊道路交通堵塞。

- In order to control traffic over the four-day holiday, the city government will provide five different free-of-charge shuttle bus routes for people conducting tomb sweeping.
  為了因應四天連續假期的交通狀況，市政府將提供五條不同路線免費的接駁巴士給掃墓的民眾。

- Some people fly kites at Ching Ming Festival's night. A string of little lanterns tied on the thread or the kite and look like shining stars in the sky.
  有些人會在清明節晚上放風箏。並且在風箏上或是線上綁上一串小燈籠，看起來就像是天空中閃爍的星星。

- Lumpias and red sticky rice cakes are the two most common foods eaten on the Tomb Sweeping Day.
  潤餅捲和紅龜粿是清明節時應景的食品。

- To worship ancestors on the Ching Ming Festival is a way for us to show filial piety.
  在清明節時祭拜祖先是我們表達孝道的一種方式。

互動時刻真有趣

清明　杜牧

清明時節雨紛紛
路上行人欲斷魂
借問酒家何處有
牧童遙指杏花村

The drizzling rain falls on the Ching Ming Festival. Travelers move along the way with deep sorrow and grief. Where can I find a tavern? The shepherd boy points at the distant village amidst apricot blossoms.

清明節時正下著毛毛細雨，正在路上趕路的行人因為無法回家與家人團聚，而感到無比的感傷。向人打聽哪兒有酒家可供他休息，並飲酒暖暖身。小牧童手指向不遠處那杏花盛開的小村落中。

寒食　韓翃

春城無處不飛花
寒食東風御柳斜
日暮漢宮傳蠟燭
輕煙散入五侯家

Petals fly through all over the capital city in spring as the east wind bends the royal willows on the Hanshi Festival. Candles are rewarded by the Emperor at dusk. Smokes rise in the houses of the five marquises.

春天的京城百花盛開，繽紛的花瓣四處飛舞，在寒食節時吹起了東風將御花園中的柳枝給吹斜了。在黃昏的時候，從宮中送出了皇帝御賜的蠟燭，清煙飄散進了新封的五個侯爺府中。

Boys' Festival
男孩節（日本）

節慶源由──簡易版

Boys' Festival in Japan is on May 5th. Boys are honored because they are strong. They work hard. Families put a cloth carp, a kind of fish, on their roof. The carp fills with wind and seems to swim in the air. The carp is a strong fish. It can swim up streams and waterfalls. The carp stands for courage and reaching for high goals. It is a good way to remind boys to work hard. It reminds boys to keep trying even if something is hard.

在日本的男孩節是在 5 月 5 日。男孩們因為身強體壯被表揚。他們努力工作。家人們將鯉魚布放在他們的屋頂上。鯉魚充滿了風並像是在空氣裡游泳一樣。鯉魚是一種強而有力的魚。牠可以在溪流和瀑布裡游泳。鯉魚代表著勇氣和達到高標。這是個提醒男孩們努力工作的好方法。這提醒男孩們持續嘗試，即使是某件很困難的事。

Inside, families set up a doll. It is a symbol of a strong and healthy boy. The doll is a child from long ago. He was strong. He rode a bear instead of a horse. He played with animals. Families eat sweet rice cakes. They wish for their boys to be strong like the carp.

在家裡，每個家庭會擺放娃娃。這是強壯和健康的男孩的象徵。這個娃娃是個來自很久以前的小孩。他很強壯。他騎著一頭熊，而不是馬。他和動物們一起玩耍。家人們吃甜年糕。他們希望他們的男孩能夠像鯉魚一樣強壯。

單字大集合

1. Carp　*n.* [C]　鯉魚

The carp is a fish.

鯉魚是一種魚。

2. Swim　*vi. vt.*　游泳；游過

I can swim in a pool.

我可以在水池裡游泳。

3. Strong　*adj.*　強壯的

My legs are very strong.

我的腿很強壯。

4. Stream　*n.* [C]　小河

I sat by a stream in the woods.

我坐在樹林裡的小河邊。

5. Waterfall　*n.* [C]　瀑布

There is a waterfall on the river.

那有個在河上的瀑布。

6. Healthy　*adj.*　健康的

I eat lots of fruit to be healthy.

我為了健康吃了很多水果。

節慶源由──精彩完整版

Boys' Festival is celebrated on what is now known as Children's Day in Japan. At first, it was on the fifth day of the fifth lunar month. When Japan started using the 12 month calendar, the holiday was placed on May 5th. It is a day to celebrate the hard work and strength of boys.

男孩節在現在被日本稱為兒童節的那天慶祝。最初，它是在農曆的五月初五。當日本人開始使用 12 個月的日曆，這個節日便被安排在 5 月 5 日。這是個慶祝努力工作的男孩的日子。

The carp has become the symbol of Boys' Festival. The Japanese consider it the most spirited of all fish. It is full of energy and strong enough to fight its way up swift streams and waterfalls. It stands for courage and the ability to reach high goals. The carp is a good symbol to encourage boys to work hard. It encourages them to overcome life's difficulties.

鯉魚已經變成男孩節的象徵。日本人覺得牠是所有魚類裡最生氣蓬勃的。牠充滿能量且足夠強壯到去對抗湍急的溪流及瀑布。牠代表勇氣和達到高標的能力。鯉魚是個用來鼓勵男孩們努力工作的優良象徵。牠鼓勵他們去克服人生的許多困難。

Beginning in late April, families fly colorful carp-shaped streamers. They fill with wind and seem to swim through the air. They fly from the rooftop with red and white ribbons. Families fly one carp for each boy.

從 4 月下旬開始，許多家都飄揚著五顏六色的鯉魚形飄帶。牠們充滿了風並且看起來像是在空氣裡游泳。牠們藉由紅色和白色的絲帶飛揚。家人們為每個男孩懸掛一個鯉魚。

Inside the house, families display a doll. This doll represents a child who was a hero long ago. He was famous for his strength. It is said that he rode a bear instead of a horse. He played with animals in the mountains when he was young. The display also includes a traditional Japanese military helmet. This doll and helmet are symbols of a strong and healthy boy.

在家裡，每個家庭會陳列一個娃娃。這個娃娃代表一個在很久以前是個英雄的小孩。他因為他的力量而聞名。據說，他騎著一頭熊，而不是馬。在他年輕時，他在山裡和動物們嬉戲。陳列裡還包含一個傳統的日本軍用頭盔。這個娃娃和頭盔都是強壯與健康男孩的象徵。

It is traditional on Boys' Festival to eat sweet rice cakes and sweet rice dumplings wrapped in iris leaves. The leaf of the Japanese iris is long and shaped like a sword. The name of the iris in Japanese means to strive for success.

傳統的男孩節吃虹膜葉包裹的甜年糕和甜粽子。日本的虹膜葉片長且形狀像把劍。虹膜在日語意味著努力爭取成功。

No one knows for sure when Boys' Festival began. Some think it came from royal Chinese guards who wore helmets and carried bows and arrows. This later became popular in Japan. Others think it came from farmers scaring away insects from their plants. They tried to scare them away with bright banners and frightening figures. Others believe the flags and streamers were flown to celebrate victory over invaders. In every case, the day celebrates being strong and overcoming struggles.

沒有人能確定男孩節起源於何時。有些人認為，這來自中國王室戴著頭盔並佩帶弓箭的侍衛。之後在日本受到歡迎。有其他人認為，來自於農人們為了嚇跑躲在農作物裡的害蟲。他們試著用鮮亮的旗幟和令人恐懼的人型嚇跑牠們。有些則相信旗幟和橫幅飛揚是用來慶祝戰勝侵略者。在每個說法裡，這天都是用來慶祝堅強和克服難關。

單字大集合

1. Symbol *n.* [C] 象徵

The flag is a symbol for our country.
國旗是我們國家的象徵。

2. Spirited *adj.* 生氣蓬勃的

Their voices were very spirited because they were so excited.
他們的聲音很生氣蓬勃，因為他們很興奮。

3. Represent *vi. vt.* 代表；作為……的代表

He represents his class with honor.
他帶著榮譽代表他的班級。

4. Famous *adj.* 出名的

The singer was famous for her excellent voice.
這位歌手因為她卓越的嗓音而出名。

5. Military *n.* [C, the S] 軍人；軍隊

The military had to go to war.
軍隊必須去打仗。

6. Succeed *vi. vt.* 成功；繼承

The team had succeed this season.
這隊伍在本賽季成功了。

7. Frightening *adj.* 令人恐懼的

I heard frightening sounds in the night.
我在晚上聽到令人恐懼的聲音。

8. Invader *n.* [C] 侵略者

Some invaders came in to take over the country.
有些侵略者進入並接管了國家。

閱讀測驗

1. Which fish is the symbol of Boys' Festival? 哪一種魚是男孩節的象徵？

   (a) Any fish that is bright red. 任何亮紅色的魚。

   (b) The salmon. 鮭魚。

   (c) The carp. 鯉魚。

2. What does the carp encourage boys to do? 鯉魚鼓勵男孩們去做什麼？

   (a) To work hard and overcome difficulties. 努力工作並度過難關。

   (b) To play hard and have fun every day. 努力玩樂並每天享樂。

   (c) To be kind to their fathers. 對他們的父親溫柔。

3. What are the doll and helmet symbols of? 娃娃和頭盔是什麼的象徵？

   (a) A boy going off to war. 進入戰爭的男孩。

   (b) A strong and healthy boy. 強壯健康的男孩。

   (c) A boy playing with animals. 和動物一起玩樂的男孩。

4. What did farmers scare insects away with? 農夫用什麼嚇跑蟲？

   (a) Loud music 大聲的音樂。

   (b) The biggest sticks they could find. 他們所能找到的最大的棍子。

   (c) Bright banners and frightening figures. 鮮亮的旗幟和令人恐懼的人型。

5. What is the traditional food, eaten on Boy's Festival?
   什麼是男孩節所吃的傳統食物？

   (a) Sweet rice cakes 甜年糕

   (b) Sweet rice dumplings 甜粽子

   (c) (a) and (b) 上述二選項皆是

活動慶典和習俗

　　在日本，每年 5 月初有一個長達約一個星期左右的連續假期，一般稱做「黃金周」（Golden Week）。而在這段假期中的最後一天則是 5 月 5 日兒童節，也是日本的男孩節（Boy's Day）及端午節。由於受到中國文化的影響，所以在西元 834 年時，將中國傳來的節日，如農曆新年、上巳節、端午節等訂為節日，在明治維新之後，更改實行西曆，停用農曆，便將這些節日調整至相應的西曆日期。

　　在端午節時懸掛的菖蒲在日文中與「尚武」同音，所以在安平時代便流行在端午節時舉行騎射的活動以驅除惡鬼，再加上在中國文化中認為五月五日為陽氣最盛的日子，因此被視為是男孩的節日。

　　日本人在四月底時便會開始懸掛鯉魚旗（Koinobori / Carp streamers）。而在蔚藍天空中迎風飛舞，由七色彩旗的真鯉還有紅黑兩色的緋鯉組成的鯉魚旗，則是一般人們對日本男孩節最深刻的印象，因此這一天也被稱為鯉魚旗祭（Feast of Banners）。懸掛鯉魚旗的習俗可以追溯至室町時代，那時只有武士家才能懸掛，而到了江戶時代，將軍幕府規定將軍家有兒子出生要懸掛旗幟，且有中國鯉魚躍龍門的說法傳入，所以鯉魚被日本人視為是好運及勇氣的象徵，因此有男孩的家庭開始流行立起鯉魚旗，祈求上天保佑男孩健康平安及能出人頭地。

　　在男孩節這一天，仍保留著原有端午節的習俗，會吃粽子或柏餅，掛菖蒲，已浸泡過菖蒲的水沐浴。另外還會擺放「五月人形」（May Dolls），人偶的主角則以日本歷史上有名的武士為主，最普遍的為金太郎及弁慶，而我國的鍾馗，因其打鬼的傳說被日本人視為孩童的守護神，因此成為五月人形中的主角之一。而有些家庭則不放人偶，而是擺飾武士的頭盔，鎧甲及武具。

實用生活會話

Q1: What are those fish-shaped kites?

那些魚形風箏是什麼啊？

A1: They are carp streamers. From the end of April to May 5, Japanese families with boys raise the carp-shaped windsocks outside their houses to wish a good future for boys.

那是鯉魚旗。有兒子的日本家庭會在四月初到五月五日之間在家外面立起鯉魚旗希望兒子能前途似錦。

Q2: How many streamers for a set?

一組裡有幾面鯉魚旗呢？

A2: Three or more. The large black one represents father, red for the mother, the small one represents son of the family and always in color green or blue. A new streamer is added when there's a new born boy in the family.

三面或是更多。其中大隻黑色的代表父親，紅色的代表母親，小的綠色或是藍色的則代表兒子。當家中有新生的男嬰時，便會再增加一面鯉魚旗。

Q3: Is there any other custom for the Japanese Boy's Day?

那日本男孩節還有其他的習俗嗎？

A3: They also display Kintaro dolls or traditional Japanese samurai helmets and armors and weapons at home.

他們還會在家中擺放金太郎人偶或是傳統的日本武士盔甲及武器。

實用單句這樣說

- Kintaro is the childhood name of Sakata Kintoki who was a hero in the Heian Period.
  金太郎是坂田金時的小名，他是平安時代的英雄。

- On Boy's Day, there is a custom to take a bath with floating calamus leaves.
  在男孩節時，有以菖蒲泡澡入浴的習俗。

- Kashiwamochi is a traditional food that eaten on the Boy's Day. It is a steamed sticky rice cake with sweet stuffing and wrapped with oak leave.
  柏餅是在男孩節時的傳統食物。它是一種包有甜餡，以橡樹葉包著的麻糬。
  （註：日文中的柏指的是槲櫟，又稱白橡樹）

- During the Golden Week, you can see flying colorful carp streamers everywhere in Japan. Some are flown above the roof, and some are hanged down like laundry.
  在黃金週假期中，你在日本到處都可以看到隨風飛揚的彩色鯉魚旗。有些在屋頂上飛揚，有些則像是剛洗好的衣物被倒掛著。

- Carps jumping over the Dragon Gate is a legend that handed down in China for generations.
  鯉躍龍門在中國是個流傳已久的傳說。

- In 1948, the Boy's Day was renamed Children's Day, and the Japanese government decreed this day to be a national holiday to celebrate the happiness of all children and to express gratitude toward mothers.
  在 1948 年時，日本政府將男孩節更名為兒童節，並將其訂為國定假日讓所有兒童一起歡樂慶祝，並表達對母親的感謝。

互動時刻真有趣

鯉魚旗製作 Carp Streamer (Koinobori) Craft

　　色彩鮮豔，造型可愛的鯉魚旗非常受到孩子們的喜愛，請試著與孩子一起製作簡易的鯉魚旗勞作，感受一下男孩節的氣氛。

1. 將下列圖樣放大至所需大小後印出，並在圖樣上著色後沿虛線剪下。
2. 將剪下的鯉魚旗捲成筒狀，並以膠水將鯉魚旗左右兩邊黏合，簡單的鯉魚旗完成！

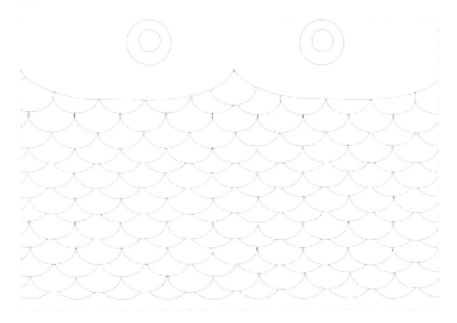

進階版

1. 可將著色完成的圖樣貼在家用捲筒衛生紙的捲筒上；或是每一面鯉魚旗選擇 3 到 4 種顏色的棉紙或是色紙，剪下直徑約 5 公分以內的圓形（約 20 個），並剪成半圓形，當作是鯉魚旗的魚鱗貼在捲筒上，請記得由鯉魚旗的尾端開始貼起。以各 2 個白色大圓及黑色小圓做為鯉魚的眼睛。如要製造飛舞的感覺，則可以長形紙條貼在尾端（捲筒內）。
2. 取一根約 20 公分長的棉線綁在竹筷上，棉線兩端各留有約 9 公分長，將兩端用膠帶貼在鯉魚旗捲筒內，頭部約兩眼的位置，一根竹筷約可綁上三面捲筒鯉魚旗。

Mother's Day
母親節

節慶源由──簡易版

In most countries, Mother's Day is a new holiday. Some countries had a day to honor all mothers. But people wanted a day to honor their own mothers.

在許多國家，母親節是個新的節日。有些國家有表揚所有母親的日子。但人們想要有表揚自己母親的專屬日。

In Taiwan, Mother's Day is the second Sunday of May. This is also Buddha Day and Tzu Chi Day. Tzu Chi is a group that works to take care of poor people. Buddha says there are three things you must do to be wise. You must be thankful. You must show respect. You must help others. Mother's Day is a day to be thankful. Buddha Day is a day to show respect. Tzu Chi Day is a day to help others.

在台灣，母親節是在 5 月的第 2 個禮拜天。這也是佛誕節，慈濟日。慈濟是照顧貧窮人民的團體。佛說有三件事情為了成為智慧的是你必須做的。你必須是感恩的。你必須表現尊敬。你必須幫助其他人。母親節是個感恩的節日。佛誕節是展現尊敬的日子。慈濟日是幫助其他人的日子。

People give their mother white flowers. White is a sign of being pure. It is a sign of a mother's long lasting love. Some people give money to the poor. Kids might kneel before their mothers to show them honor.

人們給他們的母親白色花朵。白色是純潔的象徵。這是一個母親持久的愛的象徵。有些人會捐錢給貧窮人。孩子們會跪在他們的母親前，以顯示他們的榮譽。

單字大集合

1. **Buddha** *n.* 佛

   Many people in Asia believe in Buddha.

   許多亞洲人民相信佛。

2. **Thankful** *adj.* 感激的

   I am thankful that it is not raining today.

   我很感謝今天沒有下雨。

3. **Respect** *n.* [U] 尊重

   I show respect by doing what my mom asks.

   我藉由作我媽媽要求地事情來展現尊敬。

4. **Money** *n.* [U] 錢

   They did not have money to buy food.

   他們沒有錢買食物。

5. **Kneel** *vi.* 跪

   It hurts my knees to kneel for a long time.

   跪了長時間傷害了我的膝蓋。

6. **Before** *prep.* 在……以前

   Before I go to bed, I brush my teeth.

   在我睡覺之前，我刷我的牙。

節慶源由——精彩完整版

In most countries, Mother's Day is a fairly new holiday. The first country to make the day a holiday was the United States. As it was adopted by other countries, Mother's Day was often connected to an existing cultural celebration. These older celebrations honored motherhood in general. The new holiday is a day to honor your own mother.

在多數國家，母親節是一個相當新的節日。第一個使用這天的國家是美國。由於這是被其他國家正式通過的，母親節常常被連接為一個現有的文化慶祝活動。這些舊的慶祝活動通常是表揚母親的身分。新的節日是用來表揚你自己的母親的日子。

In Taiwan, Mother's Day has been connected with both Buddha Day and Tzu Chi Day. They are all celebrated on the second Sunday of the month of May. Tzu Chi is a worldwide group that works to take care of the poor. It began long ago when 30 housewives set aside some of their grocery money every day to buy food for poor families. Buddhist culture highlights three things that are important in order to cultivate wisdom. They are to be thankful, to be reverent and to show compassion to others. Recognizing Mother's Day represents gratitude and honor. Recognizing Buddha Day represents reverence. Recognizing Tzu Chi Day represents compassion. In Buddhist culture, celebrating these three days together helps you become a wise person.

在台灣，母親節已經和佛誕節和慈濟節做連結。他們都在 5 月的第 2 個禮拜天慶祝。慈濟是個照顧貧窮人民的世界性組織。它始於很久以前，當 30 名家庭主婦每天撥出一些他們的雜物錢來買食物給貧窮人民。佛教文化點出為了培養智慧，有三件事情是非常重要的。他們感謝的、虔誠的並且向其他人表現憐憫心。認識到母親節表示感謝和榮譽。認識到佛誕節表示崇敬。認識到慈濟節表示憐憫。在佛文化裡，一起慶祝這三天幫助你成為一個智慧的人。

On Mother's Day, roads and buildings are decorated with lights, portraits and garlands. In the morning, there is a small parade in the capital. Politicians, soldiers, students, teachers and others march from the clock tower to the to the Palace. There is a band, and there is much singing and dancing. In the evening, there are fireworks.

People honor their mother by giving her flowers. White jasmine is the typical Mother's Day flower. Its white color is a sign of purity and the everlasting love of a mother. It is said that florists deliver a record number of flowers on Mother's Day in Taiwan. Some people give money to the needy. This is for the well being of their mothers and also a part of the Tzu Chi tradition. Kids might kneel before their mothers to show them honor and loyalty. In addition to flowers, gifts include chocolates, cake, stuffed toys and cards.

在母親節，道路和建築物被用燈、人像和花環裝飾。在早晨，首都會有個小遊行。政治家、士兵、學生、老師和其他人從鐘樓聚集到皇宮。會有樂隊，有許多唱歌和跳舞。在晚上，會有煙火。人們藉由給母親花來表揚她們。白茉莉是典型的母親節花朵。它的白色是純潔和母親不朽的愛的象徵。在台灣，有人說花店提供了創紀錄數量的鮮花。有些人將錢給了貧窮的人。這是幸福的母親和慈濟傳統的一部分。孩子們會跪在他們的母親錢來表示他們的尊重和忠誠。除了花朵，禮物還包括巧克力、蛋糕、填充玩具和卡片。

Here are some questions for you to discuss:
這裡有些供你討論的問題：

1. What do you usually give as a present to your Mom?
   你通常都送母親什麼禮物呢？

2. What is the greatest thing your Mom has done for you?
   什麼是你的母親為你做過最偉大的事？

單字大集合

1. Adopt *vi. vt.* 過繼；採取

Their second son was adopted when he was a baby.
他們的第二個兒子被收養，當他還是寶寶時。

2. Cultural *adj.* 文化的

There are many cultural differences between countries.
在國家間有許多不同的文化差異。

3. Motherhood *n.* 母親的身分

The young bride was looking forward to motherhood.
年輕的新娘在期盼著母親的身分。

4. Worldwide *adj.* 世界範圍的

Our group promotes worldwide peace.
我們的團隊致力於在世界各地的和平。

5. Cultivate *vt.* 加強；耕作

The teachers hope to cultivate friendships between the students.
老師們希望加強和學生間的友誼。

6. Reverent *adj.* 虔誠的

We must be very reverent when we go to the temple with Grandmother.
我們必須非常虔誠，當我們和祖母一起去廟宇時。

7. Compassion *n.* [U] 同情；憐憫

I feel compassion for all the children without parents.
我對所有沒有父母的孩子感到同情。

8. Politician *n.* [C] 政治家

Luckily, the politicians in our country make good laws.
幸運地，我們國家的政治家制定了好的法律。

閱讀測驗

1. In what country did Mother's Day first become a holiday?
   在哪一個國家母親節第一次成為節日？
   (a) In Taiwan 在台灣。
   (b) In China 在中國。
   (c) In the United States 在美國。

2. What three things do Buddhists believe bring you wisdom?
   哪三件事是佛教徒相信可以帶給你智慧的？
   (a) Thankfulness, reverence and compassion 感恩、崇敬和憐憫心。
   (b) Being kind to your father, your mother and your teacher.
      溫柔對待你的父親、你的母親和你的老師。
   (c) Growing corn, beans and peas in your garden.
      種玉米、大豆和豌豆在你的花園裡。

3. What does the white color of jasmine represent? 白色的茉莉花代表什麼？
   (a) A clean house. 一間乾淨的房子。
   (b) Purity and the everlasting love of a mother. 純潔和母親不朽的愛。
   (c) The coming of spring. 春天的到來。

4. How did the Tzu Chi get started? 慈濟是如何開始的？
   (a) From 30 housewives' benevolent actions. 從 30 個家庭主婦的善行開始。
   (b) From someone who took care of kids. 從某個關懷孩子的人開始。
   (c) From the beginning of this century. 從本世紀起始開始。

活動慶典和習俗

　　我國的母親節（Mother's Day）是訂在 5 月的第二個星期天，與國際上大多數的國家相同，而這個日子則是由美國的安娜・賈維斯所發起的，在 1913 年時，由美國國會確定將每年 5 月的第二個星期天為法定的母親節。而母親節的起源可以追溯到古希臘時期，古希臘人會舉行春季節日，並在這一天向希臘眾神之母希拉（Her(a)致敬，而在 17 世紀中葉，流傳到英國，在每年大約是 2 月底至 4 月初之間的四月齋的第四個星期日（The fourth Sunday in Lent）訂為母親日（Mothering Sunday），在這一天，長大離家的孩子們必須回家，並送禮物給母親。

　　康乃馨（carnation）是母親節的代表花朵，據說是安娜的母親最喜歡的花，在安娜向社會大眾遊說訂立母親節時，她會在教堂分送白色的康乃馨，以紀念她的媽媽。於是康乃馨成了母親節的象徵，配戴紅色康乃馨為母親建在，配戴白色花朵則是紀念已過世的母親。除了康乃馨之外，自古以來，中國就以萱草（orange daylily）又稱金針花來代表母親。古代遊子在離家前會在家中先種植萱草，希望母親因照顧萱草而心靈上有所寄託，而欣欣向榮的萱草也象徵著遊子在外一切安好，減輕母親對孩子的思念。

　　在中華文化中，孝道（filial piety）被認為是最重要的品德（moral），是實踐在每日生活當中，所以目前在大中華地區中均無法定的母親節。在台灣，慶祝母親節的風氣是源自於美國，又適逢假日，帶母親上餐館慶祝，讓媽媽休假一天是最常見的慶祝活動。另外在學校還會教做母親節賀卡（Mother's Day Car(d)，紙康乃馨等，孩子們會準備禮物或禮金送給媽媽，也常會準備蛋糕慶祝，據業者統計，母親節當天的蛋糕銷售量常為全年之冠。

實用生活會話

在國外，母親節前，老師會給孩子們一份母親節問卷（Mother's Day Q&A）作為回家功課，試試看，你有多瞭解媽媽？或是孩子對媽媽的瞭解有多深？相信我，看起來很簡單，但實際上並不是這麼容易，標準答案以媽媽的為準！

Q1: What is your mother's favorite food?
你母親最喜歡的食物？

Q2: What is your mother's favorite color?
你母親最喜歡的顏色？

Q3: What is your mother's favorite activity?
你母親最喜歡做的事？

Q4: What is your mother's favorite song?
你母親最喜歡的歌？

Q5: What is your mother's favorite food to cook to you?
你母親最喜歡煮給你吃的食物是？

Q6: What is your mother's favorite saying?
你母親最喜歡說的話？

實用單句這樣說

- Daughters and sons should fulfill their filial duty to their parents.
  兒女需對父母恪盡孝道。

- Oh, today is Mother's Day. Happy Mother's Day, mom!
  喔，今天是母親節耶。媽，祝妳母親節快樂！

- What are recommended Mother's Day gifts for my mother-in-law?
  有推薦送婆婆的母親節禮物嗎？

- Is Mother's Day a public holiday in Taiwan?
  母親節在台灣是國定假日嗎？

- Tzu Chi, the largest charity organization in Taiwan, celebrates Mother's Day, Buddha's Birthday and Tzu Chi's Day all together on the second Sunday of May.
  台灣最大的慈善團體，將母親節，佛陀誕辰紀念日及慈濟日一起在 5 月的第二個星期天慶祝。

- In Thailand, the white jasmine flowers are the symbol of maternal love. The white color of the flower symbolizes the purity of mother's true love will never change.
  在泰國，白色的茉莉花代表著母愛。這白色的花朵象徵了母親純潔的真心將永不改變。

互動時刻真有趣

● 母親節習俗大不同

　　印度（India）：母親節也是訂在 5 月的第二個星期天，但是在印度教的傳統上，在 9 月 10 月之間舉行 9 天的杜爾迦女神節（Worship of Durga）被認為是傳統的母親節。杜爾迦女神被視為萬物之母，在祭典的最後一天，信徒會抬著杜爾迦女神的塑像，送入女神位於江河湖海中的家，而婦女也會在這一天相互塗抹一種紅色顏料，以示祝福。

　　塞爾維亞（Serbia）：在每年聖誕節前的第二個星期天，為塞爾維亞的母親節。在這一天，孩子們會圍繞在母親身邊，趁媽媽不注意時，伺機將媽媽的雙腳綁起來， 對媽媽喊著 "Mother's Day, Mother's Day, what will you pay to get away?" （母親節，母親節，你要拿什麼來讓我鬆開你腳上的結？），這時媽媽會拿出事先準備好的小禮物來作為「贖金」（ransom）。

　　瑞典（Sweden）：母親節是在 5 月的最後一個星期天，除了一般的慶祝活動，瑞典紅十字會則會在母親節前夕販賣塑膠花朵，將其收入所得捐給貧窮的母親及兒童。

　　中非（Central Africa Republic）：在 5 月 29 日這一天，中非共和國會慶祝傳統的媽媽節，在這一天，所有的媽媽會盛裝打扮，並帶著孩子們參加遊行，國家首領及政府官員也會參加這項活動，已是對全國所有母親的重視及感謝。

　　泰國（Thailand）：泰國的母親節是在 8 月 12 日，這一天也是泰國皇后的生日。會有慶祝皇后誕辰的遊行，會施放煙火，而孩子們早上時會跪坐在母親身邊，獻上象徵著母愛的白色茉莉花。而在當天從事慈善活動、捐獻、或是供養和尚都會被視為是感謝母親的表現。

Dragon Boat Festival
端午節

節慶源由──簡易版

Dragon Boat Festival is a day to remember a Chinese poet. This poet was upset that his state had been taken over by another state, so he threw himself into the river to protest. People liked this man and wanted to find his body. They wanted to give him a proper burial. They threw rice dumplings in the water. This way the fish would not eat the poet's body. They searched in boats for days. All they had to eat were rice dumplings.

端午節是用來紀念一位中國詩人的日子。這位詩人因為他的國家被別的國家接收感到沮喪，因此他投河以抗議。人們欣賞這位詩人並且想找到他的肉體。他們想給他一個適當的葬禮。他們將粽子丟入河中。這個方法可能可以讓魚不吃掉詩人的身體。他們在船上搜尋了好幾天。所有人都必須吃粽子。

On Dragon Boat Festival, people eat rice dumplings. Teams of rowers race boats shaped like dragons. The front of the boat is carved like a huge dragon head. The body of the boat is brightly painted. As people cheer for their team, they clang cymbals and gongs. It is a very fun and noisy day!

在端午節，人們吃粽子。一隊隊的槳手比賽划著像龍的船。船的前方被雕刻成一個巨大的龍頭。　船身則被鮮豔的彩繪。當人們為自己的隊伍加油助威，他們敲鈸和鑼。這是非常有趣且喧鬧的一天！

單字大集合

1. Poet *n.* [C] 詩人

I have always wanted to be a poet.

我總是想要成為一位詩人。

2. Himself *pron.* 他自己

He could not bake the cake by himself.

他無法自己烤蛋糕。

3. Burial *n.* [C,U] 喪禮；埋葬

It was a proper burial for a king.

這是個國王的適當喪禮。

4. Search *vi. vt.* 搜尋；搜查

I searched for my dog, but could not find him.

我搜尋了我的狗，但找不到牠。

5. Cymbals *n.* [C] 鈸

The boy loved to play the cymbals in the band.

男孩愛在樂團裡敲鈸。

6. Gongs *n.* [C] 鑼

Gongs are too loud for me!

鑼對我來說太大聲了！

節慶源由──精彩完整版

Dragon Boat Festival began in China. It is a holiday to remember the Chinese poet Qu Yuan. He lived in the time of the Warring States. All the states in China were fighting each other. Qu did not like this and he was thrown out of government. That is when he started writing poetry. When Qu's state was taken over by another state, he was very upset. He threw himself into the river to protest evil government. People liked this man and wanted to find his body. They wanted to give him a proper burial. They threw rice dumplings in the water so fish would not eat the poet's body. People searched in boats for days, trying to find his body. All they had to eat were rice dumplings, probably filled with meat.

端午節起始於中國。是個用來懷念中國詩人屈原的節日。他身處於戰國時代，所有在中國的國家都在互相爭鬥。屈原因為不喜如此，被趕出了朝廷。這就是他開始寫詩的時候。當屈原的國家被別的國家接管的時候，他覺得非常沮喪。他投河以抗議邪惡的政府。人們欣賞這位詩人並且想找到他的肉體。他們想給他一個適當的葬禮。他們將粽子投入河裡，這樣魚就不會吃掉詩人的身體。人們試著找了他的身體好幾天。所有人都必須吃粽子，也可能是有肉的。

At first, Dragon Boat Festival was a very solemn day to remember Qu Yuan. Today, it is a fun family event. People eat rice dumplings and watch dragon boat races. A dragon boat is very long and slim. The front of the boat is carved like a huge dragon head. The body of the boat is brightly painted. Teams of rowers race the dragon boats. It can take up to seventy men to row each boat. Traditionally, all rowers were men. In some places today, there are also races with women rowers. As people cheer for their teams, they clang cymbals and gongs. It is a very fun and noisy day!

起初，端午節是個懷念屈原，非常莊嚴的日子。在今天，它是個有趣的家庭活動。人們吃肉粽並且看龍舟比賽。龍舟很長且纖細。船的前方被雕刻成一個巨大的龍頭。船身則被鮮豔的彩繪。一隊隊的槳手比賽划龍舟。每艘龍舟可能需要 70 個人划。傳統上，所有槳手皆為男性。今天在某些地方，也有和女性槳手一起的比賽。當人們為自己的隊伍加油助威，他們敲鈸和鑼。這是非常有趣且喧鬧的一天！

Dragon Boat Festival is celebrated on the fifth day of the fifth lunar month. Sometimes it is called Double Fifth. This is near the day of the summer solstice. Summer solstice is the day when the sun is at its strongest north of the equator. Daylight is longest on that day. Both the sun and the dragon represent the energy of men. That is why the dragon is a symbol for this holiday.

端午節在農曆的 5 月 5 日被慶祝。有時也被稱作雙五。這是接近夏至的日子。夏至是太陽最接近赤道以北的日子。那天是白晝最長的一天。太陽和龍兩者都代表男性的能量。這也是為什麼龍是這個節日的象徵。

Here are some questions for you to discuss:

這裡有些供你討論的問題：

1. Do you like to eat rice dumplings?

   你喜歡吃粽子嗎？·

2. Have you ever joined the dragon boat race?

   你有參加過龍舟比賽嗎？

3. What's the most special thing on the Dragon Boat Festival?

   什麼是端午節最特別的事情呢？

單字大集合

1. **Fight** *vi. vt.* 打架；與……作戰

   My brother likes fighting with me.
   我的兄弟喜歡與我一起作戰。

2. **Government** *n.* [C] 政府

   We like the government that is ruling our country now.
   我喜歡現在管理我們國家的政府。

3. **Poetry** *n.* [U] 詩歌；韻文

   Poetry is very interesting to read.
   詩讀起來很有趣。

4. **Protest** *vi. vt.* 抗議；聲明

   I would protest if my parents did not let me go to school.
   如果我的父母沒有讓我去上學，我會抗議。

5. **Dumpling** *n.* [C] 粽子

   Dumplings are my favorite holiday food.
   粽子是我最喜歡的節慶食物。

6. **Seventy** *adj.* 七十的

   My grandfather is seventy years old.
   我的奶奶 70 歲。

7. **Rower** *n.* [C] 槳手

   The rowers must be in good shape to race so fast.
   槳手必須處於好的狀態才划得快。

8. **Energy** *n.* [U] 活力；能量

   My dad always says I have too much energy!
   我的爸爸總是說我有太多的能量！

閱讀測驗

1. What happened during the time of the Warring States?
   在戰國時期發生了什麼事？
   (a) All the Chinese states fought against each other.
       所有在中國的國家相互對抗。
   (b) China went to war against Japan. 中國對抗日本。
   (c) Families all fought against their neighbors. 所有家族反抗他們的鄰居。

2. Why did Qu Yuan throw himself into the river? 為什麼屈原將自己投入河裡？
   (a) He loved to swim. 他喜歡游泳。
   (b) He wanted to see what kind of fish lived in the river.
       他想要看看什麼樣的魚生活在河裡。
   (c) It was to protest evil government. 抗議邪惡的政府。

3. How many people does it take to row a dragon boat? 需要幾個人划一艘龍舟？
   (a) It only takes two people. 只需要兩個。
   (b) It can take up to seventy people. 可能需要到 70 人。
   (c) You can row with hundreds of people. 你可以和數百人一起划。

4. What is the summer solstice? 什麼是夏至？
   (a) The day everyone goes swimming in the ocean.
       每個人去海洋裡游泳的日子。
   (b) The last day of school for the year. 一年在學校的最後一天。
   (c) The day the sun is strongest north of the equator.
       太陽最靠近赤道以北的一天。

活動慶典和習俗

　　端午節（Dragon Boat Festival, 或是 Duanwu Festival）是在農曆五月五日，所以也稱重五（Double Fifth）亦做重午。因時值初夏，容易滋生病菌，而古時候的衛生條件較差，醫藥也沒有那麼的發達，端午節原本是一個驅病防疫（avoidance of diseases）的節日，但在楚國詩人（poet）屈原因為看著祖國漸漸走向滅亡，但卻無力挽救而選擇在這一天投江自盡後，端午節便成了紀念屈原的節日了。

　　一般普遍認為在端午節吃粽子及划龍舟的兩大重要傳統，是源於在屈原死後，人們感念他的愛國情操，於是用竹筒盛裝煮好的糯米投入江中，為了不讓魚蝦吃他的身體。另外還划船找尋他的屍體。但根據考證，早在屈原之前，古代中國南方的吳越人，會在每年五月五日時舉行迎濤神祭圖騰的儀式，他們將食物用葉子或是竹筒裝著做為給龍神祭品（offerings），將其投入江中，以祈求龍神能保佑風調雨順，避免災難。他們還會在那天划著獨木舟（canoe）拜訪親友，也會進行獨木舟比賽。學者推論端午節便是源自於這個祭圖騰的儀式。

　　除了吃粽子及划龍舟之外，在端午節時，我們還會在大門口懸掛用艾草（Mugwort）、蒼蒲（Calamus）和榕樹葉（Banyan leaves）所做的蒼蒲掛，利用其揮發的氣味來淨化空氣，殺菌。也會利用蒸煮過蒼蒲及艾草的水來沐浴及洗頭。另外還會讓孩童配戴香包（sachet/scented bag），香包中所使用的香料大多能驅蚊避穢。還有一項大家都知道的端午習俗，那就是飲用雄黃酒（realga wine），但因為雄黃中含有砷，具毒性，食用可能會傷害人體，所以現在大多已經沒有飲用雄黃酒的習慣。

實用生活會話

Q1: Why do Chinese celebrate the Dragon Boat Festival?

　　為什麼中國人要慶祝端午節？

A1: To commemorate a great patriotic poet- Qu Yuan.

　　為了要紀念一位愛國詩人- 屈原。

Q2: What do you do on the Dragon Boat Festival?

　　那端午節時你們通常都會做什麼？

A2: We eat Zongzi and watch the dragon boat race.

　　我們會吃粽子還看龍舟競賽。

Q3: What is Zongzi?

　　什麼是粽子？

A3: It's a traditional Chinese food, made of sticky rice and stuffed with many different fillings such as meat, seafood, yolk, peanuts, chestnut etc. and wrapped in bamboo leaves. They are cooked by steaming or boiling.

　　它是一種中國的傳統食物，是用糯米，還有加入許多不同的餡料，例如有肉、海鮮、蛋黃、花生、栗子等，然後用竹葉包好。再用蒸的或是水煮熟。

Q4: What could you wear on the Dragon Boat Festival?

　　你在端午節可以配戴什麼呢？

A4: I could wear a special sachet on my neck.

　　我可以在脖子上配戴特別的香包。

實用單句這樣說

- In the Legend of the White Snake, the White Lady- Bai Suzhen reveals her true form as a large white snake after drinking the realga wine on the Duanwu Festival.

  在白蛇傳中，白娘子（白素貞）因為在端午節時喝了雄黃酒，而現出大白蛇的原形。

- The dragon boat race is about to start.

  龍舟比賽就快要開始了。

- The dragon boat race is the biggest event on the Dragon Boat Festival.

  龍舟競賽是端午節時最大的盛事。

- Dragon boat race is the highlight event during the Duanwu Festival. In the race, competing teams drive their boats forward rowing to the rhythm of pounding drums.

  龍舟競渡是端午節中的重要項目。在比賽中，各家參賽選手都跟著鼓聲的節奏划動他們的龍舟。

- Today you may see zongzi in different shapes and with a variety of fillings.

  現代的粽子有多種不同的形狀及各式各樣的餡料。

- Apart from the ordinary sourvy and sweet rice dumplings, that restaurant also has a purple sticky rice dumpling.

  除了一般的鹹粽和甜粽，那家餐廳還有紫米粽。

- It's almost 12 o'clock, I'm getting ready to stand an egg on its end.

  快要 12 點了，我準備好要立蛋了。

- In some areas, hanging up icons of Zhong is a common activity during the Dragon Boat Festival.

  在某些地區，貼鍾馗像是端午節的習俗之一。

互動時刻真有趣

● 端午節立蛋習俗 Stand an egg on end

　　一般認為在端午節正午時，陽氣最重，能輕易的將蛋立起來。而能將蛋成功立起來的人，將為其帶來一年的好運。而另有一個根據科學角度的說法，據說在端午節當天因太陽直射北半球，所以造成地心引力與太陽引力互相拉扯，在正午十二點時正巧形成兩股反方向平均拉扯的力量，在這個時候立蛋，這兩股平均拉扯的力量作用在蛋上，便能輕易的將蛋立起。

　　但有趣的是在西方國家中傳說將蛋立起來最好的時機是在春分或秋分的時刻。讓人不禁懷疑難道是因為地理位置的不同嗎？其實不然，經科學家證實，端午節時的引力和平時並無不同，立蛋的訣竅是在於耐心及細膩的手部平衡感。

● 立蛋小撇步 Tips for stand an egg on end

1. 抓一小撮鹽放在硬的，平坦不傾斜的表面。

   Make a small mound of salt on a hard, smooth and level surface.

2. 小心的將蛋立在鹽堆上，再輕輕地將多餘的鹽吹掉。

   Carefully balance the egg on the top of the salt, and gently blow away the excess salt.

3. 祝好運！

   Good luck!

Ghost Festival
中元節

節慶源由──簡易版

Ghost Festival is in the seventh lunar month. To the Chinese, ghosts are living people who have become a spirit. They must eat and drink like people. Chinese believe these ghosts come back to earth to visit this month. People want to please the spirits. They give them food and money. Every day in the temples, there are prayers. Lanterns hang on poles outside the temples. The ghosts see the lanterns and come into the temples.

中元節在農曆七月。對中國人來說，鬼是活著的人變成的靈魂。他們必須像人一樣吃喝。中國人相信這些鬼魂在這個月回到人間造訪。人們想要討好這些靈魂。他們給靈魂食物和錢。每天在寺廟有許多祈禱者。燈籠掛在寺廟外的柱子上。鬼魂們看到燈籠並且進入寺廟內。

At home, families make foods and burn incense. Sometimes, paper items are burned as gifts to the ghosts. After the festival, people float lanterns in water outside. The lanterns help the ghosts in water can be prayed.

在家裡，家庭會準備食物並燒香。有時，紙作的物品也會被燃燒當作是給鬼魂的禮物。在節慶過後，人們在外面放水燈。這些燈籠幫助水裡的鬼魂可以被普渡。

單字大集合

1. Live *vi. vt.* 活著；度過

They are living in the house on Park Street.
他們住在公園街上的房子裡。

2. Drink *vi. vt.* 飲

I like to drink tea.
我喜歡喝茶。

3. Believe *vi. vt.* 相信；信任

Do you believe in ghosts?
你相信鬼魂嗎？

4. Prayer *n.* [C,U] 祈禱；祈禱者；禱告

The priests say prayers for the people.
牧師為了人們念禱文。

5. Marry *vi. vt.* 結婚；和……結婚

They are getting married in June.
他們在六月結婚。

6. Incense *n.* 香

We adore the ancestors by burning incense.
我們以燒香的方式來崇拜祖先。

7. Lanterns *n.* 燈籠

Lanterns can be the colorful decorations as some festival's coming.
當一些節慶到來時，燈籠可以是五彩繽紛的裝飾。

節慶源由──精彩完整版 ●

Ghost Festival（or the Hungry Ghost Festival）is in the seventh lunar month. To the Chinese, ghosts are living people who have passed on to a spirit form. They must still eat and drink like people. Chinese people believe these ghosts come back to earth to visit during this month. They wander the earth seeking food and entertainment. People want to please the spirits. They give them food, wine and money. Because the ghosts are wandering freely, it is considered bad luck to get married in this month. It is also bad luck to start something new.

中元節在農曆七月。對中國人來說，鬼是活著的人變成的靈魂形式。他們仍然必須像人一樣吃喝。中國人相信這些鬼魂在這個月回到人間造訪。他們在人間遊蕩找尋食物和娛樂。人們想要討好這些靈魂。他們給靈魂食物和錢。因為這些鬼魂四處遊蕩，因此這個月被認為是不宜結婚的。也不宜開始新的東西。

At temples, lanterns hang on poles outside. The ghosts see the lanterns and come inside. Once inside, monks perform rituals to rid the dead of their suffering. Every day prayers are said. Sometimes the monks throw rice or small food into the air in all directions. This is food for the ghosts.

在廟宇，燈籠掛在外面的柱子上。鬼魂看到燈籠並進到廟宇裡。一進到裡面，僧侶會舉行儀式以讓他們擺脫死去的痛苦。禱文每天都被誦讀。有時僧侶們會丟米或是小的食物到空氣裡的各個方向。這是給鬼魂的食物。

At home, families make ritual foods and burn incense. Incense stands for prosperity, so families believe they will be more prosperous if they burn more incense. Sometimes, paper items are burned as gifts to the ghosts. These items are believed to have value in the afterlife. People burn houses, cars, fine clothes and gold, all made out of paper to please the ghosts. Families also pay tribute to unknown wandering ghosts so that these homeless souls do not interrupt their lives or bring misfortune.

在家裡，各家會準備儀式的食物和燒香。香代表繁榮，因此各家相信如果他們焚燒更多的香將會更加興旺。有時，紙作的物品也會被燃燒當作是給鬼魂的禮物。這些物品被相信在來世是有價值的。人們焚燒紙作的房子、車子、漂亮的衣服和黃金討好鬼魂。各家也有供品給不知名遊蕩的鬼魂，這樣這些無家可歸的靈魂便不會打擾他們的生活或帶來厄運。

　　Fourteen days after the festival, to make sure all the hungry ghosts in water can be prayed , people float lanterns in water outside.

　　節日後的 14 天，為了確定所有在水裡的餓鬼都能被普渡，人們點起水燈。

Here offer some questions for you to discuss:

這裡有些問題提供您討論：

1. Are there really ghosts existing on earth?

   這世上真的有鬼嗎？

2. What's your viewpoint of the gods and the ghosts?

   你對於鬼神的看法是？

3. What's the meaning of worshiping idols on Ghost Festival?

   中元節拜拜的意義是？

4. Do you think the way to worship the ghosts ought to be improved?

   你認為拜拜的方法應該有改進嗎？

5. According to the costumes in your hometown, what are the cultural and artistic activities on Ghost Festival?

   依據你家鄉的傳統，中元節有那些的藝文活動呢？

單字大集合

1. Hungry *adj.* 飢餓的

I was so hungry, I could eat a whole pizza.
我非常飢餓，我可以吃掉一整個披薩。

2. Entertainment *n.* [C,U] 消遣；娛樂

The games were great entertainment for the kids.
這些遊戲對孩子們來說是很棒的娛樂。

3. Wander *vi. vt.* 閒逛；徘徊於

They were wandering all over looking for their lost cat.
他們四處遊蕩以找尋他們的失蹤的貓。

4. Consider *vi. vt.* 考慮；細想

She considered whether to move or not.
她在考慮是否要搬家。

5. Ritual *n.* [C,U] 儀式；典禮；習慣

It is a ritual for us to eat rice cakes on holidays.
在節日吃年糕對我們來說是個習俗。

6. Elaborate *adj.* 精巧的

The palace had very elaborate furniture.
這間皇宮有非常精巧的家具。

7. Tribute *n.* [C,U] 貢物；禮物；敬意

We paid tribute to our friend by singing his favorite song.
我們給我們的朋友的禮物是唱他最喜愛的歌。

8. Misfortune *n.* [C,U] 災難；不幸

The travellers ran into misfortune and missed their plane.
旅客們遇到了不幸並且錯過了他們的飛機。

9. Harm *vt.* 損害

The nice dog will not harm you.
這隻很棒的狗不會傷害你。

閱讀測驗

1. What are ghosts, according to the Chinese? 對中國人來說，什麼是鬼魂？
   (a) People who are living as a spirit form. 活著的人變成的靈魂形式。
   (b) All dead people. 所有死去的人。
   (c) Only bad spirits. 只有惡靈。

2. What are the ghosts looking for as they wander? 鬼魂在遊蕩時在尋找什麼？
   (a) A warm place to spend the night. 一個溫暖的地方過夜。
   (b) Money that people have dropped on the ground. 人們掉在地上的錢。
   (c) Food and entertainment. 食物和娛樂。

3. Why do stores close during Ghost Festival? 為何商家在中元期間關門呢?
   (a) So the shopkeepers can celebrate with their families.
       所以店主可以和家人一同慶祝。
   (b) To give the ghosts room to walk the streets. 給鬼魂行經街道的空間。
   (c) Because no one wants to buy anything then.
       因為沒有人在那期間想買任何東西。

4. How do the floating lanterns help the ghosts? 漂浮水燈能幫助鬼魂什麼？
   (a) They help the ghosts be prayed. 它們幫助他們被普渡。
   (b) They make the streets look pretty for the ghosts.
       為了鬼魂使街道看起來更美麗。
   (c) They help ghosts see the doorbell better. 幫助鬼魂看得到門鈴。

活動慶典和習俗

　　用一句司馬爺爺常說的話：「中國人怕鬼，西洋人也怕鬼，全世界的人都怕鬼。」無論是在東方或是西方的宗教信仰中，都有鬼的存在。在西方有萬聖節，而我們的則是中元節（Ghost Festival / Chungyuan Festival）。我們一般稱農曆七月為鬼月（Ghost Month），在這一個月中，陰間的鬼魂（ghosts and spirits）會被釋放進到人間（the realm of the living），有子孫後人祭祀的鬼魂會回家接受香火供養，而無主的魂魄則會到處遊蕩，到有人跡的地方尋找吃的東西。所以在七月時各地會舉辦祭典活動，尤其是以七月十五日中元節的中元普渡最為盛大及熱鬧。中元普渡（ChungyuanPudu）是我國的重要民俗活動，起源於佛教中布施餓鬼（food offerings for hungry ghosts）的盂蘭盆會（Ullambana），到了宋朝又結合了道教中元節的祭祀亡靈，及儒家思想中祭拜祖先的活動，形成了今日在兩岸三地及東亞文化圈（East Asia cultural sphere）中的重要祭祀活動。

　　從台灣社會的發展歷史來看，從 17 世紀起，便有大量人口自大陸移入台灣開墾拓荒，也因此造成有許多客死異鄉，無人收埋的亡魂。基於宗教及同情心（compassion），人們會集資安置這些屍骨。而也因為這些無主孤魂大多是與我們的祖先來台拓荒時相互如兄弟般相處及照顧的拓墾者（pioneer），所以在台灣我們一般稱中元普渡為「拜好兄弟」，有別於閩南地區所稱的「拜人客（外地人）」。中元普渡是在下午二點之後做祭拜，地點則是自家門外。祭拜的供品必須是熟食，數量為奇數，在每一樣供品上插上一柱香，另外還要擺放一個盛半盆水的新臉盆及一條新毛巾，請前來的好兄弟們先洗手潔面後再享用大餐。由於正值盛夏，所以一般供品除了必備的牲禮及水果之外，現今家庭大多會選擇保存期限較長的泡麵、零食及罐頭食品。而各行各業也因為屬性不同因此在供品的選擇上也有所不同。例如消防隊的普渡絕對不能選擇鳳梨及旺旺仙貝以免招來過多業務。而八大行業因為拜天蓬元帥的關係，所以在普渡時會有煙和酒，但絕對不能拜豬肉。而工程師則會擺上乖乖以求永不當機。

實用生活會話

Q1: Tsk tsk tsk... What a long grocery list. Are you going to set up a supermarket?

嘖嘖嘖……這張購物清單怎麼這麼長啊？妳是準備要開家超市嗎？

A1: Hi, Mark. I am going to buy these snacks and drinks for the company's ChungyuanPudu rite. I need a hand, do you want to go with me?

嗨，馬克。我是要為了公司的中元普渡採買這些零食及飲料。我需要幫手，要跟我一起去嗎？

Q2: Sure, no problem. So what's the meaning of ChungyuanPudu?

當然沒問題。那什麼是中元普渡啊？

A2: Oh, Chungyuan means Hungry Ghost Festival, and the Pudu rite is a ritual of sacrificing rich food offerings for ghosts.

喔，中元節就是中國的鬼節，普渡就是獻祭豐盛的食物供品給鬼魂。

Q3: When is the Chungyuan Festival?

那中元節是在什麼時候？

A3: It occurs on the fifteenth day of the seventh month in the Chinese lunar calendar, it falls on next Wednesday this year.

它是在農曆的七月十五日，今年的話則是在下個星期三。

實用單句這樣說

- According to our custom, the seventh lunar month in generally is regarded as the "Ghost Month".
  根據我們的習俗，農曆七月普遍被認為是鬼月。

- People release lanterns on the river to light the way for the deceased during the Ghost Month.
  人們會在鬼月時放水燈為亡靈指引方向。

- "Chiang Gu" is the liveliest activity in the ChungyuanPudu Rite.
  搶孤是中元普渡中最熱鬧的活動。

- The seventh lunar month is the time to make food offerings to all departed spirits.
  農曆七月時是向亡靈獻祭食物的時間。

- There are many taboos during the Ghost Month.It is because during the seventh month, the gates of hell are open up and ghosts are free to wander here and there to seek food and entertainment.
  在鬼月時有許多的禁忌。因為在七月時鬼門大開，鬼魂可以自由的四處遊蕩去找食物及娛樂。

- Saying the word "ghost" is a no-no during the seventh month, we prefer to use "good brother" to avoid luring the evil spirits.
  在七月時不可以說「鬼」這個字，我們傾向於稱「好兄弟」來避免吸引惡靈靠近。

互動時刻真有趣

紙錢的由來

In Eastern Han Dynasty, CaiLun invented the papermaking process, and gained great wealth. CaiLun's sister-in-law HuiNiang urged her husband Cai Mo, CaiLun's brother to learn the skill of papermaking. Having learnt the skill, Caimo and his wife set up the papermaking factory. However, their paper did not sell well due to the poor quality. HuiNiang thought of a scheme to sell the paper. She pretended to die from sudden illness, and her husband cried loudly to attract their neighbors' attention.

As neighbors crowded into their house, Cai Mo burned piles of papers and said "If I can make fine quality paper, maybe you'd still be alive. I will burn out all these papers." Suddenly, HuiNiang' voice came from the coffin "Open it, I'm back." Caimo lifted the coffin lid and HuiNiang jumped out and explained what had happened to her in the underworld to those frightened people. "Don't be afraid, I am alive. I was suffering in the underworld, and then I gave all my money that my husband sent me to the ghost messenger, and he sent me back, just like the old saying goes, all things are obedient to money." "The paper you burned is the money in the underworld." After explained to their neighbors, the couple started to take out burning more papers for their deceased parents. HuiNiang's coming back to life made neighbors believed what they said. Naturally, the stock was soon sold out,and the legend spread and lived on to become a ritual until today.

東漢時，蔡倫發明了造紙術並且賺了很多錢。蔡倫的嫂嫂慧娘便讓蔡倫的哥哥蔡莫去學造紙。學會之後，夫妻倆便開起了造紙廠。然而，他們造的紙因為品質不佳所以賣的並不好。慧娘便想了一個辦法要來賣紙。她假裝因急病而過世，她的丈夫以大哭來引起鄰居的注意。當鄰居們趕到他們家時，蔡莫邊燒著紙邊說「如果我能造出品質好的紙張，也許妳就不會死了。我要把這些紙都燒光。」突然間，慧娘的聲音從棺材中傳出來「快打開，我回來了。」蔡莫趕緊將棺材蓋打開，慧娘便爬了出來並向那些被嚇壞了的鄰居們解釋在冥間發生的事。「別怕，我還活著。我在冥間受苦時，將我丈夫燒給我的錢全給了鬼差，所以他就放我回來了，就像俗話說的有錢能使鬼推磨。那些你燒的紙就是在可以在冥間用的錢。」向鄰居解釋之後，夫妻倆便開始搬出一堆紙要燒給他們過世的父母。慧娘的起死回生讓鄰居們都相信他們夫妻倆所說的。自然而然的，他們積存的紙很快就銷售一空，而這個傳說也廣為流傳並成為一種儀式直至今日。

Chinese Valentine's Day
七夕情人節

節慶源由──簡易版

　　Chinese Valentine's Day takes place in August.　On this night, young girls pray to find a good husband.　Couples go to the temple.　They pray about getting married. Newly married women pray to have a child soon. Valentine's Day is also celebrated by giving gifts to the one you love.　Chocolate, cards or flowers are common gifts. Couples spend time together. They share their gifts and show how much they care for each other.

　　七夕情人節發生在 8 月。在當晚，年輕女孩們祈禱可以找到一個好老公。情侶們去寺廟。他們祈禱能結婚。新婚的女人祈禱可以很快有小孩。情人節也藉由送禮給那個你愛的人來慶祝。巧克力、卡片或鮮花都是很常見的禮物。情侶們花時間在一起。他們分享他們的禮物並且表現出到底有多在乎對方。

　　There is an old love story for this day. It is about the daughter of the Emperor of Heaven. Seven daughters visited earth.　They were bathing in a river.　A cowherd in the field saw them.　He liked one and they got married. But, the Emperor wanted his daughter back.　He made them live on two separate stars in the sky. On the seventh night of the seventh moon, they can see each other again.

　　那天有個古老的愛情故事。是關於玉皇大帝的女兒。七個女兒拜訪了人間。她們在河裡沐浴。田裡有個放牛的牛郎看到了她們。他喜歡上了其中一位並且他們結婚了。但玉皇大帝想要祂的女兒回來。祂讓他們兩個住在天空不同的星系裡。在第 7 次月亮的第 7 晚，他們可以再次相見。

單字大集合

1. **Couple** *n.* [C] 一雙；一對

   The couples walked in the park together.
   情侶們在公園裡一起散步。

2. **Newly** *adv.* 最近；以新的方式

   We love our newly built home.
   我們喜歡我們最近新建立的家。

3. **Common** *adj.* 常見的

   It is common for girls to have long hair.
   女孩們有長頭髮是常見的。

4. **Daughter** *n.* [C] 女兒

   My daughters all go to the same school.
   我的女兒們全部上同一所學校。

5. **Emperor** *n.* [C] 皇帝

   The emperor ruled for many years.
   皇帝統治多年。

6. **Bath** *n.* [U] 沐浴

   My father says bathing must be done at night.
   我爸爸說沐浴必須在晚上。

節慶源由——精彩完整版

Chinese Valentine's Day is on the 7th day of the 7th lunar month. It takes place sometime in August. It is sometimes called The Daughter's Festival. Long ago, Chinese girls wanted to learn good household skills, like embroidery. This skill was essential for their future family.　On this night, unmarried girls pray to a star called Vega（the Weaving Maid star）to help them learn embroidery. When the star is high up in the sky, girls put a needle on the surface of water. If the needle doesn't sink, the girl already knows enough.　She is ready to find a husband.　Single women pray for finding a good husband in the future. Sometimes, couples go to the matchmaker's temple together.　They pray for their possible marriage.　And newly married women pray to become pregnant quickly.

七夕是在農曆的 7 月的第 7 天。有時在 8 月發生。它有時被稱為女兒節。很久以前，中國女孩想學習良好的生活技能，如刺繡。這些技能在她們未來的家庭裡是需要的。在當晚，未婚女孩向織女星（the Weaving Maid star）祈禱幫助他們學會刺繡。當星星高掛天空時，女孩們將細針放在水的表面。如果針沒有沉下去，女孩們知道的已經足夠了。她已經準備好尋找他的丈夫。單身女性祈禱在未來能找到好丈夫。有時，情侶們會一起去媒人的寺廟。他們為他們可能的婚姻祈禱。新婚的女性祈禱很快能成為孕婦。

Today, Valentine's Day is also celebrated by giving gifts to the one you love. Chocolate, cards or flowers are popular gifts.　Couples spend time together in the evening, sharing their gifts and showing　how much they care for each other.

在今天，七夕也藉由送禮給你愛的人來慶祝。巧克力、卡片或是花是受歡迎的禮物。情侶們在晚上花時間在一起，分享他們的禮物並且表現出他們有多麼在乎對方。

A love story for this day is about the 7th daughter of the Emperor of Heaven and an orphaned cowherd. The seven daughters of the Emperor caught the eye of a cowherd during one of their visits to earth. The daughters were bathing in a river and the cowherd decided to have some fun.　He hid their clothes and told the youngest he would not return them unless she promised to marry him.　They were married for many years.　Then, the Emperor asked the girl's grandmother to go to earth and bring his daughter back. As they were flying back up to heaven, the cowherd chased them. The grandmother made the Milky Way with a hairpin, separating the two forever. The daughter was forced to move to the star Vega and the cowherd moved to the star Altair. On the seventh night of the seventh moon, the stars Altair and Vega are high in the night sky. Magpies form a bridge with their wings for the wife to cross over to see her husband. Therefore, another common name for this festival is the Seven Sisters Festival or the Magpie Festival.

　　這天的愛情故事是關於玉皇大帝的第 7 個女兒和孤兒的牛郎。在造訪人間的期間時，7 個女兒被牛郎瞧見。女兒們在河裡沐浴，牛郎決定找點樂趣。他躲在她們的衣物裡，並且告訴最年輕的女兒他不會規還她們的衣物，除非她承諾嫁給他。他們結婚了很多年。然後，玉皇大帝要求女孩的祖母到人間來帶回他的女兒。當他們返回天上時，牛郎追逐著他們。祖母用髮夾做了一條銀河，將他們永遠分開。女兒被強迫搬到織女星，而牛郎則搬到牛郎星。在第 7 次月亮的第 7 個晚上，牛郎星和織女星會高掛在夜晚的天空。喜鵲用牠們的翅膀形成一個橋梁讓妻子穿越去看她的丈夫。因此，另一個這個節日常見的名字是七姊妹節或情人節。

Here are some questions for you to discuss:
這裡有些供你討論的問題：

1. Which places are suitable for lovers to go on Chinese Valentine's Day?
   有哪些合適的地方值得情人們在七夕情人節去逛逛？

2. How to express your love to your lover?
   該如何向心上人表達你的愛意呢？

單字大集合

1. Household *adj.* 家庭的

Cooking and cleaning are good household skills for anyone to know.
烹飪和打掃是是任何人都知道良好的持家技能。

2. Embroidery *n.* [U] 刺繡

My grandmother made lots of embroidery for us.
我祖母為了我們做了許多刺繡。

3. Essential *adj.* 必須的

Working hard is essential if you want to make money.
認真工作是必須的，如果你想要賺錢。

4. Matchmaker *n.* [C] 媒人

The young girls all hoped the matchmaker would find them a boy to marry.
年輕女孩們都希望媒人幫他們找到可以嫁過去的男孩。

5. Chocolate *n.* [U] 巧克力

You can give me chocolate anytime!
任何時候你都可以給我巧克力！

6. Cowherd *n.* [C] 牧牛者

The cowherd was dirty from being in the field all day.
牛郎因為整天待在田裡因此很髒。

7. Milky Way 銀河

We must get away from the city lights to see the Milky Way in the sky.
我們必須遠離城市燈光才能看到天空中的銀河。

8. Hairpin *n.* [C] 髮夾

I bought my mother a new hairpin for her birthday.
我因為媽媽的生日買了一個新髮夾給她。

閱讀測驗

1. What does it mean if the needle floats in the water?
   如果針漂浮在水面上意指什麼？
   (a) The girl knows enough embroidery and is ready to get married.
   那位女孩已經學會足夠的刺繡並且準備好出嫁了。
   (b) The needle is very light weight. 那隻針的重量非常輕。
   (c) The water is clean. 那水是乾淨的。

2. What were the seven daughters doing when the cowherd saw them?
   7 個女兒在做什麼，當牛郎看到她們時？
   (a) They were combing their long hair. 她們在梳她們的長髮。
   (b) They were singing a beautiful song. 她們在唱美麗的歌曲。
   (c) They were bathing in a river. 她們在河裡沐浴。

3. How did the grandmother's hairpin separate the cowherd and his wife?
   祖母的髮夾是如何分開牛郎和他的妻子？
   (a) They got in a fight over it and wouldn't talk to each other.
   他們為了它吵架並且不跟對方說話。
   (b) The grandmother used it to form the Milky Way between them.
   祖母用它形成他們之間的銀河。
   (c) It turned into a river too wide to cross.
   它讓河流變得太廣闊而無法穿越。

活動慶典和習俗

　　在中國古老的神話傳說中，牛郎（Cowherd）與織女（Weaver Girl）是一對相愛的夫妻，有一雙可愛的兒女。但卻因為荒廢了工作，引起天帝大怒，而命令兩人分開居住於天河的兩岸。牛郎帶著兒女為了要見到織女，而拼命的想要舀乾天河的水，此舉感動了天帝，答應讓他們每七日見一次面，但是傳話的喜鵲卻說成每七夕見一次面。所以他們每年只能在農曆七月七日這一天見面，喜鵲為了贖罪，便發動所有喜鵲在七夕這一天搭鵲橋（the bridge of magpies），讓牛郎與織女能快點相見，這便是七夕情人節（Chinese Valentine's Day-中國情人節）的由來。

　　七夕情人節一般又可稱做七夕節（Qixi Festival）或是乞巧節（Qiqiao Festival）。大約從晉代開始就有在七夕觀星祈願的習俗，到了南朝，則形成穿針，乞巧（beseeching skills）的習俗，而在古代，針線活（needlework）被認為是能求得好姻緣的重要才能（talent）之一，所以乞巧的習俗中也包含有能獲得美好姻緣的含意存在，於是未婚女子會在七夕向織女獻祭，以求得如織女一般的心靈手巧。

　　相傳織女是玉皇大帝最小的女兒，排行第七，別名七星娘娘、七星媽、七仙姑，廣東港澳地區則暱稱織女為七姐。而在台灣，我們尊稱織女為「七娘媽」。在台灣民間信仰傳說中，未滿 16 歲的孩子都是由鳥母（仙鳥）來照顧的，而鳥母則是受了七娘媽的託付，所以七娘媽便成了孩子的保護神。一般拜七娘媽時，我們會準備麻油雞酒、油飯、胭脂水粉、鮮花（以雞冠花和圓仔花為主）、針線、鏡子及湯圓，祭拜後，會焚燒金紙及一種以五色紙製的七娘媽紙。如果家中有滿十六歲的孩子，則需由父母陪同前往供奉七娘媽的廟宇向七娘媽亭祭拜，行禮祭拜完，則由父母將由五色彩紙和竹片糊成的七娘媽亭抬起，孩子鑽過七娘媽亭後即被視為成年，隨後再將七娘媽亭收入火中焚燒。這個儀式稱作「做 16 歲」，是舊時農業社會時的成人禮習俗，在 90 年代重新獲得重視，被官方及民間團體視為是重要的慶典習俗，而成為台灣的特色文化之一。

實用生活會話

Q1: Hey, Mary. I can see your sugary smile from miles away. What makes you so happy?

嗨，瑪麗。我大老遠的就看到妳笑得好甜，什麼事讓妳這麼高興？

A1: Hi, Jessie. Hmmm... it's no big deal. James just told me that we will go hunting tomorrow night.

嗨，潔西。嗯，沒什麼啦。詹姆斯剛跟我說我們明天晚上要一起去打獵。

Q2: What? Go hunting on Chinese Valentine's Day?

什麼？在七夕情人節時去打獵？

A2: Yes, and he said that he's going to shoot down Altair and Vega for me as the Valentine's gift.

對啊，他說他要把牛郎星跟織女星射下來送給我做情人節禮物。

Q3: Hahaha... What can I say? Love makes both of you dizzy.

哈哈哈… 我能說什麼呢？愛情把你們倆都弄昏頭了。

A3: He is so romantic, don't you think so?

妳不覺得他很浪漫嗎？

Q4: Maybe, it takes time to judge who a person really is.

也許吧，這需要時間來判斷一個人到底是怎樣的。

A3: I believe I have a keen eye for telling the real James.

我相信我有精準的眼光來判斷真正的詹姆斯。

實用單句這樣說

- Chinese Lover's Day is on the 7th day of 7th lunar month. So it is sometimes called Double Seventh Festival.
  中國情人節是在農曆的 7 月 7 日。所以有時會被稱為七七節。

- Young girls go to the local temple to pray to Weaver Girl for wisdom and dexterity in needlework.
  年輕女孩們會去當地的廟宇向織女祈求智慧及靈巧的刺繡手藝。

- "Tanabata" is a Japanese star festival which is originated from the Chinese Qiqiao Festival.
  七夕祭是日本有名的慶典，是源自於中國的乞巧節。

- They each wrote a wish on a colored strip of paper, and then tied the paper strip to the bamboo branch on the evening of Tanabata.
  在七夕祭的時候，他們在彩色的紙條上各自寫下一個願望，然後將紙條繫在竹枝上。

- According to the legend, the Milky Way separates Cowherd and Weaver Girl, and they are only allowed to meet once a year on the 7th day of the 7th lunar month.
  根據傳說，銀河將牛郎與織女分開，並且每年只能在農曆七月七日這一天見面。

- In Qixi Festival, girls always make wishes for marrying someone who would be a good husband.
  在七夕的時候，女孩們總是會許下願望希望能嫁個好老公。

- It was said that if it rains on the Chinese Valentine's Day that the rain is the tears of the separated couple.
  在七夕情人節時下的雨，傳說是牛郎與織女的眼淚。

- Some tales say that you can hear Cowherd and Weaver Girl talking if you stand under the grapevines on the night of Chinese Valentine's Day.
  在有些故事中說如果你在七夕情人節當天站在葡萄藤架下，你將會聽到牛郎與織女互訴衷曲。

互動時刻真有趣

● 「星星」相印

　　根據歷史推論，牛郎織女的故事大約是發生在西周時期。這個故事將當時在奴隸社會中人們渴望追求幸福及飽受壓抑的寫照藉著雙星的傳說來抒發。而選在農曆七月七日則是因為在當時七月七日的黃昏正是織女星升上一年中最高點的時刻，而藉著觀察牛郎織女星的位置，則能讓古人清楚的知道秋季的到來，也因而衍生出這樣的愛情傳說。以下則是在這段愛情故事中各星的英文名稱及簡單的介紹，希望大家能在七夕時除了歡度情人節之外，也能抬頭在星空找到那幾顆星星。

　　牛郎星 Altair：又稱做河鼓二，天鷹 α，牽牛星或是大將軍，在日文中則稱為彥星。在七夕傳說中，牛郎帶著兩個孩子，與織女遙遙相望，而牛郎星兩顆伴星——河鼓一和河鼓三就是傳說中的孩子。

　　織女星 Vega：又稱織女一，或是天琴 α，是北半球中第二明亮的恆星。

　　天津四 Deneb：天鵝座 α 星，和牛郎星及織女星形成夏季大三角（Summer Triangle），而天津四就是傳說中的鵲橋。

　　銀河 Milky Way：又稱天河或天漢，就是隔開牛郎與織女的天河。

Father's Day
父親節

節慶源由——簡易版

Father's Day is a day to honor fathers. Like Mother's Day, it first became a holiday in the United States. Father's Day is a day to spend with your dad. You might give him a card or a gift. If he is far away, be sure to call him on the phone. Sometimes, a family will cook dad the meal he loves best. Kids often make their dad a special gift. Maybe it's just a picture they draw. Their dad can keep the picture forever. He can look back at it years later. He will remember his kids when they were small.

父親節是用來表揚父親的。就像母親節，是在美國第一次成為節日。父親節是個用來陪伴你的父親的日子。你可以給他一張卡片或禮物。如果他很遙遠，務必用電話打給他。有時，家人會為爸爸煮他最喜歡的一餐。孩子們通常會為爸爸做特別的禮物。或許只是他們畫的圖。他們的爸爸就會一輩子保存它。他可以在幾年之後回過頭看。他將會想起當孩子們還小的時候的樣子。

In Taiwan, Father's Day is on August 8th. In China, the words August and eight both say "ba". August 8th is "ba ba". That is the same sound as the word father. Do you think that is why Father's Day is on August 8th in Taiwan?

在台灣，父親節是在 8 月 8 日。在中國，8 月和 8 都念起來是「爸」。8 月 8 日就是「爸爸」。跟爸爸念起來是同個音。你會覺得這就是為什麼父親節在台灣是 8 月 8 日嗎？

單字大集合

1. Spend　*vi. vt.* 花錢；花費

I like to spend time with my dad.

我喜歡花時間和我爸在一起。

2. Away　*adv.* 離開

My dad has to go away for two weeks.

我爸必須離開兩個星期。

3. Phone　*n.* [C] 電話

While he is gone, I will call him on the phone.

當他不見時，我將會用電話打給他。

4. Sometimes　*adv.* 有時

Sometimes, I miss my dad.

有時候，我會想念我父親。

5. Special　*adj.* 特別的

I am going to make him a special gift when he comes home.

我將要為他做個特別的禮物，當他回家時。

6. August　*n.* 八月

My birthday is in August.

我的生日在 8 月。

節慶源由——精彩完整版

Father's Day is a celebration honoring fathers and celebrating fatherhood. Father's Day first became a holiday in the United States. They had already made Mother's Day a holiday. Many people thought there should also be a holiday to celebrate fathers.

父親節是表揚父親們和慶祝父親身分的慶祝活動。父親節第一次成為節日是在美國。他們已經將母親節列為節日。許多人認為也必須要有節日來慶祝父親節。

The idea to recognize fathers was first introduced to the U.S. government in 1913. In 1916, the president spoke in a Father's Day celebration. He wanted to make it a holiday, but lawmakers disagreed. They thought it would just become a day for stores to make lots of money. Finally, in 1957, a politician accused the government of ignoring fathers. He said they had honored mothers for 40 years, but refused to honor fathers. Still, they did not agree to make Father's Day a holiday. Not until 1972 did it become a legal holiday.

正式認可父親的這個想法在西元 1913 年首次介紹給美國政府。在西元 1916 年，總統在父親節慶祝活動演說。他想要讓它成為節日，但立法者反對。他們認為這只會變成商家們賺大錢的日子。最後，在西元 1957 年，一位政治家指責政府忽視了父親。他說他們已經表揚母親 40 年了，但卻拒絕表揚父親。但他們仍不同意讓父親節成為節日。直到西元 1972 年它才變成法定節日。

Today, Father's Day around the world is a day to spend with your dad. People give cards or gifts to their dad. If he is far away, they are sure to call him on the phone. Sometimes, they cook him a special meal. Kids often make their dad a special gift. Maybe it's just a picture they draw that their dad can keep forever. He can always look back at it and remember his kids when they were small.

在今天，全世界的父親節是個陪伴你的父親的日子。人們送卡片或禮物給他們的父親。如果他很遙遠，他們確定會用電話打給父親。有時，他們會為他煮特別的一餐。孩子們通常為他們的父親做特別的禮物。或許只是一張他們畫的圖，他們的父親會永遠保存。他可以常常回去看它，並且想起他的孩子們小時候的樣子。

Many countries celebrate Father's Day on the third Sunday of June. But each country may choose its own day. Taiwan celebrates Father's Day on August 8th. In the Chinese dialect that many people speak there, both the words August and 8 make the sound "ba". So, August 8th is "ba ba". That is the same sound as the word father. Do you think that is why Father's Day is on August 8th in Taiwan? Lots of people there call it Ba Ba Day.

許多國家在 6 月的第 3 個禮拜天慶祝父親節。但每個國家會選擇它們自己的日子。台灣在 8 月 8 日慶祝父親節。那個許多人說中文的地方，8 月和 8 都念起來是「爸」。所以 8 月 8 日就是「爸爸」。跟爸爸念起來是同個音。你會覺得這就是為什麼父親節在台灣是 8 月 8 日嗎？許多那裡的人稱它為爸爸節。

On the Father's Day, people wear a particular flower to express their adoration towards to the fathers. People wear a red rose to show their love and honor to the living and well fathers, and put on a white rose to express their mourning to the fathers who has past away. Afterwards, the Pennsylvania state residents use dandelions to give tribute to the fathers; in Vancouver, people choose to wear white lilac. Red and white roses are publicly recognized the flowers on Father's Day. Because the businessmen and manufacturers see the business opportunities, they encourage the sons and daughters to give festive cards, and to buy some ties, sucks and small gifts to the fathers. Some kids even cook by themselves to prepare a meal full of love for their father.

父親節時，人們配戴特定的鮮花來表達對父親的敬意。人們以配戴紅玫瑰向健在的父親們表示愛戴，配戴白玫瑰則表示對父親的追念。之後，賓夕尼亞州人以蒲公英向父親表示致意，在溫哥華，人們選擇戴白丁香。紅白玫瑰是公認的父親節的花朵。因為商人和製造商看到商機，他們鼓勵兒女們給父親賀卡，且買些領帶、襪子等小禮品送給父親。有些孩子甚至親自下廚，為父親準備充滿愛心的一餐。

單字大集合

1. Fatherhood　*n.* [U] 父親的身分

His new baby welcomed him into fatherhood by crying all day.
他的新生兒以整天哭泣來歡迎他成為爸爸的身分。

2. Lawmaker　*n.* [C] 立法者

The lawmakers met for three months to work on the new law.
立法者為了運作新法會耗時三個月。

3. Accuse　*vt.* 控告；指責

My brother accused me of taking his favorite shirt.
我哥哥因為我拿他最喜歡的襯衫而指責我。

4. Ignore　*vt.* 忽略

I usually ignore my baby sister when she cries.
當我的嬰兒小妹妹哭的時候，我通常會忽略了。

5. Refuse　*vi. vt.* 拒絕

They refused to get out of the car.
他們拒絕下車。

6. Legal　*adj.* 合法的

Is it legal to ride your bike on the sidewalk?
在人行道上騎你的腳踏車是合法的嗎？

7. Picture　*n.* [C] 畫

I hung a picture of my dad on the wall in my room.
我在我房間的牆上掛上我爸的畫。

8. Dialect　*n.* [C,U] 方言；土話

I speak a different dialect of Chinese than my friends speak.
我會說的不同種的中文方言多過於我朋友說的。

閱讀測驗

1. Why did lawmakers not make Father's Day a holiday in 1957?
   為什麼在西元 1957 年立法者不將父親節訂為節日？
   (a) They didn't think fathers were important. 他們不認為父親是重要的。
   (b) They thought no one liked their dad. 他們認為沒有人喜歡他們的父親。
   (c) They thought it would only be a day for stores to make money.
       他們認為這只會成為商家們賺錢的日子。

2. What can a dad remember when he looks at the picture his kids drew years ago?
   父親會記得什麼，當他幾年後看著他小孩畫的圖時？
   (a) He can remember what his kids were like when they were small.
       他會想起他的孩子們小時候的樣子時。
   (b) He can remember how difficult it was to get his kids to listen.
       他會記得讓他的孩子們聽話是多麼困難。
   (c) He can remember what he was like when he was a kid.
       他會想起他在孩子時是什麼樣子。

3. Why do some people in Taiwan say Ba Ba Day, instead of Father's Day?
   為什麼在台灣有些人會說爸爸節，來取代父親節？
   (a) Because they can't remember what the holiday is called.
       因為他們不記得這個節日被稱為什麼。
   (b) Because in Chinese, August 8th is pronounced ba ba.
       因為在中文裡，8 月 8 日的發音是爸爸。
   (c) Because their dad's name is Baba.
       因為他們的父親的名字是爸爸。

活動慶典和習俗

　　我國的父親節（Father's Day）是在 8 月 8 日，除了是取其諧音（homophonic）"八八"和爸爸相近，將"八八"二字變化連綴起來，則是一個父字。發起的源由是在民國 34 年，正值對日抗戰白熱化時期，為了鼓勵人心，奮發團結，及紀念在抗戰期間為國犧牲的父親們，在上海發起了第一次的父親節活動。而在抗戰勝利之後，由上海名流（celebrities）聯名呈請政府准予訂立每年的 8 月 8 日為父親節，呈請獲准後，8 月 8 日就正式成為我國的父親節，在節日實施辦法中，和母親節一樣列為是具特殊意義，有慶祝或舉辦活動必要的節日之一。

　　大多數國家的父親節則是訂於 6 月的第三個星期天，這個日子是在 1910 年時由美國的一位杜德夫人（Mrs. Dodd, Sonora Louise Smart Dodd）所提議的。杜德夫人的父親曾參加過南北戰爭（American Civil War），在妻子因難產（difficult labor）而過世之後，父兼母職的將 6 個孩子扶養長大，在孩子長大成人，得以安養天年時，卻又積勞成疾而在 1909 年時辭世。身為 6 個孩子中唯一女性的杜德夫人特別能感受父親養育孩子的辛苦，於是在 1910 年時發起父親節的活動，除了感念父親的恩情也向全世界的父親致敬。在 1972 年時，由美國總統尼克森正式簽署文件將每年 6 月的第 3 個星期天訂為全美的父親節，為美國永久性的國定紀念日。

　　家庭聚會及送禮物給父親則是一般常見的父親節慶祝活動，由於我國的父親節剛好是在暑假期間，所以常在孩子們的暑假作業中列有製作父親節卡片的項目。而為了增加孩子與父親相處的機會，許多文化教育單位如科學館（science museum）、博物館等，會針對父親節設計相關的親子活動（family activity），或是展覽（exhibition），而商家、遊樂場所也多會針對父親節檔期做促銷。

實用生活會話

Q1: Lisa, I am going to the shopping mall, do you want to go with me?
麗莎，我要去購物中心，要跟我一起去嗎？

A1: Yes, I happen to be going there, too. I want to buy a gift for my father.
要，我剛好也要去哪兒。我要買禮物送我父親。

Q2: A gift for your father's birthday?
是給妳父親的生日禮物嗎？

A2: No, not a birthday gift. It's a gift for Father's Day.
不，不是生日禮物，是父親節禮物。

Q3: Oh, when is Father's Day in Taiwan?
喔，台灣的父親節是在哪一天呢？

A3: It is on August 8. August is the eighth month of a year, and the eighth day of the eighth month makes two "eight" s, which sounds similar to "father" in Chinese, so we celebrate Father's Day on August 8.
是在 8 月 8 日。八月是一年當中的第 8 個月份，而八月的第八天，則有兩個八，聽起來像是中文中的「爸爸」，所以我們選在 8 月 8 日慶祝父親節。

Q4: I want to give something meaningful to my father on August 8th.
我想要在八月八日給我父親一個有意義價值的禮物。

A4: How about a hug and a warm letter?
你覺得一個擁抱和一封溫暖的信如何呢？

實用單句這樣說

- Family gathering and the giving of gifts are common festivities for the Father's Day.
  家庭聚會及送禮物是父親節常見的慶祝活動。

- The red or white rose is recognized as the Father's Day flower.
  紅色或是白色的玫瑰花被認為是代表父親節花朵。

- According to the Federal Statistical Office of Germany, alcohol-related traffic accidents multiply by three on Father's Day.
  根據德國聯邦統計局指出，父親節時因酒醉而引起的車禍是平日的三倍。

- Tommy drew a Father's Day card with a coupon of 30 minutes massage.
  湯米畫了一張附有 30 分鐘按摩券的父親節卡片。

- Do you have any plans for Father's Day?
  你父親節有沒有任何的計畫？

- Organizing a family get-together and spending time with father is a popular Father's Day tradition.
  組織家庭聚會及陪伴父親是一個受歡迎的父親節傳統活動。

- My father is the one who held my hand when I was to cross the road, encouraged me to believe in my ability and was always there for me.
  我的父親在我過馬路時會牽著我的手，會鼓勵我要相信自己的能力，而且總是會在我需要他的時候出現。

- A neck tie is the most popular gift for Father's Day.
  領帶是父親節最常見的禮物。

互動時刻真有趣

父親節數獨遊戲 Father's Day Sudoku

以 FATHER 取代數字 1-6，填入以下空格中，使每個直行、橫列及六宮格中的字母都不能重複

Enter letters F A T H E R into the blank spaces so that each row, column, and 2X3 box contains letters F A T H E R.

F					T
		T	F		
	H	A	T	F	
	F	E	A	H	
		H	R		
A					H

Answer:

F	A	R	H	E	T
H	E	T	F	R	A
R	H	A	T	F	E
T	F	E	A	H	R
E	T	H	R	A	F
A	R	F	E	T	H

Moon Festival
中秋節

節慶源由──簡易版

Moon Festival is in the eighth lunar month. The full moon is very bright. People go out at night to look at the moon. Some climb to the top of a mountain to see the moon best.

中秋節是在農曆八月。滿月非常的明亮。人們在夜晚外出看月亮。有些人攀登到山頂，為了更棒的觀看月亮。

Friends and relatives give each other moon cakes. These are small rice cakes with sweet filling inside . There are many old stories about this day. One story tells how moon cakes saved China. Once, China was ruled by others. The Chinese wanted to rule their own country. At the Moon Festival, the Chinese hid papers in the moon cakes. These papers told about a secret plan. People used the plan to throw the leaders out of China.

朋友和親戚贈與對方月餅。月餅就是小型的甜年糕搭配甜餡。有許多關於這天的古老故事。有一個故事是講述月餅如何拯救中國。曾經，中國被其他人所統治。中國人想要掌管自己的國家。在中秋節，中國人將紙張藏在月餅裡。這些紙張上有一個秘密的計劃。人們用這個計畫將統治者趕出中國。

Another story tells about a king. He had a magic drink. It could make him live forever. His wife drank it instead. She flew to the moon. Children look for this moon lady every year.

另一個故事是有關一個帝王。他有個魔法的飲品。可以讓他長生不死。他的太太代替他喝下。她飛到了月亮上。孩子每年都找著這位在月亮上的小姐。

單字大集合

1. Mountain *n.* [C] 山

We climbed to the top of the mountain.
我們爬到這座山的最頂端。

2. Filling *n.* 糕點餡；填補物

I like the filling more than the cake.
我喜歡糕點餡勝過於蛋糕。

3. Rule *vi. vt.* 統治；管轄

I want to rule my country one day.
我想要有一天統治我的國家。

4. Secret *n.* [C] 秘密；機密

She would not tell me her secret.
她不會告訴我她的秘密。

5. Magic *adj.* 魔術的；不思議的

I wish I could do magic tricks.
我希望我可以做魔術表演。

6. Leader *n.* [C] 領導者；領袖

Our club does not have any leaders.
我們的社團沒有任何領導者。

節慶源由──精彩完整版

Moon Festival is on the fifteenth day of the eighth lunar month. It is also called Mid-Autumn Festival. It usually falls in September or October. This is when the moon is at its fullest and brightest. Many people go out at night to admire the moon. Some climb to the top of a mountain to get the best view. They carry lanterns shaped like fish or birds. Sometimes, people burn moon papers with pictures of rabbits or toads on them. In Chinese mythology, a rabbit and a three-legged toad live on the moon. They are friends of the moon.

中秋節是農曆 8 月 15 日。它也被稱作中秋節（Mid-Autumn Festival）。它通常落在九月或十月。這是月亮最滿最亮的時候。許多人在晚上外出賞月。有些人為了最棒的視野爬到山頂。他們提著像魚或鳥形狀的燈籠。有時，人們會燒上面有兔子或蟾蜍圖案的紙月亮。在中國神話裡，月亮和三隻腳的蟾蜍住在月亮上。牠們在月亮上是朋友。

Many people have a picnic at night under the full moon. They set up a table to honor the moon. On it, they set food and tea. They use moon-shaped fruit such as grapes. They thank the moon for bringing them together and send it their secret wishes.

許多人會在滿月的夜晚下野餐。他們搭起桌子讚賞月亮。桌子上，他們準備了食物和茶。他們使用形似月亮的水果，例如葡萄。他們感謝月亮讓他們齊聚一起，並且向月亮許下他們的祕密願望。

It is common for friends and relatives to give each other moon cakes. These cakes are small rice cakes. The inside is filled with sweet almond paste, red bean paste or eggs. Designs on the top may be the Chinese characters for harmony or long life.

朋友和親戚互相送月餅是很常見的。這些月餅是小型的年糕。裡面填滿甜杏仁醬、紅豆或是蛋黃。餅面的設計是和睦或長壽的中國角色。

There are many old stories about this holiday. One legend tells about how moon cakes once saved China. Once, China was ruled by foreigners. The Chinese wanted to rule their own country. At the Moon Festival, the Chinese hid messages in the moon cakes. These messages told everyone of a secret plan to regain control of their country. At the time told about in the cakes, people gathered together and overthrew the foreign leaders.

關於這個節日有許多古老的故事。一個傳說是講述月餅如何拯救中國。曾經，中國被其他人所統治。中國人想要掌管自己的國家。在中秋節，中國人將訊息藏在月餅裡。這些訊息告訴每個人有個重新掌管他們國家的秘密計劃。在月餅傳達的那個時刻，人們聚集在一起並打倒了外國的侵略者。

Another legend says that the woman named Chang-O married to an evil king. The king had a potion that could make him live forever. Chang-O was afraid for her people, so she drank the potion herself. She became the immortal one and flew to the moon, where she lives in her palace. Today, children are all looking for this moon goddess on Moon Festival.

另一個傳說則說，有個名叫嫦娥女人嫁給了一位邪惡的君王。君王有藥水可以讓他長生不死。嫦娥為她的人民擔心害怕，因此她自己喝了它。她變為長生不死並飛到月亮上，在那裏她住在她的宮殿裡。在今天，孩子們在中秋節都在尋找著嫦娥。

Here are some questions for you to discuss:
這裡有些供你討論的問題：

1. What's your favorite taste of the moon cakes?
   你最喜歡的月餅口味是？

2. Do you like to have a barbecue on the eve of the Moon Festival?
   你喜歡在中秋夜晚來頓烤肉聚餐嗎？

單字大集合

1. Mythology *n.* [C,U] 神話集；神話

We studied mythology in school.
我們在學校研究了神話。

2. Almond *n.* [C] 杏仁

The almond is my favorite nut.
杏仁是我最喜歡的堅果

3. Character *n.* [C,U] 角色；特色

We had to draw the characters from the story.
我們必須畫出故事裡的角色。

4. Message *n.* [C] 消息；訊息

The girls sent messages to each other.
女孩們互相寄訊息。

5. Legend *n.* [C] 傳說；傳奇人物

I heard a legend about the lady in the moon.
我聽過一個關於一位小姐在月亮上的傳說。

6. Potion *n.* 一劑

The magic potion tasted terrible.
這個魔法藥水嚐起來很糟。

7. Immortal *adj.* 長生不死的

I would love to be immortal.
我很樂意長生不死。

閱讀測驗

1. Why do some people burn papers with pictures of rabbits or toads on them?
   為什麼有些人會燒上面有兔子或蟾蜍圖案的紙？

   (a) Because they do not like toads. 因為他們不喜歡蟾蜍。

   (b) To get rid of the rabbits and toads in their gardens.
   為了擺脫在他們花園裡的兔子和蟾蜍。

   (c) Because in mythology, there is a rabbit and a toad that live on the moon.
   因為在神話裡，兔子和蟾蜍住在月亮上。

2. What kinds of characters might the moon cakes have on the top?
   哪一種類型的角色可能會在月餅的餅面上？

   (a) The Chinese characters for long life or harmony. 長壽或是和睦的中國角色。

   (b) Characters from a popular movie. 來自受歡迎的電影裡的角色。

   (c) Characters from their favorite children's story.
   來自他們最喜歡的兒童故事裡的角色。

3. In one legend, how did people know what time to meet to overthrow the foreign
   leaders? 在其中一個傳說裡，人們如何得知會合去打倒外國統治者的時間？

   (a) They called each other on the phone. 他們互相打電話。

   (b) They had to text each other on their cell phones.
   他們必須用手機互相傳簡訊。

   (c) They read about it on papers hidden in the moon cakes.
   他們閱讀藏在月餅裡的紙。

活動慶典和習俗

　　一般據信，中秋（Mid-Autumn）一詞最早出現在「周禮」，「禮記月令」上說：「仲秋之夜養衰老，行麋粥飲食」，而仲秋指的是則是農曆八月，但卻沒有清楚指出是在哪一天。根據考證，在商朝，人們便已經有在秋天滿月時慶祝豐收的習俗，而一直到唐代之後，中秋節（Mid-Autumn Festival）才成為固定的節日，並有唐玄宗夢遊月宮，而得到霓裳羽衣曲的傳說。在元末時期，朱元璋利用月餅傳遞起兵信息，並在登基之後，將月餅當作節令糕點賞賜群臣。一直到明清時期，中秋節已成為是中國重要傳統節日之一。

　　關於中秋節的傳說，大家最為耳熟能詳的是嫦娥奔月（The Legend of Chiang'e Flying to the Moon）的故事，傳說中，后羿（Hou Yi）因射下 9 個太陽，拯救蒼生有功，得到王母娘娘贈與能成仙及長生不老的仙藥（elixir of immortality）。但后羿不捨妻子嫦娥（Chiang'e），於是將仙藥交給嫦娥保管。而后羿的徒弟（apprentice）逢蒙心術不正，趁后羿外出時，威逼嫦娥交出仙藥，嫦娥不從，於是吞下仙藥，成仙飛天而去，但卻為了后羿，選擇住在距離較近的月亮上，獨守廣寒宮。

　　雖然這個神話在太空人登陸月球之後，讓人們少了那幾分的想像。但是中秋節在國人的心中仍佔有極大的份量，因為這一天在中國人的傳統中是個全家團圓的日子，在中秋節的晚上，全家會聚在一起賞月，分食月餅（moon cake），吃柚子（pomelo），給小孩戴柚子皮做成的柚皮帽（pomelo hat）是中秋節時固有的習俗。而在台灣各地還有著不同的中秋節習俗，如美濃的客家人會在這一天宰食水鴨公，還有宜蘭的菜餅，及南部吃麻糬及火鍋（hot pot）的習俗。而在 1980 年代中期興起的烤肉風潮更是席捲整個台灣，而一般被認同的來源說法則是當時兩家知名的烤肉醬廠商廣告炒熱了烤肉風潮，一直到現在，每當到了中秋節前一至二個星期就會開始出現其中一家廣告說的「一家烤肉，萬家香」。

實用生活會話

Q1: Josie, you have to help me. Patrick's parents invite me for dinner on the Mid-Autumn Festival. What should I do at that day?

喬絲，妳一定要幫我。派屈克的爸媽請我中秋節時去吃晚餐，我該怎麼辦？

A1: No worries, I think they just "simply" invite you for dinner. Traditionally, on the Mid-Autumn Festival, family members and friends will get together for dinner and moon gazing. I guess that they think you are the "family-to-be", and you're Patrick's very close "friend".

別擔心，我想他們只是單純的請妳吃晚餐。傳統上來說，中秋節時，我們會和家人朋友聚在一起吃飯賞月。我猜他們認為妳「即將成為家人」而且妳是派屈克非常親近的「朋友」。

Q2: So, when is the Mid-Autumn Festival?

所以中秋節在什麼時候？

A2: It's on the 15th day of the 8th lunar month in Chinese calendar, it's on next Thursday.

是在農曆的 8 月 15 日，下星期四。

Q3: I heard that they said something about "B-B-Q". Does that mean barbecue?

我聽到他們說 BBQ 之類的。是指烤肉嗎？

A3: Yes, I think so. It's quite popular to have a barbecue on the Mid-Autumn Festival in Taiwan.

我想應該是。在台灣，中秋節時烤肉非常受歡迎。

實用單句這樣說

- On the Mid-Autumn Festival, the full moon is as bright as a mirror.
  在中秋節時，圓圓的月亮跟鏡子一樣光亮。

- When one family grills, thousands of families smell the aroma.
  一家烤肉萬家香。

- In Korea, people give gifts to relatives and friends on the Mid-Autumn Festival, so we also call this occasion "Korean Thanksgiving Day."
  在韓國，人們會在中秋時送親戚及朋友禮物，所以我們也稱它做韓國感恩節。

- We enjoy the night of the Mid-Autumn Festival.
  我們享受著中秋節的夜晚。

- A rich thick filling of the moon cake usually made from red bean or lotus seed paste.
  月餅裡包的濃郁內餡通常是紅豆或是蓮容泥。

- In Chinese culture, the round shape of the moon cake symbolizes the completeness and unity.
  在中國文化中，月餅的圓形代表著完整及團結。

互動時刻真有趣

● 中秋節「怎麼說」
- Moon Festival：因為跟滿月有關，而且我們有祭月及賞月的傳統，
- Mooncake Festival：最廣為人知的中秋節傳統就是吃月餅。
- Zhongqiu Festival：直接音譯
- Lantern Festival：常用於新加坡及馬來西亞
- Reunion Festival：月圓人團圓。

● 嫦娥奔月中，你不可不知道的角色
- 后羿：嫦娥的先生。他射下了造成人間大災害的 9 個太陽。王母娘娘送他長生不老的仙藥作為獎賞。

  Hou Yi- He was married to Chiang'e. He shot down the 9 suns that were causing great disaster to people. He was rewarded by the Heavenly Queen Mother with an elixir of immortality.

- 玉兔：當嫦娥飛到月亮時，長生不老藥被咳了出來，而仙丹變成了玉兔。

  Jade Rabbit- When Chiang'e arrived at the moon, the elixir was coughed up and became the Jade Rabbit.

- 吳剛：吳剛是一個樵夫，他想要成仙，但是卻因為他的傲慢而被懲罰，他被要求要砍斷一棵桂樹，但樹幹在每砍一下之後便會自動癒合。

  Wu Gang - Wu Gang was a wood cutter who attempted to become immortality and was punished for his hubris by being required to cut down a cassia tree that magically heals itself after each cut.

Teachers' Day
教師節

節慶源由──簡易版

In many countries, teachers have a special day to be honored. Teachers' Day in Chinese countries is on September 28th. It is a day to honor the good work teachers do. Students bring gifts, flowers or a card to their teacher. Adults visit former teachers. In some schools, students perform for their teachers. They perform dances or dramas. Some host sports events for the teachers. A few teachers every year get awards for good teaching.

在許多國家，老師都有特別的一天來被尊崇。教師節在中國國家為 9 月 28 日。這天是用來尊敬老師們所作的優良工作。學生們帶禮物、花或是一張卡片給他們的老師。成年人則拜訪他們從前的老師們。在有些學校，學生為他們的老師表演。他們表演舞蹈或是戲劇。有些則主持給老師們的體育活動。幾個老師每年會因優良教學被授予獎項。

Teachers' Day also celebrates the birth of Confucius. He was the first and most important teacher in China. He taught for 40 years. Confucius taught people to have strong morals and to be honest.

教師節也是在慶祝孔子的生日。他是中國第一位也是最重要的老師。他教學達 40 年。孔子教導人們要有強烈的道德感和誠實。

In the temples, there are drums and dancers. They wear red or yellow robes. People who come believe they can gain wisdom. Rice cakes are handed out. Those who eat them hope to become as wise as the first teacher.

在廟宇裡，那有鼓和舞者。他們穿著紅色或黃色的長袍。來的人們相信他們能獲得智慧。年糕被發放。吃了那些的人希望他們能像至聖先師一樣智慧。

單字大集合

1. Adult *n.* 成年人

The adults in the room watched the kids carefully.
在房裡的成年人小心地看顧孩子們。

2. Former *adj.* 之前；以前

Mr. Stevens is my former teacher.
史蒂芬斯先生是我之前的老師。

3. Performance *n.* [CU] 表現

We were very proud of the team's performance.
我們非常以團隊的表現為榮。

4. Award *n.* [C] 獎項

I can't wait to see if I won any awards this year.
我等不及要看看今年我是否得到任何獎項。

5. Important *adj.* 重要的

It is important to go to school.
去學校是重要的。

6. Wisdom *n.* [CU] 智慧

My father has a lot of wisdom.
我的父親有很多的智慧。

節慶源由——精彩完整版

In many countries around the world, teachers have a special day to be recognized. Teachers' Day in Chinese countries is on September 28th. It is a day to honor the good work teachers do with their students and in the community. People can visit a former teacher or bring gifts, flowers or a card to their current teacher. In some schools, students entertain their teachers with traditional dances, dramas or skits. Some host sports activities for the teachers. A few teachers every year are awarded for their excellent teaching and positive influence.

在世界上許多國家，老師有個被正式承認的特別日子。教師節在中國國家為 9 月 28 日。這天是用來尊敬老師們對他們的學生和社會所作的優良工作。人們可以拜訪他們從前的老師或是帶禮物、花或是卡片給他們現在的老師。在有些學校，學生們會以傳統舞蹈、戲劇或是小喜劇娛樂他們的老師。有些會為老師主持體育活動。幾個老師每年會因他們的優良教學和正面影響被授予獎項。

Teachers' Day commemorates the birth of Confucius. He is considered the first and the most important educator in ancient China. He spent 40 years of his life teaching. Confucius taught about strong morals in personal life and in government. He taught people to have strong relationships and to be sincere.

教師節用來紀念孔子誕辰。他被認為是古代中國第一位，也是最重要的教育家。他花了 40 年在他的教學生涯上。孔子教導在私人生活和政府裡的道德。他教導人們要有良好的人際關係，並且保持真誠。

In the temples of Confucius, there is a grand ceremony. The ceremony begins with drum beats at 6 am. It usually begins with one solemn beat. Other beats follow, louder and faster, until it is a whole drum concert. Musicians and dancers dress in traditional red or yellow robes. Three animals—the cow, the goat, and the pig—are sacrificed. The hairs plucked from these animals are called the Hairs of Wisdom. The gates of the temple are opened to welcome the spirit of Confucius. To show respect to the spirit, everyone bows three times and offers food and drink to the spirit. This is called the Feast of Sacrifice. Confucius' spirit is then sent off before the main gates of the temple close.

在孔子廟裡，有個盛典。這個典禮開始於清晨六點的鼓聲。通常開始於一聲莊嚴的敲擊。其他的敲擊跟隨在後，更大聲且更快，直到成為一個鼓聲繚繞的音樂會。演奏者和舞者穿著傳統紅或黃色的長袍。三種動物——牛、羊和豬——被獻祭。從這些動物拔下的毛髮被稱為智慧之髮。寺廟的大門被敞開以迎接孔子的靈魂。為了表達對靈魂的尊重，每個人都鞠躬三次，並提供食品和飲料給靈魂。這就是所謂的宰牲節。孔子的靈魂接著被送走，在寺廟的主要大門關上後。

Some people who attend the event believe they can gain wisdom. After the ceremony, rice cakes called "wisdom cake" are given out. Those who eat them hope to become as wise as the ancient teacher. A huge crowd of students and their parents often wait to eat one. They believe that a small bite means better academic performance.

有些參加活動的人相信他們可以得到智慧。在典禮過後，被稱作「智慧糕」的年糕會被發放。那些吃了年高的人希望能變得像至聖先師一樣智慧。一大群學生和他們的家長常常等著吃上一個。他們認為，一小口意味著能有更好的學術表現。

Here are some questions for you to discuss:
這裡有些供你討論的問題：

1. Have you and your schoolmates ever celebrated for your teachers on Teachers' Day?
   你和你的學校同學有曾為老師們慶祝過教師節嗎？

2. Who is the teacher influencing you the most?
   誰是影響你最多的老師？

單字大集合

1. Community *n.* [C] 社區

We live in a very friendly community.
我們住在一個非常友善的社區。

2. Current *adj.* 當前的；流行的

I wrote a paper about current events in my town.
我寫了一份關於發生在我家鄉的事件的報告。

3. Traditional *adj.* 傳統的

I wear my traditional dress for special celebrations.
我為了特別的慶祝穿上我的傳統服裝。

4. Influence *n.* [C,U] 影響；作用

I hope to be a good influence on my students.
我希望我對我的學生是個好的影響。

5. Commemorate *vt.* 慶祝；紀念

When there is a day to remember a person from the past, it commemorates that person.
當有個用來記得過去的某個人的日子，那天就是用來紀念那個人的。

6. Relationship *n.* [C,U] 關係；人際關係

We have friendly relationships with all of our teachers.
我們跟我們所有的老師都保持友善的關係。

7. Sincere *adj.* 真誠的

What I wrote in my letter was very sincere.
我寫在我的信裡的東西非常真誠。

8. Sacrifice *vi. vt.* 獻祭；犧牲

Sometimes a soldier must sacrifice his life for his country.
有時士兵必須為了他的國家犧牲他的人生。

閱讀測驗

1. What are teachers awarded for on Teachers' Day?
   老師在教師節為了因為什麼被頒發獎項？
   (a) For being funny. 因為很風趣。
   (b) For sharing their lunch with the students. 因為和學生分享午餐。
   (c) For excellent teaching and their positive influence.
   　　因為卓越的教學和他們正面的影響。

2. Whose birth do we commemorate on Teachers' Day?
   誰的生日在教師節被我們紀念？
   (a) The birth of my grandmother. 我奶奶的生日。
   (b) The birth of my favorite school teacher. 我最喜歡的學校老師的生日。
   (c) The birth of Confucius. 孔子的生日。

3. What hairs are plucked from the cow, pig and goat?
   什麼毛髮從牛、豬和羊身上拔下？
   (a) All the hairs on their heads. 所有他們頭上的毛髮。
   (b) The hairs of wisdom. 智慧之髮。
   (c) The hair that has grown too long. 長得太長的毛髮。

4. How many years did Confucius spend his lifetime on teaching?
   孔子花了一生多久的時間在教學上？
   (a) 30 years
   (b) 40 years
   (c) 50 years

活動慶典和習俗

在 1994 年時，聯合國教科文組織定下每年的 10 月 5 日為「世界教師日」（World Teachers' Day）。而我國卻早在 1931 年時，就有一些教育家在中央大學發起建立，主旨為「改善教師待遇，保障教師工作與增進教師修養」，並定在 6 月 6 日為教師節（Teacher's Day），1932 年時由教育部認可。1939 年時改定 8 月 27 日的孔子誕辰為教師節。但在經過曆數及考紀學者推算及考證之後，認為孔子誕辰在轉換成國曆生日後應是在 9 月 28 日。所以在 1952 年時由行政院提請總統明令，9 月 28 日為我國的教師節及孔子誕辰紀念日。

在教師節這一天，全國各地會舉行「慶祝教師節大會」，會頒獎給資深及優良教師，表揚教師們對社會的貢獻。而在各地的孔廟則會舉行祭孔大典（Confucius Memorial Ceremony）又稱作釋奠禮（Shidian Ceremony）。釋、奠二字具有設置、呈獻的意思，代表在祭典中設置音樂與舞蹈並且呈獻牲禮、酒等祭品，以表達對孔子崇高的敬意。在祭孔典禮中最受人注目的是釋奠佾舞（Shidien Yi Dance）又稱丁祭佾舞。佾舞一般分做四級，有二、四、六、八之分，根據周朝的禮法規定，天子用八，諸侯用六，大夫四，士二，但也可被視為是根據被祭祀者的德行的高低，對國家社稷的貢獻有多少。孔子曾被唐玄宗追封為文宣王，地位等同於諸侯，依禮法應呈獻六佾舞，但因為孔子對後世影響深遠，所以從唐朝開始就有以八佾舞（Ba Yi Dance）祭孔的編制。時至今日，形成了在不同孔廟的釋奠禮上有六佾或是八佾的不同編制，一般來說會以展演八佾舞來表示對至聖先師孔子的尊崇，但也常因受限於展演的場地而以六佾舞呈獻。佾是指隊伍的行列，八佾則是指由八行八列共 64 人所形成的隊伍，而六佾則是 36 人的陣容。在台南孔廟的祭孔典禮結束後，還會有拔牛毛長智慧的儀式，民眾會以徒手拔取，也有人以剪刀剪下，以減少牛隻的疼痛。取下的牛毛被稱為智慧毛（wisdom hair）。台北孔廟在 1990 年之後已以發放智慧糕的方式來取代這個儀式。

實用生活會話

Q1: Do you know when is the Teacher's Day celebrated in Taiwan?
你知道台灣的教師節是在什麼時候嗎？

A1: Yes, I know. It is on September 28th. It's also Confucius' birthday.
我知道啊。是 9 月 28 日，同時也是孔子誕辰。

Q2: Who's Confucius?
誰是孔子呢？

A2: Confucius was a remarkable teacher, and he's also a philosopher and politician of the Spring and Autumn period of Chinese history.
孔子是在中國春秋時期時一個非常了不起的教育家，而他也是一個哲學家及政治家。

Q3: How do they celebrate Confucius' Birthday?
他們通常都怎麼慶祝孔子誕辰？

A3: The Grand Ceremony Dedicated to Confucius is held annually on Confucius' Birthday to pay homage to Confucius.
每年在孔子誕辰時都會舉行祭孔大典以示後人對孔子的崇敬。

實用單句這樣說

- We wish to show our gratitude with this gift. Happy Teacher's Day.
我們希望能藉由這個禮物來表達我們的感激之意。教師節快樂。

- We are more thankful than we can express.
我們的感謝之意無法言傳。

- The primary purpose of the education is not to teach you to earn your bread, but to make every mouthful sweet.　　　　　　　　　～James Angel
教育最主要的目的並不是教你如何謀生，而是要讓你的生活更有滋有味。

- What sculpture is to a block of marble, education is to the soul.

  雕塑用的是大理石，而教育雕塑的是靈魂。　　　　～ Joseph Addison

- One good teacher in a lifetime may sometimes change a delinquent into a solid citizen.　　　　　　　　　　　　　　　　～Phillip Wylie

  一個好的老師具有化腐朽為神奇的力量。

- Education is not the filling of the pail, but the lighting of a fire.

  ～ William Butler Yeats

  教育不是灌滿一桶水，而是點燃生命的一團火焰。

- Teacher's Day is a special day for the appreciation of teachers.

  教師節是一個特別的日子用以表達對教師們的敬意。

- Confucius is the most extraordinary educator in Chinese history, so we choose his birthday to celebrate Teacher's Day.

  孔子是中國歷史上最成就非凡的教育家，所以我們選在他的誕辰來慶祝教師節。

互動時刻真有趣

　　祭孔大典流程複雜，但卻十分具有教育意義，而且西方人也相當好奇這個流傳已久的儀式。在這裡我們用簡單的中英文介紹，希望大家能有初略的認識。

- 祭孔大典流程（Confucius Memorial Ceremony Program）

1. 釋奠典禮開始	The ceremony begins.
2. 鼓初嚴	First drum roll.
3. 鼓再嚴	Second drum roll.
4. 鼓三嚴	Third drum roll.
5. 樂生、佾生就位	Musicians and dancers take positions
6. 執事者各司其事	Ceremonial attendants take their designated positions.
7. 糾儀官就位	The ceremonial supervisor takes his designated position.
8. 陪祭官就位	The assistant sacrifice officers take their designated positions.

9. 分獻官就位	The collateral presentation offices take their designated position.
10. 正獻官就位	The principal presentation officer takes his designated position.
11. 啟扉	Opening the gates.
12. 瘞毛血	Burying the sacrificial remnant.
13. 迎神	Welcoming the spirit.
14. 三鞠躬	Three bows.
15. 進饌	Presenting the sacrificial feast.
16. 行上香禮	Offering incense.
17. 行初獻禮	Initial principal presentation.
18. 行初分獻禮	Initial principal presentation to other ancient philosophers and worthies.
19. 恭讀祝文	Chanting the blessing.
20. 三鞠躬	Three bows.
21. 行亞獻禮	Second principal presentation.
22. 行亞分獻禮	Second principal presentation to other ancient philosophers and worthies.
23. 獻花	Offering flowers.
24. 行終獻禮	Final principal presentation.
25. 行終分獻禮	Final principal presentation to other ancient philosophers and worthies.
26. 飲福受胙	The principal presentation officer accepts the sacrificial wine and pork.
27. 三鞠躬	Three bows.
28. 行撤饌禮	Removing the remnants of the sacrificial feast.
29. 送神	Escorting the spirit.
30. 捧祝帛詣燎所	Taking the sacrificial silks to the furnace.
31. 望燎	Burning silks.
32. 復位	Resuming positions.
33. 闔扉	Closing the gates.
34. 撤班	Withdrawing positions.
35. 禮成	The ceremony concludes.

　　瘞毛血：瘞讀音同「易」，是指將毛、血埋入土中，滋養土地，使萬物生生不息並有潔淨的含意。

　　獻禮：獻禮及分獻禮有分為初、亞、終三階段，皆為獻上祭祀所用的酒及絲帛。獻禮祭獻的對象是孔子，而分獻禮則是向其他的先聖先賢獻祭。

National Day
國慶日

節慶源由──簡易版

National Day is on October tenth. It is the most important holiday in Taiwan. Make people remember when the Republic of China（Taiwan）began. The holiday begins when the flag of Taiwan is raised. It is raised in front of the President's Building. Sometimes, there is a large parade of soldiers. The President makes a speech. There are many flags flying in the street.

國慶日在 10 月 10 日。這是在台灣最重要的節日。讓人們記得中華民國是何時開創。這個節日始於中華民國國旗升起時。國旗在總統府前被升起。有時，那裡會有龐大的士兵遊行。總統會發表演說。有許多國旗飄揚在街上。

The main event in each city is a large parade. This parade includes people who work in different types of jobs. There are also drummers and marching bands. After the parade, large dance groups perform. There is often a dragon dance and lion dance. In this dance, the leader of the dragon wears a large dragon head. Behind him come 24 people. They wear bright cloth. They are the body of the dragon. At night, the sky is lit up by fireworks.

每個城市最重要的事情便是遊行。這個遊行包含了做著不同類型工作的人們。也有鼓手和軍樂隊。在遊行之後，是大型的舞蹈團體表演。通常是舞龍舞獅。在舞龍舞獅裡，領導的人會戴著一個巨大的龍頭。在他身後有 24 個人。他們穿著閃亮的衣服。他們是龍的身體。在晚上，天空會被施放煙火。

單字大集合

1. October *n.* 十月

I like the weather in October.
我喜歡 10 月的天氣。

2. Republic *n.* [C] 共和國；共和政體

The country became a republic.
這個國家變成共和國了。

3. Building *n.* [C] 建築物

There is a new building for our school this year.
今年在我們學校有個新建築。

4. Speech *n.* [C,U] 演講；致詞

I am scared to make my speech at school.
我害怕在學校作演說。

5. Event *n.* [C] 事件

We are planning an exciting event.
我們正在計畫一個令人興奮的大事。

6. Parade *n.* [C,U] 遊行；行進

I can't wait to see our band in the parade.
我等不及在遊行裡看到我們的樂團。

節慶源由——精彩完整版

　　National Day is on October tenth.　October is the tenth month in the 12 month calendar.　Therefore, National Day is also known as Double Ten day.　National Day is one of the grandest celebrations of the year in Taiwan.　It marks the fall of the Ching Dynasty in China in 1911.　It marks the establishment of the Republic of China （Taiwan）on January 1, 1912.　This is not a holiday in mainland China.　However, some towns there do have a ceremony that commemorates the fall of the Ching dynasty.　There are also large Double Ten Day parades in the Chinatowns in Chicago and San Francisco in the United States.

　　國慶日在 10 月 10 日。十月是 12 個月制裡的第 10 個月。因此，國慶日又稱雙十節。國慶日是台灣一年當中最盛大的慶祝活動之一。它代表著西元 1911 年在中國的清朝的衰敗。它記錄了西元 1912 年 1 月 1 日中華民國的建立。這在中國大陸並不是節日。然而，有些鄉鎮會舉辦儀式紀念清朝的衰退。在美國芝加哥和舊金山的中國城也有盛大的雙十節遊行。

　　In Taiwan, National Day begins with the raising of the national flag of the Republic of China.　It is raised in front of the Presidential Office Building. Sometimes, there is a large military parade.　The soldiers are in full military dress. Even if there is not a military parade, the national anthem is sung. Then the President makes a speech to the country.　There are many national flags flying in the streets.

　　在台灣，國慶日始於中華民國國旗的升起。它在總統府前被升起。有時，那裡會有龐大的士兵遊行。士兵們著全套軍裝。甚至如果沒有士兵遊行，國歌也會被頌唱。接著，總統會對全國進行演說。會有許多國旗飄揚在街道上。

　　Around the country, the main event in each city is a large parade.　This parade includes people who represent many different types of jobs. There are also drummers and traditional musicians.　There are modern marching bands, too.　After the parade, there are large performances by dancing groups.　There is usually a dragon dance and lion dance. In this dance, the leader of the dragon wears a large dragon head.　Behind him come up to 24 people wearing colorful cloth to make up the body of the dragon. Other events are martial arts exhibitions and folk dances.　At night, traditional arches are lit in many streets.　The sky is lit up all over the country by large fireworks displays in all the major cities. The evening ends with an elaborate National Day concert. It is the most colorful and the most important of all the holidays in Taiwan.

　　在全國各地，每個城市的主要大事是大遊行。這個遊行包含代表不同類型工作的人們。也有鼓手們和軍樂隊。也有現代軍樂隊。在遊行後，會有很多舞蹈團體的巨型表演。通常是舞龍舞獅。在舞龍舞獅裡，領導的人會戴著一個巨大的龍頭。在他身後有 24 個人，穿著五顏六色的衣服扮演龍的身體。其它還有武術展覽和民間舞蹈。在晚上，許多街道上傳統的拱門會被點亮。所有重要的城市天空中會施放遍及全國的煙火。夜晚以精心準備的國慶日音樂會做結尾。這是所有台灣節日裡最繽紛及最重要的節日。

Do you know where the only pure states' National Day's activities locate? It's in Taichung, and be hosted by the American Chamber of Commerce in Taichung. It not only celebrates the National Day but also presents all kinds of industrial culture as well. They offer the American stylish furnishing, American country music, and the most popular hamburger and lemonade sales and so on. There are big-sized showcase of the products of American enterprise and the flights the airlines provide. This kind of activity draws near the distance between American and the Taiwanese, and helps the Taiwanese get to know more about the things and culture in the US.

　　您知道台灣唯一的「純美式」美國國慶日活動在那裡嗎？在台中，由台中美國商會主辦。不只是慶祝美國國慶日，也要同時展現美國的各種產業文化。有美式風格的佈置，美式鄉村音樂、販賣漢堡和檸檬水等最受歡迎的美式餐飲，還會有大型美國企業展示商品，還有航空公司提供的美國行程。這樣的活動，拉近了美台之間的距離，也讓台灣民眾更加了解美國的事物與文化。

單字大集合

1. Dynasty *n.* [C] 朝代

A dynasty is rulers that all come from the same family.
一個朝代的統治者都來自同一個家庭。

2. Establishment *n.* [C,U] 建立的機構；建立

We are working toward the establishment of a new government.
我們正致力於建立一個新的政府。

3. Presidential *adj.* 總統的；總統制的

The Presidential palace is very elaborate.
總統府是非常複雜的。

4. Soldier *n.* [C] 士兵

Soldiers marched on the streets to keep the people safe.
士兵在街上遊行，以保護人民的安全

5. March *n.* [C,U] 行程；行軍

The band had fun marching in the parade for the first time.
樂團在遊行裡第一次有有趣的行程。

6. Exhibition *n.* [C] 展覽；展覽品

You can see exhibitions of traditional dance at the museum.
你可以在博物館裡看到傳統舞蹈的展覽。

7. Chinatown *n.* 中國城

My relatives in the United States live in Chinatown.
我在美國的親戚住在中國城裡。

8. Concert *n.* [C] 演唱會

The concert was the best music I have ever heard.
這場音樂會是我有史以來聽過最棒的音樂。

閱讀測驗

1. Why is National Day also known as Double Ten day?
   為什麼國慶日又稱作雙十節？
   - (a) Because ten year old children get ten gifts that day.
     因為當天 10 歲的小孩可以得到 10 份禮物
   - (b) Because it is on the tenth day of the tenth month.
     因為它在 10 月的第 10 天。
   - (c) Because ten people thought of ten names for the day.
     因為 10 個人在那天想到 10 個名字。

2. How many people might follow the head of the dragon?
   可能有幾個人跟隨著龍頭？
   - (a) Up to 24 people make up the body of the dragon.
     24 個人扮成龍身。
   - (b) Everyone watching the parade can join the line .
     每個看遊行的人都可以加入行列。
   - (c) No one, because they are all afraid of the dragon.
     沒有人，因為所有人都害怕龍。

3. .What makes the sky light up all over the country at night?
   是什麼照亮整個國家夜晚的天空？
   - (a) The stars.
     星星。
   - (b) Lights from all the lanterns people are holding.
     光來自於人們提著的燈籠。
   - (c) Fireworks.
     煙火。

活動慶典和習俗

在 1911 年時由革命黨人發起的辛亥革命成功之後，1912 年的 1 月 1 日建立了中華民國。而在辛亥革命當中第一個起義的地點是在武昌，稱為武昌起義（Wuchang Uprising），發起的日期是在農曆的 8 月 19 日，即為國曆 10 月 10 日。而在之後的兩個月中，中國各地的革命都陸續成功，終於推翻了腐敗的滿清（Qing Dynasty）政府。為了紀念這個偉大的里程碑（milestone），於是將辛亥革命發起的第一天 10 月 10 日定為中華民國國慶日（National Day of the Republic of China），又稱雙十節（Double Tenth Day/ Double Ten Day）、雙十國慶及辛亥革命紀念日。

在國共內戰（Chinese Civil War）失敗之後，中華民國政府於 1949 年遷移至台灣，每年都會在總統府前的廣場舉行慶典來慶祝雙十國慶。首先會以升旗典禮（flag raising ceremony）來揭開序幕，接著是配合當年時事訂立主題（motif）的國慶典禮（National Day ceremony），此時會在凱達格蘭大道上出現不同的遊行及表演的隊伍，由三軍樂儀隊、學校學生及民間團體所組成。在政府遷台後初期，一年一度的國慶閱兵（National Day military parade）也因為時代的演變，而改為在新任總統就職當年或是建國「逢十」週年國慶時才舉行。而最近的一次就是在 2011 年建國百年的國慶日上。國慶日晚上會有由國軍主導設計的國慶煙火（National Day firework display）每年選在不同的縣市施放。在雙十節這一天，總統府前的升旗典禮及晚上的煙火施放地點總會吸引許多的民眾前往參加，成為當天社群網路上最熱門的打卡（check-in）地標。而各縣市政府在這一天也會舉辦升旗典禮、慢跑、藝文等各式各樣的國慶活動，也有民眾以懸掛國旗的方式來慶祝國家的生日。在海外各地，許多僑胞則會組織雙十國慶遊行及升旗典禮來共同慶祝。

實用生活會話

Q1: What wrong with you? You look exhausted.

怎麼啦？你看起來很累的樣子。

A1: Don't worry, I'll be okay. I just need a cup of coffee. I went to the National Day Firework Show yesterday and took a lot of photos.

別擔心，我只是需要一杯咖啡來提提神。我昨天去看國慶煙火秀了，還拍了許多的照片。

Q2: And then?

然後呢？

A2: I got stuck in the traffic jam after the firework show.

煙火秀之後我被堵在路上了。

Q3: Oh, it's really bad, isn't it?

喔，真糟糕，不是嗎？

A3: Yes, it is. It took me almost 5 hours to get home. It was a painful experience, and killing my valuable sleeping time cruelly.

你說的沒錯。我花了快 5 個小時的時間才到家。那真是個痛苦的經驗，並且慘忍的扼殺了我寶貴的睡眠時間。

實用單句這樣說

- Tomorrow is the Double Ten Day. I will have to get up very early to attend the National Day Flag Raising Ceremony at the plaza in front of the Presidential Building.
  明天是雙十節。我必須很早起床去參加在總統府前廣場的國慶日升旗典禮。

- Today, we are gathered here to hold the celebration to mark the 102nd anniversary of the founding of the Republic of China.
  今天，我們在此一同慶祝中華民國建國 102 週年。

- Double Tenth Day is the day for us to celebrate the birth of our nation.
  雙十節是我們慶祝國家生日的日子。

- Long live the Republic of China. Long live the democracy in Taiwan.
  中華民國萬歲。台灣民主萬歲。

- Sizable Double Ten Day Parades occur annually in the Chinatowns of Chicago and San Francisco.
  在芝加哥及舊金山的唐人街，每年都會舉行具有相當規模的雙十國慶遊行。

- Many supporters of the Republic of China in Hong Kong would display our national flags to celebrate the Double Ten Day before 1997.
  1997 年之前，支持中華民國的香港民眾會懸掛我國的國旗來慶祝雙十國慶。

互動時刻真有趣

● 認識我們的國旗（Flag of the Republic of China）

中華民國國旗是由藍、白、紅三色組成的。

There are three colors in the national flag of the Republic of China: blue, white and red.

用中文來說，我們通常稱它做青天白日滿地紅。

It is commonly described as Blue Sky, White Sun and Wholly Earth Red in Chinese.

藍色代表的是自由，白色代表平等，紅色代表的是博愛。

Blue symbolizes liberty; white symbolizes equality; and red symbolizes fraternity.

青天白日旗是由革命先烈陸浩東所設計的。

The "Blue Sky with a White Sun" flag was designed by Lu Hao-tung, who was a revolutionary martyr of the Republic of China.

在他的設計中，白日的十二道光芒代表的是十二個月及十二個時辰。（一個時辰等於兩個小時）

In his design, the twelve rays of the White Sun represent twelve months and twelve traditional shichen. (One shichen equals two hours.)

國旗「滿地紅」的部分則是我們的國父孫中山先生所加上的，用以象徵為了創建民國，革命先烈們犧牲生命所流下的鮮血。

The "Red Earth" field of the national flag was added by our national founding father, Sun Yat-sen, to signify the blood of the revolutionaries who sacrificed themselves to create out nation.

國旗的長寬比是 3：2。

The ratio of our national flag is 3:2.

旗面的四分之一是深藍色的，其中包括著有 12 道三角形光芒的白日圖案。

A quarter of the flag is navy blue which contains the "White Sun" with twelve triangular rays.

Western Festival
西方節慶

New Year's Day
新年

節慶源由──簡易版

In western countries, New Year's Day is on January 1st. It is a big celebration. There are many New Year's Eve parties. As the clock reaches midnight, confetti flies through the air. Couples have a new year's kiss. Songs play about old friends and saying goodbye to the old year. There are often fireworks.

在西方國家裡，新年是在 1 月 1 日。它是個大慶典。有許多除夕派對。當時鐘到了午夜，五彩碎紙在空中飛揚。情侶們會來個新年之吻。歌曲撥放著有關老朋友及向舊年份說再見。那通常會有煙火。

In London, England, the New Year begins when Big Ben（a large clock tower）strikes twelve. In Greece, families switch off the lights at midnight. They cut a pie with a coin in it. If the coin is in your piece of pie, you will have good luck.

在倫敦，英國的新年始於大笨鐘（a large clock tower）敲響 12 點鐘時。在希臘，家庭在半夜關燈。他們切開裡面有錢幣的派。如果你那塊派裡有錢幣，你將會得到好運。

On New Year's Day, there are parades and lots of sports. On New Year's Day, many people promise to change. They promise to eat better. Or to exercise more. Change seems easy on New Year's Day. But they soon forget this promise.

在新年，會有遊行和許多運動。在新年，許多人承諾要改變。他們承諾要吃得更好。或做更多運動。改變在新年看來很容易。但他們很快就會忘記這個承諾。

單字大集合

1. Party　*n.* [C]　派對

Kids love going to birthday parties.
孩子們喜愛去生日派對。

2. Midnight　*n.* [C]　午夜

I have never stayed up until midnight.
我從沒有熬夜到午夜。

3. Goodbye　再見

I said goodbye to my friend when she moved.
我向我朋友說再見，當她搬走時。

4. Tower　*n.* [C]　塔

We can see the top of the tower from our window.
我們可以從我們的窗戶看到塔的頂端。

5. Strike　*vi. vt.*　打；擊；敲

The clock strikes twelve times at midnight.
時鐘在午夜敲響 12 點鐘。

6. Promise　*vi. vt.*　允諾

I promise I will never tell a lie.
我承諾我將不會再說謊。

節慶源由──精彩完整版

Western countries today all celebrate New Year's Day on January 1st. However, most of the celebrating happens on December 31st, New Year's Eve. There are many New Year's Eve parties. As the clock reaches midnight, there are many traditions. In the United States, New York City puts up a giant ball. Thousands of people gather to watch as it drops slowly to the ground. It counts down the last minute before midnight. When it reaches the bottom, confetti flies through the air. Some people make a toast to the new year. They hold their drink glasses in the air, and wish each other a good year. Then, they all take a small drink at the same time. Some have a new year's kiss. Songs play about old friends and saying goodbye to the old year. Big cities almost always have fireworks.

西方國家在今日都在 1 月 1 日慶祝新年。然而，大部分的慶祝都發生在 12 月 31 日，除夕夜。會有許多除夕夜派對。當時鐘到達午夜時，會有許多傳統。在美國，紐約市建造一個巨大的球。上千名民眾聚在一起觀看它慢慢掉落到地面上。在午夜前的最後一分鐘會倒數。當它到達底部時，五彩碎紙在空中飛揚。有些人向新年舉杯。他們在空中舉起他們的玻璃杯，並且希望彼此有個美好的一年。然後他們會同時喝一小杯。有些人會有新年之吻。歌曲撥放著有關老朋友及向舊年份說再見。大城市們幾乎都有煙火。

In London, thousands of people gather along the River Thames to watch fireworks. The New Year officially begins when Big Ben（a large clock tower）strikes twelve. In Greece, families switch off the lights at midnight. They celebrate by cutting open a pie which usually contains a coin. If you get the coin in your piece of pie, you can expect luck for the whole year.

在倫敦，上千名民眾聚集在泰晤士河畔觀看煙火。新年正式開始於大笨鐘（a large clock tower）敲響 12 點鐘時。在希臘，家庭在半夜關燈。他們藉由切開通常含有錢幣的派慶祝。如果你那塊派裡有錢幣，你可以期待一整年有好運氣。

On New Year's Day, there are parades and sports competitions. In the US, college football teams play championship games. Ice hockey teams have an outside game in the cold winter weather. In England, there is also a football tournament. But this is European football, which is called soccer in the United States. Around the world, in cold wintery cities, Polar Bear Clubs have their annual Polar Bear Plunge. This is where people in summer swimsuits plunge into a freezing cold lake to show how tough they are. Sometimes, the ice must be chipped away to make a hole to jump in.

在新年，有許多遊行和體育競賽。在美國，大學橄欖球隊比冠軍賽。冰上曲棍球隊在寒冷的冬季氣候裡有戶外比賽。在英國，那也有橄欖球隊比賽。但那是歐洲橄欖球，在美國被稱為足球。在全世界的寒冷的冬日城市，北極熊俱樂部會有他們年度的北極熊跳躍賽。這是人們穿著夏季泳衣跳入一個寒冷的湖，以表示他們是多麼結實。有時，冰必須被鑿開來挖個洞以便跳入。

Many people make New Year's resolutions on New Year's Day. They promise to themselves that they will try something new this year. Usually, it is to eat better or to exercise more. It is always something that will make them a better person in the new year. However, these resolutions are typically only followed for a short time before they are forgotten.

許多人在新年會許下新年的決心。他們承諾自己會在新的這年嘗試某事。通常，是吃得更好或做更多運動。通常是能讓他們在新的一年將變得更好的某件事。然而，這些決心通常只被遵守一小段時間，在它們被忘記以前。

Here are some questions for you to discuss:
這裡有些供你討論的問題：

1. Could you describe the New Year's Eve at Taipei 101?
   你可以描述一下台北 101 的新年前夕嗎？

2. What's your new year's resolution?
   您新年的新願望是？

單字大集合

1. Confetti *n.* [U] 五彩碎紙

We cut up lots and lots of paper to make confetti.
我們剪碎很多很多的紙張來作五彩碎紙。

2. Officially *adv.* 正式地

Officially, he will not be the president until tomorrow morning.
正式地，他到明天早上將不是總統了。

3. Competition *n.* [C] 競賽

We love to watch all kinds of sports competitions.
我們喜歡看所有種類的體育競賽。

4. Championship *n.* [C] 冠軍稱號

We are cheering for our team to win the championship.
我們都在歡呼我們的隊伍贏得了總冠軍。

5. Tournament *n.* [C] 聯賽

How many teams are playing in the tournament?
共有幾個隊伍在這聯賽裡比賽？

6. European *adj.* 歐洲的

Do you know how many European countries there are?
你知道那裡共有幾個歐洲的國家嗎？

7. Plunge *vi. vt.* 跳入；使投入

I never plunge into cold water!
我從沒有跳入冷水裡！

8. Resolution *n.* [C] 決心

This year, I plan to keep my resolutions all year.
今年，我準備持定我所立定心志的計畫一整年。

閱讀測驗

1. What happens when the giant ball in New York hits the ground?
   紐約的巨球擊中地面時會發生什麼？
   (a) It breaks. 它損壞了。
   (b) Everyone cries. 每個人哭了。
   (c) Confetti flies through the air. 五彩碎紙在空中飛揚。

2. When does the new year officially begin in London?
   在倫敦的新年何時正式開始？
   (a) When your mom says it does. 當你的媽媽說開始時。
   (b) When Big Ben strikes twelve. 當大笨鐘敲響 12 點。
   (c) After you have eaten all your dinner. 在你已經吃完你所有的晚餐後。

3. What happens in the Polar Bear Plunge? 在 Polar Bear Plunge 會發生什麼？
   (a) Everyone walks around like a polar bear. 每個人像北極熊到處走。
   (b) People throw things at polar bears in the zoo.
      人們丟東西在動物園的北極熊身上。
   (c) People in summer swimsuits jump into a freezing cold lake.
      人們穿著夏季泳裝跳入冰冷的寒湖。

4. What kind of sport activity would be held in the U.S. on New Year's Day?
   那種運動活動在美國的新年會舉辦？
   (a) Polar Bear plunge 北極熊跳躍賽
   (b) Basketball games 籃球比賽
   (c) College football teams play championship games.
      大學橄欖球隊比冠軍賽。

活動慶典和習俗

　　隨著台灣社會的逐漸西化，人們除了重視農曆新年之外，在國曆新年時，也出現了越來越多的慶祝活動。其中以台北 101 所舉辦的跨年煙火秀（Taipei 101 New Year's Firework Show）最廣為人知。而在台北市首創由官方主辦的跨年晚會之後（Taipei New Year's Eve Countdown Party），打開了跨年晚會舉辦的風氣。而現今最流行的模式則是以 SNG 連線的方式，將在各縣市舉辦的跨年晚會作串連，一同倒數迎接新年。除了台北 101 的跨年煙火秀之外，近幾年，台北市美麗華、雲林的劍湖山世界、高雄夢時代及義大世界的摩天輪（Ferris Wheel）環狀煙火秀也相當受到台灣民眾注目。

　　世界上最有名的跨年倒數，莫過於是在紐約時代廣場（Times Square）所舉行的降球（Ball Drop）儀式。從跨年夜的 23:59:00 開始，重 1070 磅，長 6 英尺的水晶球（Crystal Ball）便會時代廣場的頂處緩緩降下，並於 00:00:00 剛好到達底處。

　　在巴西里約熱內盧的科巴卡巴那海灘的慶祝活動則是吸引全世界最多遊客參與的跨年會，除了大型的煙火表演之外，還有精彩的歌舞表演助興。第二大的跨年夜慶祝活動則是在澳洲雪梨，由於澳洲接近國際換日線，是在主要國家中第二個迎接新年的。傳統上，會在進入 1 月 1 日的那一刻起，開始展開雪梨港灣的大型煙火匯演（massive firework display），沿著港灣大橋（Harbour Bridge）及沿岸 6 公里處分別設有 4 個煙火發射點，同時發射超過 8 萬發的煙火。除了在雪梨港方圓 16 公里內觀賞煙火秀之外，還可以考慮乘坐遊艇，能在雪梨港上更近距離的觀賞。

　　隨著時代的進步，在以前人們用以表達祝賀的新年卡片逐漸被電子賀卡然後是簡訊（text message）所取代，而這幾年則又流行以 WhatsApp, Line 等通訊軟體來拜年，可說是科技進步所帶來的新風俗。

實用生活會話

Q1: It's New Year's Eve. Do you have any plans for it?

今天是跨年夜，你有沒有什麼計畫？

A1: Well, nothing special. I'll probably stay at home, and watch the countdown party show on TV and then sleep.

嗯，沒什麼特別的計畫。可能會待在家裡，看跨年晚會電視轉播，然後就睡覺吧。

Q2: I'm going to see the Taipei 101's Firework Show at the Elephant Mountain. Do you want to go with me?

我要去象山看台北 101 煙火秀，要不要跟我一起去？

A2: That sounds interesting. Ok, I change my mind, I'll go with you.

聽起來不錯。好吧，我改變主意了，我跟你一起去。

Q3: Can I sleep over at your house after the firework show?

那在煙火秀之後，我可不可以在你家睡？

A3: No problem, be my guest.

沒問題，請便。

Q4: Wow, it's so nice of you.

喔，你人真好。

A4: Since you're my friend, what a friend for!!

因為你是我的朋友，朋友就是這樣的嘛！

實用單句這樣說

- The countdown event at Taipei 101 was selected by CNN as one of the ten best places in the world to welcome the New Year.
  台北 101 的跨年倒數晚會被 CNN 評選為是世界上前十名最佳迎接新年的地方。

- Have you made any resolutions for this new year?
  你有為這新的一年定下任何新的目標嗎？

- New Year's Day celebrations vary widely across different cultures.
  在不同的文化中，新年的慶祝方式也會有所不同。

- New Year's Day Parades are held in some countries, and some parades are televised.
  在有些國家會舉行新年大遊行，而有些遊行會以電視轉播。

- Black-eyed peas are the traditional food for the New Year's meals in the southern United States.
  米豆是美國南方在新年時必吃的傳統食物。

- First-footing is an ancient New Year's tradition in Scotland. If the first person to enter your house after midnight on the first day of the year is a male with dark hair, you'll have good luck all year.
  首次拜訪是蘇格蘭古老的新年傳統。如果在午夜過後新年的第一天，第一個上門拜訪的人是個有著深色髮色的男性，將會帶來一整年的好運。

- Many people who were up on the New Year's Eve to celebrate the New Year and have a day off work have the chance to sleep in and spend the remainder of the day relaxing.
  許多在跨年夜熬夜慶祝新年的人，在不用上班的元旦當天有機會可以睡懶覺，及輕鬆的度過一天中剩下的時光。

- Since 2011, a 3D light and sound show has been held at the Bund in Shanghai, a few minutes before the New Year's Day.
  從 2011 年開始，在新年元旦的前幾分鐘會於上海外灘展出 3D 聲光秀。

互動時刻真有趣

● 新年新希望的前 10 大排行榜
The 10 most common New Year's Resolutions

1. 吃的健康及持之以恆的運動 Eat healthy and exercise regularly.

2. 少喝點酒 Drink less.

3. 學習新事物 Learn something new.

4. 戒煙 Quit smoking.

5. 在工作及生活中取得平衡 Better work/life balance.

6. 做義工 Volunteer.

7. 節省開支 Save money.

8. 整理東西或是人際關係 Get organized.

9. 多讀點書 Read more.

10. 完成家中的所有待辦事項。Finish those around the house "to-do-list".

Martin Luther King, Jr. Day
馬丁路德‧金恩紀念日

節慶源由──簡易版

　　Martin Luther King, Jr. Day is a U.S. holiday. It honors a man who changed history. It is observed on the third Monday of January. In the 1960's in the United States, black people were not free to do what they wanted. Blacks were not allowed in schools for white children. Black people had to sit at the back of the bus.

　　馬丁路德‧金恩紀念日是一個美國的假日。它用來讚揚一位改變歷史的人。它在 1 月的第 3 個禮拜一被慶祝。在 1960 年代的美國，黑人沒有做他們想要做的事的自由。黑人不被允許與白人小孩在同一間學校。黑人必須坐在公車的後方。

　　Martin Luther King, Jr. did not think this was right. It was a sad way for black people to live. He spoke out for peaceful change. He told black people to disobey the laws. They were not to fight. They were to disobey in peace. He told black people to stop riding the bus. King gave a famous speech. He spoke about his dream for blacks and whites to live peacefully together. Some people did not like Dr. King. He was shot and killed because of what he believed.

　　馬丁路德‧金恩博士不認為這是對的。這是一個讓黑人很悲傷的生活方式。他大聲疾呼要和平變革。他告訴黑人違反法律。他們不戰鬥。他們平靜地違抗。他告訴黑人停止搭公車。金恩發表一個著名的演講。他談及他的夢想是黑人與白人和平的共存。有些人不喜歡金恩博士。他因為他的信念而被射殺。

單字大集合

1. **History** *n.* [U] 歷史

   History is full of famous people.
   歷史充滿了知名人士。

2. **Observe** *vi. vt.* 慶祝；觀察

   I observed the holiday by going to the parade.
   我藉由參加遊行來慶祝節日。

3. **Allow** *vi. vt.* 容許；准許

   No one is allowed to be in this room.
   沒有人被允許待在這間房間。

4. **Peaceful** *adj.* 和平的

   It is very quiet and peaceful here.
   那裡非常安靜和和平。

5. **Disobey** *vi. vt.* 不服從；不違抗

   I never disobey my parents.
   我從不違抗我的父母。

6. **Law** *n.* [C] 法律

   Laws help us do the right thing.
   法律幫助我們做對的事。

節慶源由──精彩完整版

Martin Luther King, Jr. Day is a national holiday marking the birth of an important person in recent U.S. history.　It is observed on the third Monday of January, near the birthday of Dr. King.　In the 1960's in the United States, black people were not free to do what they wanted. Blacks were not allowed in schools for white children.　Sometimes, they had to drive right by the school for white children to get to their school.　Black people had to sit at the back of the bus.　If no seats were available for a white person , the black person had to give up his seat.

馬丁路德‧金恩紀念日是一個標記一位美國近代史重要人物生日的國定節日。它在 1 月的第 3 個禮拜一被慶祝，在金恩博士生日的附近。在 1960 年代的美國，黑人沒有做他們想要做的事的自由。黑人不被允許與白人小孩在同一間學校。有時候，為了讓白人小孩到他們的學校，他們必須靠右開車。黑人必須坐在公車的後部。如果白人沒有位子坐，黑人必須放棄他的座位。

Martin Luther King, Jr. did not think this was right.　It was a sad way for black people to live.　He began to speak out for peaceful change.　He encouraged black people to disobey the laws that kept them separated.　They were not to fight, but to quietly disobey.　He led a bus boycott in which black people refused to ride on buses. They would refuse to ride until laws for black people riding the bus were changed. The public bus system faced a serious loss of income if the black people continued to boycott.　Soon the laws were changed.

馬丁路德金恩博士不認為這是對的。這是一個讓黑人很悲傷的生活方式。他開始大聲疾呼要和平變革。他鼓勵黑人違反讓他們被隔離的法律。他們不戰鬥，但平靜地違抗。他領導對公車的抵制，黑人拒絕搭公車。他們拒搭公車直到黑人搭公車的法律改變。如果黑人繼續抵制，公眾公車系統會面臨嚴重的支出損失。很快地法律改變了。

King also led the March on Washington in 1963.　More than 250,000 people filled the area near the capital in Washington D.C.　They demanded an end to segregation in schools.　They spoke out for new laws.　They wanted it to be illegal to discriminate against blacks in the workplace.　Martin Luther King, Jr. gave his most famous speech that day.　It is called his "I Have a Dream" speech.　He spoke about his dream for a United States where blacks and whites could live freely together.

金恩也帶領了西元 1963 年在華盛頓的遊行。超過 25 萬人擠進華盛頓哥倫比亞特區國會大廈附近的空地。他們要求終止學校隔離。他們為了新的法律大聲疾呼。他們想要使在工作場合歧視黑人是不合法的。當天馬丁路德・金恩博士發表了他最著名的演講。叫作「我有一個夢」的演講。他談及他的夢想是在美國讓黑人與白人自由地共存。

On October 14, 1964, King became the youngest recipient of the Nobel Peace Prize. He received this world honor for fighting racial wrongs through nonviolence. King, however, never saw his dream come true. He was shot and killed in 1968. Martin Luther King, Jr. Day was first observed on January 20, 1986. At first, some states resisted observing the holiday. It was officially observed in all 50 states for the first time in 2000. Today, school children learn about Dr. King during January. Schools and many businesses are closed on his holiday in honor of the work he did.

在西元 1964 年 10 月 14 日，金恩成為最年輕的諾貝爾和平獎受獎者。他因為藉由非暴力與種族錯誤奮戰得到這份世界榮耀。金恩，然而，沒有看見他的夢想成真，他在 1968 年被槍殺。馬丁路德金恩博士紀念日第一次被舉行在 1986 年 1 月 20 日。起初，一些州抗拒舉辦這個假日。它在 2000 年在美國 50 州正式地慶祝。時至今日，學童在 1 月期間學習金恩博士的事蹟。學校和許多企業在他的紀念日都會放假紀念他的所作所為。

單字大集合

1. **Available** *adj.* 有空的
She was not available when I called.
當我打給她時她沒有空。

2. **Boycott** *vt.* 抵制
If you want to boycott a store, you must not ever shop there.
如果你想要抵制一個店家，你必須再也不去那購物。

3. **Segregation** *n.* [U] 種族隔離
Segregation was common in the southern United States.
種族隔離在美國南部是很常見的。

4. **Discriminate** *vi. vt.* 區別
I hope you do not discriminate against people that are different than you.
我希望你不要歧視不同於你的人。

5. **Illegal** *adj.* 非法的
It is illegal to steal.
偷竊是非法的。

6. **Recipient** *n.* [C] 收件人
The recipient of my letter did not write back.
我的信沒有寫收件人。

7. **Nonviolence** *n.* [U] 非暴力
It is good when change can happen with nonviolence.
當改變可以伴隨著非暴力發生是很好的。

8. **Resist** *vi. vt.* 抵抗；抗拒
My dog resisted when I tried to pull him my direction.
我的狗抵抗，當我試圖把他拉到我的方向。

閱讀測驗

1. What did a black person have to do if there was not a seat for a white person?
   當沒有位子給白人坐時，黑人必須做什麼？
   (a) Wave a flag in the air. 在空中搖旗子。
   (b) Ask the person next to him to move over. 要求他旁邊的人移開。
   (c) Give up his seat for the white person. 為了白人放棄他的位子。

2. Why did black people stop riding the buses? 為什麼黑人停止搭公車？
   (a) They got too hot on the bus. 他們在公車裡太熱。
   (b) They held a boycott until the laws were changed.
       他們發起抵制直到法律被改變。
   (c) They got new cars and didn't need the bus.
       他們得到新車，不需要公車。

3. What was Martin Luther King, Jr.'s dream? 馬丁路德‧金恩的夢是什麼？
   (a) That whites and blacks could live peacefully together.
       白人和黑人可以和平共處。
   (b) That people could travel the world more often.
       人們可以更常環遊世界。
   (c) That his family had a better house to live in.
       他的家庭有更好的房子可以住。

4. Martin Luther King Hr. became the youngest recipient of the Nobel Peace Prize
   because _____.
   馬丁路德金恩博士成為最年輕的諾貝爾和平獎得主是因為_____。
   (a) He was a doctor. 他是一個博士。
   (b) He gave a tremendously wonderful contribution on his studies.
       他在研究上做出超棒的貢獻。
   (c) He fought racial wrongs through nonviolence.
       透過非暴力的方式為種族錯誤奮戰。

活動慶典和習俗

　　由著名的網際網路服務提供商，美國線上（AOL Inc.）在 2005 年時所舉辦的票選活動中，馬丁·路德·金恩（Martin Luther King, Jr.）被選為美國最偉大的人物第三位。而定在 1 月第三個星期一的馬丁·路德·金恩日（Martin Luther King, Jr. Day），則是用來紀念這位在美國歷史上有著深遠影響的黑人民權運動領袖（leader in the African-American Civil Rights Movement）。甚至有學者認為如果沒有馬丁·路德·金恩致力於推動黑白種族平等，及黑人自由工作的權力，那今日的美國就不會有歐巴馬這位美國歷史上第一位非裔的總統。而在 2009 年時，歐巴馬總統也選擇在他就職的前一天向這一位偉大的黑人導師致敬。

　　馬丁·路德·金恩生於 1929 年 1 月 15 日，是一位牧師，因為採用「非暴力」（Nonviolence）方式來推動美國的民權運動而舉世聞名，其中以他在 1963 年時「向華盛頓進軍」（March on Washington）這一場美國歷史上最盛大的人權政治集會中所發表的「我有一個夢想」（I have a dream）演說最為撼動人心，在他的演說中深切的刻畫出種族和諧的美好遠景。金恩牧師在 1964 年得到了諾貝爾和平獎（Nobel Peace Prize），成為當代自由主義的象徵。而美國國會也在當年通過民權法案，宣布種族隔離（racial segregation）及歧視（racism/ racial discrimination）政策為非法政策。在 1968 年 4 月 4 日，金恩牧師被白人優越主義者刺殺（assassinate）身亡。1986 年，由雷根總統簽署法令，定立一月的第三個禮拜一為馬丁·路德·金恩日為聯邦法定假日，但受到幾個州的反對，一直到 2000 年，才完成在全美 50 州同時放假紀念。但目前仍有幾個州沒有以金恩牧師之名來紀念。

　　在馬丁·路德·金恩日前一天的禮拜天，教堂會舉行金恩牧師的追思會，而在紀念日當天，全美 398 個國家公園以免費入園的方式紀念金恩牧師，提倡以參觀國家公園，或是歷史紀念地，來瞭解美國民權運動及非裔美國人的卓越貢獻。而各地也會有遊行，及在聚會中討論金恩牧師的貢獻，不分種族的美國夢（American dream）實現，談談生活中的事，將這一個沈重的話題以生活化的方式融入，就像閒話家常一般。

實用生活會話

Q1: Katy, I need your help. Mike's preschool class has been talking about the M.L.K. Day. What is M.L.K. Day?

凱蒂，我需要你的幫助。麥克的中班課程已經在教 M.L.K. 日了。M.L.K. 日是什麼節日啊？

A1: It is the day to commemorate Martin Luther King, Jr.

是紀念馬丁・路德・金恩的節日。

Q2: Oh, I think I know him. We call him Dr. King, and he's the one who delivered "I have a dream" speech on 1963. Am I right?

喔，我想我知道他。我們叫他金恩博士，他在 1963 年時曾發表「我有一個夢想」的演說。對嗎？

A2: Yes, that's correct.

是的，完全正確。

Q3: How should I explain this holiday to Mike?

那我應該如何向麥克解釋這個節日？

A3: hmmm... It's a good question. You can explain to him about the segregation, and how wrong-headed that was. Use some examples, and let him understand that all men are created equal.

嗯……這是個好問題。妳可以跟他解釋什麼是種族隔離，及這個政策有多麼的不合理。用幾個例子，來讓他瞭解人人生而平等的道理。

實用單句這樣說

- King organized the 1963 March on Washington, and delivered his "I have a dream" speech.
  金恩牧師組織了 1963 年的「向華盛頓前進」的活動，並且發表了「我有一個夢想」的演說。

- Martin Luther King, Jr. considered himself as a disciple of Gandhi.
  馬丁‧路德‧金恩自認為是甘地的信徒。

- Dr. King was the leader of the civil rights movement.
  金恩博士是民權運動的領袖。

- Martin Luther King, Jr. Day is an American federal holiday marking the birthday of Rev. Dr. Martin Luther King, Jr. （Rev.- Reverend 牧師; Dr.- Doctor 博士）
  馬丁‧路德‧金恩日是以牧師馬丁‧路德‧金恩博士的生日來作為美國聯邦假日。

- The Martin Luther King, Jr. Day is observed on the third Monday of January which is around the time of King's birthday, January 15.The floating holiday is similar to holidays set under the Uniform Monday Holiday Act.
  馬丁‧路德‧金恩日被定在一月的第三個星期一，是在金恩生日 1 月 15 日的前後。跟其他美國統一假期法案所制訂的假日一樣，沒有固定的日期。

- Martin Luther King, Jr. Day is the latest Federal Holiday.
  馬丁‧路德‧金恩日是最新的聯邦假日。

互動時刻真有趣

● 我有一個夢想 I have a dream

　　每個人都有夢想，那你的夢想是什麼呢？金恩博士在 1963 年時發表了「我有一個夢想」的演說，下面節錄了部分的演說內容。請和孩子一同分享，看看致力於民權運動的金恩博士的訴求吧！

Let us not wallow in the valley of despair. I say to you, my friends, we have the difficulties of today and tomorrow.

讓我們不要陷入絕望的深淵。聽我說，我的朋友，我們今後仍有無數的困難。

I still have a dream. It is a dream deeply rooted in the American dream.

我仍然有一個夢想。這個夢想深深的扎根在美國的夢想之中。

I have a dream that one day this nation will rise up and live out the true meaning of its creed: "We hold these truths to be self-evident, that all men are created equal."

我夢想有一天，這個國家會站起來，實踐其信條的真諦。「我們認為這些真理是不言而喻的，人人生而平等」。

I have a dream that one day on the red hills of Georgia, the sons of former slaves and the sons of former slave owners will be able to sit down together at the table of brotherhood.

我夢想有一天，在喬治亞的紅山上，昔日奴隸的兒子和昔日奴隸主人的兒子能同聚在一桌共敘兄弟情誼。

I have a dream that one day even the state of Mississippi, a state sweltering with the heat of injustice, sweltering with the heat of oppression, will be transformed into an oasis of freedom and justice.

我夢想有一天，甚至是在密西西比州，這一個正義蕩然無存，到處充滿壓迫的地方，也能成為自由與正義的綠洲。

I have a dream that my four little children will one day live in a nation where they will not be judged by the color of their skin but by the content of their character.

我夢想有一天，我的 4 個孩子所居住的國度不會依他們的膚色，而是以他們的品格優劣來做評價。

Groundhog Day
土撥鼠節

節慶源由——簡易版

There is really only one thing people do on Groundhog day. They wait to hear if winter is over. If it is cloudy when a groundhog comes out from its burrow on February 2nd, spring will come early. If it is sunny, the groundhog will see its shadow. When he does, he will retreat back into his burrow. Winter will continue for six more weeks.

在土撥鼠節人們真的只做一件事。他們等著聽到冬天是否結束了。如果是陰天，當土撥鼠在 2 月 2 日從洞裡出來，春天將會提早來臨。如果是晴天，土撥鼠會看到自己的影子。當他看到自己的影子，牠將會撤退回牠的洞穴，冬天將會再繼續六個禮拜。

What is a groundhog? It is a common rodent. They are native to most of Canada and the eastern U.S. They are mainly seen in fields and by streams. Groundhogs eat grass and other plants all summer. They hibernate from the first frost in the fall until spring.

什麼是土撥鼠？牠是一種常見的囓齒動物。牠們大部分原生於加拿大和美國東部。牠們主要在田野和小河流旁被看見。土撥鼠整個夏天吃草和其他植物。牠們從秋天第一次霜凍冬眠到春天。

The most well-known groundhog is Phil. For over 100 years, he has been the one to watch on Groundhog Day. Is there any truth to the story? Since 1887, Phil's weather prediction has been correct less than half the time.

最知名的土撥鼠是菲爾。在過去一百年，牠在土撥鼠節一直是被關注的對象。這故事有任何的真實性嗎？從西元 1887 年起，菲爾的氣候預測已經準確了少於一半一點點的次數。

單字大集合

1. Cloudy　*adj.*　多雲的

If it is a cloudy day, it might rain.
如果是陰天，可能會下雨。

2. Burrow　*n.* [C]　洞穴

How does an animal dig a hole for its burrow?
動物如何為自己的住處挖洞？

3. Shadow　*n.* [C,U]　陰暗處；影子

My dog is always afraid of his shadow.
我的狗總是害怕牠的影子。

4. Native　*adj.*　本土的；原生的

If you are born in Taiwan, you are native to Taiwan.
如果你出生在台灣，你就是原生於台灣。

5. Frost　*n.* [C,U]　霜

I love seeing frost on the ground in the fall.
我喜歡看在秋天看地上的霜。

6. Correct　*adj.*　正確的

My answer is always correct.
我的答案總是正確的。

節慶源由──精彩完整版

Groundhog Day is a unique day. There is really only one thing people do on Groundhog day. They wait to hear if winter is over. Hopefully, spring is on the way. Folklore says that if it is cloudy when a groundhog emerges from its burrow on February 2nd, then spring will come early. If it is sunny, the groundhog will see its shadow. When he does, he will retreat back into his burrow. Then, winter will continue for six more weeks.

土撥鼠節是個獨特的日子。在土撥鼠節人們真的只做一件事。他們等著聽到冬天是否結束了。抱著希望地期待春天已經在路上了。民間傳說如果是陰天，當土撥鼠在 2 月 2 日從洞裡出來，春天將會提早來臨。如果是晴天，土撥鼠會看到自己的影子。當他看到自己的影子，牠將會撤退回牠的洞穴。然後，冬天將會再繼續六個禮拜。

What is a groundhog? It is a common rodent, also called a woodchuck. They are native to most of Canada and the eastern U.S. They are mainly seen in fields and by streams. Groundhogs gorge themselves on grass, vegetables and tree bark all summer. Then, they hibernate from the first frost in the fall until spring.

什麼是土撥鼠？牠是一種常見的囓齒動物，也叫作 woodchuck。牠們大部分原生於加拿大和美國東部。牠們主要在田野和小河流旁被看見。土撥鼠整個夏天讓自己在草、蔬菜和樹皮裡狼吞虎嚥。然後，牠們從秋天第一次霜凍冬眠到春天。

The most well-known Groundhog Day celebrations are in the state of Pennsylvania, in the U.S. There are large events with speeches, food and entertainment. At some events there, the only language that can be spoken is German. If you speak English, you must pay a nickel, dime or quarter for each word you speak.

最知名的土撥鼠節慶典在美國的賓州。有演講、餐飲、娛樂的大型活動。在那裏有些活動的唯一語言是德文。如果你說英文，你必須為你說的每個字付 5 分鎳幣、1 角硬幣或 25 分硬幣。

Pennsylvania is also home to the most famous groundhog. His name is Phil. He has been the official weather predicting groundhog for over 100 years. If Groundhog Day is on a Saturday, up to 15,000 people will gather to watch him to emerge from his stump.

賓州也是最有名的土撥鼠的家。牠的名字是菲爾。牠成為正式的天氣預報土撥鼠已經持續超過 100 年了。如果土撥鼠節是在禮拜六，多達 15000 人將聚集在一起，觀看牠從樹的根株裡出現。

One newspaper reported that people come from all over the world to see it. They say they "can't believe we do this every year. They can't believe we stand out in the cold and wait for a rodent to emerge from a stump." This tradition is thought to come from ancient Europe. In folklore there, a special bear was the indicator of spring, instead of the groundhog.

有一報紙報導全世界的人們都在觀看這個。他們說他們「不相信我們每年都這麼做。他們不相信我們在寒冷中還站在外面，並等待囓齒動物從根株裡出現。」這個傳統是從古歐洲那想出來的。在那的民俗，一隻特別的熊，反而是春天的指標，而不是土撥鼠。

So, is there any truth to the legend? According to records kept since 1887, Phil's weather predictions have been correct 39% of the time.

這故事有任何的真實性嗎？從西元 1887 年起，菲爾的氣候預測已經準確了 39% 的次數。

單字大集合

1. Unique *adj.* 獨特的

The colors used in this painting are very unique.
用在這張水彩畫的顏色非常獨特。

2. Folklore *n.* [U] 民間傳說

The truth of folklore can always be questioned.
民間傳說的真實性總是被打上問號。

3. Emerge *vi.* 出現

This flower emerges in the same place every spring.
這朵花每個春天都出現在同一個地方。

4. Rodent *n.* [C] 囓齒動物

Some examples of a rodent are mice and groundhogs.
囓齒動物的一些例子有小老鼠和土撥鼠。

5. Gorge *vi. vt.* 狼吞虎嚥

If I gorge myself on all food, I will feel sick!
如果我讓自己在所有食物裡狼吞虎嚥，我將會生病！

6. Hibernate *vi.* 冬眠

I would like to hibernate all winter, like some animals do.
我喜歡整個冬天冬眠，像有些動物做的一樣。

7. Predict *vi. vt.* 作預料；預料

The weather man is predicting rain for the weekend.
天氣預報員正在預測週末會下雨。

8. Indicator *n.* [C] 指標

Dark clouds are a good indicator of rain to come.
黑雲是大雨將至的一個好指標。

閱讀測驗

1. What will happen if the groundhog sees its shadow?
   如果土撥鼠看到牠的影子，將會發生什麼事？
   (a) It will get scared. 牠會變得害怕。
   (b) There will be six more weeks of winter. 冬天將會多六周。
   (c) He will get really hungry. 牠將會變得非常飢餓。

2. At some groundhog events, what must you do if you speak English?
   在有些土撥鼠活動上，如果你說英文的話就必須要做什麼？
   (a) Eat a whole pie. 吃下一整個派。
   (b) Tell everyone you're sorry. 跟每個人說你很抱歉。
   (c) Pay money for each word you say. 為你說的每個字付錢。

3. What is the name of the official weather predicting groundhog?
   正式的天氣預測土撥鼠的名字是什麼？
   (a) Thomas 湯瑪士。
   (b) Phil 菲爾。
   (c) Mary 瑪莉。

4. How many percentage did the groundhog's weather prediction have?
   土撥鼠的天氣預測是多少百分比呢？
   (a) It had 45%
   (b) It had 39%
   (c) It had 35%

活動慶典和習俗

傳說中，在賓州（Pennsylvania）龐斯塔維尼（Punxsutawney）小鎮有一隻十分厲害的土撥鼠，已經活了一百多歲了，他最重要的工作就是在每年的 2 月 2 日出來預測今年的天氣，而這一天被稱為土撥鼠節（Groundhog Day）。其實菲爾這一種品種的土撥鼠壽命大約是在 6 至 8 年左右，但在小鎮居民及菲爾廣大粉絲群的心中認為，菲爾在每年的夏天都會喝下一小口的神奇的混合飲料靈藥（a sip of magic punch），一小口就能延長 7 年的壽命，所以這一百多年來的傳統活動，都是由同一位菲爾來負責的。至於其他地區的土撥鼠預報，僅供參考，要聽就聽菲爾的，因為「薑是老的辣」（Experience talks）。而且菲爾在龐斯塔維尼小鎮可是有「先知中的先知、土撥鼠之王、鐵嘴中的鐵嘴」（Seer of Seers, King of Groundhogs, Prognosticator of Prognosticators）的封號。

其實這一個盛行於北美洲的傳統活動，最初是源自於德國，被德國的移民帶入北美洲，是農民用以觀測天氣的一種方式。在德國則是用獾（badger）或是刺蝟（hedgehog）來觀察影子，藉以預測天氣。一般認為選在 2 月 2 日則是與聖燭節（Candlemas）有關，在歐洲的古老傳統中會以聖燭節當天的天氣，來推測春天是否即將到臨。

在每年 2 月 2 日的早上 7 點半，在龐斯塔維尼小鎮的氣象預報儀式就會開始，而許多民眾則是在半夜就會到菲爾的洞穴附近屏息以待。15 位身穿燕尾服（tuxedo）及頭戴禮帽的土撥鼠俱樂部成員出現後，會在太陽升起之後，由主持人持樹枝敲擊菲爾的洞口，等待他出洞口預測今年春天是否會提早降臨。

實用生活會話

A1: Oh, Phil's on TV. Give me the remote control. I want to see Phil's weather forecast.

喔，菲爾上電視了。給我遙控器。我要看菲爾的氣象預報。

Q1: Phil Who? Is he famous?

哪個菲爾？他有名嗎？

A2: Yes, he is very famous. He is a celebrity groundhog.

對，他名氣可大了。他是一隻名人級的土撥鼠。

Q2: What? How can a groundhog make the weather report?

什麼？一隻土撥鼠怎麼播報氣象？

A3: It is an old tradition in Pennsylvania. According to the tradition, if Phil sees his shadow and returns to his hole, he has predicted 6 more weeks of winter-like weather.

這是賓州的流傳已久的傳統。根據傳統，如果菲爾看到他自己的影子就會鑽回洞穴裡，代表著冬天還會再持續 6 個星期。

Q3: How about if he does not see his shadow?

那如果他沒有看到他的影子呢？

A4: Good question. If he doesn't see his shadow and emerges from his hole, he has predicted an "early spring".

這個問題很好。如果他沒有看到他自己的影子，從洞裡出來的話，那代表春天即將到來。

實用單句這樣說

- If Candlemas be fair and bright, winter has another flight. If Candlemas brings clouds and rain, winter will not come again.
  如果聖燭節當天天氣晴朗，冬天還會持續。如果聖燭節當天陰雨連綿，冬天即將遠離。

- Punxsutawney Phil, WiartonWille and Balzac Billy are the three most famous groundhogs of weather prophets.
  龐斯塔維尼的菲爾、威爾頓的威力及巴爾札克的比利是最出名的 3 隻土撥鼠天氣預報者。

- Phil has been making predictions since 1887 and will probably continue.
  菲爾從 1887 年就開始做預測，並可能會一直持續下去。

- Groundhog Day is a 1993 classic American comedy film.
  土撥鼠節（中文名稱是今天暫時停止）是一部 1993 年的經典美國喜劇電影。

- According to the Groundhog Club, Phil speaks to the Club President in "Groundhogese" after making the prediction, and his prediction is translated by the Club President for the whole world.
  據土撥鼠俱樂部表示，在做出預測之後，菲爾會用「土撥鼠語」告知俱樂部主席結果，再由主席翻譯將預測的結果告知全世界。

- Weather Groundhog Phil was "indicted" by being accused of fraud as winter continues.
  氣象主「撥」菲爾被「起訴」，罪名是詐欺，因為冬天仍持續當中。

互動時刻真有趣

　　美加地區最具人氣的土撥鼠氣象主播，不但長相可愛討喜，連土撥鼠日的童詩也十分有趣，請帶著孩子一起唸唸看喔！

Groundhog, groundhog what do you see? I see the sunshine looking at me! Sunshine, sunshine what do you see? I see a shadow looking at me! Shadow, shadow what do you see? Six more weeks of winter there will be!	土撥鼠，土撥鼠你看到什麼？ 我看到陽光正看著我！ 陽光，陽光你看到什麼？ 我看到影子正看著我！ 影子，影子你看到什麼？ 六週的冬天多停留！
I see a little groundhog, fat and brown. He's popping up to look around. If he sees his shadow, down he'll go. Six more weeks of winter- oh, no!	我看到一隻小土撥鼠， 褐色的毛毛，圓又胖。 探出頭來四處望， 如果看到影子就往洞裡走。 再多六週的冬天怎麼過！

Valentine's Day
西洋情人節

節慶源由──簡易版

Valentine's Day is on February 14th. It is celebrated in many countries, but mostly in the west. Around Valentine's Day, you start to see hearts of all shapes and sizes. People give heart-shaped cards called valentines. Chocolate comes in red heart-shaped boxes. People hang red paper hearts in their windows.

2 月 14 日是西洋情人節。西洋情人節被許多國家慶祝,但主要是被西方國家。快到西洋情人節的時候,你開始會看到各種形狀大小的愛心。人們贈送稱為「情人卡」的心型卡片。巧克力放在紅色心型盒子。人們在窗戶掛紅色的紙愛心。

Children give and receive the most valentines. In many schools, students give a valentine to each person in their class. The card is often attached to a small box of heart-shaped candy. Parents often give valentines to their kids, too. The children might even get a valentine from their grandparents. And grandparents like to put a few dollars in the card, too!

孩子們贈送和收到最多情人卡。在許多學校,學生送每個班上同學一張情人卡。這張卡時常被貼在裝滿心型糖果的小盒子。父母也時常送情人卡給他們的小孩。小孩們甚至會收到來自祖父母的情人卡。祖父母也喜歡放一些硬幣在卡片裡!

In the evening, couples go to a nice restaurant to eat. It is common for the guy to give his girl a red rose(or a dozen red roses）to show his love. If he doesn't do this, he should at least give her chocolate!

晚上，情侶們會去一家好的餐廳用餐。男生給他的女孩一朵紅玫瑰（或一打紅玫瑰）表示他的愛意是很常見的。如果男生沒有這麼做，他應該至少送女孩巧克力！

單字大集合

1. Size *n.* [C,U] 尺寸；大小；多少

The shirts came in many different sizes.
許多不同尺寸的襯衫。

2. Window *n.* [C] 窗戶

You can see the sunset if you look out the front windows.
如果你看一下前面的窗口，你可以看到日落。

3. Receive *vi. vt.* 收到

I hope to receive many valentines this year.
我希望今年收到很多情人卡。

4. Student *n.* [C] 學生

This year's students are the best I have ever seen.
今年的學生是我見過最棒的。

5. Grandparent *n.* [C] 祖父；祖母；祖父母

My grandparents live very far away.
我的祖父母住得非常遙遠。

6. Dollar *n.* [C] 美元

I got twenty-five dollars for my birthday.
我因為生日得到 25 美元。

節慶源由——精彩完整版

Valentine's Day is actually Saint Valentine's Day. It is named after a saint from long ago whose name was Valentine. There are three different Saint Valentines named in church history. Very little is known of any of them. Then how did Valentine's Day become so popular? Several poets in the 1300's wrote about love coming on Valentine's Day. By the 1400's, it had become an occasion on which people expressed their love for each other. They did this with cards known as valentines. From that time on, Valentine's Day has been connected with love.

西洋情人節事實上是聖范倫坦斯日。它是以一位很久以前叫范倫坦斯的聖徒命名。有三個不同的聖范倫坦斯日命名於教會歷史。非常少人知道它們任何一個。然後西洋情人節是如何變得如此流行呢？許多 14 世紀的詩人寫到有關於西洋情人節的愛意。到了 1400 年代，西洋情人節已經變成一個讓人們互相表示愛意的節慶。人們藉由大家熟知的情人卡來展現愛意。從那個時候開始，西洋情人節已經與愛有連結。

Today, Valentine's Day is celebrated on February 14th. It is celebrated in many countries, but mostly in the west. Modern Valentine's Day symbols include hearts of all shapes and sizes. People give heart-shaped valentines. Chocolate comes in red heart-shaped boxes. People hang red paper hearts in their windows and on the walls. The winged Cupid is also popular. It is said that if Cupid sends his arrow through your heart, you will fall in love with the next person you see.

時至今日，西洋情人節於 2 月 14 日被舉行。它在許多國家被慶祝，但主要是被西方國家。現代的西洋情人節符號包括各種形狀大小的愛心。人們贈送心型的情人卡。巧克力放在紅色心型盒子。人們在窗戶或在牆上掛紅色的心紙。有翅膀的邱比特也很流行。據說如果丘比特用他的箭射穿你的心，你就會愛上你下一個看見的人。

The people who give and receive the most valentines are certainly children. In many schools, students give a valentine to each person in their class. This way no person will feel left out on Valentine's Day. The card is often attached to a small box of heart-shaped candy. Parents often give valentines to their kids, too. If the children are really lucky, they will even get a valentine from their grandparents. And grandparents like to put a few dollars in the card, too!

孩子們贈送和收到最多情人卡。在許多學校，學生送每個班上同學一張情人卡。這樣子就沒有人在西洋情人節感覺被冷落。這張卡時常被貼在裝滿心型糖果的小盒子。父母也時常送情人卡。如果小孩們非常幸運，他們甚至會收到來自祖父母的情人卡。祖父母也喜歡放一些硬幣在卡片裡！

In the evening, couples go to a nice restaurant to eat. It is common for the guy to give his girl a red rose（or a dozen red roses）to show his love. Most women love to receive chocolate, as well.

晚上，情侶們會去一家好的餐廳用餐。男生給他的女孩一朵紅玫瑰（或一打紅玫瑰）表示他的愛意是很常見的。大部分女生也喜歡收到巧克力。

In the 1980s, the diamond industry began to promote Valentine's Day as an occasion for giving jewelry.

In the past, women made fancy Valentines with paper and lace. What used to be a homemade holiday has become one that can cost you a lot of money, if you are in love!

在 1980 年代，鑽石工業開始促進西洋情人節成為一個送珠寶的節慶。在過去，女生會用紙與蕾絲做高級情人卡。以前手工製禮的節日如今變成一個得花大把錢的節日，如果你正在戀愛的話。

單字大集合

1. Occasion *n.* [C] 場合

I wore my best dress for the occasion.
我為了這個場合穿了我最好的禮服。

2. Express *vt.* 表達

She expressed concern for her friend who was sick.
她對她生病的朋友表達關心。

3. Cupid 丘比特

Girls like to think that Cupid will shoot his arrow at the boy they like.
女孩想著丘比特將祂的箭射向她喜歡的男孩。

4. Certainly *adv.* 無疑地

You certainly did a beautiful job on your project!
你無疑地在你的項目上做得很好！

5. Attach *vi. vt.* 附屬；繫上

We attached the balloon to the flowers.
我們將花繫上氣球。

6. Restaurant *n.* [C] 餐廳

There is an Italian restaurant nearby that we really like.
有一間附近的意大利餐廳是我們真的很喜歡的。

7. Jewelry *n.* [U] 珠寶

She always wears fancy jewelry.
她總是佩戴華麗的珠寶。

8. Homemade *adj.* 自製的

The kids gave homemade cookies to their teachers.
孩子送手工餅乾給他們的老師。

閱讀測驗

1. How did Valentine's Day become popular?
   情人節是如何變得受歡迎的？
   (a) Kids started to give their friends chocolate on that day.
       孩子開始在那天給他們的朋友巧克力。
   (b) Poets in the 1300's wrote poems about love coming on Valentine's Day.
       1300 年代的詩人寫了關於西洋情人節愛意的詩。
   (c) Saint Valentine started giving cards to all the girls he loved.
       聖范倫坦斯開始送卡片給所有他愛的女生。

2. What is the most common symbol of Valentine's Day?
   西洋情人節最常見的符號是什麼？
   (a) A red heart. 紅色的心型。
   (b) A red cat. 紅色的貓。
   (c) A red dress. 紅色的禮服。

3. What do guys commonly give their girls on Valentine's Day?
   小伙子在情人節通常送他們的女孩什麼？
   (a) A new car 一輛新車。
   (b) A new house 一棟新房子。
   (c) A red rose（or a dozen of them!）一朵紅玫瑰。（或一打！）

活動慶典和習俗

根據台灣媒體在 2013 年 2 月時所做的調查，情人節（Valentine's Day, Saint Valentine's Day）是全台灣上班族最討厭過的節日，理由則是對單身族群（singles）帶來心理上的壓力，而對有另一半的上班族（salarymen）則帶來財政上的壓力。原因應是來自於情人節的「過度商品化」（over commercialization），商家總是會在情人節到來之前，推出五花八門的促銷策略（promotion strategy）。而深受日本流行風潮影響的台灣，除了我國傳統的七夕情人節之外，再加上西洋情人節及日本流行的白色情人節，一年 3 次的情人節，著實讓人有些吃不消。

撇開情人節的商業化行為不論，情人節其實是一個具有美好含意的日子。一般人所熟知的情人節起源的版本是在西元三世紀時，古羅馬皇帝認為未婚男子才能成為優良的士兵，於是頒佈了禁婚令，但有一位叫瓦倫丁（Valentine）的修士，不畏威脅，仍然為相愛的情侶證婚，主持婚禮，此舉為他帶來牢獄之災，並因此在 2 月 14 日這一天被處以死刑。根據記載，教宗在西元 496 年時廢除牧神節（有部分學者推測古代慶祝情人節的習俗與這節日有關），把他被處決的那一天訂為聖瓦倫丁日，隨著時代的演變，聖瓦倫丁不顧禁令為相愛的情侶證婚而犧牲的精神，讓原本為宗教節日的的 2 月 14 日逐漸的在中世紀時期以情人節的姿態而盛行起來。

中世紀時，情人節在英國最為盛行。當時流行將未婚男女的名字依性別放入兩個不同的盒子，同時抽出一對男女互換禮物，在未來的一年中，女子為該名男子的 "Valentine"，女子會在男子的衣袖上秀上自己的名字，而男子則必須盡到保護和照顧 Valentine 的任務，之後 Valentine 在許多詩人的歌頌中成為情人的代言詞，而情人節卡片在英文中也稱做是 valentine。而在情人節時送花、糖果點心類的禮物及約會等的習俗則是在當時的英國就已盛行並一直沿用至現在。

實用生活會話

Q1: What's wrong with you? You look horrible. Does anyone owe you money?
你怎麼了？你看起來有點糟，有人欠你錢不還嗎？

A1: Oh, it's you. I just got dumped.
喔，是你啊。我剛被甩了。

Q2: Why she broke up with you on Valentine's Day?
她為什麼選在情人節這一天和你分手啊？

A2: Sigh, I forgot today is Valentine's Day. Amy said that I'm not romantic, and I don't care about her.
唉，我忘了今天是情人節。艾美說我不夠浪漫，不夠在乎她。

Q3: I think she's just too angry. Maybe you should try to apologize properly, if you really do care about her. Do you agree with me?
我想她應該是太生氣了，也許你應該好好地跟她道個歉，如果你真的在乎她的話。你同意我的話嗎？

A3: Yes, I think you are right; it's all my fault, I shouldn't make her feel ignorant. I want to apologize to her again. Thanks, buddy!
對，我想你是對的，都是我的錯，我不應該讓她感覺被忽略了。我要再跟她道個歉。謝啦，兄弟！

Q4: Cheer up! Things will go by well. Don't worry too much.
加油！事情會進行的順利的。不要太擔心。

A4: Thanks! Your encouragement makes me take a breath at ease.
謝謝！你的鼓勵讓我鬆了一口氣。

實用單句這樣說

- In South Korea and Japan, women give candies or chocolates to men on Valentine's Day.
  在南韓及日本，在情人節時女性會送男性糖果或是巧克力。

- In 18th-century England, lovers express their love for each other by gifting flowers, confectionery, and sending greeting card on Valentine's Day.
  在 18 世紀的英國，情侶之間會在情人節時互相送鮮花、糖果類的點心，及寄情人節賀卡。

- Heart-shaped outline, doves, and figures of the winged Cupid are the symbols of Valentine's Day.
  心形圖案、白鴿及有翅膀的邱比特是情人節的象徵圖案。

- How do you spend this Valentine's Day? Being single or double?
  你情人節怎麼過的？一個人還是兩個人過？

- If you plan to dine out on Valentine's Day, you should probably nail down a reservation soon.
  你如果在情人節時打算出去外面吃飯的話，你應該要趕緊的去確認訂位。

- Valentine's Day is considered by some people to be a "Hallmark Holiday" due to its commercialization.
  由於過度的商業化，有些人認為情人節是「賀曼日」。（Hallmark 是美國具百年以上歷史的賀卡大廠，除了賀卡之外，還販售許多種商品，有衣服，文具，玩具，3C 配件等，Hallmark Holiday 一般用來稱過度商業化而失去其宗教性或是紀念意義的節日。）

互動時刻真有趣

● 國際樂單日（International Quirkyalone Day）

在 1999 年跨年夜時，Sasha Cagen 跟她的朋友們在紐約地下鐵的月台上，他們是一群快樂的單身貴族，在談話之間，Sasha 發想出了 "quirkyalone" 這一個字，並在雜誌中發表了這個名詞，並衍生出完整的概念及定義。

Quirkyalone 在中文中稱樂單族：是指享受單身生活，也不會排斥與人交往，不願意單純只因為在意別人的眼光而約會

Quirkyalone: Someone who enjoys being single（but is not opposed to being in a relationship,）and generally prefers alone rather than dating for sake of it.

在世界各地，單身人口有日漸增加的趨勢。而在這些未婚人口中有相當高的比例是樂單族。而這個族群的特徵大約可歸納成以下 7 點
1. 自戀
2. 善於安排生活，並享受獨處
3. 教育程度高，涉獵的知識面廣泛
4. 理想主義者
5. 喜歡追求美好級奢華的事物
6. 興趣愛好十分廣泛
7. 有自己的社交圈及知己好友

她的概念受到美國相當多樂單族的支持，進而在 2003 年發起了國際樂單日，訂在每年的 2 月 14 日，成為厭倦過度商業化的情人節的人士歡迎，並在美國，加拿大，澳洲及英國都有相關的慶祝活動。

St. Patrick's Day
聖派翠克節

節慶源由──簡易版

St. Patrick's Day used to be a church holiday. It honored Saint Patrick, a famous holy man. He died on March 17th. On that day every year, Irish families went to church in the morning. In the afternoon, they danced, and feasted on Irish bacon and cabbage.

聖派翠克節過去是一個教堂節日。它用來紀念聖派翠克，一個知名的聖人。他死於 3 月 17 日。每年的那一天，愛爾蘭家庭早上上教堂。下午，他們跳舞，享用愛爾蘭培根與甘藍菜。

In the 1800's some Irish people moved to America. They held parades every year, playing bagpipes and drums. Today, St. Patrick's Day is very popular in Ireland, the U.S., and Canada. You do not have to be Irish to enjoy it!

在 19 世紀一些愛爾蘭人遷至美洲。他們每年舉辦遊行，演奏風笛與鼓。今日，聖派翠克節在美國，愛爾蘭與加拿大非常地風行。即使你不是愛爾蘭人你也可以樂在其中。

Green is the color of the Irish. On St. Patrick's Day, people dress in green clothes and hats. They paint their faces green. Even some rivers are colored green for the day. There are parades and feasts of corned beef and cabbage. St. Patrick's Day is not a legal holiday, but it is very popular.

綠色是愛爾蘭的顏色。在聖派翠克節，人們穿綠衣戴綠帽。他們將他們的臉塗成綠色。在那天有些河甚至被塗成綠色。許多的遊行與有鹽醃牛肉跟甘藍菜的盛宴。聖派翠克節不是一個法定假日，但它非常地流行。

單字大集合

1. Patrick 派翠克

We named our baby boy Patrick.

我們將我們的男嬰兒取名為派翠克。

2. Holy　*adj.* 聖潔的

The holy men gathered at the temple.

聖人聚集在廟宇裡。

3. Irish　*n.* [U] 愛爾蘭人

If you are born in Ireland, you might be Irish.

如果你出生在愛爾蘭，你可能是愛爾蘭人。

4. Bacon　*n.* [U] 培根

I don't like pigs, but I like to eat bacon!

我不喜歡豬，但我喜歡吃培根。

5. Popular　*adj.* 受歡迎的

The smart kids are very popular at school.

聰明的小孩們在學校非常受歡迎。

6. Corned Beef 鹽醃牛肉

Not many people like to eat corned beef.

不是許多人喜歡吃鹽醃牛肉。

節慶源由──精彩完整版

St. Patrick's Day was at first a church holiday. It honored Saint Patrick of Ireland. Saint Patrick was actually born in Great Britain. He was kidnapped and brought to Ireland at age 16. He later escaped, but returned to Ireland to bring the Christian faith to its people. He died on March 17th. On that day every year, Irish families remembered his death. They would attend church in the morning. In the afternoon, they would dance, drink and feast on Irish bacon and cabbage. It has been a holiday in Ireland for over 1000 years.

聖派翠克節起初是一個教堂假日。它用來紀念愛爾蘭的聖派翠克。聖派翠克事實上出生在英國。他在 16 歲的時候被綁架帶到愛爾蘭。隨後他逃跑，但隨即返回愛爾蘭帶給愛爾蘭人基督信仰。他死於 3 月 17 日。每年的那天，愛爾蘭家庭記得他的死去。他們早上上教堂。中午，他們跳舞、喝酒與享用愛爾蘭培根與甘藍菜。它在愛爾蘭超過 1000 年以來一直是個節日。

In the 1800's the potato famine hit Ireland. Many Irish people survived by eating potatoes. When all the potatoes rotted in the fields, people had nothing to eat. More than one million people died from starvation. Another million Irish fled their country to find a better life. As Irish immigrants began to live in America, they started "Irish Aid" groups to help their people. They held annual parades featuring bagpipes and drums. Today, St. Patrick's Day celebrations are very popular in the U.S., Canada and Australia. You do not have to be Irish to enjoy them!

在 19 世紀時，馬鈴薯荒襲擊愛爾蘭。許多愛爾蘭人靠著吃馬鈴薯生存。當所有馬鈴薯在田中腐爛，人們沒有東西可吃。超過一百萬人死於飢餓。另外一百萬愛爾蘭人逃離他們的國家去尋找更好的生活。當愛爾蘭移民開始生活在美洲，他們創建「愛爾蘭援助」機構幫助他們的人。他們舉辦一年一次以風笛與鼓為特色的遊行。今天，聖派翠克節慶在美國與加拿大還有澳洲都非常風行。即使你不是愛爾蘭人你也可以樂在其中。

Green has become the color of the Irish. On St. Patrick's Day, people dress in green clothes and hats. They paint their faces green. They decorate with shamrocks. The shamrock is an Irish plant that is green with four leaves. In Chicago, in the United States, even the river is colored green for the day. There are parades and feasts of corned beef and cabbage, traditional Irish foods. Many people drink green beer. St. Patrick's Day is not a legal holiday, but it is very popular.

綠色是愛爾蘭的顏色。在聖派翠克節,人們穿綠衣戴綠帽。他們將他們的臉塗成綠色。他們用酢漿草裝飾。酢漿草是一種綠色四葉的愛爾蘭植物。在美國芝加哥,在那天有些河甚至被塗成綠色。許多的遊行與有鹽醃牛肉跟甘藍菜的傳統愛爾蘭食物盛宴。許多人暢飲綠啤酒。聖派翠克節不是一個法定假日,但它非常地流行。

In Ireland today, the government uses St. Patrick's Day as a tool to promote tourism. They want to promote Ireland and Irish culture to the world. The St. Patrick's Festival in Ireland's capital city of Dublin lasts several days. Millions of people from around the world take part. There are parades, concerts, outdoor theater and fireworks.

今日在愛爾蘭,政府利用聖派翠克節為工具來推廣觀光業。他們想要將愛爾蘭與愛爾蘭文化推廣至全球。聖派翠克節在愛爾蘭首都都柏林為時數天。有數以百萬從世界各地來的人們參加。有許多遊行、音樂會、戶外戲院與煙火表演。

單字大集合

1. Kidnap *vt.* 綁架

A strange man kidnapped the boy, but the boy got away.
一個陌生男子綁架了男孩，但男孩離開了。

2. Escape *vi. vt.* 逃跑

The tiger has escaped from the cage at the zoo.
老虎已經從動物園裡的獸籠逃跑了。

3. Cabbage *n.* [C,U] 甘藍菜

My kids don't like to eat cabbage.
我的孩子不喜歡吃甘藍菜。

4. Famine *n.* [C,U] 饑荒

If there was a famine here, we would all starve.
如果那裡有饑荒，我們全部都會挨餓。

5. Starvation *n.* [U] 飢餓

Many children in Africa die from starvation.
許多在非洲的小孩因為飢餓而死亡。

6. Bagpipe *n.* [C] 風笛

Bagpipes have a very unusual sound.
風笛有著非常奇特的聲音。

7. Shamrock *n.* [C] 酢漿草

My grandmother grows shamrocks in her garden.
我的奶奶在她的花園裡栽種酢漿草。

8. Tourism *n.* [U] 旅遊業

We support tourism when we travel around our country.
當我們在我們的國家四處旅行時，我們支持了旅遊業。

閱讀測驗

1. Was St. Patrick born in Ireland? 聖派翠克出生在愛爾蘭嗎？
   (a) No, he was born in the United States. 不，他出生在美國。
   (b) Yes, he was born in Dublin. 是，他出生在都柏林。
   (c) No, he was born in Great Britain. 不，他出生在英國。

2. Why did more than one million people die in Ireland in the 1800's?
   為什麼超過一百萬的人在 1800 年代死於愛爾蘭？
   (a) The potatoes rotted in the fields and there was nothing to eat.
   　　馬鈴薯在田裡腐爛，那裡沒有東西可以吃了。
   (b) They were killed in a war. 他們在戰爭裡被殺害。
   (c) They caught a disease that killed them all.
   　　他們得到殺了他們所有人的疾病。

3. On St. Patrick's Day, what color clothes do people wear?
   在聖派翠克節，人們穿什麼顏色的衣服？
   (a) Purple 紫色。
   (b) Black 黑色。
   (c) Green 綠色。

4. Why does the Irish government celebrate St. Patrick's Day today?
   為什麼今日愛爾蘭政府慶祝聖派翠克節？
   (a) They want to please all the people. 他們想要使所有人高興。
   (b) They want to promote tourism. 他們想要推廣觀光業。
   (c) They like the color green. 他們喜歡綠色。

活動慶典和習俗

　　每到了三月，在歐美國家會有許多富含宗教意義及慶祝新生的節日，例如是齋戒月前的狂歡節，月底的復活節，西班牙迎接春天的火節。熱鬧的節慶再加上春天萬物復甦，百花盛開，為三月增添了許多繽紛的色彩。但 3 月 17 日卻是一個單一色彩，十分綠意盎然的節日，那就是聖派翠克日（Saint Patrick's Day），是為了紀念愛爾蘭的守護者，聖派翠克主教的節日。

　　聖派翠克出生於西元四世紀末的英國，在 16 歲時被海盜賣到愛爾蘭作奴隸負責牧羊。他在睡夢中受到上帝的指引，離開前往蘇格蘭的修道院學習。之後在西元 431 年時重返愛爾蘭宣揚天主教教義，並建立許多教堂及學校，也成功的將天主教教義帶到愛爾蘭的每一個角落，今日的愛爾蘭仍有 95%的民眾篤信天主教。3 月 17 日這一天是聖派翠克的忌日，在這一天，愛爾蘭人會用遊行的方式以示紀念。由於在聖派翠克主教宣揚天主教教義時曾以在愛爾蘭到處可見的酢漿草（Shamrock），簡單明瞭的闡釋了天主教中重要的聖父、聖子、聖靈「三位一體」（Holy Trinity）的重要教義，其形象深植於愛爾蘭民眾的心中，於是三葉草便成了聖派翠克節的重要神聖代表。1997 年，愛爾蘭政府將這一個隆重的國家紀念盛會節日更名為 "Saints Patrick Festival"。並從 2000 年開始展開為期 4 天（3 月 16～19 日）國際性規模的盛會，包含有音樂、舞蹈、運動、露天電影（open-air cinema）、煙火大會及化裝遊行（costume parade）。

　　聖派翠克節的慶典隨著愛爾蘭移民（Irish emigrants）一同傳到了其它國家。以美國為例，這一天雖然不是法定節日，但每年都會有不分族群的數百萬人上街遊行一同慶祝。除了遊行之外，還會上教堂做禮拜及聚餐，當然不可或缺的是要穿著綠色衣物及配戴三葉草飾品。在這一天，商家會絞盡腦汁的將所有商品加上綠色，以刺激銷售量。餐廳及酒吧會賣綠色的啤酒，而最值得一提的就是那「綠油油」的芝加哥河。將芝加哥河染成綠色來慶祝聖派翠克節已經有 50 年以上的歷史了，下次如果有機會在 3 月 17 日時到芝加哥的話，不妨去看看這一條「綠河」。

實用生活會話

Q1: What festival is it today? There are so many "green" people with shamrock decorations on the street.

今天是什麼節日啊？街上有好多佩帶著酢漿草裝飾的「綠人」喔。

A1: It's Saint Patrick's Day, we also call it Paddy's Day or Patty's Day. I think those people are going for the parade.

今天是聖派翠克節，也叫做 Paddy 或是 Patty 日。我想那些是去參加遊行的人。

Q2: Oh I see. What are we going to do today?

喔，那我知道了。我們今天要做什麼呢？

A2: I'm going to take you to the Chicago River.

我要帶你去看芝加哥河。

Q3: It's cold outside. Can we stay at home?

外面好冷喔，我們可以待在家嗎？

A3: Nope. Trust me, you'll gonna love it. They are going to turning the river green starting at 10 a.m.,I think we'll make it if we hurry.

不行。相信我，你一定會喜歡的。他們在今天的 10 點鐘會將河水染成綠色，如果我們動作快一點，應該趕得上。

實用單句這樣說

● Originally, the color associated with Saint Patrick was blue.
起初與聖派翠克有關的顏色是藍色。

● The use of green on St. Patrick's Day started from the 17th century.
開始在聖派翠克節使用綠色是從西元 17 世紀開始的。

● In 1903, the Saint Patrick Day became an official Irish public holiday.
在西元 1903 年，聖派翠克節正式成為愛爾蘭的國定假日。

● The Saint Patrick's Day Parade in Montreal has been held every single year since 1824. It is the oldest St. Patrick's Day parade in Canada.
一年一度的蒙特婁聖派翠克節遊行是從 1824 年開始舉辦的。是加拿大史上最悠久的聖派翠克節遊行。

● Saint Patrick's Day is widely celebrated by the Irish diasporas around the world, especially in Britain, Canada, the United States, Argentina, Australia and New Zealand.
聖派翠克節被居住在世界各地的愛爾蘭後裔廣為慶祝，特別是在英國、加拿大、美國、阿根廷、澳洲及紐西蘭。

● St. Patrick Day occurs on March 17 and is the day to commemorate one of Ireland patron saints, Saint Patrick.
聖派翠克節是在 3 月 17 日，用來紀念愛爾蘭守護聖徒之一的聖派翠克。

互動時刻真有趣

　　在聖派翠克節時，除了三葉草之外還常會看到一個紅鬍子及穿著整齊的綠衣及綠帽的矮精靈（Leprechaun）。在愛爾蘭傳說中，矮精靈非常會製作及修補鞋子，他們只有小指頭這樣的大小，但卻非常聰明也非常狡猾。他們最喜歡收集黃金，而且會把一整罐的金子（a pot of gold）藏在彩虹的盡頭（the end of rainbow）。在愛爾蘭的傳說中，只要能捉住矮精靈，便能得到一筆可觀的財富，會比世界上任何一個國王還要有錢。而一般認為三葉草及穿綠色的衣服會引起矮精靈的注意，所以在聖派翠克節時最容易發現矮精靈的蹤影。所以在派翠克節的傳統習俗中，孩子們會事先準備抓矮精靈用的餌及陷阱。

　　一般會用鞋盒、面紙盒甚至是牛奶盒來製作抓矮精靈的陷阱（Leprechaun trap）。再來就是替盒子做裝飾，請記得要用綠色，並發揮想像力。接下來要把抓矮精靈的餌（Leprechaun bait）放置在陷阱上。我們整理出來有 5 點：

1. Gold coins—金幣，或是假的金幣，如做成金幣包裝的巧克力；或是可以將豆子、小石子漆成金色。
2. Rainbows—彩虹，矮精靈將黃金藏在彩虹的盡頭，所以他們很容易被彩虹所吸引。在陷阱上放置彩虹裝飾，或是用畫的。
3. Shamrocks—三葉草，可以放真的三葉草或是裝飾。
4. Warning Signs—警告標語，放上一些「禁止進入」或是「請勿攀爬」的標誌，因為矮精靈生性多疑，這些標語反而會吸引他們去做被禁止的事。
5. Yourself—你自己，因為矮精靈喜歡偷捏沒有穿綠色衣服的人，所以記得不要穿綠色衣服，將自己擺在陷阱旁。

　　祝好運！

April Fools' Day
愚人節

節慶源由──簡易版

April Fools' Day is celebrated in many countries on April 1st. It is known as a day to play tricks on other people. How the holiday began is not known for sure. Some think it started long ago. The new year used to start on April 1st. It was changed to January 1st. Some people forgot. They celebrated it in April and were called April Fools.

愚人節在許多國家於 4 月 1 日被慶祝。這是大家都知道可以捉弄其他人的日子。這個節日確定是不知道怎麼開始的。有些人認為開始於很久以前。新年以前習慣始於 4 月 1 日，已經改為 1 月 1 日。有些人忘記了。他們在四月慶祝新年並被稱為愚人。

People all over the world enjoy tricking their friends on April Fools' Day! In France, people try to tape a paper fish to another person's back without them knowing it. In the United States, children like to fool their parents. Sometimes, they put sugar in the salt shaker. Or, they loosen the lid on the salt shaker, so that when you shake it, a pile of salt comes out. The tricks are almost never mean. It is a day of fun!

全世界所有人都享受在愚人節捉弄他們的朋友！在法國，人們在別人不知情的情況下，將紙做的魚貼到別人的背後。在美國，小孩喜歡捉弄他們的父母。有時，他們把糖放到鹽罐裡。或是他們會旋鬆鹽罐的蓋子，這樣當你搖動它的時候，就會有一堆鹽跑出來。這些玩笑幾乎都不是惡劣的。這是個有趣的一天！

單字大集合

1. **Trick** *n.* [C] 惡作劇；把戲

   The students loved playing tricks on their teachers.
   學生們愛捉弄他們的老師。

2. **Forget** *vi. vt.* 忘記

   I forgot to do my homework.
   我忘記做我的作業。

3. **Fool** *n.* [C] 傻瓜

   I don't ever want to look like a fool.
   我再也不想看起來像個傻瓜。

4. **Without** *prep.* 沒有

   It's hard to walk on rocks without shoes.
   沒有鞋子在石頭上走是很困難的。

5. **Know** *vi. vt.* 知道

   She came to school already knowing how to read.
   她來學校時已經知道如何閱讀。

6. **Shaker** *n.* [C] 搖動的容器

   The salt shaker is always on our dinner table.
   鹽罐總是在我們的晚餐桌上。

節慶源由——精彩完整版

April Fools' Day, or All Fools' Day, is celebrated in many countries on April 1st. It is not a national holiday but is widely recognized as a day to play tricks or practical jokes on each other. The origin of the holiday is not known for sure. Some think it dates back to the 1500's when the new year began on April 1st. In the mid-1500's, the calendar was changed so that New Year 's Day fell on January 1st. Those who forgot and celebrated it in April were called April Fools. Others think it dates back much farther than that. The new year in the ancient country of Persia（where Iran is today）was on April 1st or 2nd. It was a day for pranks. Iranian people still play jokes on each other on that day.

愚人節（All Fools' Day），在許多國家在 4 月 1 日被慶祝。它不是國定假日，但是個被認定可以互相惡作劇的日子。這個節日的起源確定是未知的。有些人認為它的歷史可以追溯到西元 1500 年，當時的新年開始於 4 月 1 日。在西元 1500 年年中，曆法被改變，因此新年落到了 1 月 1 日。那些忘記並在 4 月慶祝的人被稱為 4 月愚人。其他人則認為它可以追溯到比這更久以前。在古代波斯（今天的伊朗）新的一年是 4 月 1 日或 2 日。這是一個惡作劇的日子。伊朗人民仍在那一天彼此打趣逗笑。

Whatever the reason for the holiday, people all over the world enjoy tricking their family and friends on April Fools' Day! There is one story of a school teacher who would write the day's assignments upside down on the blackboard on April Fool's Day. When her students asked, she told them she stood on the ceiling to write it.

不管這個節日的成因是什麼，全世界所有人都享受在愚人節捉弄他們的家人和朋友！這有個故事說，有個學校老師在愚人節當天將功課顛倒著寫在黑板上。當他的學生詢問時，她告訴他們她是站在天花板上寫的。

Sometimes, even the media has played tricks on the public. In 1957, the British Broadcasting Company（BBC）announced that the mild winter had destroyed the dreaded spaghetti weevil. They said Swiss farmers were enjoying a wonderful spring crop of spaghetti. They even showed pictures of Swiss peasants pulling strands of spaghetti down from trees. Lots of TV viewers were tricked. They called the BBC wanting to know how they could grow their own spaghetti trees. Rarely are the tricks harmful. It is a day for fun! Who will you try to fool on April Fools' Day?

　　有時，甚至是媒體也會捉弄大眾。在西元 1957 年，英國廣播電視公司（BBC）宣布暖冬已經摧毀可怕的義大利麵象鼻蟲。他們說瑞士的農民正享受義大利麵這個美好的春季作物。他們甚至秀出了瑞士農民從樹上拉下義大利麵條的圖片。許多電視機前的觀眾被欺騙了。他們打電話到 BBC 想要知道如何栽種他們自己的意大利麵樹。很少數的玩笑是有害的。這是個有趣的一天！你會想要在愚人節捉弄誰呢？

There was some astonishing matters happening on the April Fools' Day, too. In 2003, SARS spread over in Hong Kong. A high school student delivered a post of the false news on his own website to point out that due to the pervasion of SARS, Hong Kong turned out to be the affected area and the main roads was immediately congested. This news was originally a April Fools' Day's joke to pass to his schoolmate through the ICQ; as a result, it caused the panic of the public and the crowds gathered to grasp the food at the supermarkets. Later on, the mistake maker was captured.

　　但愚人節也發生了一些令人錯愕的事。在 2003 年，SARS 在香港蔓延開來，一名中學生在自己的網站裡發出一則假新聞，指出因 SARS 在香港蔓延，香港成為疫區，各要道即時封閉。而這本是一則愚人節笑話只經過 ICQ 傳給他自己的同學，結果引起大眾的恐慌，紛紛到超級市場搶購食物。於是該名學生就被拘捕起來了。

單字大集合

1. Recognize *vi. vt.* 承認；認識

I recognized her from school.
我從學校認識她。

2. Practical *adj.* 實用的

Writing is a very practical skill for school.
寫作在學校是個非常實用的技巧。

3. Blackboard *n.* [C] 黑板

The teacher wrote us a note on the blackboard.
老師在黑板上寫下給我們的筆記。

4. Ceiling *n.* [C] 天花板

I saw a spider crawling on the ceiling.
我看到有隻蜘蛛在天花板上爬。

5. Medium *n.* [C] 媒體

TV and computer are just two of the many forms of media.
電視和電腦只是眾多媒體種類裡的其二。

6. Broadcast *vi. vt.* 廣播

The news was broadcasting updates about the typhoon.
新聞正在播放颱風的更新。

7. Dread *vi. vt.* 懼怕；擔心

I dreaded the homework project for this week.
我擔心這個禮拜的家庭作業項目。

8. Spaghetti *n.* [U] 義大利麵條

Spaghetti sauce is my favorite topping for noodles.
義大利麵醬是我最喜歡用在麵條裡的。

閱讀測驗

1. Where was the ancient country of Persia? 古代波斯在哪裡？
   (a) Just across the street from your house. 就在你的房子對面的街道。
   (b) Where the country of Iran is today. 在今天的伊朗所在地。
   (c) Somewhere in Antarctica. 在南極洲的某個地方。

2. What do kids some times put in the salt shaker on April Fools' Day?
   兒童有時在愚人節會放什麼在鹽罐裡？
   (a) Milk 牛奶。
   (b) Flowers 花朵。
   (c) Sugar 糖。

3. What did the BBC show being picked from trees on April Fools' Day in 1957?
   BBC 在西元 1957 年的愚人節播放了什麼東西從樹下被拉下來？
   (a) Spaghetti 義大利麵條。
   (b) Oranges 橘子。
   (c) Cats 貓。

4. What did a lot of viewers call BBC for on April 1st in 1957?
   為何有許多的觀眾在 1957 年的四月一日打電話給 BBC？
   (a) They wanted to know a big breaking news more clearly.
   他們想更清楚的知道一則大新聞的最新消息。
   (b) They wanted to do the TV - purchase.
   他們想要電視購物。
   (c) They wanted to know how they could grow their own spaghetti tree.
   他們想知道如何栽種他們自己的義大利麵樹。

活動慶典和習俗

　　4 月 1 日，眾所皆知的是西方傳統節日中的愚人節（April Fool's Day 亦可稱 All Fools' Day）。在這個節日裡，人們開周圍朋友甚至是陌生人的玩笑（People play pranks on friends and even strangers.），且在他們上當後告知今天是愚人節，上當者多會在恍然大悟之際也同時會心一笑。但切記務必要拿捏好尺度，免得玩笑開得太大而造成謠言，甚至是恐慌（panic），那可就得不償失。

　　愚人節的由來，大約有 5~6 種說法，而其中較具有歷史證據的是法國國王查理九世在 1565 年時下令採用新的曆法，將一年的開端從 4 月 1 日移至 1 月（January）1 日。但在新曆法推行後，仍有部分的守舊派人士仍執意在 4 月 1 日送新年禮及慶祝新年。此舉引起改革派人士以送假的新年禮物，或是舉辦假的新年派對來嘲弄守舊人士。並稱上當者為 Poisson d'Avril，四月魚（April Fish）。時至今日，在法國仍然稱那些在愚人節上當的人為四月魚。

　　傳統的愚人節，在不同的國家有著不同的時間限制（timeframe）。在英格蘭，惡作劇的時間僅限於中午 12:00 之前，而在蘇格蘭，人們則有 48 小時的時間可以惡作劇。時至今日，則不再受限於中午之前，而也不再有整整 2 天的時間來惡作劇了。

　　幾乎在各種文化中都會有個節日（festival）來慶祝冬天的結束，迎接春天的到來。例如印度的侯麗節（Holi）或是古羅馬的嬉樂節（Hilaria）等，而與愚人節則有時間點上的相似，都選擇在春分（vernal equinox）前後。在這個節日，除了惡作劇之外，人們也會舉行派對慶祝，而愚人節也不例外。傳統上，通常會組織家庭聚會，以水仙和雛菊佈置環境。也有人會製造聖誕節或是新年的氛圍（atmosphere），待客人的到來，並祝賀他們聖誕快樂或是新年快樂。而在聚會上的菜色則是別出心裁，以各式偽裝來點綴料理。例如鋪滿青椒（Green Pepper）的沙拉下藏著生蠔雞尾酒（Oyster Cocktail），或是用甜麵包屑及新鮮磨菇做成的「馬鈴薯泥」（Mushed Potatoes）。

實用生活會話

Q1: Do you know why people call the April fools "April Fish" in France?
你知道為什麼在法國稱在愚人節上當的人為四月魚嗎？

A1: Because they tape a paper fish to their friends' backs, and when he or she finds it, they shout "April Fish".
因為他們會在朋友的背上貼上一張紙做的魚，當朋友發現時，惡作劇的人則會大喊四月魚。

Q2: Do you know your mother just called? And she sounds very angry.
你知道你母親剛打電話過來嗎？而且她聽起來非常生氣。

A2: Oh, why don't you tell me earlier? I have to return her call right now.
喔，你為什麼不早一點告訴我？我得馬上回她電話。

Q3: Got you! Happy April Fool's Day! Why are you so anxious about your mother's call? Did you do something that ignored her?
騙到你了！愚人節快樂！為什麼對你母親的電話感到焦慮？你是不是惹惱她了？

A3: Yes, I did. I played a prank on her this morning, and she was very angry.
是的，沒錯。我今天早上對她惡作劇了，她非常的生氣。

Q4: Be careful! Try to apologize for your trick! Otherwise, you will have a hard time under the same roof still.
小心點！試著為你的惡作劇道歉！要不然，住在同一個屋簷下的日子可不好過阿！

A4: I see. But what should I make up for the mistakes?
我了解。但我應該如何彌補這個錯誤呢？

實用單句這樣說

- On April Fool's Day, forms of behavior that are normally not allowed such as lying, playing pranks become acceptable.
  在愚人節時，一般不被允許的行為例如說謊或是惡作劇變成是可接受的。

- We played a practical joke on our English teacher on April Fool's Day.
  我們在愚人節時開了我們的英文老師一個小玩笑。

- She pretended that she's very angry, and fooled us. Then she shouted "Happy April Fool's day"！
  她假裝她很生氣，並嚇到我們了。然後她大喊著"愚人節快樂"！

- Have you ever heard about the Google Nose? It's a program that lets you search by scent.
  你有沒有聽說過谷歌的嗅覺測試？它是一種可以氣味來搜尋的程式。

- They always take April Fool's Day very seriously.
  他們總是非常認真的對待愚人節。

- Even though I was pranked by my friends on April 1st, I enjoyed the fun they brought to me.
  雖然我在四月一日被朋友惡作劇了一番，我仍喜歡他們帶給我的樂趣。

互動時刻真有趣

● 愚人節小故事（惡搞版）

　　有一個傳說愚人節是起源自一個不幸的故事。話說在 1545 年時，有一個住在英國的挪威科學家名叫 Loof Lirpa，他寫信給英王亨利八世，宣布他發明了飛行器，並請國王參加在 4 月 1 日的飛行表演。國王及其他官員在 4 月 1 日時站在宮殿外等候 Loof Lirpa 及他的飛行器，但卻一直沒有等到，後來在 4 月 1 日當天開玩笑便逐漸成了傳統。但有證據顯示 Loof Lirpa 並沒有開玩笑，而是他的飛行器撞到了樹，而 Loof Lirpa 成了歷史上第一個空難的罹難者。而現在在挪威，有一種用魚，香蕉，蜂蜜及巧克力做成的 Loof Lirpa 餅，據說就是 Loof Lirpa 所發明的。

● 愚人節作業（惡搞版）

尋找 Loof Lirpa 鳥

1. Yell "Loof Lirpa" three times outside.
   在外面大喊 "Loof Lirpa" 三次。

2. If it doesn't work, yell "Woo! Woo! Woo!"
   如果沒用的話，大喊嗚！嗚！嗚！

3. If the bird doesn't appear, please look in the mirror and yell "Loof Lirpa" three times.
   如果還是沒出現的話，請對著鏡子大喊 Loof Lirpa 三次。

4. If it doesn't work, please spell "Loof Lirpa" backwards!
   如果 Loof Lirpa 鳥還是沒出現，請將 "Loof Lirpa" 倒著拼。

Easter Day
復活節

節慶源由──簡易版

Easter is a church holiday.　Jesus lived a long time ago.　Many people did not like him.　They nailed him to a cross.　They buried him in a tomb. Three days later, he came alive again. This is what the church celebrates on Easter.

復活節是一個教會的節日。耶穌生活在很久以前。許多人不喜歡他。他們將他釘在十字架上。他們把他葬在墳墓裡。三天後，他再次復活了。這就是教堂在復活節慶祝的事情。

But many people celebrate Easter, even if they do not go to church.　They color Easter eggs.　First, they boil the eggs.　Then, they dye or paint them bright colors. They have a game called Easter egg hunts.　The eggs used in this game are plastic eggs.　They are filled with candy or money.

但許多人慶祝復活節，即使他們不上教堂。他們彩繪復活節彩蛋。首先，他們煮雞蛋。接著，他們染或塗上鮮艷的顏色。他們有個叫尋找復活節彩蛋的遊戲。用在這個遊戲裡的蛋是塑膠蛋。它們被填滿糖果或錢。

On Easter morning, children find a basket in their bedroom. The Easter Bunny left it there for them.　No one ever sees the Easter Bunny.　He comes at night, when the kids are sleeping.　The baskets are filled with candy and toys.　Later, there is a big Easter dinner.　Families eat ham and potatoes, and a sweet dessert.

在復活節早上，孩子會在他們的寢室發現一個籃子。復活節兔子為了他們將籃子留在那裏。沒有人曾經看過復活節兔子。他在晚上到來，當孩子們都在睡覺的時候。籃子被填滿糖果和玩具。之後，會有個盛大的復活節晚餐。家人們吃火腿和馬鈴薯，以及甜點。

單字大集合

1. Church　*n.* [C]　教堂

We go to church on Sundays.
我們在禮拜天去教堂。

2. Nail　*vt.*　釘

I nailed a board for the new wall.
我為新的牆面釘上板子。

3. Dye　*vi. vt.*　被染色；染

I want to dye my hair red.
我想要將頭髮染紅。

4. Plastic　*adj.*　塑膠的

Most plastic toys break easily.
大部分的塑膠玩具很容易損壞。

5. Basket　*n.* [C]　籃子

Mom sells a basket of fruit at the market.
媽媽在市場上銷售一籃水果。

6. Bunny　*n.* [C]　兔子

I wish I had a pet bunny.
我希望我有隻寵物兔。

節慶源由──精彩完整版

Easter is a Christian holiday.　It is celebrated in countries where many of the people are Christians.　Christians are those who follow the teachings of Jesus Christ. The Bible tells the story of Jesus' life.　Many religious people of his time did not like him.　They killed him by nailing him to a cross.　When he was dead, they put his body in a tomb.　He died on a Friday, and on Sunday morning, he came alive again. This is what Christians celebrate on Easter.

復活節是基督教的節日。它在有許多人民為基督徒的國家被慶祝。基督徒是那些追隨耶穌基督教導的人。聖經描述耶穌一生的故事。在耶穌那個時期，許多篤信宗教的民眾不喜歡他。他們藉由將他釘在十字架上殺害他。當他死去，他們將他的身體放在墳墓裡。他在星期五死去，在星期日早晨，他再度復活了。這就是基督徒在復活節慶祝的事情。

Christians celebrate by going to church on Easter morning.　They sing songs about the resurrection of Jesus.　Often, little girls get new dresses for Easter Sunday. However, even people who do not believe in Jesus celebrate Easter.　A common thing to do before Easter is to boil eggs and dye or paint them in bright colors.　This started because the eggs remind Christians of the new life of Jesus.　But most people don't think about this when they are coloring their eggs.　They are simply fun to color. Once they are colored, some are put around the house for decoration. Some are saved to eat at Easter dinner. The day before Easter, many churches and parks offer egg hunts for kids.　Some families have egg hunts at home, too.　The eggs used in egg hunts are plastic eggs that are filled with candy or money and hidden outside.

基督徒在復活節早晨藉由上教堂慶祝。他們唱著有關耶穌復活的歌曲。通常，小女孩會因為復活節星期日得到新的裙裝。然而，甚至那些不相信耶穌的人也慶祝復活節。在復活節前最常見的事情變是煮蛋、染或是將它們塗上鮮艷的顏色。這件事的開始，是因為蛋提醒基督徒耶穌的新生。但大部分的人們不會想到這些，在他們彩繪他們的彩蛋時。他們只是簡單享受彩繪的樂趣。當雞蛋被彩繪好，有些會被放在房子四周當作裝飾。有些會被保存到復活節晚上食用。在復活節前，許多教堂和公園會提供尋找復活節彩蛋給孩子們。有些家庭在家裡也會有尋找復活節彩蛋。用在尋找復活節彩蛋的蛋是被填滿糖果或錢的塑膠蛋，它們被藏在戶外。

On Easter morning, children find an Easter basket in their bedroom. They believe the Easter Bunny has put it there for them. No one ever sees the Easter Bunny. He comes at night, when the kids are sleeping. He leaves baskets filled with candy and small toys or cute little stuffed bunnies. In the afternoon, there is always a big Easter dinner. Many families eat ham and potatoes, followed by a delicious sweet dessert.

在復活節早晨，孩子會在他們的寢室發現一個籃子。他們相信是復活節兔子為了他們放在那裡的。沒有人曾經看過復活節兔子。他在晚上到來，當孩子們都在睡覺的時候。他留下被填滿糖果、小玩具或可愛的填充小兔子的籃子。在下午，通常有個盛大的復活節晚餐。許多家庭吃著火腿、馬鈴薯，接著是好吃的甜點。

Easter falls on a different date each year, but it is always sometime between mid-March and mid-April. It is always on the first Sunday after the full moon following the first day of spring. Because Easter is always on a Sunday, the Monday after Easter is a national holiday. On Easter Monday, even the President of the United States holds an Easter egg hunt for children on the lawn at the White House, where he lives.

復活節在每年都落在不同的日期，但通常在 3 月中到 4 月中的某時。通常在春天的第一天滿月後的第一個星期日。因為復活節總是在星期日，復活節後的禮拜一變成為國定假日。在復活節的禮拜一，甚至連美國總統都在他住的白宮的草地上，為兒童舉行尋找復活節彩蛋。

單字大集合

1. Christian *adj.* 基督教的

There is a Christian church on the corner of our street.
在我們巷子的轉角有個基督教的教堂。

2. Religious *adj.* 宗教的

Religious people often go the church or temple.
篤信宗教的人們通常去教堂或廟宇。

3. Tomb *n.* [C] 墳墓

Many people are buried in a tomb.
許多人們被埋葬在墳墓裡。

4. Resurrection *n.* [U] 復活

Resurrection is coming back to life after you have died.
復活是在你已經死去後又回到人生裡。

5. Decoration *n.* [U] 裝飾

We hung lots of bright lights outside for decoration.
我們為了裝飾掛上許多明亮的燈

6. Hide *vi. vt.* 隱藏；把……藏起來

The eggs were hidden so well, the kids had a hard time finding them.
彩蛋被藏得太好了，孩子很難找到它們。

7. Afternoon *n.* [C,U] 下午

The kids should be tired, since they ran around all afternoon.
孩子們一定累了，因為他們整個下午到處跑。

8. Delicious *adj.* 好吃的

Mom made a delicious cake!
媽媽做了個好吃的蛋糕！

閱讀測驗

1. How does the Bible say Jesus was killed? 聖經說耶穌是怎麼被殺害的？

   (a) He was nailed to a cross. 他被釘在十字架上。

   (b) He died of a heart attack. 他死於心臟病發作。

   (c) He had a car accident. 他發生了車禍。

2. After the eggs are boiled, what do people do with them?
   雞蛋被煮熟後，人們會對它們做什麼？

   (a) They put them in the garbage. 他們把它們放在垃圾裡。

   (b) They color them in bright colors. 他們用鮮豔的顏色彩繪它們。

   (c) They hang them on their Christmas tree. 他們把它們掛在聖誕樹上。

3. Who hides Easter baskets in the kids' rooms?
   誰將復活節籃子藏在小孩的房間裡？

   (a) Santa Claus 聖誕老人。

   (b) The kids hide them there themselves. 孩子們自己把它們藏在那。

   (c) The Easter Bunny 復活節兔子。

4. What season of the year begins just before Easter?
   一年中哪個季節在復活節前剛好開始？

   (a) Winter 冬天。

   (b) Christmas 聖誕節。

   (c) Spring 春天。

活動慶典和習俗

在西方國家，一般到了 3 月，商家便會開始以白色百合花（Lily）和顏色粉嫩繪有各式各樣圖案的彩蛋，還有造型討喜可愛的復活節兔子（Easter bunny）來做裝飾，而且也會開始販售一些做成彩蛋或是兔子形狀的巧克力。每逢看到這類的裝飾及商品，人們就知道復活節（Easter）即將到臨。

復活節是在每年春分（vernal/spring equinox）滿月過後的第一個星期天，所以在國曆上的日期則會落在每年的 3 月 22 日到 4 月 25 日之間。根據聖經記載，耶穌被釘死在十字架（Crucifixion）上，在 3 天後復活（resurrection），復活節因而得名，具有重生（rebirth）與希望的象徵。復活節在古英文中是 Ēostre，是西歐異教中的春天女神，源自於古巴比倫的掌管愛情、生育與戰爭的女神 Ishtar。傳說中 Ēostre 救了一隻翅膀凍傷的鳥，將其變成兔子，但卻仍然保有生蛋的能力。而兔子變成了復活節的使者，為乖孩子們帶來復活節彩蛋（Easter egg），而這些彩蛋在傳說中是兔子的蛋。復活節習俗與春天和重生相關，蛋在許多國家的文化當中包含有豐饒及重生的意義，而兔子也因其多產而成為豐饒具生產力的象徵。

傳統習俗中，孩子們在復活節前會在雞蛋上畫各式各樣的花紋，並在復活節前夕準備好復活節籃子（Easter basket），放在床前，在復活節早上便會發現一籃滿滿裝有復活節彩蛋，兔子及毛絨小雞娃娃還有一些小玩具。在美國，還會為孩子們設計尋找復活節彩蛋的活動（Easter Egg Hunt），找到最多彩蛋的人在這一年一切都能平安喜樂。在白宮（White House）還會舉行復活節滾蛋大賽（Easter Egg Roll），許多的父母會帶著孩子在白宮的草坪上享受著滾蛋的樂趣。而這一天也會有遊行活動（parade）來慶祝復活節。在英國，除了「滾蛋」之外，在孩子間還流行一種碰蛋（Egg tapping）的遊戲，兩人持蛋相互碰擊，蛋殼先裂開的一方便算輸了。而在義大利則會在復活節當天帶 100 隻以上的蛋到教堂請神父祝福後再帶回家中，成為復活節大餐中的主要食材。

實用生活會話

Q1: When do you celebrate Easter?
復活節是在哪天？

A1: We celebrate it on the first Sunday after the Paschal full moon, and it's on March 31 this year.
復活節是在春分滿月後的第一個星期天，今年是在 3 月 31 日。

Q2: How do you celebrate it?
那你們都怎麼慶祝？

A2: We paint eggs with many different patterns before the Easter, and bring children to attend a variety of activities such as Egg Rolling, Egg Hunt on the Easter.
我們會復活節前在蛋上畫上各種圖案，復活節當天會帶孩子去參加滾蛋、尋找彩蛋等的活動。

Q3: That sounds very interesting. Can Molly and I go with you on the Easter?
聽起來好有趣喔。我和莫莉在復活節時可以跟你們一起去嗎？

A3: Sure, I'll give you a call then.
沒問題，那我會再打電話給你！

Q4: Don't you think the Easter bunny really cute?
你不覺得復活節的兔子真可愛嗎？

A4: Depends. I myself like the little bear Winnie better.
看情況。我個人比較喜歡維尼熊。

實用單句這樣說

- Egg tapping, also known as Egg fight, is a traditional Easter game.
  碰蛋也可稱做鬥蛋是一種傳統的復活節遊戲。

- In the United States, the Egg Rolling is an annual event that is held on the White House lawn for children and their parents.
  在美國，在白宮的草坪上舉辦的滾蛋大賽是個年度盛事，參賽對象則是孩童及他們的父母。

- In the Egg Rolling, children have to bring their decorated eggs to join in game.
  在滾蛋大賽中，孩子們必須帶他們畫好的蛋來參加比賽。

- An Egg Hunt is a game during decorated eggs of various sizes, are hidden for children to find, both indoor and outdoor.
  尋找復活節彩蛋是讓孩子們找出藏在室內外各種大小彩蛋的遊戲。

- The losers of the Egg Tapping contests get to eat their eggs.
  碰蛋比賽中輸掉的人要把他們的蛋吃掉。

- Easter is a religious holiday that commemorates the resurrection of Jesus Christ.
  復活節是紀念耶穌基督復活的宗教節日。

互動時刻真有趣

● 製作復活節彩蛋

需要的材料

全熟的水煮蛋

杯子或碗（可供浸入整顆雞蛋）

1/2 杯開水

1 小匙白醋

食用色素（液體約 20 滴）

1. 將煮熟的水煮蛋放涼。

Start with cool hard-boiled eggs.

2. 將水，白醋及食用色素倒入杯中混合。

Fill the cup with the mixture of water, vinegar and food coloring.

3. 把蛋放入杯中浸泡，偶爾翻動。浸泡時間最少需要 5 分鐘，浸泡時間越長，顏色會越深。

Place the egg in the cup and dunk, turning occasionally. Keep in the dye for at least 5 minutes. The egg will soak up more color the longer you wait.

4. 小心的將蛋取出，並在旁晾乾。

Remove the egg carefully and set aside to dry.

● 注意事項：

1. 材料的份量僅供染一種顏色，如要染 3 種顏色，則材料份量需準備 3 份，以此類推。

2. 在染色前，將橡皮筋捆在蛋上，不同的捆法會染出不同的線條花樣。但請小心不要弄破蛋。

3. 染色後需完全晾乾，可用紙巾沾食用油擦拭蛋殼，可讓彩蛋增加光澤。

4. 也可在晾乾後，以油蠟筆或油彩在蛋殼上畫上圖案，或是貼上蕾絲或是紙膠帶，黏上亮粉等，可讓孩子自由發揮。（以蠟筆，油彩等裝飾的彩蛋則不建議食用。）

Passover
逾越節

節慶源由──簡易版

Passover is a Jewish festival in April or May. The Jews are people who first lived in Israel. They believe in the God told about in the Bible. Passover is a time to remember their history.

> 逾越節是個猶太節日，在 4 或 5 月。猶太人是第一個住在以色列的人。他們相信聖經裡訴說的上帝。逾越節是用來紀念他們的歷史。

The people of Israel were slaves in Egypt. God helped the people of Israel escape. He caused all of Egypt's first-born children to die. God told the Israelites to mark the doorposts of their homes with the blood of a lamb. The death passed over their houses and their children were safe. When this happened, the slaves were set free.

> 以色列的人在埃及是奴隸。上帝幫助以色列的人民逃離。他使埃及的第一個出生的孩子死亡。上帝告訴以色列的人在他們的門柱上用羊血做記號。死亡會踰越他們的家，且他們的孩子會安全。當這發生，奴隸便獲得了自由。

During the Passover, Jews eat the bread of Passover is called matzo. Some of it is hidden in the house. The story of the Passover is told. Children are to ask questions to learn their history. They are rewarded with nuts and candies. They are the ones to hunt for the hidden matzo, also. The one who finds it receives a prize.

> 在逾越節期間，猶太人吃叫無酵餅的麵包。有些無酵餅被藏在房子裡。逾越節的故事被傳頌。孩子問問題，以了解他們的歷史。他們被用堅果和糖果獎勵。他們也是找尋藏起來的無酵餅的人。找到的人會得到獎勵。

單字大集合

1. Jew *n.* [C] 猶太人

There are many Jews in Israel.
有許多猶太人在以色列。

2. Blood *n.* [U] 血

There is some blood where I scraped my knee.
我刮到膝蓋的地方有些血。

3. Lamb *n.* [C] 小羊

The lamb was born in the spring.
小羊在春天誕生。

4. Flat *adj.* 平坦的

The land is very flat here.
那裡的陸地非常平坦。

5. Question *n.* [C] 問題

Why do you have so many questions today?
為什麼你今天有那麼多問題？

6. Reward *vt.* 報答；獎勵

We rewarded our dog when she did what we told her to.
我們獎勵我們的狗，當她做了我們告訴她的。

節慶源由──精彩完整版

Passover is a Jewish festival. The Jews are people who first lived in Israel. They believe in the God written about in the first five books of the Bible. Passover commemorates a time in their history, called the Exodus. The Exodus was when the ancient Israelites were freed from slavery in Egypt. Passover begins on the 15th day of the month of Nisan in the Jewish calendar. This is in April or May. It is celebrated for seven or eight days. It is one of the most widely observed Jewish holidays.

逾越節是個猶太節日，猶太人是第一個住在以色列的人。他們相信聖經前 5 冊裡訴說的上帝。逾越節紀念了他們的歷史，稱為《出埃及記》。《出埃及記》是說古代以色列人從埃及的奴役中解放出來。逾越節開始在猶太歷第 7 個月的第 15 天。通常是在 4 或 5 月。它被慶祝 7 到 8 天。這是最廣泛的猶太人的節日之一。

In the story of the Exodus, the Bible tells that God helped the people of Israel escape from Egypt. Pharaoh（the Egyptian leader）would not release his Israelite slaves. God caused ten very bad events, called ten plagues, to happen to the Egyptians. The tenth plague was the worst of all. It was the death of all the first-born children of the Egyptians. God told the Israelites to mark the doorposts of their homes with the blood of a lamb. Then, the plague would pass over their houses and their children would be safe. When this happened, Pharaoh finally let the slaves go free.

在《出埃及記》的故事裡，聖經講述上帝幫助以色列的人民從埃及逃離。法老（埃及領導人）不會釋放他的以色列奴隸。上帝引起 10 件不好的事情，稱作瘟疫，發生在埃及人身上。第 10 災是所有裡最糟糕的。是所有埃及人第一個出生的孩子的死亡。上帝告訴以色列的人在他們的門柱上用羊血做記號。然後，死亡會踰越他們的家，且他們的孩子會安全。當這發生，奴隸便獲得了自由。

During the Passover celebration, Jews cannot have any yeast in their home. When the Israelites left Egypt they had to leave quickly. They did not have time to bake bread with yeast in it. So, the bread of Passover is called matzo. On the first night of Passover there is a special dinner. The father speaks a blessing. Bitter herbs are dipped in salt water. This is to remember the suffering and tears of the Israelites.

在逾越節期間，猶太人在他們的家裡不能有任何的酵母。當以色列人離開埃及時，他們必須快速地離開。他們沒有時間讓酵母在麵包裡烘烤。所以，在逾越節吃的麵包被稱為無酵餅。在逾越節的第一晚會有個特別的晚餐。神父說禱詞。苦菜浸泡在鹽水中。這是用來記得以色列人的苦難和淚水。

They eat matzo and some of it is broken off and hidden in the house. The story of the Passover is told. Children are encouraged to ask questions and participate in the discussion. They are rewarded with nuts and candies when they do. They are the ones to hunt for the hidden matzo, too. The one who finds it receives a prize.

他們吃無酵餅且有些被折斷的被藏在屋裡。逾越節的故事被傳頌。孩子們被鼓勵問問題及參與討論。當他們這麼做時被堅果和糖果獎勵。他們也是找尋藏起來的無酵餅的人。找到的人會得到獎勵。

Here are some questions for you to discuss:
這裡有些供你討論的問題：

1. What's the special meaning that the Passover provides to the Jews?
   逾越節帶給猶太人的特別意義是？

2. Through the way that the God saved the Jews, do you think He is too cruel or not?
   藉由上帝拯救猶太人的方式來了解，你認為祂會太殘忍或不會呢？

單字大集合

1. Jewish *adj.* 猶太人的

Jewish people live in many countries of the world today.
猶太人在今日住在世界的許多國家裡。

2. Israel 以色列

The country of Israel is often in the news.
以色列的國家常常出現在新聞裡。

3. Exodus *n.* [U] 《出埃及記》；外出

There was a mass exodus of people during the flood.
在洪水期間有大量外出民眾。

4. Slavery *n.* [U] 奴役身分

Black people in the U.S. were once in slavery.
在美國的黑人曾經在奴役身分裡。

5. Plague *n.* [C] 瘟疫；災害

Life changes when plagues come, like the Black Plague that brought death to many long ago.
當瘟疫降臨時生活便改變了，像是黑死病在很久以前帶來死亡。

6. Doorpost *n.* [C] 門柱

Sometimes, people paint their doorposts red.
有時，人們將他們的門柱漆成紅色的。

7. Yeast *n.* [U] 酵母

If I had some yeast, I would bake some bread.
如果我有一些酵母，我會烤一些麵包。

8. Bitter *adj.* 苦澀的

I spit the bitter fruit out of my mouth!
我從我的嘴裡吐出苦澀的水果！

閱讀測驗

1. What country did the people of Israel escape from?
   以色列的人民要從哪個國家逃離？
   (a) The United States 美國。
   (b) China 中國。
   (c) Egypt 埃及。

2. Why did they want to escape? 為什麼他們想要逃跑？
   (a) They did not want to be slaves anymore. 他們再也不想要成為奴隸。
   (b) They thought it was too hot in Egypt. 他們認為埃及太熱了。
   (c) They wanted to go home to see their mothers. 他們想要回家看他們的母親。

3. Who died in the tenth plague? 誰在十災中死亡？
   (a) All the neighborhood dogs. 所有鄰居的狗。
   (b) Everyone who was outside. 所有在外面的人。
   (c) All the first-born children of the Egyptians. 所有埃及人第一個出生的孩子。

4. Why do Jews eat matzo during Passover?
   為什麼猶太人在逾越節期間吃無酵餅？
   (a) It is their favorite bread. 這是他們最喜愛的麵包。
   (b) They can't eat yeast during Passover, and matzo is made without yeast.
       他們在逾越節不能吃酵母，無酵餅是無酵母製成的。
   (c) Matzo is less expensive to buy than other bread.
       買無酵餅較其他麵包不昂貴。

活動慶典和習俗

　　逾越節（Passover 亦稱 Pesach），在大家所熟悉的達文西名畫「最後的晚餐」（Last Supper）中，耶穌在受難前與其門徒（disciples）共進的便是逾越節宴席。逾越節開始於尼散月（Month of Nisan）十五日（在 3 月至 4 月之間），在以色列境內為接連 7 天，而境外則是 8 天。根據舊約聖經中的出埃及記記載，「這血要在你們所住的房屋上作記號；我一見這血，就越過你們去。我擊殺埃及地頭生的時候，災殃必不臨到你們身上滅你們。你們要記念這日，守為耶和華的節，作為你們世世代代永遠的定例。」而句中的越過，英文為 pass over，便是命名為 Passover（逾越節）的由來。

　　逾越節是紀念在離開埃及的前一夜，後來猶太人將其與除酵節合而為一，除酵節持續 7 天，而逾越節是在除酵節的第一天。在逾越節期這一週，不能吃任何含有酵母（yeast）的食物，是為了紀念當時匆忙離開埃及，甚至無法讓麵發酵的苦境。而在聖經中，酵也含有邪惡、惡毒意味，所以在逾越節前，必須將家中徹底打掃乾淨，清除所有沾染有酵的物品。而也會象徵性的留下一小撮酵，在逾越節晚餐前，由父親帶著兒子點燃蠟燭，用羽毛將最後一塊刷掉。接下來就是逾越節晚餐（Seder），以特殊的食物及晚餐儀式來提醒世代記住神領以色列人出埃及的神蹟。晚餐會家中婦女點燃蠟燭開始，餐桌上必備羊脛骨、一顆水煮蛋、一大疊無酵餅（Matzah）、青菜、苦菜（Bitter herb / Maror）、甜沙拉（Chaoset）、葡萄酒，以及一碗鹽水。羊脛骨代表逾越節的羊羔，水煮蛋是唯一一種越煮越硬的食物象徵著猶太人愈挫愈勇，所以是不能吃的。先吃青菜沾鹽水，鹽水是在埃及被奴役時的淚水。再嘗無酵餅分別沾苦菜及甜沙拉，提醒子孫，祖先在埃及受的苦及現在生活的甜美都要好好記在心中。在這兩道菜中間，會進行藏餅（Afikomen）的儀式，將三張無酵餅中間那張取出，先感恩，弄碎，放在白布中藏起。晚餐後，讓孩子找出，可得到一份小禮物。這在猶太教中，認為是在尋找彌賽亞，而在基督教中認為耶穌就是彌賽亞，但並不被以色列人所認同。餐中會佐以 4 杯酒（Four Cups），第 1 杯，為家中長者為節日祝福，第 2 杯是在講述逾越節的故事之後。第 3 杯是對上帝的感謝，第 4 杯是在歌曲及讚美詩之後，並互祝來年能在耶路撒冷共聚。

　　由於猶太教對於逾越節晚餐的儀式及次序有嚴格的規範，在被稱做哈卡達（Haggadah）的一份解釋說明中有詳盡的流程。而逾越節期間不吃發酵食品及某些由 5 種穀物製作的東西，這些都被稱做「chametz」。為了避免觸犯規則，一般猶太人會選擇食物上有標示符合猶太教規（kosher）的食品。餐點上的變化並沒有我們想像中的單調，而節日的氣氛也十分歡樂，在節期中也不行做粗重的工作，因為是要紀念脫離奴隸的身份，也十分類似我國在過年期間休養生息的習俗。

● **逾越節四問** The four questions on Passover

在逾越節晚餐中，有一個儀式，由最年幼的孩童發問今天晚上和其他晚上有什麼不同，通常有 4 個問題，被稱為逾越節 4 問（The four questions on Passover）。孩童會以吟唱的方式，而答案則是從在晚餐說的逾越節故事中獲得。

實用生活會話

What makes this night different from all other nights?
今晚與其他晚上有什麼不同？（這一句是引導用的問題）

Q1: On all other nights we do not dip our vegetables in salt water even once, but on this night we do so twice?
在所有的晚上我們都不用沾醬，但為什麼今晚我們需要用蔬菜沾醬在鹽水中兩次呢？

Q2: On all other nights we eat bread or matzah, but on this night we eat only matzah?
在所有的晚上我們吃麵包或是無酵餅，但為什麼今晚只吃無酵餅？

Q3: On all other nights we eat any kind of vegetables and herbs, but on this night we only eat bitter herbs?
在所有的晚上我們吃各種蔬菜，但為什麼今晚只吃苦菜？

Q4: On all other nights we eat sitting upright, but on this night we all recline?
在所有的晚上我們正襟危坐的吃飯，但為什麼今晚卻要倚著吃飯？

實用單句這樣說

- No leaven shall be eaten and no leaven shall be seen of yours in your possession during the Passover
  在逾越節期間，不能吃含酵食品也不能擁有任何與酵相關的物品。

- Chametz is any food made from wheat, barley, rye, oat or spelt which has risen.
  有酵食物是所有用小麥、大麥、黑麥、燕麥或是斯卑爾麥製作，且經過發酵的食品。

- Passover commences on the 15th day of Hebrew month of Nisan, and lasts for 7 days in Israel
  逾越節期是從希伯來尼散月的第 15 天開始，在以色列是接連著 7 天長的期間。

- His parents go to Jerusalem every year at the feast of Passover.
  他的父母每年會在逾越節時去耶路撒冷。

- Many Jewish people spend the Passover with families and close friends.
  許多猶太人在逾越節期間會和家人及好友共度。

- Many Jewish people use grated horseradish, or romaine lettuce for the moror.
  很多猶太人用辣根泥及蘿蔓葉來當作苦菜。

互動時刻真有趣

● 逾越節單字表

Passover 逾越節	yeast 酵母	leaven 發酵	bitter 苦	herb 香料
wheat 小麥	barley 大麥	rye 黑麥	oat 燕麥	matzah 無酵餅

下列的字母順序被打散了，請填上正確順序的單字。可以參考上面表格中的單字

Unscramble the words. Use the words in the textbox to help you.

Unscramble words

1. aazhtm　＿＿＿＿＿＿＿＿＿＿＿＿

2. ery　＿＿＿＿＿＿＿＿＿＿＿＿＿＿

3. brhe　＿＿＿＿＿＿＿＿＿＿＿＿＿

4. sorevPsa　＿＿＿＿＿＿＿＿＿＿

5. atyes　＿＿＿＿＿＿＿＿＿＿＿＿

6. thwae　＿＿＿＿＿＿＿＿＿＿＿＿

7. aot　＿＿＿＿＿＿＿＿＿＿＿＿＿＿

8. nlaeev　＿＿＿＿＿＿＿＿＿＿＿

9. ribtet　＿＿＿＿＿＿＿＿＿＿＿＿

10. yrabel　＿＿＿＿＿＿＿＿＿＿＿

Answer:

1. matzah

2. rye

3. herb

4. Passover

5. yeast

6. wheat

7. oat

8. leaven

9. itter

10. barley

Memorial Day
陣亡將士紀念日

節慶源由——簡易版

Memorial Day is a national holiday in the United States. It is on the last Monday of May. It is a day to think about soldiers who have died. The first Memorial Day was after the U.S. Civil War. This was the war between the north and the south in the 1860's. People wanted to remember those who had died in that war. They put flowers on soldiers' graves.

陣亡將士紀念日是美國的國定節日。它在 5 月的最後一個禮拜一。是個感念死去將士的日子。第一次的陣亡將士紀念日是在美國內戰後。這個戰爭是在 1860 年代的南部與北部間。人們想要記得在這場戰爭死去的士兵們。他們將花擺放在士兵的墳上。

Some people still visit soldiers' graves. A United States flag is flown on each grave in the national graveyards. Cities large and small have parades. Most have marching bands. Soldiers march and drive cars and trucks from some of the wars. Speeches honor brave men and women.

有些人仍會造訪士兵們的墳墓。美國國旗飛揚在國家公墓裡的每個墳墓上。大和小的城市都有遊行。大多數都有軍樂隊。士兵們行軍並開著來自某些戰爭的車輛和卡車。演講讚揚著勇敢的男女。

Memorial Day is also the beginning of summer. Families and friends gather. Many go camping or to the beach. They have the first barbecue of the summer. The smell of hotdogs and hamburgers is everywhere!

陣亡將士紀念日也是夏天的開始。家人們和朋友們齊聚。許多人去露營或到海邊。他們有了夏天的第一次烤肉。到處都有熱狗和漢堡的氣味！

單字大集合

1. Die *vi. vt.* 死；死於

My cat ran away and died.
我的貓逃跑並死去了。

2. Flower *n.* [C] 花

Pink flowers are my favorite.
粉紅色花朵是我的最愛。

3. Fly *vi. vt.* 飄揚；駕駛飛機

The flags have flown on the poles all week.
旗子已經飄揚在柱上整個禮拜了。

4. Graveyard *n.* [C] 墓園

I stay away from graveyards at night.
我在夜間遠離墓園。

5. Barbecue *vt.* 烤

I can't wait to barbecue hotdogs!
我等不及要烤熱狗了！

6. Hamburger *n.* [C] 漢堡

Mom and dad eat hamburgers, but I like hotdogs.
媽媽和爸爸吃漢堡，但我喜歡熱狗。

節慶源由──精彩完整版

Memorial Day is a national holiday in the United States. It is always on the last Monday of May. This holiday provides a day to remember people who have died while serving in the U.S. military. The first Memorial Day was after the American Civil War. This was the war between the north and the south of the United States in the 1860's. People wanted to remember those who had died in that war. It was called Decoration Day, because it was a day to decorate soldiers' graves with flowers. In 1868, the commander of the U.S. Army declared that Decoration Day should be observed nationwide every year. By the 1900's it had grown to include Americans who died in all wars. After World War II, Memorial Day became the common name. It became an official holiday in 1971.

陣亡將士紀念日是美國的國定節日。它在 5 月的最後一個禮拜一。這個節日提供了一個懷念在美國軍隊服務時死去的人們的日子。第一次的陣亡將士紀念日是在美國內戰後。這個戰爭是在 1860 年代的南部與北部間。人們想要記得在這場戰爭死去的士兵們。它被稱為裝飾節，因為他是用花朵裝飾士兵墳墓的日子。在西元 1868 年，美國軍隊的指揮官聲稱裝飾節應每年全國性的被慶祝。在 1900 年代，它已經成長為包括在所有戰爭裡死去的美國人。在第二次世界大戰後，陣亡將士紀念日變成了常見的名稱。在西元 1971 年，它變成一個正式的節日。

On Memorial Day, many people visit cemeteries and war memorials. Often, they place flowers on the graves of people they knew. Many volunteers place a United States flag on each grave in the national cemeteries. The people buried in national cemeteries are only those who have died in battle. Both cities and small towns have celebrations. There are thousands of parades held all over the country. Most of these feature marching bands and a military theme. Current military personnel and veterans of the armed forces march. Some drive military vehicles from various wars.

在陣亡將士紀念日，許多人參觀墓地和戰爭紀念館。通常他們擺放花朵在他們知道的人的墳上。許多志願者將美國國旗放在國家公墓的每個墳上。在國家公墓埋葬的人，只有那些死在戰場上。城市和小鎮都有慶祝活動。有上千個遊行在全國各地舉行。大多數以軍樂隊和軍事的主題為特色。軍隊遊行有現役軍人和退伍軍人。有些開著來自各種戰爭的軍事車輛。

After the parades, there is often a speech by a member of the military. These speeches honor the bravery of soldiers. They encourage Americans to uphold freedom in the world. There is also a National Memorial Day Concert held on the lawn of the United States Capitol.

在遊行之後，通常會有軍隊成員的演說。這些演說尊敬的勇敢的戰士。他們鼓勵美國人崇尚自由世界。在國會大廈的草坪上也有陣亡將士紀念日的音樂會被舉辦。

Memorial Day weekend is a long weekend. Since the holiday is on a Monday, people have three days for gatherings with family and friends. This weekend is considered the beginning of the summer season. Therefore, many people go camping or go to the beach. They have the first barbecue of the summer. The smell of hotdogs and hamburgers is in the air.

陣亡將士紀念日週末是個長週末。因為節日是在星期一，人們有三天的時間和家人及朋友齊聚。這個週末也被認為是夏季的開始。因此許多人去露營或到海邊。他們有了夏天的第一次烤肉。熱狗和漢堡瀰漫在空氣裡。

單字大集合

1. Civil *adj.* 國內的；國民的

A civil war is a war between citizens of the same country.
內戰是在同一個國家的公民之間的戰爭。

2. Commander *n.* [C] 指揮官

The commander led his soldiers into battle.
指揮官帶領他的士兵投入戰鬥。

3. Cemetery *n.* [C] 墓地

Many people choose to be buried in cemeteries.
許多人選擇被埋葬在墓地裡。

4. Volunteer *n.* [C] 志願者

It takes a lot of volunteers to make the parade a success.
要使一場遊行成功需要耗費許多志願者。

5. Feature *vi.* 以……為特色

The movie will feature a popular movie star.
這部電影將以有一個當紅影星為特色。

6. Personnel *n.* [U] 人事部門；員工（總稱）

All office personnel are invited to the picnic.
所有的辦公室人員被邀請去參加野餐。

7. Veteran *n.* [C] 退伍軍人

All veterans should march in the parade.
所有的退伍軍人應在遊行中行軍。

8. Bravery *n.* [U] 勇氣

The boys were honored for their bravery during the storm.
男孩們因為他們在暴風雨裡的勇敢而被表揚。

閱讀測驗

1. When was the first Memorial Day? 第一次的陣亡將士紀念日是何時？
   (a) The day my father was born. 我爸爸出生那天。
   (b) After the American Civil War. 美國內戰後。
   (c) After World War II. 第二次世界大戰後。

2. Why was it first called Decoration Day? 為什麼它第一次被稱作裝飾節？
   (a) Because all the kids decorated their rooms that day.
       因為所有孩子在那天裝飾他們的房間。
   (b) Because girls made Christmas Decorations that day.
       因為女孩們在那天做聖誕節裝飾品。
   (c) Because the graves were decorated with flowers.
       因為墳墓被用花朵裝飾。

3. What is placed on each grave in the national cemeteries?
   什麼被擺放在國家公墓的每個墳上？
   (a) Candy for the soldiers to eat. 給將士吃的糖果。
   (b) Flowers. 花朵。
   (c) A United States flag. 美國國旗。

4. Memorial Day starts from _____ in a week.
   陣亡將士紀念日從一週的 _____ 開始。
   (a) Sunday 星期日
   (b) Monday 星期一
   (c) Friday 星期五

活動慶典和習俗

　　根據詹森總統在 1966 年發表的官方版本中，最早紀念陣亡將士的地方是在 1866 年，南北戰爭（Civil War）結束後不久，紐約州滑鐵盧（Waterloo）鎮的一個藥店（drugstore）老闆亨利.韋爾斯提議全鎮商店關門一天，為在戰爭中犧牲的戰士們默哀一天，並在同年的 5 月 5 日舉行紀念活動。而在同一天，指揮北方軍隊的洛根將軍宣布於 5 月 30 日紀念在戰爭中犧牲的士兵，並在那一天帶領退伍軍人到阿靈頓公墓（Arlington National Cemetery）為南北雙方犧牲的士兵獻上鮮花及在墓碑前插上美國國旗。這兩個日子在 1868 年時合併，並被人們稱為裝飾日（Decoration Day）。而到了 1971 年，聯邦政府將這一天定在 5 月的最後一個星期一，為陣亡將士紀念日（Memorial Day），全國放假一天，讓更多的人可以一起紀念這個日子。而紀念的對象也不僅限於在南北戰爭中犧牲的士兵，而是廣泛包含在所有戰爭中犧牲的美國士兵。

　　在陣亡將士紀念日這一天，全美各地會舉行遊行及煙火秀等活動，其中最特殊的是在華盛頓特區的滾雷巡遊（Rolling Thunder Motorcycle Rally）以摩托車遊行的方式來紀念失蹤及陣亡的士兵，並呼籲人們重視他們及其家屬的權益。除了現役及退伍軍人（veteran）會到戰死的士兵墓碑前表示敬意之外，也有些民眾會利用這一天前往墓園探視已故親人。而由退伍軍人組織的支持性團體會在這一天販售由殘疾退伍軍人製作的紙虞美人花（paper poppy）為慈善活動募款。當天全美各地會以在中午之前降半旗的方式來表示默哀，隨後會將國旗升至頂端。而白宮紀念委員會將當天的下午三點鐘定為國家紀念時刻（National Moment of Remembrance），呼籲民眾在此時停止活動一分鐘，向犧牲將士們致意。陣亡將士紀念日普遍的被美國民眾認為是夏季的開始，所以出遊，接受陽光洗禮也成了這個假期中最多人從事的活動，除此之外出外野餐（picni(c)，在家烤肉或是辦家庭聚會都是不錯的選擇。

實用生活會話

Q1: Sweetheart, can we have a barbecue on Saturday?
甜心，我們星期六來烤肉好嗎？

A1: No, I don't think so. That is not a good idea to have a barbecue on the Memorial Day weekend.
不好吧。在陣亡將士紀念日假期中烤肉不是個好主意。

Q2: Why? I think you like barbecue.
為什麼？我想你喜歡烤肉啊。

A2: Memorial Day is a solemn event. It makes me feel guilty to have a barbecue on the Memorial Day weekend.
陣亡將士紀念日是個莊嚴的日子。在這個假日中烤肉讓我感到有罪惡感。

Q3: That's why I choose Saturday, because I want to take you and kids to the Memorial Day parade. We'll also raise a flag to a half staff until noon to commemorate those heroes. Does that make you feel better?
所以我才選在星期六啊，因為在陣亡將士紀念日的時候，我要帶妳跟孩子們去參加陣亡將士紀念日遊行。我們那天還會升旗，並以降半旗方式直到中午來紀念那些英雄。這樣妳有沒有覺得好點？

A3: Yes. You should tell me about Monday plan first.
有。你應該要先告訴我你星期一的計畫。

Q4: Sorry, I am too excited about having a vacation.
抱歉，我對於這假期有些太興奮了。

A4: That's all right. After all, after a period of hard-working, you can take a break.
還好。畢竟，在一段時間的努力工作後，你可以休息一下了。

實用單句這樣說

- Memorial Day is a day to memorize the men and women who died while serving in the United States Armed Forces.
  陣亡將士紀念日是為了紀念那些在美國陸海空三軍服役時過世的男性及女性。

- We fly the flag at half staff until noon and then raise it to the top of the staff until sunset on the Memorial Day.
  我們在陣亡將士紀念日會降半旗至中午，然後將國旗升至頂端一直到日落。

- There will be no school on the Memorial Day.
  在陣亡將士紀念日那一天不用上課。

- Memorial Day is a United States federal holiday, formerly known as Decoration Day.
  陣亡將士紀念日是個美國聯邦假日，之前被稱做裝飾日。

- Johnny said the commemoration today made clear for him the meaning of the Memorial Day.
  強尼說今天的紀念會讓他清楚的瞭解到陣亡將士紀念日的含意。

- Rolling Thunder is an annual motorcycle rally that is held in Washington DC during the Memorial Day weekend to call for the government's recognition and protection those Missing in Action and Prisoners of War.
  滾雷巡遊是每年在陣亡將士紀念日假期時於華盛頓特區舉行的摩托車集會，是為了要喚起政府對戰俘及失蹤士兵的肯定及保護。

互動時刻真有趣

● 虞美人花 Poppy

　　在第一次及第二次世界大戰的協約國的國殤日（11 月 11 日）及美國的陣亡將士紀念日及退伍軍人日時，常會看到這種花的出現。通常人們會將它別在胸前衣襟上以示哀悼之意。在第一世界大戰期間，法蘭德斯戰場（Flanders Fields）被認為是最慘烈的戰場。而一位加拿大籍的軍醫約翰麥克雷（John McCrae）在這場戰役中目睹了他的戰友死亡，而寫下了「在法蘭德斯戰場」（In Flanders Fields）這一首詩。詩中提到，在法蘭德斯，開滿了虞美人花。而虞美人花的紅色被認為像是士兵們留下的鮮血，因此被選擇配戴來紀念為國捐軀的將士們。虞美人花是罌粟科罌粟屬，但跟一般認知中可提煉鴉片的罌粟花（opium poppy）是不同種。在 2010 年 11 月時英國當時新上任的首相卡麥隆率團訪問中國，因為正值英國國殤日，因此全體團員皆配戴虞美人花在衣襟上。中國官員誤認為是罌粟花，為了避免讓人聯想到在清代，中英兩國間的鴉片戰爭，所以請團員將花取下，但被英國首相府人員拒絕。虞美人花在古代中國就已經有大量培植，相傳是虞美人自殺後，流在地上的鮮血長出了鮮紅色的花朵，因而得名，有代表對愛情的忠貞及家國摯愛的含意。所以下次如果看到有人配戴時，請記得它是虞美人花。

In Flanders fields the poppies blow　在法蘭德斯戰場 虞美人隨風搖曳
Between the crosses, row on row,　綻放在十字架之間 一排排一行行
That mark our place; and in the sky　標示著我們斷魂的所在
The larks, still bravely singing, fly　雲雀仍舊在天空勇敢高歌 飛翔
Scarce heard amid the guns below.　歌聲卻淹沒在漫天的砲聲之中

We are the Dead. Short days ago　我們已逝 就在幾天之前
We lived, felt dawn, saw sunset glow,　我們曾活著 感受曙光也看過璀璨夕陽
Loved and were loved, and now we lie,　愛過也被愛 但我們現在長眠
In Flanders fields.　在法蘭德斯戰場上

Take up our quarrel with the foe:　繼續和我們的敵人戰鬥吧
To you from failing hands we throw　用我們顫抖的雙手拋給你們
The torch; be yours to hold it high.　那熊熊的火炬 讓你們將它高舉
If ye break faith with us who die　如有違背與我們立下的誓言
We shall not sleep, though poppies grow　我們將無法安息 儘管虞美人依然綻放
In Flanders fields.　在法蘭德斯戰場上

Independence Day
獨立紀念日

節慶源由──簡易版

The 4th of July is Independence Day in the United States. In 1776, there were 13 British colonies in America. They wanted to be free of the King of England. There was a long war between England and the colonies. The colonies won the war and declared freedom. It was July 4th, 1776.

7 月 4 日是美國的獨立紀念日。在 1776 年，美國有 13 個英屬殖民地。他們想要從英國國王手裡獲得自由。在英國與殖民地間有長期的戰爭。殖民地贏得了戰爭並且宣告自由。在 7 月 4 日，1776 年。

July 4th is a national holiday most known for its fireworks. During the day there are speeches and parades. There are concerts, picnics and baseball games. Since it is the middle of summer, most celebrations take place outdoors.

7 月 4 日是一個以煙火表演聞名的國定節日。白天會有許多演講與遊行。有音樂會、野餐、棒球比賽。因為這一天是仲夏，大部分的慶祝活動在戶外舉辦。

At night, the fireworks include songs about America. This always includes The Star Spangled Banner, which is the national anthem.

晚上，煙火表演會包含有關美國的歌。總是會有美國國歌──星條旗永不落。

Families often celebrate Independence Day by having a picnic or barbecue. They have the day off to spend with family and friends. Paper streamers, balloons, and paper plates all shine in red, white, and blue, the colors of the U.S. flag.

家庭們通常藉著野餐或是烤肉慶祝獨立紀念日。他們用那天休假來陪家庭與朋友。紙幡、氣球、紙盤通通閃耀著紅、白、藍，美國國旗的顏色。

單字大集合

1. **British** *adj.* 英國的

   British people are from Great Britain.
   英國的人民來自於大不列顛。

2. **Declare** *vi. vt.* 聲明；宣布

   I declared a day off for all workers.
   我向所有的勞工宣布放假一天。

3. **Freedom** *n.* [C,U] 獨立自主；自由

   We are hoping for freedom from homework.
   我們正在希望從功課裡得到自由。

4. **Baseball** *n.* [C] 棒球

   In a baseball game, players run around the bases.
   在棒球賽中，選手們繞著壘包跑。

5. **Banner** *n.* [C] 旗幟

   They hung a banner in the window.
   他們在窗口掛上一面旗幟。

6. **Streamer** *n.* [C] 旗幟

   Paper streamers blew in the wind.
   紙幡在風中隨風飄動。

節慶源由——精彩完整版

The 4th of July is Independence Day in the United States. It commemorates the day the Declaration of Independence was signed. In 1776, there were 13 British colonies in America. They wanted to be independent of the British King. They declared their independence on July 4th, 1776. This started the American Revolution, the war between England and the colonies. The Colonial soldiers won that war and the United States was born.

7 月 4 日是美國的獨立紀念日。它慶祝著美國獨立宣言被簽屬的那天。在西元 1776 年，美國有 13 個英屬殖民地。它們想要從英國國王手中獨立。它們在 1776 年 7 月 4 日宣布它們的獨立。這開啟了美國革命，一場英國與殖民地的戰爭。殖民地的士兵們贏了戰爭，美國誕生。

On the one year anniversary of independence, thirteen gunshots were fired in salute. This was done once in the morning and once again as evening fell. There were prayers, parades and fireworks. Ships in harbor were decorated in red, white and blue, the colors of the United States flag.

在獨立的一周年，發射 13 記槍砲致敬。這在早上做一次，並在日落前再做一次。有禱告、遊行與煙火表演。在海港的船隻被裝飾成紅、白、藍，美國國旗的顏色。

Today, it is a national holiday most notably known for its patriotic displays and fireworks. During the day there are political speeches and ceremonies. Many politicians make it a point to appear at a public event to praise the nation's laws, history and people. There are parades, concerts, picnics and baseball games. A salute of one gunshot for each state in the United States is called a "salute to the union". It is fired on Independence Day at noon by all military bases. Since it is the middle of summer, most celebrations take place outdoors.

在今日，這個國定節日尤其以愛國表演與煙火表演聞名。白天會有許多政治演講與典禮。許多政治人物利用這天出現在公眾事件讚揚國家的法律、歷史與人民。有遊行、音樂會、野餐與棒球比賽。每發向美國各州致敬的槍砲被稱為「向美國致敬」。獨立紀念日中午由所有軍事基地開火。因為這一天是仲夏，大部分的慶祝活動在戶外舉辦。

On the lawn of the nation's Capitol in Washington, D.C., there is always a free concert before the fireworks. It attracts over half a million people annually. Independence Day fireworks are often accompanied by patriotic songs. This always includes The Star Spangled Banner, which is the national anthem. Other patriotic songs might include God Bless America, America the Beautiful and This Land is Your Land.

在華盛頓哥倫比亞特區的美國國會大廈草坪，在煙火表演之前總有免費的音樂會。這每年吸引了超過 50 萬人。獨立紀念日煙火表演常常伴隨著愛國歌曲。總是會包含美國國歌──星條旗永不落。其他愛國歌曲可能包含「上帝保佑美國」、「美哉美國」、「這是你的土地」。

Families often celebrate Independence Day by hosting or attending a picnic or barbecue. They take advantage of the day off and the long weekend to gather with relatives and friends. Paper streamers, balloons, paper plates, napkins and sometimes even people's clothes are red, white, and blue.

家庭通常藉由舉辦或參加野餐、烤肉慶祝獨立紀念日。他們利用休假與長期的周末與親戚朋友團聚。紙幡、氣球、紙盤、餐巾，甚至有時人們的衣服都是紅、白、藍色。

單字大集合

1. Declaration *n.* [C,U] 宣布；宣告

When the kids made a declaration of independence, their mother was worried.
當孩子做了獨立宣言後，他們的母親很擔心。

2. Independence *n.* [U] 獨立；自主

All kids want independence from their parents as they get older.
所有孩子都想從他們的父母那獨立，當他們年長時。

3. Revolution *n.* [C] 革命

Many countries have a revolution to gain freedom.
許多國家為了得到自由有了革命。

4. Colony *n.* [C] 殖民地

The colonies were formed by people looking for a new country.
殖民地是尋找新國家的人們所組成的。

5. Patriotic *adj.* 愛國的

I feel patriotic when I hear our national anthem.
當我聽到我們的國歌時，我覺得我很愛國。

6. Political *adj.* 政治的

There are lots of political people in the parade today.
今天的遊行裡有很多政治人物。

7. Salute *vi. vt.* 行禮；向……誰行禮

The soldiers always salute their leader.
士兵總是向它們的領袖行禮。

8. Annually *adv.* 每年地

We have a birthday party annually.
我們每年都有生日派對。

閱讀測驗

1. How many British colonies were there in America in 1776?

   在西元 1776 年在美洲共有幾個英屬殖民地？

   (a) Too many to count. 太多數不清。

   (b) 50. 。

   (c) 13.

2. Why were ships decorated in red, white and blue?

   為什麼船隻被用紅、白和藍色裝飾？

   (a) The captains' favorite colors were red, white and blue.

   　　船長最喜歡的顏色是紅、白和藍色。

   (b) Those are the colors of the United States flag.

   　　這些是美國國旗的顏色。

   (c) Those were the only decorations they could find.

   　　這些是他們所能找到的唯一裝飾。

3. What is a salute of one gunshot for each state in the U.S. called?

   向美國每個州致敬的槍響被稱為什麼？

   (a) The Star Spangled Banner. 星條旗永不落。

   (b) The soldiers salute. 士兵們致敬。

   (c) A salute to the union. 向美國致敬。

4. What is the name of the U.S. national anthem? 美國國歌的名字是什麼？

   (a) America the Beautiful 美國的美麗。

   (b) God Bless America 神佑美國。

   (c) The Star Spangled Banner 星條旗永不落。

活動慶典和習俗

　　在 18 世紀中葉，英屬北美 13 個殖民地與大不列顛王國間爆發嚴重衝突，歷經美國革命（American Revolution），在 1776 年 7 月 2 日大陸會議上表決通過宣示獨立的決案，在 7 月 4 日發表獨立宣言（Declaration of Independence），正式宣告獨立，13 個殖民地合併成為美利堅合眾國（United States of America）簡稱美國。在 1783 年的獨立戰爭結束後，7 月 4 日被正式定為美國獨立紀念日（Independence Day）是美國的國慶日，在 1941 年宣告成為聯邦假日。

　　1776 年的 7 月 8 日，大陸會議的代表在宣讀獨立宣言之前曾敲響自由鐘來召集費城的民眾。因此，自由鐘便成了美國獨立紀念日活動中代表性的象徵之一。其中最引人注目的就是在鐘下方的裂痕，事實上，自由鐘在第一次試敲時，就已經產生了裂痕，在重鑄兩次之後正式使用，在 1835 年再次裂開，1846 年最後一次被敲響時，已嚴重損壞。政府官員擔心這個極具歷史意義的鐘會因此而毀損，所以將其從鐘塔取下，放在紀念館中供人參觀。鑄鐘公司曾提出願意負擔所有費用將此鐘重鑄，但被美國政府拒絕了，因為鐘身上的裂痕就像是在建國之初，就像是祖先們所受的磨難，及付出的血淚代價，是歷史的一部份，是美國人的驕傲。

　　美國獨立日早期的慶祝活動大多是遊行及演說，並帶有宗教色彩，慢慢的加入了戶外活動，如棒球賽、亞利桑納州的馬術競技賽等，讓慶祝活動多元化，也更活潑生動起來了。在活動中常可看到以美國國旗的紅、白、藍三色為主，飾以星星及條紋的圖案被廣泛的利用在活動的服裝、緞帶、氣球等物品。在賓州立提茲市（Lititz）的人會在獨立日晚上會將自家製作的蠟燭點燃，放到水面上任其漂浮，類似我們的水燈祈福儀式。而晚上在全美各地所舉辦的煙火大會則是慶祝的最高潮，在紐約市由梅西百貨所贊助的煙火晚會號稱是 7 月 4 日最大規模的煙火秀，也有電視轉播。除了這一些五花八門的慶祝活動之外，民眾還喜歡在公園的草地上野餐，或是在戶外烤肉，為這個激發民眾愛國心的節日增添許多溫馨氣氛。

實用生活會話

Q1: Dad, what is "Old Glory"?

爹地，什麼是「昔日輝煌」啊？

A1: Old Glory is the fond nickname for the U.S. flag.

「昔日輝煌」是人們對美國國旗的暱稱。

Q2: Is there any other names for the flag?

那還有其他的稱法嗎？

A2: Yes, we also call it "Star-Spangled Banner", "Red, White and Blue", and "Stars and Stripes".

有，我們還會稱它做「星條旗」、「紅白藍」及「星星和條紋」。

Q3: How many stars are on the U.S. Flag?

在美國國旗上有幾顆星星呢？

A3: There are 50 white, five-pointed small stars on the flag.

一共有 50 顆白色的小五角星。

實用單句這樣說

- I love Independence Day. We celebrate it on the fourth of July.

  我愛美國獨立紀念日。我們在 7 月 4 日慶祝。

- Independence Day, commonly known as the Fourth of July, is a federal holiday in the United States.

  美國獨立紀念日，一般稱為七四節，是美國的聯邦假日。

- There are many celebration activities on the Independence Day, such as political speeches, parades, baseball games, carnivals, concerts, family reunions and etc.
在美國獨立紀念日會有許多的慶祝活動，像是政治演說、遊行、棒球賽、嘉年華會、音樂會、家庭聚餐等等。

- Like the other summer-themed events, Independence Day celebrations always take place outdoor.
如同其他的夏季活動，美國獨立紀念日的慶祝活動多半在戶外舉行。

- Firework Shows on the Independence Day are often accompanied by patriotic songs, for example, the national anthem "The Star-Spangled Banner", "America the Beautiful" and etc.
美國獨立紀念日的煙火大會通常在施放時會以愛國歌曲為伴奏，例如是美國國歌「星條旗」、「美哉美國」等等。

- The Liberty Bell is the iconic symbol of American Independence.
自由鐘是美國獨立戰爭的象徵性代表。

互動時刻真有趣

在自由鐘裡找出下列與美國獨立紀念日有關的單字、詞

Find words from the Liberty Bell

AMERICA 美國	BILL OF RIGHTS 人權法案	BLUE 藍色
CONSTITUTION 憲法	EAGLE 老鷹	FIREWORKS 煙火
FLAG 旗	FREEDOM 自由	INDEPENDENCE 獨立
JULY 七月	OLD GLORY 美國國旗	PARADE 遊行
PICNIC 野餐	RED 紅色	STARS 星星
STRIPES 條紋	WHITE 白色	

```
                              X B L U E
        F C J T K A X T P G K E F J V M X S W E T
      M F B V C X Z A W E R F I R E W O Y R S K F Q X T H S S D
      F J K C O L D F G L O R Y S F H O A H I O S S R A E D E
      G C B H I E T J S A C B N M A E R Y I G B B S V E A L K E
      C Q B R R E D D R T Y W G A J I O P G B S S P R H J Q E L
    C V B R H L K Y W                       S V E E A F H K E U
    A J J U L D V                             Q E Q W S K Y T U A
    E F T U D M             J I G C I T Y           S F T H O P
    X K O N M         S E H N F N Q E Q F Q
                    E U C G A D S I A F S F A E
                    E W C O F T G E H C H E L Q Q E R
                    E R O N S G A P R Y T A P W A Z G
                    R T Y S T G S E N U M J R O F S S
                    T Y S T S F N D S D E T Y G N S L
                    L U I S A K E P E S R R H B I S S
                    L K I O U H U C N O R F G I Y G P T
                    J J O U T U C I T R H S C V O R I
                    H H P L I Q E U Y E E A D A D I P
                  T G G L J W E Q J E W Q G D C P E E
                  R R F F J O H D I D Y Y J A V E E O
                  E E D H G H H C P O I U I Q B S S
                Q W W S G A Q X D L M J L O P N A E Q
              O P P Q A F E R Y H D F P A R A D E P O V
                W H I T E G J A S D F G H J K
                    J U L Y E T Y U P
```

Answer:

```
                              X B L U E
        F C J T K A X T P G K E F J V M X S W E T
      M F B V C X Z A W E R F I R E W O R K S A H T S S D
      F J K C O L D G L O R Y S F H O Y S F Q X T S D E
      G C B I L L O F R I G H T S G E A H L T Q A S D E
      C Q B H J E T J S A C B N M A E R Y I O P R A R E E
        R E D D R T Y W G A J I O P G B S S H J Q E L
    C V B R H K Y W                         E A G L E A
    A J J U L D V                           E F H K Y U O P
    E F T U D M             J I G C I T Y     Q W T U E O P
    X K O N M         S E H N F N Q E Q F Q     S F T H P
                    E U C G A D S I A F S F A E
                    E W C O F T G E H C H E L Q Q E R
                    E R O N S G A P R Y T A P W A G H
                    R T Y S T G S F N U M J R O F S L
                    T Y S T S H D S D E T Y G N L
                    L U I S A K E P E S R R H B I S
                    L K I O U H U N O R F G I Y G P T
                    J J O U T U C I T R H S C V O R I
                    H H P L I Q E U Y E E A D A D I P
                  T G G L J W E Q J E W Q G D C P E E
                  R R F F J O H D I D Y Y J A V E E O
                  E E D H G H H C P O I U I Q B S S O
                Q W W S G A Q X D L M J L O P N A E Q
              O P P Q A F E R Y H D F P A R A D E P O V
                W H I T E G J A S D F G H J K
                    J U L Y E T Y U P
```

Labor Day
勞動節

節慶源由──簡易版

　　Labor Day is a national holiday in the United States. It is the first Monday in September. People celebrate the work that is done all year. At first, Labor Day had parades. There were festivals for workers and their families. There were speeches by prominent men and women.

　　勞動節在美國是國定節日。在 9 月的第一個禮拜一。人們慶祝完成全年的工作。首先，勞動節有遊行。有給勞工和他們家人的慶祝活動。有傑出男性和女性的演講。

　　Today, Labor Day has lost much of that meaning. There still have some speeches or parades. But mostly, it is a day to rest and play. People have picnics and barbecues. Families might spend the day on the lake. Families with school-age children might travel. Soon children will be too busy with school to travel. For some, school has already started. It is seen as a transition to fall activities.

　　在今天，勞動節已經失去許多它的涵意。仍然有些演講或遊行。但大多數地，這是休息和玩樂的日子。人們野餐和烤肉。家庭們可能會在湖上花上一整天時間。有在學兒童的家庭可能會旅行。很快地，孩子會因為學校太忙而無法旅行。對有些人來說，學校已經開學了。這個節日被認為是到秋季活動的過渡時期。

　　Because many people are off work, stores think it is a perfect shopping day. This is bad news for people who work in sales. They have to work long hours on Labor Day.

　　因為許多人休假，店家們認為這是個完美的購物日。這對從事銷售的人來說是個壞消息。他們得在勞動節工作很長的時數。

單字大集合

1. Worker　*n.* [C]　勞工

It takes many workers to run the factory.
這需要許多勞工來使工廠運作。

2. Meaning　*n.* [C,U]　涵義；意思

What is the meaning of this word?
這個字的涵義是什麼？

3. Travel　*vi. vt.*　旅行；在……旅行

Do you want to travel to India?
你想要到印度旅行嗎？

4. Busy　*adj.*　忙碌的

I am too busy to come over today.
我今天忙到無法從順道拜訪。

5. Already　*adv.*　已經

I have already seen that movie.
我已經看過那部電影。

6. Perfect　*adj.*　完美的

That costume would be perfect for Halloween.
這將是完美的萬聖節前夕服裝。

節慶源由──精彩完整版

Labor Day is a national holiday in the United States. It is the first Monday in September. People celebrate the economic and social contributions of all workers. In the beginning, Labor Day was to have street parades and festivals for workers and their families. There were speeches by prominent men and women. On September 5, 1882, 10,000 workers assembled in New York City to participate in America's first Labor Day parade. After marching from City Hall through the city, the workers and their families gathered in a park for a picnic, concert, and speeches. It first became a state holiday in Oregon in 1887. Not until 1894 did it become a national holiday.

勞動節在美國是國定節日。在 9 月的第一個禮拜一。人們慶祝所有勞工的經濟和社會貢獻。一開始，勞動節有街頭遊行和給勞工和他們家人的慶祝活動。有傑出男性和女性的演講。在西元 1882 年 9 月 5 日，一萬名勞工聚集在紐約市參加美國第一次勞動節遊行。從市政府行經整個城市後，勞工和他們的家人們為野餐、音樂會和演講聚在公園。它在西元 1887 年首次在美國俄勒岡州成為州節日。直到 1894 年，它成為一個全國性的節日。

On Sep. 4, 1882, one of the laborers' leader suggested to have a big parade during this day in order to ask for more reasonable working conditions from the management, and presents the New Yorkers' strength and unity of the laborers. Therefore, there are 20 thousand more of New York City's laborers to join this parade. They lifted up the sign of "the labor makes everything", and proclaimed the slogan of "8 hours work, 8 hours rest, 8 hours entertain", walking through the Broadway Boulevard. And the other cities in the states also didn't start to imitate until the Congress approved that the first Monday of every Sep. was designated as the national Labor Day.

在 1882 年的 9 月 4 日，紐約市的工人領袖建議在這一天舉行盛大的遊行，向資方要求更合理的工作條件，也向紐約市民展現工人的力量與團結。因而，總共有兩萬多名紐約工人參加了遊行。並且高舉「勞動創造一切」的標語，呼喊著「8 小時工作、8 小時休息、8 小時娛樂」的口號，在百老匯大道上一路走過。而美國其他的城市也就開始仿效，直到國會通過，把每年 9 月的第一個星期一指定為全國的勞動節。

Today, Labor Day has lost much of its original meaning. There still have some speeches or demonstrations. But mostly, the holiday is thought of as a day of rest and recreation. It is mostly celebrated with picnics and barbecues. Families might spend the day on the lake. Families with school-age children use it as the last chance to travel at the end of summer vacation. For some, school has already started. This three-day weekend is the last weekend before school children get busy with school activities. It is seen as a transition to fall activities.

在今天，勞動節已經失去許多它的涵意。仍然有些演講或示威遊行。但大多數地，這被認為是休息和娛樂的日子。它主要是野餐和烤肉慶祝。家庭們可能會在湖上花一整天。有在學兒童的家庭利用這最後的機會在暑假的尾聲去旅行。對有些人來說，學校已經開學了。這三天的週末是在學兒童開始忙碌學校活動前的最後一個週末。

Since it is a holiday for workers, many people are off work that day. However, because so many people have the day off, stores see it as a perfect shopping day. Labor Day has become an important sale weekend. Some store owners claim it is one of the largest sale dates of the year. This is bad news for people who work in retail sales. Not only do they have to work on Labor Day, they also work long hours.

因為這是勞工的節日，許多人在那天休假。然而，因為許多人在那天有休假，店家們認為這是個完美的購物日。勞動節已經變成一個重要的銷售週末。有些店家老闆聲稱這是他們一年當中其中一個巨大的銷售日。這對從事零售銷售的人來說是個壞消息。他們不僅得在勞動節工作，還得工作很長的時數。

單字大集合

1. Economic *adj.* 經濟上的

The economic situation in the world today is uncertain.
今日世界經濟上的情勢是不穩定的。

2. Social *adj.* 社交的；社會的

I love to go to social events.
我喜歡參加社交活動。

3. Contribution *n.* [C] 貢獻

Children make many funny contributions to their families.
孩子們對他們的家人做了許多有趣的貢獻。

4. Prominent *adj.* 突出的；卓越的

Prominent people are very well known.
卓越的人都非常有名。

5. Assemble *vi. vt.* 集合；聚集

The students were all assembled for the first day of school.
學生們因為開學第一天全部集合在一起。

6. Participate *vi. vt.* 參加；分享

Will you participate in the game?
你會參加比賽嗎？

7. Demonstration *n.* [C] 展示；實地示範

We are going to have lots of art demonstrations this year.
我們今年將會有許多藝術展示。

8. Transition *n.* [C,U] 轉變；過渡時期

It is time to transition from spring to summer.
這是春天到夏天轉換的時刻。

閱讀測驗

1. Who were the labor day parades and festivals for?
   勞動節遊行和慶祝活動是為了誰？
   (a) Workers and their families. 勞工和他們的家人。
   (b) Grade school children. 小學生。
   (c) Poor people in the community. 社區裡的窮人。

2. Where did the first Labor Day parade take place?
   第一次的勞動節遊行在哪裡舉辦？
   (a) At a large school for girls. 在大型的女校。
   (b) In New York City. 在紐約市。
   (c) In Chicago. 在芝加哥。

3. What is Labor Day thought to be today? 在今天，勞動節被怎麼認為的？
   (a) A day to go to work for the first time. 第一次工作的日子。
   (b) The first day of summer. 夏天的第一天。
   (c) A day of rest and recreation. 休息和娛樂的日子。

4. To whom it is a bad news to have to work on Labor day?
   對誰而言，必須在勞動節工作是個壞消息呢？
   (a) Teachers. 老師們。
   (b) Politicans. 政治人物們。
   (c) People who work in retail sales. 從事零售銷售的人。

活動慶典和習俗

　　在 1882 年 9 月 5 日時，紐約各工會組織發起第一次的勞動節（Workingmen's Holiday）的活動，其訴求則是以「8 小時標準工作日」為主題的立法活動，要求將原先長達 12 至 16 鐘頭的工時縮短為 8 小時。中央工會（Central Labor Union）在 1884 年時選擇 9 月的第一個星期天來慶祝勞動節，並推動這活動，希望其他地方也能像紐約一樣來慶祝。而在 1885 年開始，在美國許多工業重鎮也開始跟進在 9 月初慶祝勞動節。而在 1894 年時，美國國會確定每年 9 月的第一個星期日為全國性慶祝的勞動節（Labor Day）。

　　大多數的美國人會將每年 5 月的陣亡將士紀念日（Memorial Day）視為是夏季的開始，而 9 月份的勞動節則是夏季結束的象徵。多數的私立學校及大學會在勞工節前一週開學，而大部分的公立學校則在勞動節過後開學，有著三日週末連休（three-day-weekend）的勞動節是夏天的最後一個假日。所以許多美國人會抓緊這三天的假期，不論是在家看遊行、辦烤肉或聚餐活動、野餐、露營、划船或是到海灘或是主題樂園（theme park）遊玩，藉以放鬆心情，準備迎接秋季的到來。而在紐約布魯克林舉行的勞動節嘉年華遊行/西印裔美國人嘉年華（Labor Day Carnival Parade/West Indian Carnival），每年會吸引超過 3 百萬人次參加，是美國勞動節一大盛事之一。除了遊行之外，在各地也會有煙火秀表演。還有一個特殊的慶祝活動，相信會受到大多數女性的歡迎，那就是在美國每逢假日必有的促銷活動，勞動節特賣（Labor Day Sales）緊接在 8 月份開始的返校日特賣（Back to School Sales）的後面，各商場間的折扣戰爭可說是在每年的 8、9 月間達到最高潮，因此在勞動節假日期間，在各商場總是能看到滿滿的購物人潮，可說是勞動節新型態的慶祝活動。

實用生活會話

Q1: Honey, do you have any plans for the long weekend?

親愛的，這個週末有什麼計畫嗎？

A1: Nope, I think we better stay at home. You know, school will begin on the next week, and I want to bring kids' minds back to study.

沒有，我想我們最好待在家。你知道的，下星期就開學了，我想讓孩子們能收心。

Q2: So, what's your plan?

所以你的計畫是？

A2: Hmmm… nothing special, just stay at home and read.

嗯，沒什麼特別的，就是待在家看書吧。

Q3: Come on, that sounds boring. We have three days' vacation. How about go camping? Kids will love it. I guarantee that they'll be fine in the school, just make sure that they get enough sleep.

拜託，聽起來真無聊。我們有 3 天假期耶。要不然我們去露營，好嗎？孩子們一定會很高興的。只要讓他們有充足的睡眠，我保證孩子們去學校後會沒問題的。

A3: All right, let's go camping. I think I'm just too nervous.

好吧，就去露營吧。我想我太緊張了。

實用單句這樣說

- In Taiwan, we celebrate Labor Day on May 1.
  在台灣，我們在 5 月 1 日慶祝勞動節。

- Tomorrow is May Day, we are going to make a day of it.
  明天是 5 月 1 日勞動節，我們要好好的玩上一整天。

- Labor Day, the first Monday in September, is a United States federal holiday to celebrate the achievements of workers.
  勞動節，九月的第一個星期天，是一個慶祝勞工成就的美國聯邦假日。

- Labor Day generally marks the end of the summer season, and the beginning of the school year.
  勞動節通常代表著夏季的結束，及新學期的開始。

- Many people use the Labor Day holiday as part of the long weekend where they can relax, spend time with families, play or watch sport, or have barbecues.
  許多人會利用勞動節的長假來放鬆心情、陪伴家人、去運動或是看運動節目、去烤肉等。

- During the Labor Day vacation, government offices are closed, as are post offices, schools and many businesses.
  在勞動節假期間，政府機關、郵局、學校及許多公司都不上班。

互動時刻真有趣

　　在美國，勞動節之後就是大多數學校開學的日子，而在台灣，開學日也大多訂在 9 月初之前。由於是新的學年度，孩子要面對的也許是新的班級，新的同學或是新的學校。所以許多家長會擔心在暑假過後，孩子們會在學校適應不良，也就是所謂的返校憂鬱（Back to School Blues），專家提出，充足睡眠（enough sleep）及豐富的早餐（good breakfast）是必備的要件來對抗返校憂鬱，而多陪伴及充分準備也有所幫助。所以在美國，有一項新興的勞動節親子活動就是一同準備開學所需的東西。不過，請記得先痛痛快快的玩完之後再來準備喔！

● 開學用品（請視個人需要及學校要求做增減）
- 書包 bookbag/backpack
- 鉛筆數隻 pencils
- 橡皮擦 eraser
- 彩虹筆 rainbow crayon
- 蠟筆一組 crayons
- 口紅膠 glue stick
- 白膠 Elmer's glue/ craft glue
- 兒童安全剪刀 child safety scissors
- 彩色筆一組 colored markers
- 尺 ruler
- L 型資料夾 L shape file folder
- 牙刷及牙膏 tooth brush and paste
- 衛生紙 tissue

Columbus Day
哥倫布日

節慶源由──簡易版

Columbus Day is a U.S. holiday to honor Christopher Columbus. It is on October 12th, the day Columbus landed in America in 1492. He was sent from Spain by the King and Queen . He planned to discover a western route over the ocean to China and India. The King and Queen wanted him to find the gold and spice islands of Asia. Instead, he landed in the Americas.

哥倫布日是尊崇克里斯多夫‧哥倫布的美國節日。它在 10 月 12 日，哥倫布在西元 1492 年登陸美洲的日子。他從西班牙被國王和皇后派遣。他計畫找到西方航線穿越大洋到達中國和印度。國王和皇后想要他發現亞洲的黃金和香料群島。相反的，他著陸於美洲。

Later that month, Columbus sighted Cuba and thought it was mainland China. He started a Spanish village in what he thought was Japan. On his third journey to the Americas he realized it was not Asia at all. He finally knew that he had stumbled upon an unknown continent.

當月稍晚，哥倫布發現了古巴，並認為那是中國大陸。他在一個他以為是日本的地方發展一個西班牙小鎮。在他第三次到美洲的旅程上，他意識到那裡不是亞洲。他終於知道他已經偶然發現了一個未知的大陸。

For many years, Columbus Day was a national holiday. But today, little is done to celebrate. Other holidays have been given more importance.

多年來，哥倫布日是一個全國性的節日。但在今天，已經很少被拿來慶祝。其他的節日被賦與更多重要性。

單字大集合

1. Land　*n.* [U]　陸地

We were excited when our ship landed on the shore.
我們很興奮，當我們的船在岸上登陸時。

2. Discover　*vt.*　發現；找到

I want to discover a new land some day.
我想要有一天能發現一個新大陸。

3. Western　*adj.*　西部的

We live on the western side of the mountains.
我們住在山脈的西邊。

4. Island　*n.* [C]　小島

Everyone in the islands knows the sound of the sea.
小島上的每個人都知道海的聲音。

5. Stumble　*vi. vt.*　絆倒；使絆倒

I stumbled down the rocky hillside.
我從許多岩石的山坡上跌跌撞撞地下來。

6. Unknown　*adj.*　陌生的

That person is unknown to me.
那個人對我來說是陌生的。

節慶源由──精彩完整版

Columbus Day is a U.S. holiday that commemorates the landing of Christopher Columbus in the New World. It was on October 12, 1492. The explorer had set sail two months earlier. He was sent from Spain by the King and Queen . He intended to discover a western sea route to China and India. He hoped to find the fabled gold and spice islands of Asia. Instead, he landed in the Americas, becoming the first European to explore this part of them.

哥倫布日是個紀念克里斯多夫‧哥倫布著陸於新世界的美國節日。這是在西元 1492 年，10 月 12 日。探險家提早兩個月起航。他從西班牙被國王和皇后派遣。他打算找到西方航線穿越大洋到達中國和印度。他希望可以發現寓言裡亞洲的黃金和香料島嶼。相反的，他著陸於美洲，成為探索這其中一部分的第一個歐洲人。

Later that month, Columbus sighted Cuba and believed it was mainland China. In what he thought was Japan, he established a Spanish colony with 39 of his men. In March 1493, the explorer returned to Spain in triumph, bearing gold, spices and "Indian" captives. It was not until his third journey to the Americas that he realized it was not Asia at all. He finally figured out that he had stumbled upon a continent previously unknown to Europeans.

當月稍晚，哥倫布發現了古巴，並相信那是中國大陸。在一個他認為是日本的地方，他與 39 個他的人，建立了一個西班牙殖民地。在西元 1493 年 3 月，探險家凱旋回到西班牙，帶了黃金、香料和「印地安」俘虜。但直到他第三次美洲之旅，他才意識到這不是亞洲。他終於知道他已經偶然一個歐洲人未知的大陸。

Columbus Day was unofficially celebrated in a number of cities and states as early as the 18th century（1700's）. It did not become a national holiday until the 1937. For many years, it was a national   holiday. Schools, banks, post offices and all government offices were closed. In some states, there were large parades and other recognitions of the holiday. Most of those events have dwindled in importance today.

在 18 世紀早期（西元 1700 年），哥倫布日在一些城市和州是被非正式慶祝的。它並沒有成為國定節日，直到西元 1937 年。多年來，它政府訂定的節日。學校、銀行、郵局和所有政府部門都會關閉。在有些州,會有大型遊行和其他被准許的假期。這些事在今天的重要性已經減少。

There is not a whole lot done to celebrate Columbus Day anymore. In some states, schools still close for the day, though. In some states, it is still a government holiday. But, in many states, there is little recognition of Columbus Day at all. Most school children still learn about Christopher Columbus and the part he played in the exploration of the Americas. But, as more recent holidays have been added to the year, this is one that has lost some of its importance.

已經沒有這麼多用來慶祝哥倫布日的事了。然而在一些州,學校仍會在那天關閉。在有些州,它仍然是政府訂定的節日。但在許多州已經很少承認哥倫布日了。大部分上學的孩子仍會學習有關克里斯多夫·哥倫布和他探險美洲的部分。但當越來越多節日被加到一年之中,哥倫布日也就減少了一些它的重要性。

In the year of 1972, the United States initiated the Columbus Day. It is the 300th anniversary to celebrate the discovery that Christopher Columbus found the land of America. The tradition of this celebration thus spreads out through the whole American continent. Countries in the areas of the North and South America and Caribbean Sea and so on will hold memorial activities on this day.

1972 年,美國首先發起哥倫布日。剛好是哥倫布發現到美洲大陸的 300 週年紀念日。這個節慶的傳統也由此傳遍整個美洲。像南北美洲,加勒比海地區的國家都會在此節日舉行紀念活動。

As for the Europeans, the big gate of the immigrant to the Continent of America gets to open. However, for the aboriginals, as we know, the Indians, they suffered a huge invasion. Therefore, when the Columbus Day comes each year, there are no less of Indians to hole activities to resist against the colonial rules.

對歐洲人來說,殖民美洲的大門就此開啟,但對原住民,也就是印第安人來說,則是受到很大的侵略。所以每年到了哥倫布節,就有為數不少的印第安人舉行活動來抗議殖民統治。

單字大集合

1. Explorer *n.* [C] 探險家

I hope to be a great explorer in the space one day.
我希望有天可以成為一位優秀的太空探險家。

2. Intend *vt.* 打算

I intended to be on time, but my car ran out of gas.
我打算準時，但我的車沒油了。

3. Fabled *adj.* 寓言中的

Since the spice islands are fabled, I wonder if they really exist.
因為香料島嶼是在寓言裡，我在想它是否真的存在。

4. Mainland [the S] 中國大陸

Many people from mainland China return home to Taiwan for Chinese New Year.
許多人為了農曆新年從中國大陸返家回台灣。

5. Continent *n.* [C] 大洲；大陸

Do you know which continent you live on?
你知道你住在哪一大洲嗎？

6. Previously *adv.* 以前地

I took this class previously, so I don't need to take it now.
我以前上過這門課，所以我現在不需要上了。

7. Dwindle *vi. vt.* 漸漸減少；使減少

The number of cookies dwindled as the children ate them.
餅乾的數量減少，當孩子們在吃它們的時候。

8. Exploration *n.* [C,U] 勘查；調查

I am studying the exploration of North America.
我正在研究探索北美洲。

閱讀測驗

1. What did Columbus intend to discover on his journey?

   哥倫布打算在他的旅程上找尋什麼？

   (a) Diamonds in the desert. 沙漠裡的鑽石。

   (b) A western sea route to China and India. 到中國和印度的西方航線。

   (c) A new language. 新的語言。

2. How many journeys did it take to realize he was not in Asia?

   總共幾次的旅程讓他了解他並不在亞洲？

   (a) He knew it right away on the first journey.

   在第一次的旅行他就立刻知道了。

   (b) He never figured that out. 他從來沒想通這點。

   (c) Three 三次。

3. Do most school children still learn about Christopher Columbus?

   大部分學校的孩子仍學習有關克里斯多夫‧哥倫布嗎？

   (a) Yes, but some don't get the day off of school anymore.

   是的，但有些再也沒得到學校的放假。

   (b) No, they are too busy to learn history.

   不，他們忙到無法學習歷史。

   (c) No, because they don't go to school in October.

   不，因為他們 10 月不去學校。

活動慶典和習俗

　　克里斯多福・哥倫布（Christopher Columbus）出生在 15 世紀中葉的熱那亞共和國（Republic of Genoa），今義大利西北部。他是一個探險家（explorer）、航海家（navigator）及殖民家（colonizer）。在 15 世紀的時後，人們大多相信世界是平的，但仍有部分受過教育的人相信地圓說，而哥倫布就是其中一位。他說服了西班牙女皇伊莎貝拉（Queen Isabella），認為向西航行，能更容易到達亞洲。他在 1492 年時首次登陸美洲，之後又從歐洲連續探訪了美洲沿岸三次。但他一直認為他所到達的地方是印度，一直到他過世之前，他都還不知道他四次造訪的是一處鮮為人知的新大陸。

　　哥倫布並不是第一位發現美洲的探險家，歷史上記載，早在 11 世紀時，北歐的維京人就已經發現北美洲。但哥倫布卻是第一位帶動了歐洲與美洲持續接觸的人。並開拓接下來延續了好幾個世紀的歐洲探險及海外殖民的新領域，對西方的歷史有著深遠的影響。哥倫布在 1492 年的 10 月 12 日第一次登陸美洲，在 1792 年時，在美國紐約第一次發起紀念哥倫布發現新大陸 300 週年的慶祝活動。1866 年的 10 月 12 日，基於對同胞的驕傲，紐約的義大利後裔發起的第一屆的發現美洲慶祝會。在 1862 年時，舊金山的義大利後裔將 10 月 12 日這一天成為哥倫布日（Columbus Day）。在 1905 年，科羅拉多州（Colorado）成為第一個將哥倫布紀念日納為正式節日的地方。1937 年時，哥倫布日正式成為聯邦假日，從 1971 年開始，這個紀念日被正式定在 10 月的第二個星期一。慶祝活動大多是以餐會、遊行及舞會的方式呈現，但最特別的是融合了美國及義大利的文化傳統。因為哥倫布紀念日是由美國的義大利後裔所發起的，一般認為如果哥倫布不是生在義大利的話，那美國就不會有哥倫布日了。所以在哥倫布日的慶祝活動中，同時也是義大利裔民眾展示傳統習俗的時刻。

實用生活會話

Q1: I have a question. What is the Columbus Day?
我有問題。什麼是哥倫布日？

A1: Columbus Day is the day to celebrate the anniversary of Christopher Columbus'
first arrival in the Americas.
哥倫布日是慶祝克里斯多福・哥倫布首次登陸美洲的週年紀念日。

Q2: Is it an official holiday.
那是個正式的節日嗎？

A2: Yes, it is. It is a United States federal holiday.
是正式的節日。它是美國聯邦假日。

Q3: How do you celebrate it?
那你們一般都怎麼慶祝？

A3: We usually have some parades on this day.
我們通常在這一天會有遊行慶祝活動。

實用單句這樣說

- Columbus Day may top the list of contentious federal holidays. It stirs up the angers of American-Indians.
  哥倫布日大概是最具爭議的聯邦假日。這個節日激起了美國印地安裔民眾的憤怒。

- South Dakota does not recognize Columbus Day at all.
  南達科他州不認同哥倫布日。

- "Fall Weekend" takes place of the holiday formerly known as "Columbus Day" at Brown University.
  在布朗大學，用「秋季週末假日」來取代之前的「哥倫布日」。

- Columbus Day was first celebrated in 1792, but a lot has changed then, including the image and reputation of Columbus.
  哥倫布日從 1792 年開始被慶祝，時代在變，哥倫布在人們心中的形象及聲譽也隨著改變。

- Some people believe that Columbus' arrival symbolize the start of the terrible centuries-long slaughter of native inhabitants.
  有些人認為哥倫布的登陸象徵性的開啟了延續幾個世紀殘忍的原住民大屠殺。

- The date Columbus arrived in the America is celebrated in many Latin American countries.
  在拉丁美洲的許多國家都有慶祝哥倫布登陸美洲的日子。

互動時刻真有趣

下列表格有 10 個與哥倫布日相關的英文單字，可以在為孩子解說哥倫布日的由來時使用。下面的活動請讓孩子練習填上正確的單字，以加深印象。

ocean 海洋	ships 船隻	sailboats 帆船	gold 金子	Queen 皇后 / 女王
world 世界	round 圓的	maps 地圖	trip 旅遊	explorer 探險家

下列的字母順序被打散了，請填上正確順序的單字。可以參考上面表格中的單字

Unscramble the words. Use the words in the textbox to help you.

1. amsp　＿＿＿＿＿＿＿＿＿＿＿＿＿＿
2. pitr　＿＿＿＿＿＿＿＿＿＿＿＿＿＿
3. naoec　＿＿＿＿＿＿＿＿＿＿＿＿＿＿
4. owdrl　＿＿＿＿＿＿＿＿＿＿＿＿＿＿
5. enQue　＿＿＿＿＿＿＿＿＿＿＿＿＿＿
6. rprxeeol　＿＿＿＿＿＿＿＿＿＿＿＿＿＿
7. ssabltiao　＿＿＿＿＿＿＿＿＿＿＿＿＿＿
8. dnour　＿＿＿＿＿＿＿＿＿＿＿＿＿＿
9. phsis　＿＿＿＿＿＿＿＿＿＿＿＿＿＿
10. dlgo　＿＿＿＿＿＿＿＿＿＿＿＿＿＿

Answer:

1. maps
2. trip
3. ocean
4. world
5. Queen
6. Explorer
7. Sailboats
8. Round
9. Ships
10. gold

Halloween
萬聖節

節慶源由──簡易版

Halloween can be a fun and scary holiday. It is on October 31st. Children and adults like to dress up in costumes. Often the costumes are scary. Some people like to be a ghost, a witch, or a devil. Others like less scary costumes. They might be a princess, a movie star or an animal.

萬聖節前夕可以是一個既有趣又可怕的節日。它在 10 月 31 日。小孩們與大人們喜歡用服裝打扮。這些服裝通常很嚇人。有些人喜歡扮成鬼、女巫、或一個惡魔。其他的人喜歡比較不可怕的服裝。他們可能會扮成公主、電影明星或動物。

Kids love to trick-or-treat. They walk from house to house. They say "trick or treat," at each door. They get candy or money.

小孩們喜歡玩"不給糖就搗亂"。他們挨家挨戶地走。他們會在每家門前說「不給糖就搗亂」。他們會得到糖果或是錢。

Many people carve pumpkins. They clean out the inside of a pumpkin. They carve a face in it. It can be a fun or a scary face. People put a candle inside the pumpkin on Halloween night. People might sit around a big fire. They might go to a costume party. Some tell scary stories. Halloween around the world is a mix of fun and fright.

許多人刻南瓜。他們清空南瓜的內部。他們在南瓜刻一張臉。它可以是一張有趣或是可怕的臉。人們在萬聖節前夕夜晚放置蠟燭在南瓜內。人們可能會圍著旺火坐。他們可能會去服裝派對。有些派對會講鬼故事。全世界的萬聖節前夕是樂趣與可怕的結合。

單字大集合

1. **Scary** *adj.* 可怕的

   It is scary to go out in the dark.
   在黑暗裡外出很可怕。

2. **Witch** *n.* [C] 女巫

   She was a nice witch for Halloween.
   她在萬聖節前夕是個棒女巫。

3. **Devil** *n.* [C] 魔鬼

   The devil was dressed in red.
   魔鬼打扮成紅色的。

4. **Carve** *vi. vt.* 做雕刻工作；雕刻

   You must be careful when you carve.
   你在雕刻時必須小心。

5. **Candle** *n.* [C] 蠟燭

   The candle lit up the dark room.
   蠟燭照亮了黑暗的房間。

6. **Fright** *n.* [C,U] 恐怖；驚嚇

   I had a fright when I heard the noise.
   當我聽到聲響時，我覺得驚恐。

節慶源由──精彩完整版

Halloween is an interesting holiday observed in many countries around the world. It has origins in both Christian and non-Christian practices. Halloween is October 31st, the night before the western Christian feast of All Hallows（or All Saints Day）. Thus comes the name All Hallows Eve, or Halloween. It is a time when the human and the spirit worlds were thought to be closest together.

萬聖節前夕是一個被世界許多國家慶祝的有趣節日。它在基督教與非基督教的常規都有起源。萬聖節前夕是在 10 月 31 日，是西方基督聖餐的萬聖節（All Saints Day）前一晚。因此有萬聖節前夕（Halloween）這個名字。這是一個人類與靈魂世界被認為最靠近的時刻。

On All Saints Day, the church would say prayers for all the saints（Christian believers who had recently died. People believed that the souls of the dead wandered the earth until All Saints Day. All Hallows Eve was their last chance to pay their enemies back for harm they had done. The next day, the souls would move on to the spirit world. Christians wanted to avoid being recognized by a soul. They would wear masks and costumes to disguise themselves. Non-Christians also believed that souls would visit their homes on All Hallows Eve. They would build big bonfires to ward off the spirits. Poor people used to go door to door asking for food on this evening. In return, they would offer prayers for the dead the next day.

在萬聖節，教堂會替所有聖徒（最近過世的基督信徒）禱告。人們相信死者的靈魂會在世間遊盪直到萬聖節。萬聖節前夕是他們報復敵人的最後機會。隔天，靈魂會移動到靈魂世界。基督徒想要避免被靈魂認出。他們會帶著面具與穿著服裝來偽裝自己。非基督徒也相信靈魂在萬聖節前夕會造訪他們家。他們會搭大營火以避開靈魂。窮人們過去時常在這個夜晚挨家挨戶要食物。他們會在隔天奉獻對死者的禱告作為回報。

Many Halloween traditions today come from these past traditions. Children and adults alike look forward to dressing up in costumes. Often these costumes have an frightening theme. Popular costumes are monsters, ghosts, skeletons, witches, and devils. Less frightening costumes are princesses, movie characters or animals. Young children especially dress in less frightening costumes.

今日許多萬聖夜前夕的傳統來自於過去的習俗。孩子與大人們同樣地期待服裝打扮。這些服裝時常有嚇人的主題。受歡迎的服裝有怪獸、鬼、骷髏、女巫和惡魔。比較不嚇人的服裝有公主、電影角色或動物。年輕的孩子尤其穿著比較不嚇人的服裝。

Kids love to go trick-or-treating in costume.　They walk from house to house saying "trick or treat," in order to receive candy or money.　"Trick or treat" actually means that if you don't give me a treat, I will play a mean trick on you.　But this rarely happens.　Mostly it is a fun activity for all.

小孩們喜歡穿著服裝去玩「不請客就搗亂」的遊戲。他們挨家挨戶地走並說：「不請客就搗亂」，為了收到糖果或錢。玩「不請客就搗亂」的遊戲實際上是指如果你不款待我，我就會給你一個卑劣的惡作劇。但是這個絕少發生。對所有人來說這大都是一個有趣的活動。

Many people make jack-o-lanterns before Halloween.　This means cleaning out the inside of a pumpkin and carving a face in it.　It can either be a fun or a scary face. Many jack-o-lanterns glow outside houses with a candle inside on Halloween night. People sometimes also have bonfires, go to costume parties and tell scary stories on Halloween.　Halloween celebrations around the world are an interesting mixture of fright and fun.

許多人製作在萬聖節前夕前製作杰克燈。這是指清空南瓜的內部並在南瓜上刻一張臉。它可以是一張有趣或是可怕的臉。許多內部有蠟燭的杰克燈於萬聖節前夕的夜晚在屋外發光。在萬聖節前夕，人們有時候也會搭營火，去服裝派對說鬼故事。萬聖節前夕慶祝活動在全世界都是既有趣又可怕的結合。

單字大集合

1. Interesting *adj.* 令人覺得有趣的

That story was so interesting.
這個故事是令人覺得有趣的。

2. Believer *n.* [C] 信徒

They are believers in working hard every day.
他們是每天辛勤工作的信徒。

3. Avoid *vt.* 避免

You should wash your hands often to avoid getting sick.
你應經常洗手，以避免生病。

4. Costume *n.* [C] 服裝

Our costumes are never scary on Halloween.
我們在萬聖節前夕的服裝從來不可怕。

5. Disguise *vt.* 掩飾

He disguised himself so well; no one recognized him.
他把自己偽裝得很好；沒有一個人認出他來。

6. Skeleton *n.* [C] 骨骼

They used skeletons to learn the bones in the body.
他們使用骨骼來學習人體裡面的骨頭。

7. Trick-or-treat 玩「不請客就搗亂」的遊戲

When I trick-or-treat, I go to all my friends' houses.
當我玩「不請客就搗亂」的遊戲，我會到我所有朋友的家。

8. Jack-o-lantern *n.* [C] 杰克燈

I like to carve jack-o-lanterns out of giant pumpkins.
我喜歡在巨型南瓜上刻杰克燈。

閱讀測驗

1. What did the church believe dead souls did until All Saints Day?
   教堂相信死者靈魂會做什麼直到萬聖節？

   (a) Sang very loud songs at night. 在晚上唱非常大聲的歌曲。

   (b) Wandered the earth. 在世間遊蕩。

   (c) Took a long nap. 睡上一個長覺。

2. Why would Christians disguise themselves?
   為什麼基督徒要偽裝自己？

   (a) So they would not be recognized by one of the wandering souls.
      這樣他們就不會被其中一個遊蕩的靈魂認出。

   (b) So they could get candy from their neighbors.
      這樣他們就可以從他們的鄰居身上得到糖果。

   (c) Because they didn't want anyone to see that they were out at night.
      因為他們不想要任何人看到他們在晚上外出。

3. What could happen（but usually doesn't）if you don't give candy to a trick-or-treater?
   如果你沒有給糖果給「不請客就搗亂」的遊戲，將會發生（但通常不會）什麼事？

   (a) You could feel very guilty. 你會覺得非常內疚。

   (b) They could clean your house the next day. 他們隔天會打掃你的房子。

   (c) They could play a mean trick on you. 他們會對你做卑劣的惡作劇。

活動慶典和習俗

　　每年的 10 月 31 日是萬聖節（All Hallows' Day/ All Saints' Day）前夕，在英文中稱 All Hallows' Eve，縮寫簡稱為 Halloween。Halloween 在中文稱法中應該是萬聖夜，但一般常習慣稱 Halloween 為萬聖節。

　　與復活節及聖誕節相同，萬聖節也是天主教將其他宗教節日融入吸收並重新詮釋的節日之一。在西元 2000 年前不列顛凱爾特人的傳統信仰中，10 月的最後一天，代表的是夏天的終結，冬天的開始。在這一天，他們會表達對太陽神的敬意，感謝太陽神讓他們古物豐收，以應付即將到臨的冬天，但這天晚上，也是惡靈力量最大的時候，因而被稱為死人之日或是鬼節。傳說在這天，死去人們的靈魂及鬼怪會出現，為了嚇走鬼魂，凱爾特人會披上動物毛皮及戴上面具。

　　孩子們穿著精心挑選的造型服（costume），臉上化著恐怖的妝容，挨家挨戶按響鄰居家的門鈴，並大喊「不給糖就搗蛋！」（Trick or Treat）成為萬聖夜時最主要的活動。主人家在這時則會拿出糖果、巧克力甚至是小禮物來分發給這些上門的小妖魔鬼怪。在美國，小孩一晚得到的糖果常需以袋來計算，收穫十分豐富。而在蘇格蘭的小孩們就沒有那麼幸運了，他們在要糖果時說的是「天是藍，草是綠，齊來慶祝萬聖夜！」（The sky is blue, the grass is green, may we have our Halloween.）然後再以歌唱舞蹈表演來得到糖果。

　　在萬聖夜時，許多美國家庭會在門外擺放傑克南瓜燈（Jack-o'-Lantern），這習俗在英國和愛爾蘭時是以蕪菁（turnip）雕刻而成，但到了美國，則因為南瓜的取得比蕪菁容易，所以南瓜燈成了普羅大眾印象中深刻的萬聖夜象徵。萬聖夜接近蘋果的豐收期，所以有些活動與蘋果有關。其中最常見的是「咬蘋果」（Apple bobbing），將許多蘋果浮在一個裝滿水的大盆子或是木桶裡，參加者必須以牙齒咬起蘋果。以前還常會以太妃糖蘋果分送給上門要糖的孩子，但在幾個將刀片或大頭針藏入蘋果中的惡作劇後，這個習慣便漸漸消失。

實用生活會話

Q1: Did you get your Halloween costume yet?
你的萬聖夜服裝準備好了嗎？

A1: Yes, I did. I ordered it several weeks ago, and got the package yesterday.
有，我準備好了，我幾個禮拜前就訂了，昨天收到包裹了。

Q2: What do you want to be this Halloween?
那你萬聖節要裝扮成什麼？

A2: I want to be a Zombie prom queen.
我要扮成僵屍舞會皇后。

Q3: Wow, where did you get the idea?
哇，你怎麼會有這個想法？

A3: Oh, Frank's going to be the Zombie prom king, so...
喔，因為法蘭克要打扮成僵屍舞會之王，所以…

Q4: I can't wait to see you two's costumes.
我等不及要看你們二人的打扮。

A4: Me too.
我也是。

Q5: Then we can take a picture and post it on FB.
然後我們可以照相，並把照片放上臉書。

A5: Yeah, it would be fun.
是的，這會很有趣的。

實用單句這樣說

- Bobbing for Apple is a game often played at Halloween party.
  咬蘋果是一個在萬聖夜派對上常玩的遊戲。

- Trick or Treat, smell my feet, give me something good to eat.
  不給糖就搗蛋，聞我的臭腳丫，給我好吃的東西。（這是一首孩童在萬聖夜常唱的歌。）

- Your costume is marvelous.
  你的造型服真是棒透了。

- The ghost story frightened the children.
  這個鬼故事把孩子們都嚇壞了。

- Take it easy, this is not a haunted house.
  放輕鬆，這不是鬼屋。

- A witch wears a broad brimming, tall black and pointed hat and rides on a broomstick.
  巫婆帶著一頂寬邊，高高的黑色尖頂帽，並騎著掃把。

- The Jack-o'-Lantern custom probably comes from Irish folklore.
  傑克南瓜燈的習俗可能是源自於一個愛爾蘭民俗傳說。

- Tony hollowed out a pumpkin to make a Jack-o'-Lantern.
  湯尼把南瓜挖空用來做成傑克燈。

互動時刻真有趣

　　很久很久以前，吝嗇鬼傑克是個喜歡作弄人的貪心老酒鬼。有一天他騙魔鬼爬上蘋果樹，當魔鬼在樹上時，他很快的在樹幹四周放十字架。魔鬼無法下來，傑克趁機要魔鬼答應永遠不會取走他的靈魂，魔鬼答應了，他便將十字架拿走。幾年過後，傑克死了，但因為他太壞，太慘忍，所以他無法上天堂。而魔鬼也答應不取他的靈魂，所以他也無法到地獄。他無處可去，他問魔鬼「沒有燈，我要怎麼看到要去哪兒呢？」魔鬼便丟給他一塊從地獄之火中取出的灰燼，傑克就把這塊灰燼放到挖空的蕪菁中，開始他永無止境的徘徊，只為了找一個棲身之地。這就是傑克燈的由來。

　　Once upon a time, Stingy Jack was a greedy, old drunk who liked to play tricks on everyone. One day he tricked the Devil into climbing up an apple tree. Once the Devil was up there, Stingy Jack quickly placed crosses around the trunks of the tree. The Devil was unable to get down, and Jack made the Devil promised not to take his soul forever. The Devil made a promise to him, and he removed crosses and let the Devil down. Years later, when Jack died, he was not allowed to enter heaven, because he was too mean and too cruel. However, the Devil had promised not to take Jack's soul, so Jack was barred from hell as well. Now he had nowhere to go, and he asked the Devil that how he could see where to go as he had no light. The Devil tossed him an ember from the flame of Hell to light his way. Jack put the ember inside a hallowed out turnip which was his favorite food, and began endlessly wandering the earth for a resting place. He became known as "Jack-o'-Lantern."

Thanksgiving
感恩節

節慶源由──簡易版

Thanksgiving is a day to say thank you. The first Thanksgiving was in 1621. Some people came by boat to live in America. It was winter. They had no homes. They had no food. Many people died. They needed help. In the spring, some Indians helped them. The Indians showed them how to grow food. They grew corn and beans. They showed them where to fish and hunt. In the fall, the new people wanted to say thank you. They made a big meal for the Indians. They ate corn, beans, deer, fish and wild birds. They ate and played games for three days.

感恩節是說謝謝的日子。第一個感恩節是在西元 1621 年。有些人藉著船來到美洲定居。那時是冬天。他們沒有家。他們沒有食物。許多人都死亡了。他們需要幫助。在春天時,有些印地安人幫忙了他們。印第安人教他們如何種植糧食。他們種植玉米和豆子。印第安人向他們展示哪裡可以漁獵。在秋天時,新住民想要感謝他們。他們為印第安人做了豐盛的一餐。他們食用玉米、豆子、麋鹿、魚和野生鳥類。他們吃喝玩樂了三天。

Today, Thanksgiving is the same. In the fall, Thanksgiving is a day to say thank you. Families may eat a big meal with turkey, corn and beans. They play games. They say thank you for good food and other good things.

在今天,感恩節還是一樣。秋天時,感恩節是說謝謝的日子。家庭們會吃大餐,有火雞、玉米和豆子。他們玩遊戲。他們向新鮮的食物和其他好的事物說謝謝。

單字大集合

1. **Winter** *n.* [C,U] 冬；冬季；冷天

   It is cold in the winter.
   冬季是寒冷的。

2. **Boat** *n.* [C] 船

   The boat was on the river.
   船在河上。

3. **Indian** *n.* [C] 印第安人

   Indians lived in America first.
   印第安人第一個居住在美洲。

4. **Hunt** *vi. vt.* 打獵；獵取

   We must hunt for meat to eat.
   我們必須為了有肉吃而打獵。

5. **Family** *n.* [C] 家庭

   Some families live in big houses.
   有些家庭住在大房子裡。

6. **Turkey** *n.* [C] 火雞

   A turkey is a big bird.
   火雞是一隻大的鳥類。

節慶源由──精彩完整版

Thanksgiving is a day to give thanks. The first Thanksgiving was in 1621. A group of people called Pilgrims moved from England to America. It was winter when their ship landed in America. They had no homes and very little food. Almost half of the Pilgrims died that winter. They needed someone to teach them how to live in their new land. Some Indians who lived in the area became friends with the Pilgrims and taught them how to grow corn, pumpkin and beans. They showed them where to fish and where to hunt. In the fall, the Pilgrims harvested enough food to help them make it through the coming winter. They wanted to say thank you for the harvest. They wanted to thank their Indian friends for helping them survive in America. They invited the Indians to a feast. They ate cornbread, pumpkin, dried fruit, deer, fish and wild birds. After the meal, there were games, races, and shooting competitions. The celebration lasted for three days.

感恩節是說謝謝的日子。第一個感恩節是在西元 1621 年。一群被稱作清教徒的人從英格蘭移居美洲。當他們的船著陸美洲時是冬天。他們沒有家，只有非常少的食物。幾乎過半的清教徒在那個冬天死亡了。他們需要有人教導他們如何在新大陸生活。有些居住在同一地區的印第安人和清教徒成為朋友，並教他們如何耕種玉米、南瓜和豆子。印第安人向他們展示哪裡可以捕魚、哪裡可以打獵。在秋天時，清教徒收穫了足夠的糧食，得以幫助他們度過即將到來的冬天。他們想要感謝收成。他們想要感謝他們的印第安朋友教導他們在美洲生存。他們邀請印第安人參加盛宴。他們吃玉米麵包、南瓜、乾果、麋鹿、魚和野生鳥類。在大餐後，他們玩遊戲、競賽和射擊比賽。慶祝活動持續了三天。

Many times after that first Thanksgiving, people in America had a similar fall celebration. Sometimes, it was to celebrate the harvest. Sometimes, it was to celebrate winning a great battle in the war for freedom. Some years, there was no Thanksgiving celebration. Finally, in 1863, President Abraham Lincoln made Thanksgiving Day a national holiday, celebrated in November each year.

在第一次感恩節之後的很多次，在美洲的人們也有類似的秋季慶典。有時候，是用來慶祝收成。有時候，是用來慶祝贏得自由的戰爭。曾經有些年，人們沒有慶祝感恩節。最後，在西元 1863 年，亞伯拉罕‧林肯總統將感恩節訂為國定節日，在每年的 11 月慶祝。

Thanksgiving is still a national holiday in the United States, celebrated on the fourth Thursday of November.　It is celebrated in the fall to give thanks for the harvest and for the good things that have happened that year.　Businesses and schools are closed so families and friends can celebrate together. In New York City, there is a large Thanksgiving Day parade, which many families watch on TV. In the afternoon, the Thanksgiving feast often includes turkey, potatoes, vegetables and pumpkin pie. Before eating dinner, the people often take some time to talk about what they are thankful for.　They might be thankful for their job, for the harvest, for good health or for many other things.　After dinner, if the weather is good, people often go outside to play football or basketball or play some other active game.　Some people choose to watch football on TV instead.　No matter how it is celebrated, it is still a day to say thanks!

感恩節在美國依舊是國定節日，在 11 月的第 4 個禮拜四慶祝。在秋天慶祝，感恩收成及在當年發生的美好事物。公司和學校都休息，這樣家人和朋友就可以一起慶祝。在紐約市，有個感恩節大遊行，許多家庭都會在電視上收看。在下午，感恩節大餐通常包含火雞、馬鈴薯、蔬菜和南瓜派。在吃完晚餐前，人們通常會花一些時間說說他們想要感激什麼。他們可能感激他們的工作、收成、良好的健康或是其他事情。在晚餐後，如果天氣是好的，人們通常會到外面去玩足球或是籃球或是其他活動。有些人選擇用在家裡的電視上看足球取代。不管是怎麼慶祝的，這仍然是個說謝謝的日子！

單字大集合

1. Pilgrim　*n.* [C]　清教徒

The pilgrims wanted to live in a new land.
清教徒想要住在新大陸。

2. Friend　*n.* [C]　朋友

I invited my friends to my party.
我邀請我的朋友來我的派對

3. Harvest　*vi. vt.*　收割莊稼；收穫

We will harvest our garden before winter.
我們將在冬天後收成我們的花園。

4. Celebration　*n.* [C]　慶祝

My family had a big celebration for Chinese New Year.
我的家人為了農曆新年有個大慶祝。

5. National　*adj.*　國家的

I learned a lot when I went to the National Museum.
我去國家博物館時學到很多。

6. Holiday　*n.* [C]　節日

Chinese New Year is my favorite holiday.
農曆新年是我最喜歡的節日。

7. Survive　*vi. vt.*　活下來；在……仍然生存

They could survive the long winter in their warm house.
在他們的溫暖的房子裡，他們可以度過漫長的冬天。

8. Pumpkin　*n.* [C]　南瓜

The big orange pumpkin grew in our garden.
有個大的橘色南瓜生長在我們的花園裡。

閱讀測驗

1. Who taught the Pilgrims how to live in the new land?

   誰教清教徒怎麼在新大陸生活？

   (a) Their parents 他們的父母。

   (b) The Indians 印第安人。

   (c) They never learned now to live there. 他們從未學習如何在那裡生活。

2. How long did the first Thanksgiving last? 第一個感恩節持續多久？

   (a) A whole week 一整個星期。

   (b) Three days 三天。

   (c) A full year 一整年。

3. What do many people eat on Thanksgiving today?

   現今多數人在感恩節那天會吃什麼？

   (a) All the fruit they find in the house 所有他們在房子裡找到的水果。

   (b) Lots of candy 很多糖果。

   (c) Turkey, potatoes and pumpkin pie 火雞、馬鈴薯和南瓜派。

4. What a day of Thanksgiving is?

   感恩節是怎樣的日子呢？

   (a) A day to celebrate. 來慶祝的日子。

   (b) A day to give thanks. 來說謝謝的日子。

   (c) A day to dance. 跳舞的日子。

活動慶典和習俗

　　十七世紀受迫害的清教徒（Pilgram）到達美州時，印第安人（Indian）教導他們種植、捕魚、守獵的生活方式，在豐收的日子，一同慶祝以感謝上天賜與好的收成。美國於每年十一月的第四個禮拜四慶祝感恩節，這個節日就如同中國的春節一樣，親人會回家團聚，一同準備小型南瓜、彩色玉米等應景的裝飾及享受豐盛的大餐。

　　這天舉國歡慶，許多城鎮會舉辦化妝遊行，尤其是以紐約市梅西百貨的感恩節大遊行（Macy's Thanksgiving Day Parade）最著名。這個活動開始於西元1924 年，通常與早上九點舉行，沿著百老匯（Broadway）大道前進，整個活動進行的時間大約是三小時。遊行中會有樂隊、花車、好幾層樓高的大型卡通人物氣球，如米老鼠（Mickey Mouse）、凱蒂貓（Hello Kitty）、史努比（Snoopy）、功夫熊貓（Kung Fu Panda）、史瑞克（Shrek）、蜘蛛人（Spiderman）等，都是相當受歡迎的迪士尼卡通或電影角色。每當這些造型玩偶出現，總是讓現場參加遊行的民眾非常興奮，歡呼聲此起彼落。無法到現場參加遊行的民眾也可在電視前欣賞轉播，每年約有四千多萬的觀眾在家中藉由電視台轉播一同感受遊行現場的歡樂氣氛。

　　感恩節當天晚上就是全家人一同聚餐且觀看足球賽事的歡樂時刻了！當天餐桌上美國的傳統菜餚當然少不了烤火雞（roast turkey）、南瓜派（pumpkin pie）、小紅莓果醬（cranberry sauce）、比司吉（Biscuit）等。大餐的主角就是烤火雞，通常會把火雞的肚子塞進撕成碎片的玉米麵包（corn bread）、蘋果丁、麵包丁、乾酪、西洋芹（celery）、核桃（walnut）等各式填充佐料，再將表皮烘烤至金黃色，配上火雞內臟煮成的濃稠醬汁（gravy）及每年九月和十月盛產的小紅莓做成的特製紅莓醬汁就完成了。每年的感恩節，美國有很多的火雞都會變成桌上美味的佳餚，大家覺得身在美國的火雞有一點可憐，所以在美國白宮草坪前舉辦一個特赦火雞的活動，美國總統會親自釋放一隻沒有被吃掉的火雞，讓這隻火雞可以會農場頤養天年，這也算是一個滿有趣的感恩節活動。在感恩節當天，許多家庭會在早上先上教堂，中午一起裝飾家裡與準備豐盛大餐，想想值得感謝的人、事、物，大家在這天享受團聚的時刻，維繫著家庭感情。

實用生活會話

Q1: What do people eat on Thanksgiving?
大家在感恩節時吃什麼？

A1: They always have turkey and pumpkin pie on Thanksgiving.
他們在感恩節總會吃火雞和南瓜派。

Q2: Who are you going to invite for Thanksgiving table?
你要請誰一起來吃感恩節大餐？

A2: I'll invite my grandparents and my cousins.
我會邀請我的祖父母和我的表親。

Q3: What do you normally do after Thanksgiving dinner?
你通常在感恩節晚餐之後會做什麼？

A3: I watch the American football game with my family.
我會跟我的家人一起看美式足球比賽。

Q4: Have you visted to Macy's Thanksgiving Day Parade before?
你曾經參觀過梅西百貨的大遊行嗎？

A4: Yes, my family have visited there twice on the trip to New York City.
是的，我們一家已經在去紐約市的旅程中參觀過兩次了。

實用單句這樣說

- Thanksgiving is coming.
  感恩節即將到來。

- My mother and I are going to prepare for our Thanksgiving dinner.
  我和我媽媽要一起準備我們的感恩節晚餐。

- Pumpkin pie is a traditional dessert for Thanksgiving.
  南瓜派是感恩節的一道傳統的點心。

- Here is the recipe from my grandmother.
  這是我奶奶的食譜。

- Just follow the steps and you can make a delicious roast turkey easily.
  只要按照這些步驟，你就可以輕鬆做出一隻美味的烤雞。

- Let's say some appreciative words to each other.
  讓我們彼此說些感謝的話。

- Most Americans enjoy playing board games with their family during holidays.
  大多數的美國人喜歡在佳節時和家人玩桌棋遊戲。

- Children can't wait to put on their Indian customs.
  小朋友們都等不及穿上印第安人服飾。

互動時刻真有趣

　　享用完豐盛的感恩節火雞大餐後，別忘了讓應時甜點為感恩夜劃下一個令人回味無窮的完美句點。現在就一起來做一個好吃的南瓜派吧！

● 食材：

南瓜泥（pumpkin puree）350 克
派皮（pie crust）1 張
紅糖（brown sugar）100 克
雞蛋（egg）2 顆
鮮奶油（whipped cream）200 克
牛奶（milk）100 克
肉桂粉（ground cinnamon）1 茶匙
薑末（ground ginger）3/4 茶匙
鹽（salt）1/2 茶匙
肉豆蔻粉（ground nutmeg）1/4 茶匙
丁香粉（ground cloves）1/2 茶匙

Step1. 將派底放置鋁箔盤裡，以 400 度溫度放入烤箱底部，烘烤 10 分鐘備用。

Step2. 用容器將南瓜泥、糖、鹽、肉桂粉、肉豆蔻粉、丁香粉混合均勻；加入蛋汁攪拌均勻，最後再加入牛奶和鮮奶油全部混合均勻，就是南瓜泥餡。

Step3. 將南瓜泥餡倒入派皮中抹平表面。

Step4. 將注入餡料的派皮，放進 180 度烤箱內約烤 30-35 分鐘就完成了。

Christmas Day
聖誕節

節慶源由——簡易版

Christmas Day is on December 25th. In church, people celebrate the birth of Jesus. Children act out the story. They dress as the shepherds and angels who came to see the baby. Others tell a story of a man who brings gifts. Some call him Santa Claus. In other countries, he is Father Christmas or Saint Nicholas. No matter which story you believe, Christmas is a time to be together with family.

聖誕節是在 12 月 25 日。在教堂裡，人們慶祝耶穌的誕生。兒童表演出故事。他們打扮成牧羊人和天使來看寶寶。其他人則說著關於一個男子帶來禮物的故事。有些人叫他耶誕老人。在其他國家，他是聖誕老人或聖尼古拉斯。不管你相信哪一個故事，聖誕節是個與家族同聚的時刻。

Some people spend all of December getting ready for Christmas. They sing Christmas songs. They send Christmas cards to their friends. They bake Christmas cookies. They put up a Christmas tree in their house. They buy gifts. The presents are wrapped and placed under the tree. On Christmas Eve, Santa or Saint Nick brings gifts to the children. On Christmas Day, people open their gifts and have a big dinner. They eat, play games and enjoy being together.

有些人會花整個 12 月為聖誕節作準備。他們唱聖誕歌曲。他們寄聖誕卡給他們的朋友。他們烤聖誕餅乾。他們在家裡擺放聖誕樹。他們買禮物。禮物被包好並放置在聖誕樹下。在聖誕夜，耶誕老人（Saint Nick）帶禮物給孩子們。在聖誕節，人們拆開他們的禮物並且吃大餐。他們吃東西、玩遊戲並且享受相聚。

單字大集合

1. **Angel** *n.* [C] 天使

   We put glass angels in our window.
   我們在窗口擺放玻璃天使。

2. **Baby** *n.* [C] 嬰兒

   The new baby will be born today.
   新生兒將在今天誕生。

3. **Cookie** *n.* [C] 餅乾

   I like to help my mom bake cookies.
   我喜歡幫我媽媽烤餅乾。

4. **Present** *n.* [C] 禮物

   I hope lots of those presents are for me.
   我希望這些禮物裡有很多是給我的。

5. **Wrap** *vt.* 包裹

   The gifts are wrapped in pretty paper.
   這些禮物被漂亮的紙包裝。

6. **Dinner** *n.* [C,U] 正餐；晚餐

   I can't wait until we eat dinner!
   我不能等到我們吃晚飯！

節慶源由——精彩完整版

Christmas is a Christian holiday that is also commonly celebrated by non-Christians. As a religious holiday, Christmas is the celebration of the birth of Jesus Christ. It is most often celebrated on December 25th.

聖誕節是基督教的節日，也普遍地被非基督徒慶祝。作為一個宗教性的節日，聖誕節是個耶穌誕生的慶典活動。大多在 12 月 25 日被慶祝。

In the Christian celebration, people have many traditions that come from the story in the Bible. According to the story, Jesus was born in a barn, surrounded by farm animals. Shepherds in the fields heard the story from angels in the sky and were the first to visit the baby. Many times in churches, children act out the story. There are the mother, father and baby Jesus. There are shepherds and angels. The people sing songs that tell the story. Sometimes, outside the church, the story is acted out with live animals, such as sheep and camels.

在基督教的慶典裡，人們有許多傳統來自聖經裡的故事。根據這個故事，耶穌出生在一個穀倉裡，周圍環繞著農場動物。原野裡的牧羊人聽到來自天上的天使的故事後，第一個拜訪了嬰兒。許多次在教堂裡，孩子們演出這個故事。裡頭有母親、父親和嬰兒耶穌。有牧羊人們和天使們。人們唱著訴說故事的歌曲。有時，在教堂外，故事會與活的動物們一起演出，像是羊及駱駝。

In the non-religious celebration, most people celebrate the story of a man who gives gifts. This person is called by several names. In some countries, he is Santa Claus. In other countries, he is Father Christmas or Saint Nicholas. In all cases, he secretly brings gifts to children. It is usually at night, when children should be sleeping.

在非宗教的慶祝活動裡，大部分的人們會慶祝一個男子發禮物的故事。這個人被稱作許多名字。在一些國家，他是耶誕老人。在其他國家，他是聖誕老人或聖尼古拉斯。不管什麼情況，他都會偷偷帶禮物給孩子們。通常是晚上，當孩子們在睡覺的時候。

Whatever you believe about Christmas, many traditions are the same. Several weeks before Christmas, people start to play special Christmas music. Sometimes, groups go Christmas caroling. They sing favorite Christmas carols（songs）door to door or outside the homes of people they know. They send Christmas cards to their friends and family. They bake special Christmas cookies. They decorate their houses and put up a Christmas tree. They buy gifts for everyone in their family. All of the presents are wrapped and placed under the tree.

不管你相信哪個有關聖誕節的，許多傳統是一樣的。聖誕節前數周，人們開始播放特別的聖誕音樂。有時，會集體去聖誕報佳音。他們挨家挨戶或到認識的人的家門口，唱著最喜愛的耶誕頌（歌曲）。他們寄聖誕卡片給他們的朋友和家人。他們烘烤特別的聖誕餅乾。他們裝飾他們的家並擺上一棵聖誕樹。他們買禮物給家族裡的每個人。所有禮物被包裝好並放在樹下。

Families gather together from near or from far away for Christmas. On Christmas Eve, those who celebrate the Christian holiday go to church. There is a special service to remember the birth of Jesus. Afterward, some families go home to open their gifts. Christmas Day begins early in the morning. Children wake up early to see what Santa brought them. Often, they have hung up a fancy stocking near the Christmas tree. Santa may have filled this with candy and small gifts. For those who wait until Christmas Day to open gifts, they usually find extra gifts under the tree that Santa has brought. After the gifts are all open, the family has a large Christmas dinner. They eat, relax, play games and enjoy being together.

來自遠或近的家人們為了聖誕節相聚在一起。在聖誕夜，慶祝聖誕節的人們會到教堂。那有個用來懷念耶穌誕生的特別儀式。在這之後，有些家族會回家去拆開他們的禮物。聖誕節始於清晨。孩子們早起去看耶誕老人帶給他們什麼。他們通常已經在聖誕樹旁掛好華麗的襪子。聖誕老人可能已經在裡面放滿糖果和小禮物。為了那些等到聖誕節當天拆禮物的人，他們通常會在樹下發現聖誕老人帶來的額外的禮物。在禮物都被打開之後，家族會有個大型的聖誕晚餐。他們吃、放鬆、玩遊戲和享受相聚。

單字大集合

1. According 根據

According to the weather report, there will be a big rain.
根據氣象報導，那裡將會有一場大雨。

2. Surround *vt.* 包圍；圍繞

Our house is surrounded by trees.
我們的房子被樹木包圍。

3. Shepherd *n.* [C] 牧羊人

The shepherds make sure wolves do not steal the sheep.
牧羊人確定野狼沒有偷走綿羊。

4. Camel *n.* [C] 駱駝

If you want to travel across the desert, use a camel.
如果你想要旅行穿越沙漠，使用駱駝。

5. Santa Claus 聖誕老人

Santa Claus is well known in the United States.
聖誕老人在美國眾所皆知。

6. Saint Nicholas 聖尼古拉斯

Saint Nicholas is popular in many countries in Europe.
聖尼古拉斯在歐洲許多國家很受歡迎。

7. Carol *vi. vt.* 唱耶誕頌歌；歡唱

Can we go caroling on our street?
我們可以去我們的街上報佳音嗎？

8. Service *n.* [C] 儀式；服務

At our church, the Christmas Eve service is at 7 pm.
在我們的教堂，聖誕夜儀式是在晚上七點。

閱讀測驗

1. In the Bible Story, who were the first people to visit the baby Jesus when he was born? 在聖經故事裡，誰是第一個在耶穌誕生時探望他的人？
   (a) His grandparents from the United States. 他在美國的祖父母。
   (b) Shepherds in the fields. 原野裡的牧羊人。
   (c) The next door neighbors. 隔壁的鄰居。

2. In the non-religious celebration, when do Santa Claus or Father Christmas bring their gifts?
   在非宗教的慶祝活動裡，聖誕老人（Father Christmas）何時帶來他們的禮物？
   (a) In the middle of the day, so everyone sees them.
      在一天的中間，這樣每個人都看到它們。
   (b) On each child's birthday. 在每個小孩的生日。
   (c) In the middle of the night when children are sleeping.
      在半夜當小孩都在睡覺時。

3. Where are the gifts placed until Christmas? 禮物直到聖誕節都會被放在哪裡？
   (a) They are left at the store. 它們被遺忘在店裡。
   (b) They are wrapped and put under the Christmas tree.
      它們被包裝好且放在聖誕樹下。
   (c) They are hidden under the bed. 它們被藏在床下。

4. What might Santa Claus put in a Christmas stocking?
   聖誕老人可能會放什麼在聖誕襪裡？
   (a) Candy and small toys 糖果和小玩具。
   (b) Puppies and kittens 小狗和小貓。
   (c) Vegetables from the garden 來自花園裡的蔬菜。

活動慶典和習俗

　　每到了 12 月，不論走到哪裡，總是會聽到悅耳的鈴聲加上溫馨的耶誕旋律，提醒著人們耶誕節（Christmas）的到來，過耶誕節儼然已成了世界各地的風俗習慣。Christmas 這個字是從古英文 CristesMæsse 演變而來，用現代英文來說就是 Christ's Mass，中文是基督彌撒的意思。因為在 12 月 24 日耶誕夜（Christmas Eve）及 12 月 25 日耶誕節凌晨兩日交接的午夜 12 點，天主教教堂會舉行子夜彌撒來慶祝耶穌基督的誕生，久而久之人們便以 Christmas 來稱呼這一個節日。而中文名稱則是源自於在清朝末年的傳教士稱耶穌為西方聖人，而在台灣，神明的誕辰用台語稱為聖誕，因此將這個節日稱為聖誕節或是耶穌節。但在 1980 年代，新聞局通令媒體不得使用方言，因此更名為耶誕節。而後禁令解除，現在則是聖誕節及耶誕節皆可通用。

　　談到耶誕節的習俗，一定就會想到耶誕禮物（Christmas Gift），從 10 月底就開始耶誕購物的旺季。商家在這時候會開始樹立耶誕樹（Christmas tree），擺放聖誕裝飾，如花環以製造濃厚的耶誕氣氛。而許多美國家庭則是在感恩節後擺放耶誕樹。而在德國則是在耶誕夜當天才擺放。一般會將耶誕樹擺到新年過後。而每個國家的耶誕大餐的主菜都不太一樣，美國流行吃火雞，英國傳統有烤乳豬，而德國、捷克及波蘭等喜歡吃鯉魚、正值澳洲則喜歡吃燒烤，種類繁多。但相同的是耶誕節是一個全家團聚的節日，家人坐在一起享用大餐，才是慶祝耶誕節最棒的方式。啊！等等，我漏了一個，拆禮物也很棒。吃完了大餐，又睡的飽飽的，在耶誕節的早晨拆開看了好久的禮物，心中滿滿的歡喜。雖然在購買禮物上，淘空了荷包，也知道在節日過後的超低折扣，但為了家人，一年一次是值得的！在耶誕夜的晚上，宗教的色彩十分濃厚，除了子夜彌撒之外，還有挨家挨戶報佳音（carol singing）的隊伍。有些家庭會在大餐後一起做餅乾或是聖誕布丁等，有點類似我國北方包餃子的習俗。在美國，只有放耶誕節這一天，好一點的，如政府機關，24 日只上半天班。而在英國及大多數英國聯邦國家如澳洲則有 2 天的假期，25 日的聖誕節及 26 日的節禮日（Boxing Day），其實單從英文上看，非常像是 26 日才拆禮物的感覺。這一天起源自英國，莊園的領主，會在這一天將許多的衣物、穀物、用具等裝箱，送給奴僕，或是把錢投到僕人帶來的盒子裡，類似我們發年終獎金及員工福利品的日子。但現在就是假日及耶誕節後商場大特價的日子。

實用生活會話

Q1: Merry Christmas! What plans do you have for this special day?

耶誕快樂！今天有沒有什麼計畫啊？

A1: I'm going back to Canberra to have dinner with my families.

我要回坎培拉跟家人一起吃晚餐。

Q2: When are you going to leave?

什麼時候要走？

A2: About 3 o'clock. I guess maybe I can finish my report before that.

3 點吧。我猜我在那之前能將報告寫完。

Q3: Well, you may not know this, but because it's Christmas Eve, almost everyone in the city gets off work early today so that they can go back home early. Starting at 3, traffic usually becomes bumper to bumper. Do you need help with your report?

嗯，你可能不知道，因為今天是耶誕夜，幾乎市區裡的每個人都提早下班才能早一點到家。從 3 點開始，交通會堵成一團。你的報告需要不需要幫忙啊？

A3: That will be great, thank you so much. So I can probably leave earlier.

這樣就太好了，真是太謝謝你了。那我也許能早點離開了。

實用單句這樣說

- We are going to Sydney for Christmas and New Year.
  我們要去雪梨過耶誕節及新年。

- Did you see the luxury watch she got for Christmas?
  你有看到她耶誕節收到的那一隻奢華名錶嗎？

- Toy stores do a roaring trade before Christmas.
  玩具專賣店在耶誕節前的生意好到嚇嚇叫。

- We use mistletoe to decorate our house at Christmas.
  我們在聖誕節時用槲寄生裝飾家中。

- A Christmas wreath is a circle of flowers and leaves which some people hang on the front door at Christmas.
  耶誕花環是以花和葉子編成的，有些人會在上耶誕節時將其掛在前門上。

- Christmas would not be the same without the eggnog.
  少了蛋酒就不是耶誕節了。

- I have to get some ornaments and a pretty star tree topper for my Christmas tree.
  我要買些裝飾品及一個放在樹頂的漂亮星星來裝飾我的聖誕樹。

- Christmas should be the time full of excitement and wonder, not just a marketing strategy.
  聖誕節應該是充滿興奮及奇妙的時刻，而不只是一種行銷策略。

互動時刻真有趣

● 你不可不知道的聖誕老人

　　談到耶誕節，相信大家腦海中都會出現聖誕老人（Father Christmas/ Santa Claus 或簡稱 Santa）送禮物的畫面。聖誕老人的概念是衍生自聖尼古拉斯（Saint Nicholas）這一位 4 世紀時會悄悄送禮物的善良主教（Bishop），Santa Claus 便是轉變自荷蘭語中的聖尼古拉（Sinterklaas）。在北美洲，孩子們會在耶誕夜（Christmas Eve）時在壁爐上放上一只襪子，期待聖誕老人帶來的禮物，還會貼心的為他準備一杯牛奶及一塊餅乾慰勞他的整夜奔波。在歐洲，孩子們收耶誕禮物的方式則是擺放空的容器或是鞋子。而目前廣為人知的穿著紅白顏色服裝的聖誕老人形象，則是可口可樂公司在 1930 年代參考法國的聖誕老人（Père Noel）所設計出的。在西方國家的購物中心及百貨公司從 12 月開始就會設置與聖誕老人合影的區域，而這時總是會有大排長龍的孩子們等待著要和聖誕老人說說話及照相。有些孩子會在耶誕節前寫信給聖誕老人，為了不讓孩子失望，有些國家的郵局還會有專人回覆這些信件。除此之外，北美空防司令部（NORAD- North American Aerospace Defense Command）還特地為孩童們提供「追蹤聖誕老人」（NORAD Tracks Santa）的服務，在耶誕節的前後，孩子能以電話或是網路來查詢目前聖誕老人的所在位置。此項服務會在每年的 12 月 1 日開始啟動，網址是 www.noradsanta.org。而目前聖誕老人的家在經過第 40 屆的世界聖誕老人會議之後，決定移居到丹麥屬地，北美洲的格陵蘭島（Greenland），大會的原因是因為當地有許多的馴鹿（reindeer）。

好書報報

好學易上手的
Hotel
英語會話

Simply Learning
Simply Best

MP3

旅館的客人有各行各業，也有為數不少來自不同國家，
因而操持著流利的旅館英語，是旅館人員不可或缺的利器，更是必備的工具！
本書內容精心安排 *6* 大主題 *30* 個情境 *120* 組超實用對話內容
　☆以中英對照的方式呈現對話內容，閱讀更舒適！
　☆精選好學易懂的key word：生字＋音標＋詞性，學習更札實！
Part I　Front Desk 櫃檯
Part II　Reservations 預約
Part III　Housekeeping Department 房務部
Part IV　Amenities 設備
Part V　Banquets 宴會
Part VI　Crisis Management 經營管理危機
作者：Claire Chang & Mark Venekamp
定價：新台幣469元
規格：504頁 / 18K / 雙色印刷 / MP3

餐飲英語
*easy*說

從不會說到說得跟老外一樣好，循序漸進做練習，職場英語一日千里！
身處餐飲英語職場環境，懂得用英語對話一一接招、讓英語交談字字精準！
老外服務生的餐飲致勝話術，國際化餐飲時代不可不學！

★基礎應對→訂位、帶位、包場、特殊節日訂位、公司行號預訂尾牙或酒會等大型活動
★餐廳前場與後場管理→擺設學問、服務生Must Know、主廚推薦、食物管理與內部清潔
★人事管理→客人生氣了、客人不滿意、遇到刁鑽的客人、部落客評論

120個餐廳工作情境 + 100%英語人士的對話用語！
擁有這一本，餐廳工作無往不利，即刻通向世界各地！

作者：Claire Chang & Mark Venekamp
定價：新台幣369元
規格：336頁 / 18K / 雙色印刷 / MP3

GET TO KNOW
THE AIRLINE INDUSTRY

航空英語會話

Live
Show

THE TOP
& THE ONLY ONE

這是第一本以航空業為背景，強調實務，從職員角度出發的航空英語會話工具書
從職員vs 同事、職員 vs 客戶兩大角度
　　呈現出100%原汁原味的航空職場情境
從前台到後台所發生的精采對話實錄
　　猶如身歷其境更能學以致用，達到全方位的學習目標
特別規劃：
★職業補給站→提供許多航空界的專業知識
★英語實習Role-play→以Q&A的方式，介紹各種可能面臨到的情況
像是免稅品服務該留意什麼、旅客出境的SOP、
違禁品的相關規定、迎賓服務的幾個步驟與重點、
飛機健檢大作戰有哪些... ，為你的職場實力再加分。
作者：Claire Chang & Mark Venekamp
定價：新台幣369元
規格：352頁 / 18K / 雙色印刷 / MP3

好書報報

要說出流利的英文，就是需要常常開口說英文!

國外打工兼旅遊很流行，如何找尋機會? 訣竅方法在這裡。
情境式基礎對話讓你快速上手，獨自出國打工，一點都不怕!
不同國家、領域要知道哪些common sense?!
出門在外，保險、健康的考量更要注意，各國制度大不同?!
貼心的職場補給站，全部告訴你!

作者：Claire Chang & Melanie Venecamp
定價：新台幣469元
規格：560頁 / 18K / 雙色印刷

心理學研究顯示，一個習慣的養成，至少必須重複21次!

全書內容規劃為30天的學習進度，讓讀者搭配進度表，
在一個月內，不知不覺中養成了英語學習的好習慣!

■圖解學習英文文法，三效合一!
　　→刺激大腦記憶 + 快速掌握學習大綱 + 快速「複習」
■英文文法學習元素一次到位:
　　→20個必懂觀念　30個必學句型　40個必閃陷阱
■流行有趣的英語不再只出現在會話書了!
　　→「那裡有正妹!」、「今天我們去看變形金剛3吧!」

作者：朱懿婷
定價：新台幣349元
規格：336頁 / 18K / 雙色印刷

用Mind Mapping來戰勝E-mail寫作

12大主題，各種情境的範例解說，
遇到各種問題都能輕鬆應對，迅速有效率!

情 ◎心智圖 + 寫作技巧錦囊
境 ◎單字、片語、實用例句
單 ◎英文範例 + 段落大意+中文翻譯
元 ◎換個對象寫寫看
介 ◎文法解析實用句型
紹 ◎心智圖動動腦 + 練習範例分享

作者：陳瑾珮
定價：新台幣349元
規格：320頁 / 18K / 雙色印刷

用英語來學節慶

作　　者／倍斯特編輯部
封面設計／高鐘琪
內頁構成／菩薩蠻有限公司

發 行 人／周瑞德
企劃編輯／倍斯特編輯部
印　　製／世和印製企業有限公司
初　　版／2013 年 10 月
定　　價／新台幣 299 元

出　　版／倍斯特出版事業有限公司
電　　話／（02）2351-2007
傳　　真／（02）2351-0887
地　　址／100 台北市中正區福州街1號10 樓之 2
Ｅ m a i l／best.books.service@gmail.com

總 經 銷／商流文化事業有限公司
地　　址／新北市中和區中正路752號7樓
電　　話／（02）2228-8841
傳　　真／（02）2228-6939

國家圖書館出版品預行編目(CIP)資料

用英語來學節慶 / 倍斯特編輯部著. — 初版. —
　臺北市： 倍斯特, 2013. 10
　　面；　公分
　ISBN 978-986-89739-3-0(平裝)

　1. 英語 2. 讀本

805.18　　　　　　　　　　　　102018744